To Suzanne.
You're a bright light in what can,
at times, be a writer's dark world.
Don't ever let that light burn out.

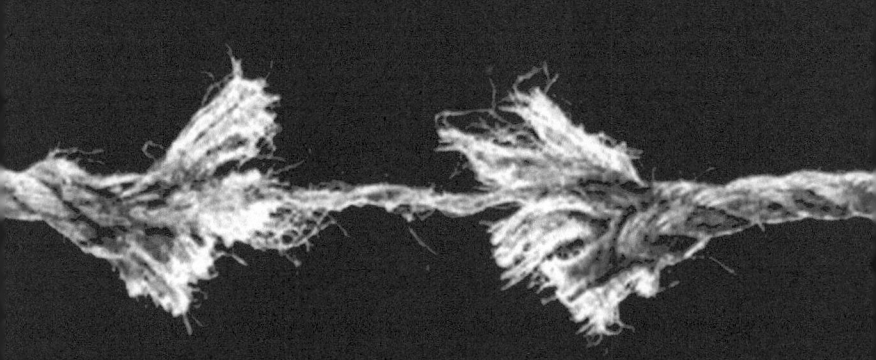

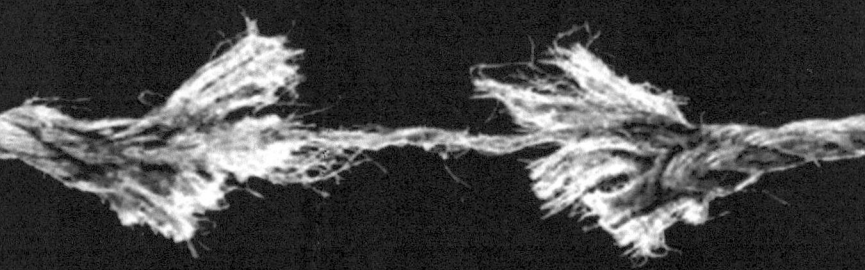

THEY THOUGHT
THE
THEIR STORY
FABLE
WAS OVER...
OF US

New York Times Bestselling Author
nicole williams

CHAPTER ONE

I couldn't breathe.

That happened every time I passed by the Charleston city limits sign. I'd spent eighteen years in Charleston—born, raised, and hazed there—but had never really learned how to breathe there.

Maybe it had more to do with the exhaling part of the breathing process. I'd spent my first eighteen years of life inhaling and holding my breath: waiting, enduring, biding

. . .

And then I'd gotten out.

Santa Barbara might have been a part of the same country, but it might as well have been halfway across the world, complete with an entirely different culture and lifestyle. Moving there had been like finding my promised land without knowing there was one to find.

I'd spent four years in college and the last few working. My family wanted to know when I would be coming "home," a question they'd been pummeling me with since the day after my graduation. Three years later, and I still hadn't worked up the nerve to tell them I *was* home.

Down here, Southerners seemed incapable of comprehending home being anywhere else. Especially when a person came from the kind of family I did, with the kind of history and status mine did, in the suffocating heat that was only outdone by the humidity.

Why my sister had decided to get married in the summer was beyond me, though I guessed it had something to do with making me as miserable as possible.

Oh God. My sister. The wedding. Family. Old friends. My mother's nitpicking and cloying perfume. My father's elbow-rubbing and cigar smoke. That house I never seemed to belong in. That city that stifled the life right out of me. That entire part of the world that seemed to eject me from it as quickly as I ejected myself.

Shit. I couldn't do this. Not after everything.

I knew the taxi driver had the air conditioning full bore. Not because I could feel its cool rush breaking across my skin, but because I'd asked him to crank it up before we'd pulled away from the airport loading zone. I'd thought it would help.

I should have known better.

Rolling down the window a couple of cranks didn't help either. In fact, it only made my suffocation worse. The heavy air oozed into the backseat, reeking of the same familiar scents I'd tried to erase from my memory. The Charleston air encased me, seeming to cling to my skin and fall into my lungs like a couple of cinder blocks.

I'd taken my first inhale in Charleston, and I'd be holding my breath until I passed that city limits sign in a week. I wouldn't be able to breathe again until I'd escaped this place, and I'd spend the next three years, or preferably decades, dodging invites home for holidays or vacations.

The blocks of concrete in my lungs weren't sitting well. I'd gone years without feeling them, and my body was fighting instead of accepting them. That had happened the last time I'd flown back here too, when it had been two years since my last visit.

When the taxi shot by another familiar sign, this one with its fresh yearly coat of paint outlining the words *The Abbott Family Welcomes You to Charleston, Their home for ten generations and growing,* I knew I needed to pull over and give myself a few more minutes to adjust before stumbling up the front steps of that house and succumbing to the whims and wills of my mom and sisters.

I couldn't pass through those double doors like this or else, like sharks sensing prey in distress, they'd see me as an easy target. Or an *easier* target.

"Excuse me," I said to the driver, my voice sounding strange to my ears. Probably because I'd been holding my breath for a few minutes now. "Would you mind pulling over? Sir." I barely remembered my Southern manners and tacked on the address.

Just because I knew this wasn't where I belonged and avoided Charleston like my very existence depended on it didn't mean I found it evil in all ways. From an objective point of view, Charleston, and the South as a whole, had plenty going for it . . . for people whose name wasn't Clara Abbott.

"We're only a few miles from the address you gave me, ma'am." The driver had a thicker accent than the locals, more New Orleans than Charleston.

"Exactly. Please pull over."

If the driver didn't detect the plea in my voice, he saw it on my face when he glanced at me in the rearview mirror. "No problem, ma'am. There's a little place right up here I can pull into if you'd like to get out and catch your breath."

I nodded my thanks but not my agreement. There'd be no breath-catching for me for seven long, gruesome days.

I knew the place just up the road he had in mind. Everyone who'd lived out here knew this place either by reputation or from personal experience. The Hide and Seek was an old hollowed-out train car that had been transformed into a bar of sorts. I didn't know exactly how a bar was "of sorts," but I thought it had something to do with the fact that while the place served shots like we were all waking up to the apocalypse, it didn't follow with the bar trend of playing music or hanging neon lights in windows or offering a dance floor.

It was frequented by those who slithered in and out of society under the cover of night and those with more tar than blood pumping through their veins. You know, from their black hearts. At least that was the story I'd been told while growing up here.

The Hide and Seek wasn't for my family and its "kind;" it was a haunt for the "other kind." No Abbott had stepped foot inside it. Until tonight.

When the driver pulled into the rudimentary parking lot, equipped with enough potholes and mud bogs to keep out the expensive imports, I threw open the door before the taxi had come to a complete stop. I was out the door the moment the tires stopped moving.

The driver threw his arm across the back of the passenger seat and twisted around to ask me, "Do you want me to wait or leave, ma'am?"

"Wait please." I was already moving toward the old train car, rusted out from age and humidity, tangled with vines and moss that had crept its way around it.

"The meter won't stop running." He pointed at the meter that was already approaching the triple-digit mark.

I nodded, continuing on my journey. "I know. I won't be long. I just think I need a drink before I go any farther."

A silver, untamed brow lifted. "Ma'am, from the look of you, you're in need of a whole fifth of drinks." The driver waved, shooing me on my way. "I'll be waiting. Take your time."

Firing off a wave at the driver as I powered toward the train car, I fought the urge to decipher "taking my time" as spending the next seven days here before staggering back to the cab and making the return trip to the airport.

It was my younger sister's wedding; I had to be there for her. The sentiment might not have been returned, and a fraction of my motivation for showing up might have been derived from the fear of our mother sending a lynch gang for me if I failed to appear, but I was going nonetheless. I just needed a shot or two of the kind of courage that came in liquid form. With my family, no one had the right to judge me for turning to a bottle to face them.

After weaving through a brigade of beat-up trucks splattered in mud and hollowing out from rust, I made it to the train car. The entrance wasn't visible from the parking lot, so it must have been hiding around the back. While most businesses would have placed a priority on putting the entrance in plain view of potential customers, The Hide and Seek seemed to want theirs to be difficult to find.

I hadn't stepped foot in the place yet, and I already

knew I liked it. Nonconformist. Waving its middle finger at the world. This relic of a train car had ten times the courage I did within these city limits.

When I stumbled around the back and almost crashed into a guy answering nature's call up against the rusty metal wall, my impression fell a few notches. When it came to nonconformism, I drew a hard line at peeing in public, setting aside the fact that the entrance of The Hide and Seek wasn't exactly the most public of places. Still . . . it was public enough to take your peeing elsewhere. Try behind that tree ten feet away elsewhere.

After I dodged the guy relieving himself, he offered a grunt that could have been an apology just as easily as it could have been a greeting. Grunts, in this part of the world, were a multi-functional form of communication.

Swinging open the screen door, I stepped inside The Hide and Seek, stitching on an expression that said I'd been here a hundred times and would come back another thousand. A quick look at the bar's patrons glancing at me told me my ruse wasn't working. With the way some of the guys were appraising me, the term *fresh meat* kept echoing in my head. Actually, when I took a second look around, it looked like I was the only woman in the place . . . or at least the only one a person didn't need to play a guessing game to identify.

Other than the door I'd just come through, there were no windows or doors cut out of the old train car that was just as rusted from the inside as it was from the outside. The lighting was somewhere on the scale between low to non-existent, and I swore I heard the whir of a generator in the background, possibly what was responsible for keeping the lights *barely* on and the beers, from the looks of the non-frosty glasses, a few degrees below room temperature.

No air conditioning pumped through the space, not that I'd expected to feel any, and even though the sun had gone down an hour or two ago, the heat was still alive and well inside of this tin can. It was a good twenty degrees cooler outside . . . and I'd been about to swelter alive out there.

Swallowing, I took a few more steps inside. The temperature crawled up a degree with every step I took, so instead of continuing toward the empty bar table at the back, I changed directions and snagged one of the empty stools lining the particle board bar, which seemed mostly held together by duct tape and rusty nails.

I shuffled through my memory, trying to find the last time I'd had a tetanus shot. Only five or six years ago, maybe. I was good.

Thankfully, the stools lining the counter were mostly empty, save for one guy at the opposite end who seemed as content to ignore me as I was to ignore him. The rest of the patrons behind me, staggered around the tables and chairs, were staring holes into my back. *Fresh meat, fresh meat, fresh meat.*

If only my parents could see me now. They'd crap their colons.

The bartender's back was turned to me for a while as he poured a line of shots from a bottle that was almost the size of my hybrid back in California. If he'd noticed me come in, it didn't show. As desperate as I might have been to grab a drink or two and get the heck out of there, I knew better than to clear my throat and throw around orders like I owned the place. The Abbott name ran deep in these waters, and just as many people would rather see us sink than swim. I'd changed a good deal from my former debutante days, but still . . . Abbott family photos had been plastered across enough billboards and newspaper articles in these parts to stick to the memories of even the most remote swamp dwellers.

I might have been of the family, but I wasn't *one* of them. I had to remind myself of that again when the bartender continued to ignore me and my lack of breathing continued to strangle my waning courage. The bartender delivered the line of shots to a few of the tables, and when he returned, he continued being oblivious to the woman practically bouncing on her stool at the end of the counter.

What was this? A boys-only club? A members-only maybe? Whatever it was, I wasn't leaving until I'd had my drink, so help me God.

"Hey, Tom, put her first drink on my tab," the guy at the opposite end of the counter said, startling me. From how still he'd been, I'd been under the impression he'd passed out in his drink. "Any woman brave enough to step foot in this place deserves her first drink free."

The bartender gave one of those infamous grunts. "Considering the tab you've run up here, you're lucky I poured you that drink you've been nursing the past two hours."

I was about to speak up—something to the gist of thanks, but no thanks—when the man at the end of the bar rose from his stool, took something from his back pocket, riffled through what I guessed was a wallet, and slammed a five dollar bill on the counter. "I said her first drink's on me."

"Tom" glanced at the bill, ambled down to that end of the counter, then tugged the five from beneath the guy's palm. "Still trying to play in a different league? I thought you would have learned your lesson with that Abbott girl, but hell, if you want to spend the last five in your wallet on a girl who wouldn't let you mow her front lawn, who am I to turn my nose up at your money?" The bartender wadded up the bill and shoved it deep into his jeans, a rattle-like chuckle rising in his chest. "You've never been one for learning your lesson, Boone."

This time I had my mouth open and was in the middle of starting my "thanks, but no thanks" speech when the words froze in my throat. It couldn't be. No how. No way. It couldn't be . . . *him*. It had been years—seven to be exact—since I'd last seen him.

His voice sounded different, yet similar in the way a person could never forget the color of the walls in their childhood bedroom. Boone. It wasn't a common name, even buried this deep in the belly of the country.

Still, I couldn't help grasping that last strand of hope that it wasn't *the* Boone as my head turned to take my first full look at the man sitting at the other end of the counter. I didn't need more than a moment to confirm who it was.

The Boone. Similar to his voice, he looked different, yet the same. The same dirty blond hair ever in need of a haircut, though now it was just long enough to be pulled back into the messiest ponytail I'd ever seen. The same wide shoulders and imposing frame that had made boys give him a wide berth. That had apparently transferred into manhood, as evidenced by the rest of the patrons staggered everywhere in the bar save beside him. The same way he held himself, like he was always ready for a fight, fists semi-curled, shoulders partially tensed.

The same way his Adam's apple bobbed before he

turned and looked at me . . .

His eyes locked onto me, boring through me in a way that made me wish I'd worn body armor before stepping into this place. Unlike the rest of him, Boone's eyes had changed. They were still the same chestnut shade, but the lights in them had burned out. That spark of trouble or excitement or whatever emotion he'd ever felt had gone out, leaving something dull and lifeless behind.

"On second thought, I'll take that five back, Tom." Boone's eyes stayed fixed on me as he held out his hand. "This woman's taken enough from me for this lifetime and my next ten. I'm not giving her anything else, the last five in my wallet included."

Tom grunted at Boone, shoving the bill deeper into his pocket before grabbing a shot glass and pouring something into it.

When I swallowed, my throat burned—parched from the memories I had of the man ten feet down from me, painful from the unpleasant memories that outweighed the pleasant ones. "That's okay. I can go."

I stood from my stool as Tom slammed the shot in front of me. It smelled like the cleaner my mom used to insist the maids use to clean the showers with—the same stuff the FDA later banned after discovering it blinded people if even a splash of it wound up in their eyes.

"No need to leave on my account, Miss Abbott. We all know you and your family come and go wherever they want, as they want, whenever they want." Boone's voice took on the sharp edge I used to hear him use with others but rarely with me. "Besides, you're an expert at pretending I don't exist. It's been a while, but I'm sure it's just like riding a bike. Carry on ignoring me. I'm confident I can return the favor." He twisted around in his seat until he was hunched over in the same position I'd found him in.

I'd known this trip would be a disaster of record-breaking proportions, but I hadn't factored in running into Boone Cavanaugh at The Hide and Seek. I didn't need another complication in this already-complicated trip home. I needed to get in, get out, and get moving on.

The frustration that was more owed to fate vented out and latched on to Boone. "Oh, give it up, Boone. Your same old 'The Abbotts Are the Root of All Evil in South Carolina' speech is old. Find some fresh material."

My eyes squeezed shut when I realized what I'd said. Usually I was a seasoned pro at biting my tongue and re-membering my manners, but with Boone, that well-honed skill had never worked. Years later and it still didn't. I said what was on my mind before thinking it through—that was always Boone's and my way.

"You're right. I am in need of fresh material, some-thing that's never in short supply when it comes to your family." From his voice, I could imagine the look on his face—one side curled into a scowl, the other flat with apa-thy. "How about this for fresh? 'Little Sister Abbott Weds Big Sister Abbott's Old Sweetheart and All-Around Butt-plug Rumored to Have Been Fucking Them Both Until Big Sister Found Out and Dreamed About Castrating ButtPlug, But Instead She Flew in To Wish Them Well in Their Forthcoming Nuptials.'" Boone cleared his throat. "How's that for new material?"

My stomach churned. In addition to my breathing problem, now I was having stomach issues. Leave it to Boone Cavanaugh to unleash the all-out body assault.

Plugging my nose to get it down, I lifted the shot

glass to my lips and drank it in one gulp. My body convulsed. The stuff tasted how I'd guess that shower cleaner had tasted too.

"If you're going for overdone and sensationalized, then I think you nailed it. Well done." Sliding a bill out of my wallet, I nodded at the bartender when his eyes dropped to my empty glass. My stomach was still twisting from what Boone had just said, from what he'd just brought up. "I'm paying for my own drinks tonight, so why don't you give Boone another of whatever he's drinking for that five he just gave you. I don't want anything from him either."

Down the counter, a harsh huff sounded.

We were quiet for a moment as Tom poured us each our drinks, but as was typical, that quietness never lasted long when Boone and I were in the same room.

"Ford McBride is pathetic. You should be thanking every deity real or imagined you aren't the sister who wound up with him."

I tried to exhale in an effort to calm myself. I couldn't do it. "Who says I'm not?"

"You do. By showing up for their wedding and plastering on a fake smile for the photographer. I mean, come on, Clara, that was the guy you were planning on marrying, and now he's marrying your little sister after going behind your back with her for God knows how long." Boone's voice rose, every word half a note louder. "If that's giving the guy your middle finger, then damn, you need a reeducation on the topic."

"I think I know where to get one if I decide for myself that I need one," I fired at him, shifting on the bar stool so I was leaning more away from him than toward him. We might have been ten feet apart, but another two inches couldn't hurt. "And where do you get off trying to paint me as the villain with everything you've got stacked up in your corner?" I tucked my hair behind my ear and shook my head. "Me and everyone else the villain and you the hero. Got that twisted around there, Boone."

When Tom slid Boone's drink in front of him, Boone shoved it back at him, which struck me as strange. I'd maybe seen Boone Cavanaugh turn down a drink . . . never. "Oh yeah. That's right. I forgot about you knowing everything about everyone. Guess I shouldn't have let that slip my mind—that being an Abbott family theme and all."

My body was so tense, my muscles felt close to snapping. I'd come into this place to find a way to relax, not to get more wound up. Massaging my temple with one hand, I took a sip of my shot with the other. My body convulsed more violently this time. This wasn't a sip-and-enjoy type of establishment.

"Is this really how we're going to do this, Boone?" I asked. "Picking up right where we left off seven years ago? Is this really how much we've matured all these years later?"

Boone's head angled my way some. He was silent for a moment, watching me. "Where else would you expect us to pick up, Clara?"

I leaned forward, curling my arms around my drink and staring at the void right in front of me. I couldn't look at him and talk rationally. That had always been the case, no matter how good or bad our relationship. "Somewhere along the lines of civil."

Boone's laugh rolled through the room. His malicious laugh, not the one I used to love. "What you did to me, how you treated me . . . you're not the person to be going on about civility. Don't you dare preach to me about being civil."

I felt the first flash of alcohol in my system, dulling my inhibitions and heightening them at the same time. "And you can just get down from that high and mighty stool down there and stop lecturing me about right and wrong. Nice try." I lifted what was left in my glass and chugged it. This drink was better than the first two—a sure sign the alcohol was doing its job. "You want to bring up the past, I'm willing to bring up a few pieces of it too."

From the corner of my eye, I noticed him shift on his stool. He was obviously under the same impression that another couple of inches of distance couldn't hurt.

"Why don't you finish your drink and leave?" he snapped, motioning at the screen door I'd come through. "This used to be the one place a person could go without worrying they'd run into an Abbott, and I'd like to keep it that way. I've put up with enough from all of you to have earned my sainthood a decade ago, so beat it." He waved again at the door, waiting for me to run off like I wanted to.

But I wasn't going to run. Not yet. I'd cut and run from Boone enough times that I wasn't going to add to that list. Besides, I wasn't leaving until I was good and marginally intoxicated so I could endure the reunion with my family.

When I slid my empty glass across the counter, Tom didn't need the nod from me. He knew what I wanted.

"Don't worry, Boone. I'm not planning on ransacking the place and spoiling your retirement plan of ruining your liver." That was, if it wasn't already permanently damaged from the bottles I'd seen him empty as a teenager. "And I'm only in town for the week, so the likelihood of us running into each other again is next to none."

"Which would be too soon for me," Boone announced to himself, though he didn't mutter or mumble. It wasn't his style to say something under his breath. If Boone had something to say, he said it for everyone to hear.

The heat pressed in around me, making it impossible for me to think straight. "Okay, you hate me. I get it." I grabbed the refilled shot glass out of Tom's hands so quickly, half of it splashed across the counter. The particle board lapped it up like it was as desperate for the drink as I was. "You've made that exceedingly clear. But why don't you stop acting like you were the only one who got hurt? You paid me back. And then some."

When I noticed my hands trembling, I tucked them into my lap. I didn't want to seem weak around him. Not after all this time. Boone already knew all of my weak parts and pieces from childhood and adolescence. I didn't want him having an education in my adult ones.

"Are you about ready to go face your ex-sweetheart and little sis, who are about to exchange I dos in a few days? Because from what I recall of your little-to-no alcohol tolerance, by now you should be shit-faced enough to do what you Abbotts have made an art form of and Pretend Everything's Just Fine and Dandy."

I stared at the screen door, wishing I'd never come through it. Part of me wished I'd never met the guy sitting six stools down from me. Right then, I was willing to sacrifice the good memories for the sake of having none of the bad ones. "Stop, Boone. Just stop. I can't do this again."

"Just getting started, Clara."

Before I could snap something back, my phone vibrated in my shorts' back pocket. The cut-offs and tee I'd slipped into in Santa Barbara had seemed like a good choice at the time, but now I was wishing I'd gone with a light, airy sundress. This heat was like nothing else, and it had been so long since I'd been in it during the summer, I guessed I'd purged those memories from my brain.

I had a new text. From my little sister. The youngest of the three Abbott girls—Avalee. In it was a picture of her hand, her nails perfectly polished in some shade of petal pink, a diamond the size of Delaware flashing on her ring finger. It was so large, it covered up most of her middle finger and all of her pinkie. The words, *Sterling asked! This was my answer!* were all that accompanied the photo that knocked whatever air I was still clinging to from my lungs.

Avalee was twenty-one. She'd graduated high school three summers ago. She was the youngest, the one who should have been the last to get married if chronology had anything to do with it, and here she was, engaged before I had one solid prospect in the queue. The middle sister, Charlotte, was getting married in six days, which left me, the oldest, as the last daughter to marry off. Or else fulfill the opening of old spinster.

I could only imagine what my mom would say when I rolled up to the curb tonight. Starting and ending with, *when are you going to get serious and settle down?*

I forced myself to stop thinking about what my mom would say, and the increased pressure, guilt, and scrutiny I'd be under from the moment I trudged into their presence until the moment I fled from it. I forced myself to type back, *Congrats! So happy for you both!* and hit send before I could change my mind.

I should have been happy for my sisters, but being happy for one another was not an Abbott sister trait. One-upping was more the thing to do, and a big reason why I got out as soon as I could. Charlotte might have wound up with Ford, and he might have been a handsome, rich son of a bitch, but there was far more to him than that—far more of the undesirable qualities in a lifetime partner. And Ava-lee might have landed the biggest diamond I'd ever seen, even after living in coastal California for seven years, but what good was a big precious gem if your husband worked all day and spent most of his nights with his mistress(es) as Sterling Beauregard Senior was infamous for?

After making sure the message had gone through, I flipped my phone over on the counter, willing it to stay silent for the rest of the night. I could have turned it off, but that seemed too easy.

Boone twisted on his stool and angled himself in my direction. "How much longer are you planning on staying tonight? Because if you're not leaving in the next five minutes, I am. I came here to forget my problems for a few hours, not resurrect a whole shitload of them."

My phone buzzed again. Repeatedly. I kept it flipped over and tried to ignore it. When I noticed the full shot glass in front of me and couldn't remember ordering it or how long it had been sitting there, I knew better than to drink it.

I knew better—but I didn't *do* better.

The chemical cleaner smell and taste had disappeared. Yet another sign that I'd exceeded my goal of getting tipsy. That might have been the reason my mouth opened and out came words I hadn't planned on saying. "Listen, I'm sorry, Boone." I twisted on my stool so I was facing him. "I'm sorry for how things went down between us. I never wanted to hurt you . . . but that didn't change that I did." I bit my lip when certain memories came flickering back to life. "And I'm sorry."

He was quiet, his expression flat and his body still. Around us, the bar echoed with noises and voices, the air filled with the scent of alcohol and body odor. This should have been the last place in the city limits I'd go to. The person sitting down from me should have been the last I'd find myself with.

I didn't know what any of this foretold about the next week, if anything at all, but I found myself wishing I could plan on more of the unexpected. What I expected was a whole lot of what I'd lived, breathed, and drowned in for eighteen years.

"That's the first time I've ever heard you apologize."

Boone's voice cleared my head some, bringing me back to the here and now instead of the there and then. No matter where I was and who I was with, I far preferred the here and now.

"Well, feel free to do the same. I've never exactly heard a string of apologies from your lips either." I twirled my hand in a proceed kind of motion, and he lifted a brow in disbelief.

"What *exactly* do you want me to apologize for?"

The blood pulsing through my veins heated. It was already at an ungodly temperature—I did not need to start heating myself from the inside out as well. Another degree or two up, and I'd be passing out.

When Boone's brow stayed elevated, implying he was innocent on all counts, I reached for the refilled shot. Screw it. "Nothing, Boone. Absolutely nothing."

After that, I twisted back around and finished my shot in one drink. When the bartender meandered over, bottle at the ready, I covered the glass with my hand and shook my head. I was already showing up alone, late, and dressed in what my mother deemed "scrubs intended for the homeless, not for an Abbott daughter." If I showed up drunk too, heads would roll. Starting with mine.

After a minute of silence, my phone started going off like a fireworks display on the Fourth of July. It was buzzing so much, so non-stop, it rocked across the counter. All I could do was stare at it and clasp my hands in my lap. I couldn't deal with them right now. I'd be forced to deal with them soon, but they weren't going to ruin my last half hour to myself.

"Your phone's about to blow up," Boone piped up, still angled my direction.

"Well aware of that. Thank you." I glared at the phone, still jumping around like it was alive.

"If you wanted to avoid your family, why the hell did you fly down here for the wedding?"

I went back to rubbing at my temples. I couldn't put this off for much longer. Rip off the bandage and suck it up. It was only a week. Seven days. I'd endured eighteen years; what was one week?

"What do you know about any of it?" I said when my phone almost vibrated off the edge of the counter, forcing me to grab it before it careened to the floor . . . also made of particle board.

"I know more about you and your family than any of

you care to acknowledge, that's what I 'know about it,'" he replied, his voice calm and even. He'd always been better about controlling his emotions . . . or masking them.

I hadn't meant to look at my phone, but after catching it screen-side-up, I'd already read a few texts before I realized I'd done it.

Avalee just told me she told you! Isn't it fabulous? Mom's first message read.

Followed by Charlotte's, *Can't wait to meet your Plus One. Where are you two? It's late.*

Followed by another from Avalee. *You're next. I know it.*

Followed by three more from my mom. *Who is this mystery man you're bringing with you? Do we know him?*

Followed by, *Is it serious? As in your father and I should keep the caterer on retainer serious?*

Followed by, *Everyone's waiting for you and your date. Please don't keep us waiting much longer.*

Followed by another half dozen messages I refused to continue scanning.

I powered off my phone, slid it into my back pocket, and let my head fall into my hands. What a fucking mess. I hadn't even shown my face at home yet and everything was in crisis mode. I knew better than to expect anything to get better once I did see my family. I knew better than to hope they'd be understanding and keep their comments and opinions about my lack of a plus one to themselves. I knew better than to expect the best when the opposite had been the theme of my formative years.

My head was swimming both from the alcohol and my family pressing down on me like a hot iron, and that might have been what was responsible for the plan formulating in my head being verbalized.

"Boone?" I said, twisting my neck to look at him. He hadn't stopped looking at me. "What are you doing this week?"

He reached for his replenished drink and lifted it in my direction. "A whole lot of this."

I swallowed when he did, but I was fighting the voice in my head that warned me this was a bad idea—quite possibly my worst idea to date. "How would you feel about earning some extra money?"

Boone settled his glass on the counter, keeping it clutched in his hands. "Who says I haven't already earned so much of it I couldn't possibly be interested in earning any more?"

Now it was my turn to lift an eyebrow in his direction. While the Abbotts were known for the wealth spilling from their ears, the Cavanaughs had been known for the past few generations for the opposite.

From his worn brown boots that probably should have been tossed out last summer, to the plaid button-down shirt I had a distant memory of him wearing back in high school, I had my answer. Plus, there was the whole issue of . . . "That last five dollars in your wallet that is now in Tom's pocket might say something about you not having so many more of those you wouldn't be interested in making more of them."

Finally his face gave way to emotion. Just a flash and only for a moment, but his eyes narrowed at the same time his forehead creased, like he was almost insulted. "You Abbotts think you can buy the world and anyone in it. I've known that about your family for years, Clara, but I guess I didn't realize that gene had been passed down to you."

I refused to back down, not after bringing it up. Besides, Boone's impressions of me couldn't get much lower.

"Ten thousand dollars," I said and shut up after that.

Boone was clearly as shocked by the number as I'd guessed he'd be. Ten grand was a lot of money to anyone anywhere. Especially to earn in one week. Down here though, working the kinds of jobs Boone had worked back in high school and probably still did, that was a third of a year's salary.

He looked away for a moment, glaring at the wall across from us, before his gaze cut back to me. His shoulders were tense, his neck so rigid that his veins and muscles were showing. Part of me knew he felt insulted that I was offering him money in exchange for a favor—part of me felt ashamed for the same—but Boone's and my relationship had been severed years ago. This was nothing more than a business transaction between a couple of acquaintances.

"You know, the last time someone offered me that chunk of change over a few drinks, it wasn't followed by an offer that was on the up-and-up." His voice was cool and removed, the way he was looking at me the same.

"What I'm about to ask isn't illegal, I promise. It's not even inside." I shook my head. "It's just . . . maybe a little deceitful."

He huffed and gave a nod. "I'd expect nothing less."

When I thought of a way to phrase what I was about to suggest, nothing sounded quite right. No matter how I worked the pieces of my proposition in my head, no arrangement made it seem less undignified. So I went with the most basic explanation.

"All I need from you is for you to pose as my plus one for the week. Nothing more. One week, ten grand. What do you think?" My words came out too fast, my voice too high. Because no matter what I tried to convince myself of, no matter how much radio silence had passed between us, Boone and I were not and would never be mere acquaintances. We had too much history to ever be "acquaintances."

Boone was silent for a minute. One long minute I thought would never pass. When he did finally say something, I'd been two seconds away from leaving and spending the next seven years trying and failing to forget about Boone Cavanaugh again.

"Let me get this straight, because I thought I understood the English language, but I cannot get my head wrapped around what you just said." Boone scooted his stool a half foot in my direction, the skin between his brows pinched in a deep line. "Are *you* asking *me* to show up at your family's place with your family inside and pose as your date for the wedding?"

I shook my head. Hard. "As my plus one. That's all." My traitor voice gave me away though. Still too high and fast.

Boone didn't miss it either. Something that resembled the stirrings of a smirk worked its way into his expression. "As your boyfriend."

He wasn't going to make this easy. Not that he had any reason to. "As my *plus one*."

Boone's smirk became as pronounced as it got. His head tipped just a bit, his eyes flashing, and his mouth turned up in a hint of a smile. "As your lover?"

My fingers curled into my palms. "As. My. Plus.

23

One."

An uneven chuckle vibrated in his chest as he studied me. He probably couldn't figure out my business deal any more than I could. "Why? Why me?" He held out his arms and shrugged. "With all the history between us and the history of your family treating mine like we were trash . . . why choose me?"

I picked at the frayed ends of my cut-offs, considering his question as much as I was considering my answer. I had too many reasons to ask him, most of those reasons ones I didn't want to legitimize by voicing . . . even to myself. When I'd left Charleston seven years ago, I'd told myself the Boone Cavanaugh chapter of my life was over. Yet here I was reopening it, or starting a brand-new chapter.

Boone continued to wait, his silence screaming at me.

He wanted to know why, so I gave him an answer, though it might have been the least honest one I had. "Limited options." I scanned the few dozen customers, most of them older than my father and most looking like addiction had played some recent role in their lives. "Running short on time." I tapped my wrist. "That's why I choose you. Now if you're done with the Q & A, what's your answer?"

My pulse was pounding in my neck as I waited. I needed him to say yes. I needed him to agree to crawl into that cab with me and pose as my plus one for the next week because even though my family weren't fans of the Cavanaughs, showing up single was a worse crime.

"Am I to understand that who you'd originally planned on bringing as your 'plus one' fell through?" Boone scooted his stool down another foot.

I couldn't decide what I wanted to do more: scoot closer or farther away. "Stop talking like an asshole. If you have a question, ask me for Christ's sake."

"I didn't think debutantes were supposed to take the lord's name in vain . . ."

I was tempted to slug the smirk right off his face, but I didn't. I needed him to agree. I needed to not show up solo and become the target of sabotage setups and sneaky double-dates the whole week.

"Fuck you, Boone Cavanaugh," I fired off before I could bite my tongue.

A second of silence passed between us, then he laughed. "There's the Clara Belle Abbott I'd been convinced had been adopted at birth. Damn, I missed her."

I found myself laughing with him, because crying seemed like the less enticing option. Laugh or cry—the beat of Boone's and my relationship. "So does that mean you'll do it?"

Boone wiped his eyes, his laugh rolling to an end. It had been forever since I'd heard him laugh, but it sounded the same. Just like I remembered. "If you answer my questions to my satisfaction."

"And there's the Boone Cavanaugh who makes so many conditions no one can ever get close enough to him to get through." I peaked a brow at him, letting him know he wasn't the only one allowed to take shots.

"You were planning on bringing some rich California boy toy with you this week?"

"I was planning on bringing my *boyfriend* who, yes, lives in California, but was a transplant from Ohio, and who was very middle class, with me this week." The three or four or five shots were making my mind muddy. I couldn't tell if I was saying too much or too little, but Boone seemed satisfied with my answer.

"But that fell through?"

I nodded, my head stuffed full of cotton and tequila.

"You broke up with him." It was a statement, not a hint of doubt in his voice.

"He broke up with *me*."

Boone's forehead creased. "How long ago?"

"Three days ago."

Boone's mouth parted some. "The guy broke up with you three days before he was planning to fly down here to support you and save you from the blood-suckers?"

"Boone—" I warned.

"Sorry, the creatures of the night," he continued, not hiding his smile when my frown deepened. "I gotta tell you, you really know how to pick 'em. First Ford McBride, the behind-your-back-fucking-your-little-sister loser, and then this prick who bailed on you a few days before you flew out to face your own personal Armageddon."

I cracked my neck from side to side. Boone wasn't saying anything I hadn't heard or told myself a thousand times, but it felt different coming from him.

"Let's not forget to toss you into that knowing-how-to-pick-'em pile," I muttered, more to myself than to him, but he didn't miss it.

"You didn't pick me, Clara. I picked you." For the briefest moment, I caught a glimpse of the Boone I remembered. The one who'd occasionally open himself up and share his world with me.

I swallowed. I'd finished my last shot minutes ago, but I felt like hundred-proof alcohol was streaming down my throat. "Any more questions? I've, or we've, got to get going unless I want my dad calling the sheriff to come looking for me."

"Wouldn't be the first time, would it?" A smile pulled at the corner of Boone's mouth.

"It wouldn't be. But at least this time the sheriff wouldn't have to lie to my daddy about how he found me, and who he found me with."

"Or where he found us . . ." Boone's gaze shifted away, staring at the wall opposite us like he was seeing something else.

"So?" I pressed.

He took another sip of his drink. "Aren't you going to ask me if I'm seeing someone? Don't you care if I've got someone in my life I'll need to explain this little week-long arrangement too?"

"Of course, yes, I should have thought of that. Do you have . . . someone? Do you think she'd care if you did this?"

Boone finished his drink before rising from his stool. He'd always been tall, but it looked like he'd stretched another couple inches in the years since I'd seen him. And that was definitely the same shirt he'd had in high school. I remembered those buttons. The shiny marbled ones that snapped closed . . . or popped open.

"I've only ever had one someone special, Clara, and she turned me off to the whole idea of ever having another." He wouldn't look at me as he talked. "So no, there's not someone special in my life to care what I do or who I do it with."

He tipped his chin good-bye at Tom as he headed toward me. I scrambled off of the stool, trying not to sway in place when I stood. I wasn't short—in fact, I was taller than average for a woman—but standing a foot across from Boone Cavanaugh, I felt very small. Almost like he could squish me between his thumb and index fingers.

"Ten thousand dollars? Seven days?" He shuffled a step closer, putting himself so close that if I kept swaying in place, I was going to sway right into his arms. That shouldn't have seemed like such an appealing option.

I nodded because I couldn't form any words I trusted to say out loud—because I'd just been hit by a familiar scent. One I'd tried to delete from my memory, and one I knew I never could. Boone smelled like my childhood. Like the best years of my life in Charleston. Salty from sweat, sweet from his mom's and sister's shampoo he used to use instead of buying something more manly, and sour with the reminder of the past. I wanted to bury my face in his shirt and breathe him in until I'd had my fill, but if this next week was ever going to work, I couldn't let past feelings and history bleed into the picture.

I couldn't wreck him again—and I couldn't let him wreck me again.

Distance. Arm's length. Collected, cool, and calm. That was my marching beat for the next week. Boone and I had started out as friends; we could do it again.

My vision was blurry from the shots, the background of the bar hazy and undefined. The only thing I could see clearly was him.

His hand lifted, moving toward my face. Just when I thought he was about to cup my cheek and kiss me, his fingers grasped a chunk of my hair swinging just above my shoulders. He studied it for a moment like he didn't recognize it. After a minute more of that, he leaned in, dropping his mouth to just outside my ear. He was messing with me. I knew that. It wasn't enough that I was paying him ten grand; he was going to cost me more by the end of this.

"You've got yourself a boyfriend. Temporarily," he whispered, his voice raising bumps on my forearms.

Lifting my shoulders, I cleared my head and slowly shoved him back until he was an arm's length away. "A plus one. Temporarily."

CHAPTER TWO

What was I doing? What was I thinking? What had I gotten myself into?

Those were the questions playing on a reel through my mind from the time Boone and I had crawled into the taxi until now, when we were a mile away from Abbott Manor, my childhood home.

I shouldn't have drunk so much. I should have shot out of my stool and left the moment I noticed Boone Cavanaugh a few stools down. I should have never opened my mouth. I shouldn't have asked him a certain question I knew he couldn't say no to. I shouldn't have stepped into that decrepit train car in the first place. No, I shouldn't have gotten on that damn plane this morning and flown down here.

I shouldn't have . . . it was the theme of my day, most of my life, and most certainly the rest of the week.

"So what's our story?"

I jumped when Boone nudged me. After I'd climbed into the cab and told the driver I was ready, not another word had been spoken. I guessed, like myself, Boone was second-guessing his decision.

"What story?" I replied.

"Our love story? The one we're going to tell your family after they come out of their shock comas and want to know how you and I, living across the country from each other and ignoring each other like we were sworn enemies for close to a decade, wound up together again?" He nudged me again with his arm. "*That* story."

Boone was large enough to take up a good half of the backseat, but he'd always taken up the space of a man twice that size, as evidenced from the way his legs were spread so far; his knee kept bumping the outside of my leg even when I was pressed up against my door. When we hit a rut in the road and his knee thumped my leg with enough force that I felt it travel up my thigh and down my calf, I pressed tighter into the door.

"Oh, our story . . . I guess I haven't really thought that part out yet." We'd need a story, and I knew that story couldn't be formulated tonight. Not with my brain marinating in a tequila bath.

"Really? You've got nothing?"

"I've got nothing tonight. I'll have it all ironed out come morning though, I promise."

Boone grunted and stared out his window. "You really didn't think this whole thing out very well, did you?"

"It was more a spur-of-the-moment type of decision."

"Nice to know I'm your Plan B. Nothing's changed . . ." Boone rolled down the window a few cranks even though the air conditioning was blasting through the taxi. He tilted his head toward the open window, letting the hot, sticky air break across his face. It looked like he could breathe again.

"Just let me do the talking tonight." I rifled through my purse for a stick of gum or a breath mint or something that would disguise the tequila on my breath. "In fact, since it's so late, most of the family will probably be asleep, so why don't you just sneak up to my old room with the luggage? I'll say a quick hi to everyone who's awake, and we can deal with the big reveal at breakfast. After a good night's sleep."

Boone's head reclined into the headrest, his knees moving closer together so I wasn't getting thumped every few seconds. "Something else that hasn't changed. Sneaking me upstairs while you distract your family. Check. Think I can manage that. Might be a little rusty, but I've got plenty of experience. Should come right back to me."

"Boone—"

"It's okay, Clara. I don't care about that shit anymore. What I care about is the ten grand."

When it was clear not a mint or stick of gum was to be found in the confines of my purse, I tossed it onto the cab floor in a frustrated fit. It wasn't the purse I was upset with—it was the purse's owner. The decisions she'd made and the consequences that had come as a result. "If we're going to do this, successfully, we're going to need to leave the past where it belongs."

"Squirming on our faces?"

I groaned. "Behind us. We can't be hashing out what happened and who's to blame and taking jabs at each other every two seconds, or we might as well ditch this whole deal now because it won't work. We need to focus on pretending to like, tolerate, and respect each other. We need to pretend there isn't history between us and that all we care about is our future together." The pep talk was just as

32

intended for myself as it was for him. "Do you think you can do that?"

"Do you think you can?" he fired back, cranking down the window another notch.

"Yes," I lied . . . I answered.

"Then so can I. No problem," he lied . . . he replied.

From the front seat, the driver gave me a funny look. I shrugged in reply. I could only imagine how perverse this conversation sounded to an outsider, and even if I had the time, I wasn't sure I could explain it.

By then though, we were pulling up to the house. The gate at the end of the driveway was operated by keypad access, but before I could tell the driver the code to enter, the gate swung open. Which meant someone was watching the security screen and had opened the gate from the house. Which meant they were waiting for us.

My heart sped up, adrenaline, or was that panic?, dripping into my bloodstream. Why was my body's reaction to coming home the same as if I were being chased by a pack of wolves in waist-deep snow? Why was my instinct to go into survival mode when I passed through that gate? Why was my fight-or-flight response triggered whenever I passed into the borders of the estate that had been in my family for five generations?

Those were questions I'd been asking myself for years. Questions that had remained unanswered for years.

My hands wrung in my lap, my legs bounced out of control, and my teeth chewed out the excess adrenaline on my lower lip.

Out of nowhere, Boone's hand appeared in my lap, weaving between mine until he had one in his grasp. His large hand swallowed mine, giving it a gentle squeeze. "It will be okay, Clara. They can't ruin your life twice."

Something inside me stilled. Boone's hand was still rough and dotted with callouses. It was still warm and solid though, anchoring me before I drifted away.

"That won't stop them from trying," I whispered as I could just start to make out the large plantation house in the distance.

Boone's jaw tightened. "Well, I won't let them ruin my life twice."

"It won't stop them from trying."

As we continued to wind up the driveway, the driver gave a low whistle. "This your home, miss?"

"No, this isn't my home," I answered. "This is my family's home. Not mine."

"This is some place," the driver continued. "Your family must be real well off."

I closed my eyes when the house came into full view. Too much, too fast. Boone beside me, that house in front of me, all of the family waiting to lash out in their passive-aggressive way. Why had I come?

"If only by their bank accounts' standards," I said as I retrieved my purse from the floorboard and got back to digging through it madly, desperate for a mint and a means of distraction.

"Here." Boone's other hand reached across our laps. In it was a white round mint.

I froze for two moments, that chalky alabaster mint bringing on another enclave of memories. These ones though, they were good. All of them.

"Thank you." I took the mint and popped it into my mouth. It wasn't mint-flavored; it was cinnamon, spicy and hot just like I remembered. With one little mint, I was whisked back to the past: to a first kiss, to the first *real* kiss, to the first time I'd ever . . .

"Fuck me." Boone whistled as we rolled to a stop in front of the house.

"What?" I asked, getting jettisoned from the past into the present. I preferred the other option.

"How many people are staying the week with your parents?" He craned his head out the window, focusing on something off in the distance.

"I don't know. I didn't ask. Both of my sisters obviously, probably my mom's parents, and maybe Aunt May, but there shouldn't be that many. That's what hotels are for." I was wringing the hell out of my purse straps, wishing I'd drained another shot or two, because from the feel of it, the adrenaline and nerves had burned it all up in the drive here.

"You better do a recount, Miss Abbott, because from the looks of the cars I can see parked around the carriage house, your place has become the Hotel Grand Charleston." Boone pointed out the window, but I couldn't see. Or maybe didn't want to see.

The thought of dozens of family members and strangers ambling around the estate made this trip even more intolerable. The house lacked no number of rooms, but it lacked in other things. Notions like privacy, which I would need if this plan with Boone was going to fly. With dozens of people wandering the estate, that meant Boone and I would have to act the part of the loving couple around the clock, no slip-ups.

Even when we'd been together, for real together, we hadn't been capable of that. How in the hell were we going to manage it now?

"You sure you want to do this?" Boone's hand dropped to the door handle, looking just as ready to open it as keep it sealed shut.

I made myself look at the house. The one I'd grown up in for eighteen years until fleeing it like the devil was chasing me. I'd been back three times since, always fleeing in much the same way. Why did I keep coming back? Why did I continue to put myself through this? Oh yeah . . .

"I don't have a choice, Boone. You of all people should remember that."

His knuckles went white as his grip tightened on the door handle. "You've always got a choice. You have a choice now, and you certainly had a choice then. Don't blame them for the choices you made."

Here we went, mucking through the past again. This wouldn't work. I should have sent Boone away right then. I should have paid him the ten grand just to leave, because showing up with Boone Cavanaugh as my date was going to drip a few more drops of nitroglycerin into the pot. My family wasn't even on curt-greeting-while-passing-on-the-sidewalk status with the Cavanaughs. Boone should have been the last person I'd picked to pay to be my date this week.

But then flashes of my sister's picture went through my head. Avalee was engaged. Charlotte was about to be married. Everyone was expecting me to show up with a date. Everyone had expected me to be the first to get married.

If I showed up alone . . . God, I didn't want to think of the comments I'd get, or imagine the potential "suitors" my mom would line up for me. No, this was a good plan.

THE FABLE OF US

At least better than showing up alone.

"I'm not blaming anyone," I said as the driver unloaded the luggage from the trunk. "I'm not blaming my parents, my sisters, you, Ford, or anyone else for anything. I'm just trying to get through this right now, so would you mind cutting me a little slack?"

His expression stayed frozen. "Does that mean we're doing this? We're going, willingly into a pit of vipers?"

I reached for the handle on my side. "We're doing this."

He sucked in a quick breath through his nose, then threw the door open. "Then let's get started so we can finish already."

His hand wove free of mine as he stepped outside to help the driver with the luggage. The luggage . . . there were only two pieces of it—my matching set. We had nothing to show for Boone, not even a small overnight bag.

This might have been the most ill-fated plan ever conceived.

"Boone!" I threw my door open and ejected from the backseat. "You have to hustle up to my room without being seen. We didn't think to pick up a suitcase for you. My family won't miss it. They'll ask questions right from the start, and I'd prefer to delay them until at least day three or four."

I threw my purse strap around my neck and shoulder, fishing around for my wallet to pay the driver. The fare had been steep, as in a couple hundred dollars steep, but I guessed that was what one could expect when they spent forty-five minutes camped out in some bar, drinking cheap tequila and bickering with an old flame.

The driver gave another low whistle after I handed him the bills. "Mighty generous tip, ma'am. Thank you much."

I nodded in his direction before zeroing in on Boone, who had a piece of luggage in each hand and was starting for the stairs. "Did you hear me, Boone? They can't see you. Not tonight."

"Yeah, I heard you. Because I don't have any luggage." He paused with his foot on the bottom step. He didn't look even a fraction hesitant about climbing the stairs to the house that had been just as responsible for eating away at him as it had me. I yearned for that kind of strength. "But who are you kidding, Clara? Your family has always lived under the impression I never had anything more to offer than the clothes on my back, so me showing up with no luggage shouldn't come as a surprise to anyone." He continued up the stairs, his boots stomping against each one like he was trying to drive his heel through them.

I rushed up beside him, grabbing his elbow when he'd stomped his way to the top stair. "Boone, please," I said, panic sharpening my voice.

He stopped long enough to glare at the large double doors in front of us before his gaze moved my way.

"Please?"

He tried holding his glare while looking at me, but it didn't last. A moment later, he sighed. "I won't be your dirty little secret this time, Clara. Not again."

My hand curved around the bend of his arm. "I know. You won't. I'm not going to keep sneaking you in through windows or lying about who I'm out with. I promise. I just need tonight to gather my thoughts and collect my wits before they start firing questions our way." I glanced at the doors, half expecting them to fly open before a stream of family came crashing around us. No one came though. "Okay?"

Boone stepped away from me until my hand fell from his arm. "I've never been able to say no to you. Why would that have changed now?"

He wasn't looking at me like I was guilty, nor did anything in his voice hint at the same, but there had been few times in my life when I'd felt more guilt. Boone was right —I'd hidden him from my family, keeping him a secret for months. Boone had it in his head that I did that because I was ashamed of him, but the truth was I'd been ashamed of *them*. Ashamed because I knew they wouldn't accept him. Ashamed because I knew they were the type of people who judged a man first by the size of his wallet and second by the size of his heart.

Ashamed because I knew they'd arrive at the conclusion that their daughter was too good for that nothing of a boy with a dead-end future, and I knew the truth—Boone Cavanaugh was too good for the likes of me.

"Thank you," I whispered before I made my way up to the door.

My parents had around-the-clock staff manning all areas of the estate, and even though I knew proper protocol was to ring the doorbell and wait for the butler to open the door and welcome us inside, we were going incognito tonight.

When I tried the door handle, I found it unlocked. It was past ten o'clock, which meant my dad was just about to doze off from his third brandy of the night, and my mom was probably layering her fifth night cream onto her face before downing a sleeping pill and passing out.

So why did I feel like I was about to be pounced on?

"You remember where my room's at?" I whispered to Boone as I opened the door as slowly and noiselessly as I could.

"Hard to forget the room of the girl I lost my—"

"Shhhh." I lifted my finger to my lips and fired a warning look back at him.

"Yes, I remember where it is," he said, his voice quiet once again.

"As soon as I open this door, I want you to run up those stairs and don't stop until you're closing my bedroom door behind you. Okay?"

His nostrils flared ever so slightly. "Whatever you say."

Once the door was all the way open, I waved him inside, rushed in behind him, and closed the door. The foyer was empty, and other than the clocks I heard ticking in the library and living room, I didn't hear a sound. Maybe everyone was already asleep.

"Hurry," I whispered, motioning toward the stairs Boone was staring at like they were insurmountable.

All he did was give me a look. That look said more than any words could have. Then he lunged up the stairs, taking them two at a time like my suitcases were empty.

Once Boone had reached the top and disappeared down the hall, I rolled my neck a few times before wandering toward the kitchen. Someone was awake and around. The gate hadn't opened itself.

The journey to the kitchen took longer than I remembered. The house had been built two hundred years ago, during a time when excess and extravagance was the thing to do for those Southern families with money and a good name. Over eight thousand square feet and with so many rooms I couldn't recall half of them, this place might have seemed like a palace for a young girl to grow up in. For me, it had been a prison keeping me jailed from the things I wanted to do and the people I wanted to be with.

"The Abbotts had all been cut from the same cloth" was the way people around here phrased it . . . save for one soul. Me. I'd never been one of them, though I might have shared their last name. Even from the time I was a child, I'd known that. Their goals weren't mine. Their ambitions weren't mine. Their outlooks on the world and views of people deviated drastically from my own.

I hadn't just been the black sheep of my family—I'd been the wolf. The very thing that threatened their existence.

At first I put up a fight when they tried to mold me into something that more closely resembled my mother and younger sisters, but after exhausting myself, I got sneakier. I played the role they wanted me to act when they were around, and I picked up the person I really was when they weren't looking.

I'd played their game for so long though, parts of me started to become like them. It had taken me a while to recognize that, but when I did, it became a big part of why I crossed the country to get away.

A big part, though not the only one.

When I reached the kitchen, I found it just as quiet as the rest of the house. I was about to slip back into the foyer and escape up the stairs to my bedroom when I heard it. That sound had been a staple in my childhood, responsible for making me want to run in the opposite direction. Given it was my mother's voice, I should have wanted to run to-ward her.

"Where is she? Where is that beautiful firstborn daughter of mine?"

The hair on the back of my neck rose on end. From the sounds of her heels echoing, she was just crossing the foyer, successfully cutting off my escape route. I was con-sidering turning and running . . . somewhere, when my opportunity disappeared. My mom had noticed me and come to a stop in the middle of the foyer, holding that all-too-familiar smile in place like it was all that kept her an-chored to the world.

Past most people's bedtimes, my mother was still dressed in a stylish light blue skirt suit and ivory heels, her makeup looking as if it had just been applied and her jew-elry sparkling as if it had just been polished. She was pris-tine. That was my mother in one word. Pristine . . . but that only applied to the surface layer. What resided below that wasn't quite so flawless

"Clara Belle," she said in that voice that held both a gentle and a sharp edge to it, making a person unable to decide whether they were being insulted or complimented. "It has been too long since we've seen that gorgeous face of yours around here. Get over here and give your mother a hug." She outstretched her arms, waving her hands in-ward, waiting for me to come to her.

That was the way it was with my mom and me—I went to her when she wanted, how she wanted. Never the other way around. This time included.

"Hey, Mom." I headed her way and put on the face that said this was no big deal, coming home with years of bad history in my room right now. "Sorry I'm so late. Delays at the airport."

Giving the cinnamon mint a hard suck right before I stepped into her arms, I lifted mine and wrapped them around her. The motion was stiff, forced. Hugging my mother came as unnaturally as breathing under water.

"But I checked your flight status all night. Not a single delay to be found." She patted my back a few times, honey in her voice, vinegar behind her words.

My shoulders tensed, but they relaxed a moment later. I might have been out of practice, but stretching, manipulating, and all-around evading the truth came right back to me. "Baggage claim hold-ups. They thought they lost my bag in Phoenix only to find out another passenger had mistakenly taken it. Thank goodness they realized it before too long and ran it back to the airport for me." I was talking too much, explaining more than needed. So maybe I was a little out of practice.

"What an unfortunate inconvenience," Mom said, winding out of the embrace and stepping back. Distance was as important to her as it was to me.

We stood like that for a minute, quiet and watching each other, waiting. Waiting for what, I didn't know, but something we'd been waiting for for years. Mom gave me a careful investigation, the one I was used to getting every time she saw me for the first time after a long stretch, and though she kept her thoughts to herself, her expression laid them all out to be read.

Sometimes I wondered if part of the reason I'd resisted my mom so much was because we looked alike. So similar in our features that when childhood pictures of her and me were put side by side, it was impossible to tell who was who. Where my sisters had taken on my father's darker features—honey brown hair and hazel eyes—I'd gotten my chunk of DNA from our mother.

Though she'd been dyeing hers for years, our hair was the same cornflower blond, a stark contrast to our deep blue eyes. We were built the same—petite with curvy figures—and I'd even been told we moved in the same way. After growing up in her shadow, being mistaken as her by old relatives nearing senility, and earning praises for my looks—which I knew my mom cared about more than my being praised for my intelligence or personality— I rebelled with what I could.

I couldn't change the way I looked, not much at least, but I could change the way I thought. I could change what I was made up of on the inside . . . and I had. Maybe a bit too late to make a difference when I'd still lived in Charleston, but enough to have made a difference in my life since.

"Look at you, already cozy in your jammies for the night." Mom pinched the hem of my T-shirt, her gaze skimming the frayed cuffs of my shorts.

In California, this was the way most of the population dressed. In the South, within the boundaries of Abbott Manor, one didn't dress like this unless they wanted the cops called on them after being mistaken as a vagrant.

"And what happened to that long, thick hair of yours?" Her hands moved to the ends of my hair, her fingers combing through it like she was hoping it would grow back to its former splendor right before her eyes. "Don't you worry though, Clara Belle. Hair grows back, and when it does, don't you dare see the butcher of a beautician who did this to you"—she gave a chunk of my hair a tug, shaking her head—"ever again. I'll have Janine do a little asking around and find out who out there in California knows a darn about women's hair."

"It's a big state, Mom. Might want to specify to Janine that I live in the Santa Barbara area, because I'm not driving to San Diego for a shampoo and style." I held my smile and took a couple steps back, far enough away that my Mom couldn't keep ripping through my just-above shoulder-length hair. The last time she'd seen me, my hair had still been long, halfway down my back, and so thick I could barely get a ponytail holder around it once. Everyone had loved my hair, touching it and claiming just how far they'd go to have the same kind. Everyone loved my hair . . . except for me.

That was why I'd walked into the beauty salon a couple years ago, had her hack off a foot to donate to Wigs for Kids, then thin out what remained attached to my head. I'd lost what felt like ten pounds of hair that day, and a thousand pounds of weight off my shoulders. I was my own person, no longer subject to the Abbotts.

"I'm sure we can find someone who will fit the bill," she said. "A new hire at SuperTrims would be an improvement." Her voice trailed off in that familiar way it had for years whenever she'd delivered an insult. She always masked it with a shrug and a just-barely audible tone, but it never tempered the intent of her message.

I made my smile stretch. Kill them with kindness—it was the Southern way. When in Charleston, do as the Charlestonians. "I've missed you so much, Mom. I'm glad to be back."

She covered her chest with her hand. "I've missed you so much too, baby. You'd better not stay away so long again or else I might just have to lock you away the next time you come visit."

I was considering replying with something along the lines of visiting family being a two-way street, then I reminded myself that I did not want my family visiting my home in California. I didn't want them to be a part of the life I'd made for myself. They belonged here, not out there.

"Girls!" my mom shouted over her shoulder. "Your sister's here at long last. You won't believe what she's gone and done to her hair." She shot me a wink and waved. "It's just hair though. It'll grow back before you know it. Don't worry a bit, Clara Belle."

"I didn't plan on it," I replied, bracing myself as I heard a duo of heel strikes heading this way. From their pace, I could tell they weren't in a particular hurry to reach me, though that might have had more to do with the height of their heels than their actual excitement, or lack thereof, to see me.

Avalee was the first to make her way into the foyer, a fairy in every way save for the pixie wings—small in size, wide and curious eyes, graceful in motion. Because of the decent enough age gap between us growing up, I'd always felt closer to Charlotte, though Avalee and I were more alike.

"Clara Belle!" Avalee gushed, rushing forward on, yep, heels that could have pierced through a rhino's hide straight to its heart. "Oh my gosh, it's really you!"

I winced as she rushed toward me. I was sure she was going to slip on the gleaming marble and crack open her skull.

"Did you see? Did you hear the good news?" Lifting her left hand, she kept rushing my way until her fist was half a foot from my face.

Given the size of the diamond projecting from her finger, I stepped back so as not to get stabbed in the cornea. "Congratulations, Avalee. That's so great."

I took hold of her hand and studied the ring long enough to mollify her. It really was a nice ring, sparkling like a disco ball and large as a quail egg, but I couldn't imagine going about a person's daily business while wearing it twenty-four hours a day. If it wasn't snagging sweaters, it would be scratching kids' faces.

"I know, right? I can't believe it finally happened to me too!" She lifted her eyes to the ceiling like she'd been waiting eons to get engaged at the ripe old age of twenty-one. Down here, that might have held some truth.

"Avalee's engaged. I'm getting married. When's it going to be Clara Belle's turn?" A different voice filled the foyer, spoken in a tone that seemed intent on rubbing my face in all of my mistakes.

"Hey, Charlotte. How are you?" I dropped Avalee's hand and angled my body in Charlotte's direction.

She was leaning against the doorway leading from the living room, arms and ankles crossed, bestowing a look upon me that made me wonder why I'd been invited to this thing in the first place.

"I'm about to marry Ford McBride. I'm doing fabulous," she replied, a smile slipping into place.

I gave myself a moment to clear my head before replying. I wasn't getting into this with her again. Ford McBride wasn't worth fighting over. Ever again. "Cold feet?"

She stuck out her foot, a pink suede heel adorning it. "Toasty warm."

"Must mean it's meant to be then. You found your soul mate."

Charlotte watched me for a moment, searching for anything that might give away that my words were anything less than genuine. She wasn't going to find anything though, no matter how hard she looked, because I'd gotten over Ford so long ago, I couldn't even remember what I'd seen in him at the time.

"Speaking of soul mates," she said, shoving off the doorway and coming in our direction, "where is this new guy of yours?" She looked over my shoulders before scanning the foyer. "He isn't the imaginary kind, is he?"

I bit the inside of my cheek. Charlotte knew how to push me—she always had, and it had only gotten worse since she'd stolen my boyfriend. "He's upstairs. Probably passed out asleep by now." My gaze wandered up the stairs. No Boone in sight. Thank god, because I could barely manage this Abbot Estrogen Reunion on its own, sans bad boy from my past. "You'll all get a chance to meet him tomorrow morning."

"What's his name?" Avalee asked, clapping in fairy-like excitement.

I shrugged. "His Name."

She shoved at my arm, smiling like I'd just made a joke. I hadn't meant to, but I'd take it if that's what they wanted to think.

"Tell us something about him," Mom piped back into the conversation now that we'd moved on to the topic of my beau. "When we found out you'd be bringing your boyfriend along, I can't tell you how excited we all were. Your father and I . . . well, we've waited for this day for a long time."

"Me to bring a boy home?" I asked, confused.

"You to finally get serious and settle down." Mom's continued smile was starting to creep me out. Upon closer inspection, it looked like a serious Botox job was responsible for the smile that redefined creepy.

"Who says I'm settling down and getting serious?" My eyes crept up the stairs again, wishing I could escape before answering any more questions.

"You do, silly girl," Mom circled her hand in the direction of my face. "It's that look on your face right now, and that sound in your voice. I haven't seen you like this with anyone since . . ." She caught herself not a word too soon. Clasping her hands in front of her, she turned to my sisters like she was looking for a little help.

Avalee and Charlotte looked as surprised by Mom's near blunder as I was. After Boone's and my fallout, speaking his name had been like high treason within these walls. Even speaking *of* him had been a crime. I'd thought with all of the time that had gone by, paired with no shortage of other drama and debacles, Boone and what had happened would seem like old, tired news. Clearly not.

Avalee was just stepping forward to give me what looked like another hug—she was the "hugger" in the family—when someone else stepped into the foyer. Someone I hadn't seen in years and someone, had he not been marrying my little sister, I would have wished to avoid for another fifty.

"Clara Belle." Ford cracked a smile and leaned into the same doorway his wife-to-be just had. "I like your hair."

Mom's and Charlotte's eyes lifted to the ceiling at the same time in the exact same way. Creepy phenomenon number two on this trip home—middle sister was becoming a clone of our mother.

"Hey, Ford." My eyes fell to the ground for a moment under the pressure of his unwavering stare. I made them realign with his. I wouldn't let him make me feel small and inconsequential again. "Congratulations. You know, since I haven't gotten a chance to tell you yet. It's really great you and Charlotte are getting married."

Tension pressed into the room. Everyone knew what had happened between Ford and two Abbott sisters, and no one wanted to bring it up and call bullshit bullshit. We Abbotts preferred making nice and turning the blind eye— if only when it came to others of our "kind," because the opposite was the way Boone had been treated.

Ford nodded a few times, not seeming to blink as he watched me. "How's California treating you?"

I raised a shoulder. I didn't want them to know how great it was or how much I loved my life out there for fear of them moving and ruining the good thing I had going. "Good. How's South Carolina treating you?"

Ford's smile went higher on one side. High enough that his dimple set into his cheek. "Good," he answered, mirroring my nonchalant tone. "How's that little business of yours coming along? Throw in the towel yet? Opening a business is always more work than people figure, and a good half of them fail in the end anyway."

A hand slid up to my hip. What I'd ever seen in the elitist, conceited Ford McBride was lost to me now, but there must have been something redeeming in him at one time. Something more redeeming than his good looks and healthy trust fund.

"Not too bad." Too much coolness in my voice. *Back*

off, Clara. Don't let them get to you on your first night. You're a wall. The Great Wall of Clara. They can't move you, no matter what kind of blows they hit you with.

"If you ever need any consulting or expertise when it comes to running a business, I'd be happy to—"

"I'm sure Clara Belle can manage just fine on her own," Charlotte cut in, marching toward Ford like he were being fondled by a house of horny sorority sisters.

"Yes, *Clara* can and has managed just fine on her own. But thanks."

I didn't know why I still tried. Clearly no one in my family would ever respect my wish to be called Clara instead of Clara Belle. Yes, that might have been the name on my birth certificate, but by my estimation, it was one name too many. Clara was my name in California, though I doubted it would ever be so here. Only one person down here had ever called me Clara.

"The first year is the hardest, you know, Clara Belle, when businesses either make or break themselves," Ford powered on, ignoring his fiancée's attempts to distract him from the topic or, more accurately, me.

Charlotte had wound up with the man, but for some reason, I got the feeling she felt like we were still fighting for him. I hadn't even fought for him when I first found out about them, so it was a one-sided match on her part.

"This is my *third* year, and believe me, I'm doing just fine. Thank you again though." I felt my jaw tightening, so I worked it as loose as I could get it. The business I'd opened back in California had been the object of ridicule, scrutiny, and contempt in my family and those twined to it. To say their attitude wore thin on my patience would have been a tender way of putting it.

"You never were one for asking for help, Clara Belle." Ford gave me a look, something meaningful in his eyes he was waiting for me to pick up on.

I pretended to ignore it while Charlotte attempted to wrestle his attention away from me with her roving hands and her body pressed against him.

"Maybe that's because asking for help wouldn't have done any good. Maybe it's because there's only helping yourself in this family—in this world," I corrected when I heard my mom inhale, like I'd just slapped her across the cheek. I wasn't saying anything that was intended maliciously, but I was voicing what we all knew to be the truth.

Ford twisted a quarter turn, freeing himself some from Charlotte's hold. "God, you look great. Different, but great. You've come into your own, Clara Belle. Good for you."

Charlotte's hand stopped rubbing his shoulder.

I crossed my arms and moved a few steps to the side so I wasn't directly in front of him. I wasn't sure if he was intentionally fucking with me to get a response out of me or if he was being as genuine as Ford McBride was capable, but he was making me uncomfortable. Especially given our history. Especially given he was marrying my sister in five days.

It was Avalee who cleared the air, and just in time from the look on Charlotte's face. I couldn't tell who she wanted to water-board first: Ford or me.

"Come on, Clara Belle, who is your guy? I can't take all of the suspense because Mom's right, this one's different. This one means something to you." Avalee paused for a moment before waving dismissively at Ford. "No offense to you, Ford. Sorry."

Ford's clear blue eyes were narrowed some. "Plenty taken. Thanks though, Avalee. Besides, I could never make Clara Belle happy in the way she wanted to be. I knew that before I asked her out on our first date. I could try, but I could never try hard enough. She wasn't meant for me."

The room got quiet. Quieter. Inside, I felt closer to exploding though. Why was he talking like he hadn't been cheating on me with my sister? Why did he get to stand there and pretend I'd broken his heart instead of the other way around? Why was everyone in this room content to go along with that and continue to play oblivious to the fact that Ford was marrying my sister after fucking her behind my back?

There was so much bullshit filling the air, I was, for once, thankful I couldn't breathe down here.

"That's because *I* was meant for you, Ford." Charlotte put herself directly in front of him again, pawing his chest like a deranged kitten. After a few more seconds, she finally got his attention.

"Lucky me, sugar," he cooed and kissed the tip of her nose as he wrapped an arm around her shoulders.

Charlotte's eyes closed as she exhaled like she was relieved or something. Watching all of this Ford push-Charlotte pull made me sad. Genuinely sad. I'd been wanting to talk to my sister about Ford for years and find out why she seemed to be under the impression he was a deity wrapped up in mortal flesh, because I knew for a fact he wasn't. Charlotte and I might have had our differences, and she might have done everything to make my life harder than it needed to be, but that didn't erase the fact that I loved her and wanted the best for her.

The man she was about to marry did not fall into that category. Or anywhere close to it.

"So come on and spill it already. No more distractions." Avalee fired a warning look at Ford and Charlotte, who were kissing a bit too feverishly and *loudly* up against that doorway.

I did the mom thing and did my best to pretend it wasn't happening.

"Who is he? Who's this guy who's got you all riled up?" Avalee waved at me like I was proving her riled-up point right now.

"You can meet him tomorrow." I crossed my arms tighter, moving toward the staircase. Enough family reunion time for one lifetime. Time to retire.

"Come on, quit being so darn mysterious. Give us something to get us by until morning. "Avalee propped a hand on her hip and tapped her foot. "Tell us what he does."

"Why does that matter?"

"Because it always matters, Clara Belle." My mom had resurfaced from her delirium now that we were talking about the man she was probably already scheming how to get me married off to, at least until she learned who it really was. She stepped up beside Avalee and adjusted her long hair held back by a couple of clips.

I didn't know I'd rolled my eyes until they had already made their revolution. Mom didn't miss it either.

"I bet he's a movie producer, or maybe one of those indie rock singers from LA." Avalee clapped a few times.

Meanwhile, Charlotte detached herself from Ford long enough to glare at her sisters like we were a couple of imbeciles. It had been a long time since I'd gotten that look from Charlotte. It had come with such frequency growing up, I'd kind of missed it.

"He's probably one of those surfer bums whose address is the beach and gets around on the bus," Charlotte added.

I continued slowly toward the stairs, my foot so close to stepping up the first one.

"No, he's probably some high-powered entertainment industry attorney or a plastic surgeon to the stars or a real estate tycoon." Ford stepped out of Charlotte's embrace and meandered closer to me. Why was he looking at me like that? Why was he acting like the other three people in this room weren't there? "Clara Belle wouldn't just settle for anyone. She always had her sights set high . . . save for that one time, that one indiscretion . . ."

My blood rolled to a boil. Ford had no right to talk about my past like he knew the whole story. He had no right to deem who was or wasn't worthy of me. He had no fucking right to call a person I'd cared about a mere indiscretion.

What a piece of work.

"Enough with the lame guesses already," Charlotte half-shouted, glaring at Ford's back as he moved my way. "Are you going to tell us what he does or not, Clara Belle?"

"I'm not." I was in the middle of shaking my head when I noticed someone move out of the shadows at the top of the stairs.

It was a large, imposing figure, and one I didn't need to look at full-on to know whose outline it was. I'd memorized all there was to know about him years ago. Those memories might have been shuffled to the back of my mind, but they'd always be there.

"Unemployed," the figure now coming down those stairs spoke up. "That's my profession at this current time. Any other questions? I'd be happy to answer them now that I've gotten me and Clara settled in."

Three sets of eyes skipped to the stairway—Avalee's widening the least, my mom's widening to the point of being legendary—followed by three mouths falling open as they watched Boone make his way down the stairs. The fourth set of eyes, belonging to Ford, stayed focused on me, narrowing a bit more with every step Boone descended.

Mine though? Mine narrowed into slivers aimed at Boone. What in the hell was he doing? He wasn't incapable of following directions, and I knew he'd heard me ask him to stay upstairs. He was doing this intentionally. He was purposely trying to make this hard on me. I'd agreed to pay him ten grand to act as my plus one for the week, but I'd forgotten to lay down a set of much-needed ground rules. It was clear he was going to spend the next week paying me back for what he deemed I owed him from our past.

I would have been better off showing up solo.

"Get the hell out of this house, Cavanaugh. You practically destroyed this family and this girl." Ford's voice filled the foyer, his finger thrusting in my direction. "You have no right to be here. Leave."

Boone paused long enough in the middle of the stairs to look at Ford. To the others in the room, I knew Boone appeared as cool and in control of himself as he ever was, but I read the finer print they had yet to learn. The way the corners of his eyes creased when he was fired up. The way his knuckles pulled through his skin like they were readying themselves for a brawl. The way the muscles in his neck stiffened just enough to be visible. Boone had never liked Ford. Ford had never liked Boone. It wasn't just teenage boy rivalry; it had gone much deeper than that.

"If messing up this family and that woman is your qualification for who does and doesn't deserve to be in this house, then you better be the first to walk out those doors." Boone's hand tightened around the bannister, looking capable of turning the redwood into sawdust.

Ford shook his head, trying to look away from Boone, but he couldn't. "I'm done talking with you. I learned years ago that trying to rationalize with a wild, savage animal is like expecting them to have a conscience. Neither is possible. It's just in the animal's nature to be wild. And savage."

"Is that a promise I can get your signature on?" Boone continued down the stairs. "Because I really think I'd like that in writing."

My poor mother was looking between Boone and me like she couldn't figure out what was happening. She backed away when Boone tromped down the last few stairs. Avalee stayed where she was, giving me a curious look, while Charlotte's head looked ready to spin.

Ford's gaze sliced in my direction. "I thought you were smart, Clara Belle. The kind of girl who learns from her mistakes and doesn't make the same one twice."

Talking to me like I was a child. Patronizing me like I wasn't in possession of a scrap of intelligence. If he wasn't so far away, I might have slapped Ford McBride right then.

"It's *you* who's implying I made a mistake in the first

place—no one else." My voice came out two keys lower.

"I wasn't exactly implying anything," Ford replied, his gaze shifting between Boone and me like he'd just witnessed a train wreck and was trying to figure out what to do next.

"And he's not exactly alone in his not implying that either," Charlotte added, coming up beside Ford and winding her arm through his.

He tried to wag it off, but Charlotte's hold was unbreakable.

"What I've never understood about you all is why you're so concerned with everyone else's business when you have no shortage of your own business that needs serious attending to." Boone leapt down the last couple of stairs to land beside me. He shot me a sideways look before continuing. "I think that's what Reverend Simmons would call fixating on the speck in your neighbor's eye while ignoring the fucking plank in your own."

"Reverend Simmons doesn't say that word," Charlotte said, like she was just as innocent of never saying it. Which she wasn't. I'd heard her moaning it a handful of times before I stumbled in on her and my boyfriend.

"He should reconsider. Packs a punch, don't you think?" Boone said, grinning at Charlotte in such a way it was clear he was teasing her.

Her eyes narrowed. "Like you've ever sat through a Sunday service in your life, Boone Cavanaugh. Who are you to preach to us about morality?"

Boone stuffed his hands into his front pockets and shrugged. "No one, but with you all being regular church-going members, I would have thought you'd be on the whole speck/plank bandwagon. But clearly I'm way off, because I could see that plank in your eyes, Charlotte, from a mile back. The one dropped there when you decided to set your sights on your sister's boyfriend and fuck him silly in your sister's—"

My mother's throat-clearing rattled the chandelier.

I nudged Boone. He hadn't accepted what I had—bringing up the past and the wrongs held within it didn't result in an apology, but it could wind up declaring war.

"So you're unemployed, Boone?" Ford said, moving closer to us while my mom started fanning herself like she was close to passing out.

What a mess. I hadn't meant for this to happen like this. I hadn't meant to shock and alienate my family from the word go.

"And I only needed to say that once. Good for you for improving your listening and comprehension skills, Ford. You get an A-plus. And that's one your daddy didn't even have to buy you." Boone kept that half-smile pasted in place, acting like this entire thing was a game he was enjoying. Actually, I knew he was enjoying messing with Ford. It was one of Boone's favorite pastimes, just like messing with Boone was one of Ford's.

"And being unemployed is something new for you? Because that's not what the unemployment office is claiming . . ."

Charlotte tugged on Ford's arm like she was trying to warn him to shut up. I would have done the same to Boone, but I was afraid to touch him. I'd never been able to *just* touch Boone Cavanaugh.

"And high marks for wit and comic relief as well." Boone clapped in Ford's direction. "On a roll tonight, McBride. Nice to see what an Ivy League education and a couple hundred grand can buy a guy these days."

"I'm pretty sure Estelle here has a gardening position open." Ford lifted his arm in my mom's direction, waiting for her to confirm.

Her lips stayed sealed. She wouldn't offer Boone anything, I knew. A job pruning her roses included.

"Should be able to score a lot of overtime this week with the wedding and all," Ford continued. "Enough for some pocket change for the next time you find yourself with a woman and consider stopping by a convenience store to pick up some supplies. You know, in case you want to learn your lesson from the first time."

I felt like I'd just been punched in the ribs. My lungs collapsed, and I wavered in place. Around the room, my mom and sisters shared a gasp, while Boone's hands curled into fists as he squared himself in front of Ford. His tense shoulders quivered with what I knew was anger. Some people trembled when they were scared; some quivered when they were sad. Boone? Anger was only that emotion that could truly shake him.

"I'm not the only one who forgot to show up with 'supplies' in our lifetimes, Ford, so step off." Boone's voice was low and rolled through the room.

Whatever Charlotte saw on Boone's face had her reaching for Ford's arm again, digging her heels into the floor as she tried to pull him back a few feet. Not that I could blame her. Boone might have been in front of me, but I knew enough about that tone to picture which expression went along with it. We also knew that when those two had gotten into it in the past, Boone had always come out the winner—at least in terms of the blood-and-sweat battle. Ford had come out on top when it came to getting out of jail free and getting a pass on detention

"When did this happen, Clara Belle?"

My mother's voice was so quiet, I wasn't sure it was her who'd spoken. Only after realizing she was waiting for me to answer did I register who had asked the question.

"When did what happen?" I asked, stepping around Boone so I had a good view of everyone in the room again.

"You and . . ." My mom seemed almost scared to look at him, but she finally did. If only for a moment. "Boone."

This was exactly why I wanted to save the big reveal for tomorrow morning: so I could have the night to work out some story. Some story that didn't have anything to do with walking into a backwoods bar and offering an old flame ten grand to pose as my plus one.

"Not too long ago," I said right at the same time Boone said, "A while now."

Four pairs of eyes shifted between Boone and me.

"Why didn't you say something? Why didn't you give me a little warning . . . so I could prepare your father and myself for this?" My mom's complexion had gone a few shades lighter.

I couldn't remember a time I'd seen her so at a loss—other than the time after I'd told her about . . . *that* time. I shook my head and let go of that thought. That was the past, and a part of the past that was too painful to hold on to. I had to let that go for good somehow.

"I'm saying something now," I answered. "Sorry if you needed a warning before finding out Boone was my plus one, but I just didn't think it was that big a deal."

"Yeah, why would Boone Cavanaugh snaking his way back into your life again be a big deal?" Charlotte said under her breath.

My reply wasn't said under my breath. "Because that was eight years ago, and some people believe in moving on. Get over it already, Charlotte. I have."

Boone gave me another one of those sideways glances. I pretended to ignore it.

"Your father . . . I don't know how he's going to handle this," Mom fretted, glancing toward his study as if he was about to come out with guns blazing. "You know how he feels about what happened . . . how he feels about him."

"*He* is right here. Ten feet in front of you, Mrs. Abbott." Boone crossed his arms and seemed to stretch to his full height. "And *he* isn't sure how he's going to handle your husband either. *He* knows how he feels about what happened . . . and how *he* feels about Mr. Abbott too."

"Then why are you here? Why come back when you know the way we feel about you and with the way you clearly feel about us?" Mom moved over to one of the decorative Parisian chairs at the bottom of the staircase and settled into it.

I hadn't expected her to take this so hard. I hadn't expected the ironclad Estelle Abbott to be dropped to sitting status a few minutes after finding Boone Cavanaugh back in her family's life.

"Because Clara asked. That's why."

"I don't know if Clara asked for what you gave her eight years ago. Nice of you to be so accommodating now. Maturity becomes you, Boone."

Boone didn't look at Ford, nor did he fire anything back. The muscles banding down his jaw tightened though. He could fool Ford into thinking that he didn't give a rat's fuck about him, but Boone couldn't fool me.

He'd never been able to.

"Then why did you, Clara Belle, ask Boone to come?" Mom continued, folding her hands in her lap then refolding them the other way. "Surely you had to know what a ruckus this would cause. Why would you invite this kind of dilemma during such a special time for your sister?"

I made myself count to five before replying because my gut response wasn't so kind. "Because he's my plus one," I said slowly, each word more cursed than spoken.

Boone shouldered up close beside me, winding his arm around my shoulder and pulling me close. "Her boyfriend." He grinned around the room like it was a proud moment.

Just enough so no one else would notice, I elbowed him in the ribs. He was in so much trouble. I couldn't believe I'd offered him ten grand to throw gasoline on this fire that had almost burned out. Why couldn't I have just come alone? Why was I so afraid of my family knowing I had no one? Why did I care that I would be the last to get married even though I was the oldest? Why did I care what they thought in the first place?

My headache started coming back, and this time I didn't have a shot of tequila to dull it down.

"You fucked her life up once already, Cavanaugh. Didn't get enough that time? Needed to do it once more?" Ford took a few long strides toward us, breaking from Charlotte's hold.

Boone stayed in place, his arm still twined around me, not even flinching. The longer Ford stared at Boone's arm draped around me, the wilder his eyes became. Before my eyes, Ford was morphing into that wild, savage animal he'd just claimed Boone was.

"You still don't know what the hell you're talking about, McBride." Boone's arm tightened around me. "I'm tired of you pointing your finger my way when you should be pointing it your way just as much, if not more."

"You can keep telling yourself you're innocent on all counts, but come on, Boone, even a loser like you has to know better. You messed up Clara Belle's life once, and I won't let you do it again. You hear me?" Ford's voice grew louder with each word, his last almost a shout.

"I messed up Clara's life? Really? And who was the boyfriend dipping his stick in her little sister?"

Charlotte gasped, her palm lifting like she wanted to slap someone's cheek.

"You need to figure out what waters you can and can't swim in, Cavanaugh." Ford pointed at Boone, waving his finger like he was scolding him. "You're a piece of trash, and trash doesn't mix with the Abbotts. Trash belongs with other trash, something there's no shortage of in and around this town. So go fuck with some other piece of trash and make more trash, but keep your pollution to yourselves. You're not welcome in this family."

"Ford . . ." I growled, shaking my head at him.

Even my mom and Avalee looked shocked by what he'd just said. It might have been the unsaid belief among the wealthy families down here, but no one voiced it. Ever.

After a few seconds, everyone's gaze shifted to Boone.

Waiting for him to holler something just as spiteful or throw Ford to the ground and start swingin'. We waited, knowing Boone wasn't reputed for his peaceful resolution of conflicts.

Boone lifted his hand, his fingers curling into a fist.

And then . . . he covered his mouth and yawned—a loud, long one—followed by giving my shoulders a squeeze. "Sweetheart, it's bedtime."

My eyebrows pulled together. This was not the Boone I remembered. Everything else about him might have been very much the same, but walking away when tensions were at peak levels was not his trademark. This wasn't the time to question it though, or to fight his suggestion.

Giving the most convincing smile I could, I waved at those in the room. "Good night."

My mom's face went blank. "He's not staying here, is he? You're not staying in the same room surely."

Boone's arm stiffened against my shoulders as we were about to head up the stairs.

"Why wouldn't he be staying here?" I said. "Why wouldn't we be sharing the same room?"

All four people in the foyer came around the stairs, following us.

My mom led the charge. "Because Boone lives here in town and can stay at his place."

"Providing he has one that isn't the bed of his truck," Ford interjected, sneering in Boone's direction.

And we'd officially hit peak bullshit levels.

"Let's see, Ford lives in town. Sterling lives in town. Are they staying at their places this week, Mom?"

She held my stare, but she shifted her weight onto her other foot. "Well, no, they're not."

Of course they weren't, because Sterling and Ford came from wealthy, well-to-do families. And because they dressed a certain way. And drove a certain kind of car. And had gone to fancy schools and had fancy degrees and had fancy-sounding jobs.

Boone had been treated like a second-class citizen as long as I could remember. No more. I was still pissed at him for surprising us all down here tonight and was more than a little conflicted about how he'd gone about everything in the past, but I was done letting my family take a shit on him whenever and however they could.

When I started to climb the stairs, Boone followed, keeping his arm glued to my shoulder and matching my ascent, step for step.

"Good night," I said again when we were halfway up the stairs.

"Yes, good, we'll talk in the morning." From the sound of my mom's voice, she was a few breaths away from hyperventilating, but no one chased us up the stairs. "Let's just get a good night's sleep, and we'll work this all out tomorrow."

I didn't look back. I just kept going. This was where I'd failed before, but I wouldn't this time. Keep going, don't let them stop you. Don't let them even slow you down.

"Can't wait," I said under my breath before taking the final step and setting foot on the second floor.

Boone stayed silent the whole time, only dropping his arm when we were out of sight of the onlookers below. I hadn't looked back to see if they were all still down there, gaping at us with varying degrees of shock and disgust, but I could feel their stares aimed at my back through the wall, they were that intense.

As Boone and I travelled down the hall to one of the last doors, he hugged the wall, seeming to want to keep as much distance between us as possible. This was the first time we'd ever walked down this hall together, side-by-side.

Even when Boone had been nothing more than my childhood friend, my parents had barely allowed him onto the front porch, and when our relationship evolved into more, they certainly didn't let him get anywhere close to my bedroom. They didn't know about the dozens of times he'd climbed the tree outside my room, thrown himself onto the roof, and climbed through my window.

When I peeked at him striding down the hallway like he couldn't get down it quickly enough, Boone almost looked uncomfortable. His forehead folded together and his neck tense, he picked up his pace when he noticed me studying him.

I had the urge to say something to comfort him or say something about letting what had been said and how he'd been treated in the foyer roll off his back, but I couldn't find the words. The only words rolling around on my tongue were ones about him not listening to me, ones having to do with him betraying me when I'd trusted him . . .

I swallowed and pushed the past back into the recesses where it belonged. This wasn't then. I wasn't the same girl I'd been then. Boone probably wasn't the same guy he'd been either.

Don't project his mistakes from the past onto him now. Don't let past choices define present actions. Those were the phrases I repeated in my mind as we took the last few steps before pausing in front of my bedroom door.

Boone waited for me to open the door, and when I did, he waited again for me to go in first. Once I stepped inside, I turned and waited for him to come in and shut the door. I was still half-expecting the cavalry to come charging after us, and until that door was shut and locked, I wouldn't be able to relax.

But Boone stayed in the hall, his hands buried in his pockets and his eyes staring at the threshold between my hall and bedroom.

"I've never seen you so undecided about coming into my room," I said when I found him in the same place after I'd slid out of my shoes.

"That's because I know better now."

His words lodged a lump in my throat. I'd hurt him back then, but he'd hurt me too. So badly the scars I wore from what Boone and I had done to each other were ones I'd carry to my grave. But I didn't want to play the blame game this week. I wanted to bury the past once and for all with him.

"Are you coming in or not? Because I'm tired, and if you're going to stay out there all night, I'll just toss you a pillow and blanket now."

"Aren't you going to invite me in? Beg and plead until I cave like you used to?" Boone's voice was low and sharp.

"No, I'm not," I answered, all emotion drained from my voice. "Because I know better now too."

A huff came from the doorway right before he took his first step inside my room. After a few more, he closed the door, sealing us inside . . . and the air went from light to so thick with tension it felt stifling.

I pretended I didn't even notice, continuing to wander about my bedroom. I unzipped my suitcases Boone had propped up over by my closet, and turned on the light in the bathroom that adjoined my room.

My parents had left my bedroom just the way I'd left

it seven years ago. No doubt waiting for their prodigal daughter to return and snuggle beneath those lavender flower sheets, cuddle the stuffed bear on her nightstand they didn't know Boone had won me at a carnival one summer, and get back to being their good, obedient daughter.

If that was what they were waiting for, it would prove to be a lifelong wait.

"Hey, thanks, by the way, for listening to me earlier and staying hidden tonight. Nothing like coming home to the firing squad that is my family and throwing you into the mix five minutes later." I pulled out a pair of pajamas from my suitcase, but it was more for a distraction.

"No problem, Clara. Glad I could be of service." Boone settled into one of the chairs in the other corner of the room and tugged off his boots.

The air might have been heavy with tension, but there was something else moving in and taking over. Anger.

"Why in the hell did you do that?" I said, my words feeling venomous in my mouth.

Boone's boots bounced across the carpet as he tossed each one. Pulling off his socks, he did the same with those. He knew I was a bit of a neat freak when it came to my room, and this was clearly another way for him to try to ruffle me. "Because I'm tired of being your dirty little secret."

I popped up, wringing the heck out of my pajamas. "I'm paying you, Boone—a hell of a lot of money too. All I asked was for you to stay here and be a 'dirty little secret' for tonight."

"That's right. Exactly." He rose out of the chair, angling himself in my direction. "This is business. Which means I'm not some star-struck boy in love with a girl and willing to do anything for her. You might have been able to ask me to stay hidden in your room when we were kids, but I'm not a fucking child anymore, so stop treating me like one."

Pacing across the room, I collected his scattered boots and socks and tucked them neatly against the wall outside the bathroom. "Oh, yeah? Stop acting like one then."

Boone fired off another huff. "You first."

"Your maturity just keeps careening," I said before slamming the bathroom door behind me and locking it. I was planning on changing into my pajamas before crawling into bed and putting this whole God-forsaken day behind me, but instead I found myself leaning into the bathroom counter and fighting an onslaught of tears I hadn't known were coming until they were close to spilling.

I wasn't sure how long I'd been locked inside the bathroom, fighting off tears as fervently as I'd been fighting off bad memories all night, when a soft knock came at the door.

"Clara?" Boone's voice was quiet, back to the same one I remembered. "I need to take a piss."

So much had changed about him . . . and so much hadn't. I shoved off of the counter and finally changed into my pajamas. "There's a plant just outside the door. I'm sure it could use a good watering."

From the other side of the door, Boone sighed. "Clara?" Another sigh. "Are you okay?"

I kept changing, focusing on stuffing my arm through a shirt sleeve and my legs through the shorts' legs. "I'm okay, Boone."

Once I was done changing, I doused some cold water

on my face, brushed my teeth, and pulled open the bath-room door.

He was still there, hovering just outside. "Hey."

"Hi," I said, slipping past him. "It's all yours. Sorry for the plant comment."

Boone chuckled as he moved inside the bathroom. "I'm not. If you had taken another minute longer, I would have gladly 'watered' that plant. In fact, I just might before I leave this week, because I can't tell you how many times I've wanted to take a piss on something of your dad's . . ."

I made a proceed motion with my hand. "Knock yourself out."

Another soft chuckle filled the room before Boone closed the bathroom door.

While he took care of his business, I headed for my bed, throwing off the decorative pillows and throws before folding down the blankets and sheet. The same flowery fabric softener lingered in the sheets, transporting me back to my childhood and adolescence.

I'd just turned off a couple of the lamps staggered around my room when the bathroom door exploded open and Boone marched out of it . . . right before pulling his shirt over his head and tossing it onto his boots. I tried not to stare. I didn't want to stare.

I couldn't help but stare.

When his hands lowered to his jeans, unfastening the button before moving to his zipper, my blood curdled. "What do you think you're doing?" My voice came out squeaky and high.

Boone paused, mid-zipper-lowering. "Getting ready for bed."

"And this requires stripping?"

His head tilted as he took a good look at me. The corners of his mouth twitched when he noticed me clutching my pillow like I was about to strangle it. "Well, yeah, unless you have another set of those pink silky jammies. I'm not exactly into wearing stiff, heavy jeans to bed." He waited—I guess giving me a minute to offer him a pair of pink silky pajamas—before tugging his jeans down his legs and stepping out of them. "There. Much better."

He curled his jeans into a ball and flung them into the same corner as the rest of his stuff, giving me a front-row seat to checking him out when he wasn't looking. My throat ran dry, my arms tightening around the pillow clutched to my chest. Boone had always been in possession of a good body. The kind a girl couldn't help staring at and wondering what it would feel like wrapped around hers.

Years later, and nothing had changed. While some guys his age were starting to show signs of a gut, Boone's was still flat and hard, carved with so many lines and planes my eyes felt close to crossing from staring at them. His shoulders had gotten wider, his back broadening too. His skin was already browned from the summer, and from what I could tell, he hadn't gone and tattooed himself up like I knew my parents and our high school teachers had predicted.

All this time had passed and I didn't have a sliver of the feelings now I'd had for him then, but I still found myself being pulled toward him. Almost like a planet orbiting the sun, I couldn't escape his pull.

I plastered on an unaffected face and got back to fiddling with the blankets. "Is that really necessary?"

"Is what really necessary?"

"Sleeping in your underwear." Talking about them made me look at them, which made my throat run dry all over again.

Boone shrugged. "I've always slept in my underwear."

"Yeah, but you're not exactly sleeping alone, free to strut around however you want."

A smile that was a bit too knowing worked into position. "I remember wearing a whole lot less whenever it was just you and me in this room, Clara. If that's what you're getting at, I can just as easily go commando . . ."

When his hands moved to the waist of his boxers, I sat up. "The boxers work just fine, thank you."

"You're welcome." Boone snatched the pillow from my arms and dropped it on the floor. "Thanks for the pillow."

I pretended to ignore the grin he fired my way, and I finished turning off the lights. I kept the small lamp glowing on the table across my room, unsure I was ready to be in a dark room with Boone again. After crawling into my bed and tucking the sheet over me, I rolled over to the edge where he was just getting settled onto the carpet below.

"Thanks for staying in my bedroom like I asked." Then I snatched the pillow right back.

His head hit the floor with a bump that was accompanied by a surprised grunt. "Is that an invitation into your bed, or are you trying to prove a point that there are consequences for not obeying your highness?"

Accompanied by the darkness, Boone's low, smoky voice brought back memories I did not want to have resurrected when he was stretched out half naked less than a few feet away and I was still two shades past tipsy.

"I think you can figure out the answer to that question on your own." I kept my eyes focused on the ceiling, the sheet tucked tight under my arms.

"I'm not sure I can. I've never had much of a talent for figuring you out."

My eyes narrowed at the ceiling. "What's that supposed to mean?"

"Exactly what you think it's supposed to mean." From the sound of his voice, I knew his back was to me.

"You're hopeless when it comes to trying, wanting, or pretending to decipher people's feelings?" I stuffed the pillow I'd just stolen back from him beneath my head and tried to get comfortable. In the few seconds it had been pressed around his head, it had taken on his scent. The one that was still the same.

No amount of punching or adjusting would make that pillow any more comfortable.

"Only with you. Only because to really know and understand a person, that person has to *want* to be known and understood. Which you didn't. Which you probably never will." Boone sounded like he was shuffling around to get comfortable on the carpet. "So there."

As I continued my stare-a-thon with the ceiling, a smile started. *So there* had always been Boone's and my way of bringing up a grievance with each other, speaking our piece on the topic, and moving on. Our way of not getting hung up on the details when there were no shortage of much larger issues impeding our relationship. *So there* had been spoken between us so many times, it had been responsible for saving us from at least a few hundred potential fights.

A few hundred and one now.

"Hey, Boone?" I whispered a few minutes later. He hadn't moved or so much as fired off one of his go-to grunts, but I knew he was still awake.

One of those grunts sounded.

"Thanks for having my back down there," I said, rolling onto my side. The side facing him. "It's nice to know there's one person in this house who's in my corner. Even if it's the one I had to pay to stand there."

"When it comes to you and your family, I'll always have your back." From the change in his voice, I knew he'd turned in my direction as well. "And that has nothing to do with our present business arrangement."

I buried my head deeper into the pillow, finally feeling comfortable. "So there."

His chuckle was the last thing I remembered hearing before falling asleep.

CHAPTER THREE

"**C**lara Belle? Wake up already." A pattern of sharp knocks outside the door and just as sharp words roused me the next morning. "It's almost eight o' clock. Breakfast is on the table in ten. It would be nice if you'd grace us all with your appearance. That's what Mom said."

I groaned and threw a pillow over my face. A three-hour time change, five hours of sleep, and too much tequila were not the recipe for putting the "good" in good morning. Not to mention the snappy sister probably tapping her foot outside my door.

"Thanks for the wake-up call, Charlotte," I replied, my voice muffled by the pillow. "We'll be down in a few minutes."

"Yippee," she replied, though her tone was the opposite of what her word choice suggested.

Giving myself a few seconds to blink my eyes awake, I rolled onto my side. "Hey, Boone," I said around a yawn. "Time to rise and shine."

It took every scrap of strength and determination woven inside me to level my tone and expression and make it seem like I was as unfazed at waking up with him in my room as I could have been. Like rolling out of bed to an ex was a weekly sort of thing I scheduled into my calendar. When he didn't say or grunt anything, I scooted farther onto the edge of the mattress to see if he was really asleep or just giving me a hard time by ignoring me.

My eyes about burst out of their sockets when I peeked down at him. Throwing myself back onto my mattress, I tried to flush the image from my head, but the damage had already been done. No amount of flushing would erase it.

"And you clearly already are *rising* and shining."

A single-noted chuckle vibrated in his chest. "Quite clearly." His voice was extra smoky, heavy with sleep.

I clamped my eyes closed and hummed *Twinkle Twinkle Little Star* in an effort to distract myself from what I'd just seen. "Could you clearly take care of that please? So I can get up and get ready for breakfast before my family decides to break through that door and drag me down?"

"Would you like to assist me in taking care of it, or would you like me to take matters into my own hands?"

I wasn't looking at him, but I'd long ago memorized the smirk I knew was holding his expression captive right now. "Control yourself. For once."

Another chuckle rattled in his chest. "Come on, Clara. Chill out. It's perfectly normal."

"No, *that* most certainly is not normal." Why couldn't I stop picturing it? Why did it seem the harder I tried, the more it pressed into my mind?

"You're right. It's above average."

I snatched one of the pillows on my bed and fired it in his direction. "No, it's *ab*normal."

My eyes were still clamped closed, but I heard him moving around. "When I fell asleep last night, I don't recall it being around a pillow and blanket."

I cleared my throat. "When I woke up in the middle of the night, I had a weak moment, seeing you all curled up on the carpet and shivering. Sorry. It won't happen again."

"I'm used to sleeping in eighty-degree temperatures and eighty-percent humidity. This air conditioning should be renamed Arctic Blasting."

I'd never been a big fan of the air conditioning either. I didn't like feeling sealed up and shut in, trapped inside something that created an artificial environment.

"You're welcome," I said as Boone let out a loud yawn.

"Thank you," he said when he was finished.

"Breakfast is in ten, according to Charlotte, and I'd like to arrive a minute early so I can make sure she doesn't sprinkle arsenic into my eggs. I'd suggest the same to you."

"Since she hates my guts?" he said.

"Only outdone by how much she hates mine."

"Then we'd better get down there quick. I've still got years of pissing people off in me. It would be a shame to go before I'd reached my full potential." Boone shuffled to his feet beside the bed, the sheet still wrapped around his waist and hanging just below his hips.

He was still having morning . . . *issues.*

"Really, Boone? Not helping." I waved in the general direction of his southern . . . region . . . area.

"Sorry. I didn't realize you'd turned into such a prude. Kind of went the opposite direction on me."

I was looking away, but I heard him moving toward the bathroom.

"Don't worry. The above-average tent pitcher is out of sight . . . but maybe not so out of mind, right, Clara?

"Boone . . ." I warned, not sure how I'd survive the day if it continued in the same manner. Morning wood and illicit comments revolving around it had exhausted me sufficiently—no need for anything else.

"You know I love it when you say my name like that."

I ground my teeth together, cursing my moment of weakness last night. Sure, he was cute when he was sleeping, but the awake version wasn't anything close.

"I'm just gonna take a quick shower, then we'll go watch for arsenic poisoning, k?"

I rose up in bed and twisted in his direction. "Not enough time . . ."

Boone was heading into the bathroom, his back to me and still clutching the sheet around his waist. However, it wasn't covering anything around his backside.

"Jesus Christ, Boone. What happened to your boxers?" I should have clamped my eyes closed again, but Boone's backside . . . yeah, it would have been a crime against humanity to divert my eyes when his ass was in view.

"I took them off. Too restrictive."

"Well, would you mind putting them back on? Preferably before I wake up and you start traipsing around my room naked?"

"I've got a sheet on." He paused outside the bathroom

door and turned around.

My eyes shot up from where they'd just been focused. I didn't want him to know I'd been checking out his ass. From the flash in his eyes, he already knew.

"A sheet only works if a person cinches it around their front *and* back." I lifted an eyebrow at him.

"Oh, well, in that case . . ." Lifting his arms in a *what the hell* kind of gesture, he let the sheet float to the floor. And now he was standing in front of me, facing me, fully naked.

I tried not to look.

I wasn't up to the task apparently.

"You've proven your point, Boone. You have nothing to hide. Would you mind covering up now?" My chest was on fire, spreading to the further reaches of my body. How I managed to sound so unaffected, I didn't know.

"Nothing you haven't seen before. Nothing you haven't done a lot worse with either." Giving another shrug, Boone disappeared into the bathroom, only closing the door halfway.

While he took his shower, I threw on a light cotton shift dress and a pair of sandals, and ran a brush through my hair a few times before I tied a scarf around it. I wanted to brush my teeth, but that would have required stepping into the bathroom, and after everything that had already happened between Boone and me this morning, I didn't need to add seeing him step out of the shower, wet and naked, to that list.

There was only so much a woman could take before she broke. I was fast approaching mine.

So the tooth brushing was delayed, temporarily filled in by a couple pieces of mint gum I'd unearthed from one of my suitcases. I'd just finished popping in my second piece when I heard the shower turn off.

I sat on the edge of my bed, having already made it, and waited for Boone to get dressed. When he emerged from the bathroom a minute later, in the same clothes he'd been wearing last night—since the whole packing a suitcase for my plus one hadn't crossed my mind—he broke to a stop when he saw me.

"You waited for me," he said, more like a question than a mere observation.

"You seem surprised."

He rolled the cuffs of his sleeves up past his elbows, giving his wet hair a shake. Droplets of water rained around my room, catching the sunlight breaking through the windows and forming hundreds of tiny prisms.

"I just assumed you would have headed down when you were ready, you know, so you wouldn't keep your family waiting." He bent over to tug on his boots, seeming grateful for the distraction.

"Yeah, well, I didn't want to throw you to the sharks all alone. This might be a business deal, but that doesn't mean I can't treat you humanely in the process."

Boone stopped in the middle of tugging on his second boot, the skin between his eyes creasing. He was going to say something—I could feel it—then the moment passed before it had a chance to take root.

Standing, he cleared his throat and headed to the door. "Rip the bandage off?" He opened the door and waited.

"Rip that sucker off."

I lifted off the bed and crossed the room toward him. When I passed by, I felt like I was passing through an energy field. Like the electricity in the air was especially concentrated around him. That wasn't something new when it came to Boone, but it was something I'd hoped would have been decommissioned after all of this time. After all of the baggage that came with the story of us.

When I stepped into the hall, I almost felt my walls lifting back into place. My body armor fit snugly around me, secured so there were no weak spots a sharp thing could penetrate. It came naturally. I'd learned long ago that the only way to survive in this family was to protect myself, invisible walls and armor included.

"Let me do the talking when it comes to us," I whispered to Boone, who'd shouldered up beside me and wasn't scanning the area like he was just waiting for some family member to pop out of one of those dozen doors and fire off one belittling comment after another.

His head shook. "Yeah, when I followed that advice from you last time, your parents called the cops, thinking I was some half-naked miscreant in your bedroom, about to defile their daughter. Instead of believing the 'alleged' miscreant was dear daughter's boyfriend who she'd just been defiling." He gave me a nudge with his elbow, his grin as wicked as they came. "For the second time that morning."

"You weren't so eager to divulge what we'd been up to that morning either, so why don't you turn that tsk-tsk tone on yourself for a change?" I scooted away from him, giving myself some space.

We were almost down the stairs and heading into the breakfast dining room—because the Abbott family had been eating their breakfasts in a separate room than their dinners for five generations—when Boone's forehead creased. "It's too quiet down here. Are you sure they weren't going out to breakfast or something?"

Now that I was paying attention, I realized I didn't hear anything either, which was unusual. Usually my dad's booming Southern voice could be heard from a few rooms back, or my mom trying to get my dad's attention by firing off question after question about whose dinner invite they should accept for the weekend, and Avalee and Charlotte could almost always be heard bickering about something. This morning though, when I knew at least a dozen extra bodies were living under this roof, I couldn't make out the sound of a spoon scraping against a bowl.

"No, I'm not sure. Since Charlotte was the bearer of the breakfast news, this could be some kind of booby trap." I craned my neck to look into the living room to see if anyone was in there. Like the rest of the house, it was empty.

"Or maybe Reverend Martin finally got it right and Armageddon arrived and took away all of the bad eggs," Boone said, checking the kitchen to find it just as empty.

The thought made me laugh. "Free at last. Thank God Almighty, and Armageddon, I'm free at last."

Boone and I were both still laughing as we rounded into the silent dining room. The breakfast dining room. Our laughs cut off mid-note.

"I don't know about bad eggs, but if they're not cold already from waiting on you two, they're about to be."

Boone cleared his throat while I slid a bit in his direction. There was a cold front directly ahead, whereas he'd always given off a warmth that bordered on sunshine.

The room had been silent before. It somehow became even more so.

At the head of the long table was my dad, untouched by age and unsoftened by experience, if his expression could be trusted. Where I was used to seeing three of the two dozen chairs staggered around the table filled, this morning, every one save for one was filled. Some faces I recognized; most I didn't.

All clearly knew who I was though. Just as clearly as they knew who Boone was. No, that wasn't the right way to put it . . . more likely, they knew *of* Boone.

Not the version I'd grown up knowing or even the one he truly was.

"Daddy," I said at last, trying on a smile because the situation warranted it. Seeing one's dad for the first time in over two years generally did . . . right? "I'm sorry I missed you last night. It's good to see you again."

"Yes, well, if someone would have arrived when we were expecting her, you wouldn't need to make an apology in front of everyone at the breakfast table, would you?" My dad's voice filled the room, bouncing off the walls and filling the empty spaces. He wasn't what I would call a hard man, just an unbending one. He knew what he knew, and what he knew was the truth. No exceptions.

That left anyone looking to have a relationship with him the person who'd have to make so many justifications and conditions until they broke. The only way to love an unbending person was to break yourself.

It was what I'd done with my father.

It was what I was hell-bent not to do again.

"Your mother had the good grace to tell me who your date was for the wedding. The same good grace you might have exercised so we had a bit of a . . ." My dad's eyes finally landed on Boone. If looks could commit murder, my dad had just earned himself a life sentence. "Warning as to what was coming."

"Don't you mean *who* was coming?" I said in a tone that got closer to snapping than saying.

My dad's gaze cut back to me, his silver brow lifting in a way that suggested he'd made no error.

Boone moved a bit closer to me, holding his head so high it looked unnatural. "I bet you never thought you'd see my face around here again," he said, managing to project in the same manner my dad had mastered.

Dad settled back into his chair, lifting the newspaper in front of his face. "More like *hoped* I never would," he said, as though he were speaking to himself. "But like my daddy always used to say, hoping is worth its weight in shit."

My eyebrows drove into my forehead. My dad was of the South, for the South, and the essence of the South, which meant he followed a certain code of conduct that was exclusive to this part of the world. Part of that code included never cursing in front of the "gentler" gender and making up for those periods of abstinence by cursing it up with the rest of the Neanderthals who considered themselves the very pinnacle of human-dom. That he'd just dropped a shit bomb in front of a roomful of women meant my dad wasn't feeling like himself. Either that, or he'd been possessed by a guy who'd spent a lifetime in a trailer park outside of Detroit.

"Why don't you take a seat so we don't starve our guests away?" Dad shook his paper open but couldn't seem to distract himself from Boone and me hovering inside the room.

"There's only one chair left." I waved my finger between Boone and myself. "And there are two of us."

Dad lifted his brow again, an expression of *So?* settling onto his face.

To my dad's left, Ford covered his mouth as a laugh erupted from him. Everyone was still staring at us, and no one was taking the initiative to make the introductions, so I continued to stand there, accepting the gaping and snickers and invisible question marks hanging above everyone's head. Waiting.

I'd spent half of my life waiting. Waiting for something that had never come to life. Waiting for something I couldn't designate with a name even.

"It's okay, sweetheart," Boone said, his voice drawing out the term of endearment longer than necessary. "You can sit on my lap. Wouldn't be the first time we've eaten breakfast like that."

When I looked at him smiling down at me like everything was coming up roses, I found my eyes starting to narrow. I caught myself before anyone else seemed to notice.

I was just about to plaster on a smile and say something along the lines of, "Not when there's company around" when my mom shot out of her seat.

"Now there's absolutely no need for anyone to be left without a chair when we've got a whole storage room packed with them." Mom lifted her eyebrows at one of the kitchen employees hovering in the corner of the room, then she plastered on a smile of her own. "I must have miscounted when I gave Frieda the number for breakfast."

"You must have," Boone replied, his smile more convincing than my mom's, though I knew what he was saying between the lines. *You didn't miscount anything, lady.*

You simply chose not to count me.

"How did everyone sleep?" Dad gave up on his paper and dropped it into a crumpled heap on the edge of the table. He couldn't stop watching Boone and me.

A chorus of "good" and "well, thank you" swept around the table. The new chair was just being nestled in beside the other empty chair. Frieda rushed back into the kitchen to grab another place setting, and Boone took my hand and walked me over to our chairs. My dad's eyes lowered to where Boone held my hand. If you could kill the same person twice, my dad had just earned himself another life sentence.

"I don't know if you want to call it sleep, per se," Boone said, firing off a wink around the table before continuing, "but I had one hell of a night if you know what I mean."

My mouth wasn't the only one that fell open. My mom's, along with a few others, followed my lead, while Dad and Ford went with something more along the lines of curling their lips while reaching for their butter knifes. As Boone slid out my chair for me, I gave him a subtle nudge before sitting. One that suggested he shut the hell up unless he wanted me to stab him in the knee with my fork if he made any more comments of that nature.

Frieda raced back into the room and set up Boone's place setting in less time than it took me to unfold my napkin and smooth it into my lap.

Breakfast was a formal affair at Abbott Manor, as most everything was. We ate our eggs with cloth napkins, drank our coffee from porcelain cups painted with gold leaf, and sipped our pressed-fresh-every-morning orange juice from imported Italian crystal. While the breakfast centerpieces were typically extravagant, from the three floral pieces lining the center of the table, I guessed my parents had had every floral shop from Charleston to Raleigh on round-the-clock mode.

"Estelle tells me you're unemployed, Boone." Now that we were seated, my dad sawed into his ham steak, though I couldn't help feeling like it was Boone's neck he was envisioning. He cut into it a bit more eagerly than breakfast ham warranted.

Boone took a sip of his orange juice, ignoring the heads turned his way. "Estelle speaks the truth."

"Is this something new?" Dad asked, before lifting a piece of ham to his mouth.

I reached for my own glass of juice. Breakfast hadn't even started, and I was already counting down the bites until it was over.

"My business just went under." Boone took another drink, draining his glass. When he was done, he slammed his glass on the table like he was in some gunslinger bar and that was the way one asked for another drink. "So yeah, new within the past few weeks."

My eyebrows came together as I processed what he'd just said. I hadn't known anything about Boone owning his own business or what that business might have been. I hadn't known that had been on his radar even. The fact that it had gone under so recently gave me fresh insight into why he'd so quickly taken the deal I offered him.

Desperation: what makes the world go round.

"What kind of business was that?" The forkful of ham stayed frozen in the air as my dad continued his interrogation.

When Frieda came up behind Boone after giving me a

side of ham and poached eggs, she waited. Boone glanced back when he noticed her, his forehead lining.

"Your napkin, Cavanaugh," Ford piped up. "It goes in your lap. It's not used for wiping your ass like I know you were thinking."

Beside him, Charlotte snickered, and across the table, Mr. McBride, who looked to have packed on fifty pounds in seven years and run his liver into the ground judging from the pale brown spots dotting his arms and face, popped off a single-noted laugh.

"Please, everyone. We're at the breakfast table, and we've got a whole tableful of guests." Mom patted the air with her hands, addressing the room like the debutante she'd been. "Now, Boone, you were telling us about the little business you started up . . ." Her hand flicked in his direction, giving him the floor.

I fought the urge to correct her for applying the word *"little"* to both Boone's and my business ventures. In Freudian terms, that pretty much meant my mom thought we were a couple of fools to think we could or should think big enough to venture into the business world. She'd never understand, because to understand, a person needed to be wired with the understanding code.

She wasn't.

Pinching his napkin, Boone simply moved it from his plate to the side of it. He didn't put it in his lap, where it so-called belonged. In his own way, a way that wouldn't earn him a reprimand from my mom, Boone was giving the finger to Ford. "I started a non-profit kids' rec center."

Guests in the process of eating their breakfasts stopped chewing. I'd been about to dive into my thick slice of buttered toast when I turned my attention elsewhere. A kids' center? A non-profit? *Come again?*

"What's that?" Dad pressed, his mustache curling higher from his half-smile. "Like a daycare?"

Again, Ford choked on a laugh, though this time he didn't seem to care about trying to hide it.

Boone grabbed his fork and cut into one of his eggs. My dad wasn't the only one venting his emotions on the breakfast food.

"No, kids could come and go as they wanted," Boone explained around a mouthful of egg, "but it gave the growing number of kids in our community who are being raised in unstable-to-volatile homes a soft spot to land for a few hours. A place where they could just be kids and get warm meals." He finished with a shrug and stuffed the other half of his egg into his mouth.

No one had anything to say, not even my dad or the laughing hyena Ford. I didn't even know what to say, because I couldn't figure out how to think about what Boone had just said. He'd owned and run a charitable program for the underprivileged kids in the community? He gave them a safe place to play and a reliable place to eat a hot meal? He had the vision to start something like that, the knowledge to see it through to completion, and the composure to explain it to a roomful of judgmental strangers, even after that business had crumbled?

Who was the person sitting beside me? What had happened to the one who had turned his back and left me when I'd needed him most? How did that kind of a person go on to build a business that revolved around supporting others and being there when others weren't?

It seemed Boone and I had more to get straight than just our fake story of how we'd reunited after all of these years.

"I take it this non-profit paid you a salary.'" Ford leaned forward in his seat, innocence pasted onto his face. Ford was so many things, and none of them included innocence.

Beside me, Boone blew out a slow breath. "Yeah, it did, and before you go and assume I was corruptly drawing six figures a year from it, my salary was twenty-four thousand." The internal gasps from the majority of guests lining the table was so loud, it almost made me jump in my seat. "It's a matter of public record. You know, just in case you don't believe me and want to double-check."

Ford exchanged a look with my dad. From the looks of it, those two were still each other's second-biggest fans —next to themselves.

"Oh no, Boone, it's clear from those boots you're still tromping around in that you were making less than the poverty line." Ford's dimple set into his cheek as he fought to suppress a smile when Charlotte laughed. "My question had more to do with why in the hell a man would open a business and welcome all the headaches that come along with that if he knew he would be making less than 25K. I mean, it's an okay weekly sort of salary, but I thought there were labor laws protecting people from that kind of atrocious annual income."

Of all the bodies at the table, only Avalee and myself were giving Ford an appalled sort of look. Probably because most of the people around the table were his family and friends . . . actually, I think just as many were members of my own family, albeit distant ones I hadn't seen in years and couldn't name if someone dangled a one-way ticket home leaving in an hour in front of my face.

Boone continued to work at his breakfast though, half of it already shoveled into his mouth. "Because maybe my kind of reasons behind doing things are entirely different than your reasons." When he returned Ford's stare, there was fire in Boone's eyes. Fire was another word for contempt. "I could explain it, but you wouldn't understand."

Charlotte rolled her eyes as she continued picking at her eggs, stabbing at them until the yolk burst and pooled in the center of her plate. Knowing Charlotte, she was probably trying to lose another ten pounds before the wedding. She wore a size 25 in jeans and had been underweight by medical standards her whole life, but if you asked her, there'd never been a time when she couldn't stand to lose ten pounds.

Me on the other hand? According to the devil—also known as the BMI chart—I was a perfectly average weight for my height, but according to my mom, my size eight was about four sizes too big. Being a non-underweight teen girl in this household had been hell. Even now, my mom couldn't help eyeing my piece of toast every time I lifted it to my mouth. You know, since carbs were the enemy.

"Speaking of business ventures, what's this I hear about your company expanding, Clara Belle?" Dad lifted his coffee cup in Frieda's direction, irritation set into his brow. Frieda bustled over with the coffee pot like the lives of an entire continent were in her hands. "Making its way down into the belly of the country here? Are my sources correct?"

All heads turned in my direction. All of them save for Ford's, who stayed focused on his plate as he cut into his ham like he was performing surgery.

"The business is thriving. Sales are soaring," I said, feeling like I was explaining it to the whole table. "My goal wasn't to just keep to California if this worked; it was to expand nationally. I just didn't think it would happen so quickly."

Boone set down his fork and angled in his seat toward me. "What kind of business, Clara?"

He realized his slip an instant after I did. His expression stayed flat though. The mistake only registered in his eyes, whereas my whole body and face went rigid with an *oh shit!* feeling.

"You don't know what Clara Belle does?" Ford wasn't focused on dissecting his ham and eggs anymore. "How long have you been seeing each other again?"

My dad pressed his forearm into the table and leaned forward. "Yes, how long?"

I took a sip of my orange juice, stalling. Boone stayed quiet, peaking his brow just enough to let me know he was heeding my warning to let me do the talking when it came to our relationship.

"Do you want to know about my business or about Boone and me?" I asked, circling my fork at my plate that had mostly gone untouched thanks to the Q & A firing squad. "Because I'd like to be able to take a bite of my breakfast sometime this morning."

My mom's eyes drifted to my half-eaten piece of toast. I knew that in her eyes, I'd already eaten enough to get me through lunch.

"Why don't you just sum it *all* up for us, Clara Belle, since it seems there's a whole lot of fuzzy area surrounding you, and we'll throw in the clarifying questions if we have any," Dad said.

93

Dad ignored Charlotte when she said something to him, no doubt trying to get his attention as she had for her entire life. What I'd come to expect was that the only thing that garnered our father's attention when it came to his family was potential scandal and anything that might tarnish the supposed pristine Abbott name. Between the three of his children, I'd been the most "problematic," and therefore received the most attention.

What Charlotte failed to realize in her jealousy was that there was a difference between good attention and *bad* attention.

"Well, the business's sales have tripled over last year and are expected to—"

"How about you start your summary with why Boone Cavanaugh is sitting at my breakfast table beside my daughter, whose heart and innocence he crushed a lifetime ago." Dad held his smile for the other guests nibbling at their breakfasts in silence, no doubt feeling like a bunch of third wheels. "That is what interests me most at the present moment. I'd like you to look me in the eyes and explain to me why that boy is the one you chose to bring as your date this week."

"My plus one," I corrected automatically.

Boone gave me a sideways look, like I'd somehow just betrayed him.

"Pray do tell, just how long have you and your 'plus one' been reacquainted? Because the last time you were able to squeeze us into your busy schedule and fly back home, I was under the impression you'd forgotten the name Boone Cavanaugh, and certainly the man behind that name."

A couple of conversations were starting to circle the

table, and I was thankful I didn't feel the pressure of two dozen sets of eyes aimed my way anymore. It made thinking on the fly much easier.

"I don't know. It's difficult to say, exactly, when we got reacquainted . . ." I fumbled for the right words to cut and paste together an airtight lie. "I guess we just sort of started talking a while ago, emails here and there, sporadic phone calls, that sort of thing . . . and you could say one thing led to another led to us sitting next to each other at your breakfast table this morning." When I finished massacring that explanation, I picked up the other half of my toast and stuffed it into my mouth to shut myself up.

Dad's forehead was creased with lines of confusion, as were Ford's, Charlotte's, and Mom's. Even Boone's forehead was creased, although his expression was less confused and more *what the hell?* I gave a just-detectable shrug, and he stabbed a chunk of ham and stuffed it into his mouth, chewing on it like he had a serious beef with his pork.

"So are you two just friends? Or is there more to it?" Dad pressed. "Because your mother tells me you two shared the same room last night, so that tells me there's *something.*"

And how about that breakfast?

I felt like I was slowly slumping into my chair, one pointed question at a time. In a few more, I'd be falling out of it, and somehow, that sounded like the most appealing option.

"I think that's difficult for either Boone or me to answer," I said once I'd finished my toast. "So maybe we could move on to discussing something more exciting . . . like the big wedding coming up." When I threw my hands in Charlotte and Ford's direction, I got nothing more than a glare and a hair swish from my sister.

"Please, darling," Boone's voice filled the room, sounding a bit more game-show-host than backwoods-Southern-boy. This wouldn't be good; the darling part gave that away. I slumped deeper into my chair. "You don't have to go and understate what we have just because few people ever get to experience the connection you and I have."

I tipped my head at him and forced a smile that was anything but benign. "What are you talking about Boone?" I added under my breath, *"Why* are you talking?"

He aimed a wink at me. "If you're going to keep on with this modest approach, let me take over and explain how it really is between us."

"Please don't," I muttered through clenched teeth, ramming my knee into his beneath the table.

He patted my leg a few times in return. "A few of you at the table know that Clara broke my heart when we were kids. Broke might be an understatement, but you get the idea. She crushed me."

Ford exhaled sharply, shaking his head. My dad was doing the same thing.

Boone continued, ignoring the varied responses circling the table, "When we reconnected, I thought I'd give us another go and, if nothing else, see if I could repay her the heartbreaking favor."

"What exactly do you call what you did to her back then?" Ford said, aiming a look at Boone like he was contemplating the quickest route to get to him so he could wring his neck.

Boone ignored Ford, holding his smile and staring at

me like I was his whole world. My knee kept ramming his, but it was getting me nowhere besides a sore leg.

"But boy, did my plans for revenge backfire," he said, almost cooing.

I felt sick. What had I done? What was I doing? Why didn't I just stand up and admit to everyone what had transpired to bring Boone to my side this morning. The truth would have been ten times better than this story he was weaving.

Dad shoved his plate away and leaned in, his gaze leveled on me. "Just how serious is this?"

He was waiting for me to answer him, but it was Boone who gave it to him. "I don't know your definition of the word, but I gotta tell ya, Mr. Abbott, there have been plenty of times I've looked into those blue eyes of hers and seen my forever in them." Flashing me another wink, he patted my cheek.

I resisted the urge to swipe his hand away. No need to further confuse everyone—they looked so confused already, eyes were close to going crossed.

"Clara Cavanaugh . . ." Boone said, nodding in approval. "It sounds pretty, doesn't it? Like some fairy-tale made-up name or something."

My dad's face was red. My mom looked closer to hyperventilating. I was both.

"No need to rush things." My father's voice made each word sound like he was cursing instead of speaking.

Boone shrugged, stuffing a piece of toast into his mouth. "No need to slow things down either."

I grabbed my fork and lowered it into my lap. If he kept going, I was going to stab him in the thigh with it.

"You don't have a job." Dad lifted one finger in the

air, then another one. "You have no way to support my daughter."

"Clara's got a job," Boone replied. "She could support me."

Ford threw down his napkin and shoved away from the table. Dad looked another word from Boone away from doing the same thing.

"Isn't that the way an *equal* marriage should work?" Boone asked.

At the word marriage, Mom looked closer to fainting than hyperventilating.

"I'm not planning on staying unemployed forever, or even for long, but in the meantime, good thing for us both she makes some serious bank." Boone nudged me with his elbow, his face glowing from the thrill of pissing off my family and throwing me for one hell of a loop at the same time.

"Which I'm sure is why she'll have you sign a prenup before that 'forever in her eyes' turns into a reality." When Frieda appeared with the coffee carafe to refill my dad's cup, he waved her away. "Isn't that right, Clara Belle?"

My dad was waiting for me to reply. To back him up. My voice, or more likely my will to project it, was gone.

"Whatever Clara wants. She's a smart girl. I trust her." Boone popped the last bite of his half piece of toast into his mouth before sliding the other half onto my plate. He must have remembered how much I loved all things bread.

My mom didn't miss it, and would no doubt ensure whatever was on my lunch plate was adjusted to include no carbs.

I wasn't sure what to think of the shared toast. Was it

just another way of him messing with me? Messing with my mom because he remembered how she'd monitored every morsel that went into my mouth back then? Or was this the Boone I remembered? The generous, kind one who would have given a friend his life or limb if they asked for it.

I didn't have time to process it though, because that was when Dad fired off more questions, hardly pausing to take a breath between each one. "Do you have an attorney back in California, Clara Belle? Do they even have any that take clients outside of celebrities? You'll need one separate from your business attorney, one well-versed in prenuptial arrangements of the kind you and Boone potentially might be drawing up."

"More like *improbably*," Ford muttered, his breakfast untouched from the looks of it, mirroring his wife-to-be's.

"Let me give Bill a call later this morning and see if he can recommend someone out in your neck of the woods. He's got plenty of connections," Dad continued relentlessly. "And remember, you want someone who represents *you,* not both of you." My dad pulled his phone from his pocket, breaking a cardinal rule of no phones at the table, either making a reminder or about to dial up Bill right this minute. "I'll ask him too if he knows of anyone who can help you with your business. While I've got him on the line."

"I have someone who sees to the legal matters around the business," I got in. My voice sounded so small, I don't think Boone even heard me.

"And if you haven't already, put together a will, Clara Belle. One that will protect your company, in the event of your death, from those close to you who might have less-than-honorable intentions when it comes to their interest in you all of a sudden."

"Am I to infer from your tone that you're referring to individuals outside of her own family who have less-than-honorable intentions?" Boone didn't hide the accusation in his tone.

"I think we've all heard enough from you for one morning, Mr. Cavanaugh. I'm talking to my daughter directly—I'm certainly not going through the snake pouring poison into her ear." Dad waved his finger between him and me, implying we had the tight bond that some dads had with their daughters. Most everyone at the table probably knew better though. "Besides, this is a family breakfast. You might be trying for a second time to weasel your way into it, but I can assure you if I have anything to say about it, you'll be as successful marrying into the Abbotts as you were the first time you made your play."

"Dad . . ." I said, but it barely registered a decibel.

Shouts and protests broke out around the table—my dad shoving out of his chair, still popping off insults at Boone; Ford beside him, adding fuel to the fire; and my mom bouncing in her seat, about to cry from the way her "perfect" wedding week kick-off breakfast was turning into a scene out of a reality television series. If the table hadn't been so large, I didn't doubt my dad wouldn't have already thrown it over.

"Dad, stop," I tried again, but it was useless.

Boone, who'd stayed calm during the first brunt of my dad's attack, was shoving out of his seat, firing back insults and accusations just as lashing. That was the point I tuned out.

I shouldn't have come back. No one really wanted me

here anyway. Charlotte had only invited me because our mom had insisted and Mom had only insisted because I was the sister of the bride and what would the five hundred guests think if the sister of the bride wasn't there? The Abbott Family Façade would no doubt be shattered for good over that scandal.

Invitation or not, I shouldn't have come. I brought dissent and disaster upon this family. They brought the same upon me. We were better off without each other, something I'd accepted the day I stepped foot into my first apartment back in California and realized it felt more like home than the one I'd grown up in ever had.

Everyone still at each other's throats, I quietly pushed out of my chair, stood, and silently left the room. If anyone noticed me leave, no one called out to me. If anyone cared I was leaving, no one expressed it.

I passed Frieda in the hall, her face settled into a concerned expression, but before she could ask me if I was okay, I nodded and kept going. I had to get out of this house and find some fresh air. Or some fresher air at least.

I went through the back of the house, shoving through the screen door the house staff were required to use. I'd always felt more comfortable passing through that old side door than the sweeping double ones at the front anyway.

The moment my feet touched the grass, I kicked off my sandals, pulled the bow out of my hair, and jogged toward the edge of the grounds. I knew where I was going, but I couldn't get there fast enough. I felt as though I had a rubber band around my waist, and the farther I got from the house and my family, the harder it fought to pull me back. The harder I had to fight to keep pulling away. If only I could just find the point where that rubber band would snap and the connection could be cut once and for all, life could be so much easier down here.

For once, I could feel as apathetic about my family as I pretended I was.

The tire swing was still there, dangling from one of the big oak trees creeping along the streambed, more of the tire covered by Spanish moss than was exposed. I supposed without me around, there was no one to climb through it and swing away hours of the day, searching for the answers to their problems in the steady pendulum of a rope tied to a circle of rubber.

The morning was warming up but still cool enough to be enjoyed, the humidity not yet sticking to my skin like an impatient lover. I approached the swing and carefully swept aside the moss, just enough to climb through the tire and swing, but not so much it would damage the tendrils of moss. Time had frayed the rope and lined the rubber with cracks, but it was still there. Still serving its purpose and persevering.

The tire swing had been one of the few things my dad had added to the grounds with his own hands and sweat and elbow grease. It had been a present for my fifth birthday, the only one I said I wanted the morning I woke up and my parents asked me what they could buy me. Since it had been a Sunday and most of the staff was off for the day, Dad had no choice but to buy the supplies himself, hang the rope, and cinch the tire tight. It was either that or deal with a disappointed daughter, and back then, our relationship had been easier.

I'd picked out the tree, and Dad had done the rest. It had taken him most of the day, and my birthday was only a couple hours away from being over by the time it was done, but I got what I wanted that day: my dad's attention —the *good* kind—and a tire swing I'd spent a year's worth of hours on since.

The rope stretched and whined when I settled my weight into the swing, but it held strong. The outside of the tire might have worn thin, but the core was still strong. Winding my arms around the rubber, giving it a gentle hug, I leaned my cheek into the tread and used my toes to swing me gently back and forth. The dew-dotted grass tickled my ankles while the sheets of Spanish moss brushed across my back. If there was one place in this state I felt at home, it was right there.

Only a minute or two had passed, and I was just starting to put the disaster known as breakfast with my family behind me, when I heard heavy footsteps crunching through the grass behind me. I didn't look over my shoulder to see who it was; I already knew. In my lifetime, only one person had come looking for me when I'd gone missing. Only one had cared enough to find me, or cared enough to notice I was gone in the first place.

The footsteps came to a stop a few lengths back, then he cleared his throat like he was announcing himself. "So . . . I'm a prick."

I continued staring at the world in front of me, refusing to look behind me at all that was there waiting.

"Already know that," I said, feeling something more closely resembling exhaustion than the outrage I'd felt earlier.

Behind me, Boone sighed. "I'm sorry. I couldn't help it. Those people . . . the way they think of me . . . the way they treat you . . . I guess I can't help but try to even the score any time I see a chance."

Back and forth. Forth and back. I kept swinging, though my toes were growing tired of bearing the weight of my body. "Already know that too"

"What does that mean?"

I caught myself about to look back. Not yet. I wasn't ready for my moment of peace to be over. There'd already been too few and far between. Twenty hours of torture to every two minutes of solace. "You know what that means, Boone."

He seemed content to let my words hang between us, not in a rush to move on or deny it. Just when I was close to checking to see if he was still there or if I'd scared him away, I heard his steps move closer.

"Enough with the heavy for one morning, okay?" he said, his fingers brushing my back when the swing swung his direction. "You want me to push you?"

I slid my hair back behind my shoulders to hide my neck. If he was paying close enough attention, I didn't want him to notice the goose bumps dotting the skin there. "I want you to push me and keep your mouth shut."

When I swung back in his direction again, Boone grabbed the rope to stop it. "I think I can manage that."

I smiled, knowing Boone might have been capable of keeping his mouth shut momentarily, but never for long. If he managed a whole minute, it was a success.

Letting go of the rope, he grabbed the tire and pulled it back as far as he could, then he lifted me even higher. When he let go of the tire, I closed my eyes and focused on the way the air felt crashing across my face. On the way it felt breaking through my hair. I focused on how some-thing so invisible to the eye and so taken for granted could become such a powerful thing.

When the tire swung back Boone's way, my smile widened as my hair whipped across my face, tangling in my eyes and darting into my mouth. Life seemed so simple from the seat of this swing. So clear that it was more simple than it was complex, more good than it was bad. Why things got so muddied when I climbed off of it, I didn't know, but maybe that was the price of gravity.

CHAPTER FOUR

"How is it, Clara Belle?" my mom asked for the tenth time in the past thirty seconds, rapping on the outside of my dressing room door. "How is the fit? Not too big, I hope. When I called in the size your sister had down for you, I figured that had to be a mistake, and you know how frumpy a too-large dress will look on your frame, sweetheart. If it's too big, I'm sure I'll be able to talk Pearl into squeezing in a quick tailoring job. The wedding pictures will be forever, and we don't want to shudder whenever we look back at the past."

After that, I tuned her out. She'd been going on and on ever since we'd rolled out of the driveway with my sisters and a couple of second cousins stuffed into her new Rolls. My mother had been a head-turner in her youth, according to my dad and her, but now that age had waved its wand of scorn her way, she had to get her head-turning in other ways. Driving a few-hundred-thousand-dollar car down the streets of Charleston included.

The guys had been set for a day of golfing and drink-ing at the country club while us girls, lucky us, got to endure a final dress fitting. Then we were having lunch at the spa my mom was an emeritus member of and an afternoon of "pampering." The other girls might have been getting hot stone massages and paraffin dips, but I'd already seen what I was scheduled for, and a full body waxing followed by a couple of seaweed-and-pineapple wraps weren't my idea of pampering.

"Come on out. Let us see it on you." My mom went from rapping on the door to twisting the doorknob. Thank God I'd triple-checked to make sure it was locked after I sojourned in here. "I've seen your sisters in their dresses already, but I'm dying to see you in yours, sweetheart. Open up already."

I couldn't stop staring at the mirror and shaking my head. This had been going on for the past five minutes, ever since I'd wriggled into this sham of a bridesmaid dress and sucked and wrestled more pieces of flesh than I'd known I had to get the zipper *mostly* up. I'd always known Charlotte had it out for me, but I hadn't known until right now that she was going in for the kill.

There was one color my mom used to forbid me to wear upon penalty of public humiliation when people saw just how pasty and yellow my skin was contrasted against aforementioned outlawed color: peach. It was sinister. Even I'd come to recognize that fact, despite my desire to never agree with my mother.

Something having to do with having light hair, combined with ivory skin with yellow undertones, just made me look ever so wrong when peach was laid across my frame. It was a masterpiece of epic disaster. The atom bomb of atrocious. The coux de *good god*.

Banning peach from my wardrobe was one of the few

things my mom had gotten right when it came to me.

So why was I stuffed in it now, from head to toe, covered in a sheen-y, sickening shade of peach? Why was my mom acting like she was on pins and needles to see me in it? Why hadn't she vetoed Charlotte's color choice when she saw what colors she'd selected for the big day?

Why was I still standing here shaking my head at my reflection and not clawing out of this thing like a feral cat stuffed in a strait jacket?

"Clara Belle. Right this minute. I'm dying out here," Mom practically squealed, her hands clapping in her excitement.

"It's to die for. I promise you that," I said flatly, unable to stop my shaking head.

It wasn't just the color, though that was unforgivable on its own; it was also the shape. Unlike my sisters, Charlotte, I hadn't been graced with a tall, lean body but a shorter, softer one. The boxy, sharp cuts the dress was styled around would have looked banging on a runway model whose hipbones would have popped through the chemise, but it made someone with my curvy frame look like someone had just tried squeezing a family of pigs into a cocktail dress.

Unflattering didn't even begin to sum it up.

Rip the bandage off . . .

"Coming out," I announced, flipping off my reflection that continued to mock me. "Brace yourselves."

My mom did the giddy clap again. "I've got my camera ready."

"That really isn't necessary," I said as I opened the dressing room door slowly and stepped out . . . even more slowly. If she'd heard my comment about the camera, she hadn't heeded it. A flash fired off in my face, blinding me. "Mom, put that thing away before you blind someone."

There was no shortage of lights in the bridal store, so why her trusty old camera deemed the lighting appropriate for flash was an indication of just how archaic that sucker really was. Let's just say her camera had been old before camera phones were around.

"I'm not sure Aunt Estelle's going to be the one responsible for blinding anyone today . . ." my cousin Cynthia said. She and Charlotte had been best friends growing up. That was enough to sum her up.

It took me a few moments to blink away my blindness, and when I did, I found every mouth in view dropping open. My mom looked closer to dismay than shock though. Tears could just be made out welling in the corners of her eyes.

"Oh no, Clara Belle, what went wrong?" She looked around the room like she was trying to locate an emergency responder to come save the day.

"Besides how much weight she gained since giving me her measurements three months ago?" Charlotte sashayed up to my mom, crossing her arms and inspecting me like she wasn't sure if she felt more like laughing or gloating—clearly a tough decision for her.

"I didn't gain any weight, but thanks for your concern. And sympathy." I circled my hand at her face. Her eyes were practically dancing inside her skull.

"And the dress didn't just cinch up a couple of sizes overnight," she replied.

Avalee joined my mom, Charlotte, and cousins in the inspection line-up. She was the only one of the bunch who looked like she felt sorry for me.

"Yeah, and something tells me by the way the sleeves feel like they're about to cut off the circulation in my arms that this isn't the way this lovely gown is supposed to fit." That was just the most noticeable place on my body tingling from decreased blood supply at the moment. Back in the changing room, I'd had to suck in my waist so much to get the zipper up the side, I almost passed out. I'd gotten used to the vacuum-packed feeling there now though, and I'd adjusted to breathing shallowly.

"I ordered it based on the measurements you gave me."

When I tried crossing my arms in Charlotte's direction, I could only get them to the halfway mark before I stopped trusting the integrity of the seams holding this thing together. "In case you're blind, Charlotte, this dress is not based on my measurements." I smacked my hips in proof, where the seams were pulling the most. "Nor is it based on just about any other average American woman's measurements."

My mom lifted her pointer finger and continued looking just over my shoulder. It was the only way she could "look" at me without getting to the cusp of bursting into tears. "We're not average, dear. We're Abbotts."

Charlotte arched a narrow brow at me like that summed it up. Game over.

"I can't wear this. Sorry." I had to shuffle to the three-way mirror because taking normal-sized strides was impossible.

"The wedding is four days away. I can't exactly just order you a new one from London and hope it makes it here in time," Charlotte said.

I continued shuffling. "Then what do you suggest,

dear sister?"

"Stop eating," she popped off. "And shapewear."

My cousins cackled beside her.

"God, Charlotte," Avalee said, "you can't seriously expect her to wear that. It's hideous." Avalee threw me an apologetic smile. "No offense, Clara Belle, it just, you know . . ."

"Should be burned after we draw a ring of salt around it?" I suggested, pinching at the fabric.

"Better make it two rings. Just to be safe," Avalee said as I shuffled the last few inches to the mirrors.

I didn't know why I was expecting anything to look different or to have loosened up—silk chemise didn't stretch—but somehow, out here under all of the shop's overhead lights, I looked even worse. This dress was birthed in the inner circle of hell.

I resisted the urge to rip it apart, piece by piece, and instead turned around so everyone could get another good look . . . because it wasn't like they'd already been gaping at me without blinking since I'd popped out of the dressing room.

"Unless you gave the shop my measurements as being 32-22-32, this was ordered in the wrong size, Charlotte. It would be nice if you could check to see if they can get the *correct* size here in time for the wedding."

My mom was bobbing her head, already reaching for her American Express.

"And don't take this as me questioning your sanity or anything, but can I ask why you picked such a long dress with long sleeves in heavy fabric for your afternoon summer wedding in Charleston?" The air conditioning was blasting in here and I could already feel sweat dripping down my back—and a few other places I didn't want to be dripping sweat from all day and night long.

"My dress isn't like that. It's much lighter and breezier," Cynthia said, like she'd just defended Charlotte instead of incriminating her.

"Yeah, neither is mine. It's strapless and mid-calf length," my other cousin, Harper, added.

When I turned to Avalee, the only one who would be on my side, and all she could do was bite her lip and look away, I knew what had happened.

Charlotte had happened.

"What do they mean *their* dresses are different than this beauty I have on now?" I heard the venom in my voice as I started in Charlotte's direction. If it weren't for the dress, I would have been tempted to wrap my fingers around her neck and squeeze until the amusement drained out of her eyeballs.

She lifted a shoulder like none of this was a big deal. Like me about to sweat myself into dehydration and have my limbs amputated thanks to lack of circulation was no big. "I decided I wanted all of my bridesmaids to wear different dresses."

Of course she did. Why the hell not? When it came to Charlotte's attempts to put me in my place—according to her, directly below her heel—she leapt at any and every opportunity.

"And I'm going to assume, because I know you wouldn't single me out like this, that everyone else's dress is still the same *lovely* shade?" Out here in the brighter lights, my skin looked yellow. I'd look like a jaundiced sausage in front of five hundred of Charleston's finest. Couldn't wait.

"Mine's mint." Cynthia grimaced when she inspected my dress again, like she couldn't decide what was more offensive: the color or the style.

"Mine's periwinkle," Harper said next.

When Avalee stayed quiet, I stared at her and waited. She was back to biting her lip, though this time she was looking over her shoulder at the door.

"Hers is lilac," Charlotte said for Avalee.

I shook my head, giving myself another internal flogging for getting on that airplane yesterday when I knew the same three-ringed circus would be waiting for me down here. Charlotte would still be out to get me. Mom would still be looking to remake me. Dad would still treat me like a child. And everyone else would still have their own personal agenda when it came to Charleston versus Clara Abbott.

Why I'd found myself hoping things would be different, why I'd expected change to even be possible in the first place, I didn't know, but this was the last time. The *last* time.

"Why did I wind up with peach then?" I asked. "Since you were clearly going with the pastel-themed color scheme, why not marigold or petal pink or eggshell? Why peach?"

My mom turned her own accusation my sister's way. She must not have had a hand in or known what dress the bride had selected for her older sister. Had she, I knew my mom well enough to know she would have gone to great lengths—a.k.a. her pocketbook—to prevent Charlotte from doing this to her . . . I mean to me.

"You know what peach does to your sister's complexion, how it washes out her hair." Mom motioned at me, waiting for Charlotte's answer.

"Technically, the stylist called the color—"

"The stylist can call it whatever she wants. You can call it whatever you want. But that doesn't change the fact that it's peach. And ugly in every last way a dress can be repulsive."

Charlotte's face fell, her eyes going glossy. And the Academy Award goes to . . .

"I picked it out myself," she said softly, still in character.

Cynthia and Harper rushed to her sides, patting her and throwing me looks.

"Yeah, that's obvious," I said.

Charlotte slid her hair over her shoulder. "Meaning?"

"Meaning you picked this out with exactly me in mind."

Charlotte's phone rang before she could reply. Not that she had any defense, because she could plead innocence all she wanted, but I knew what this was about: payback. For whatever fouls I didn't know I'd done her.

After she answered her phone and walked away, I turned to Mom. "I can't wear this."

Mom patted the air in my direction, like she was trying to calm me down when I was surprisingly calm given the circumstances. "We'll figure something out, but you're right, you can't wear that. What would the guests think? I mean, what was Charlotte thinking, knowing you would be in a good handful of the wedding photos wearing that?"

I tried crossing my arms again. The stiches whined in protest, but held, before I gave up and dropped my arms back at my sides. "Not to be forgotten is how I would feel standing up there by that altar thing right before I passed out from heat exhaustion or lack of oxygen."

Avalee took a few steps my way, tilting her head as she inspected the dress. "It's really not so bad. With a few modifications, I think we can make it much better."

"Avalee, I love you, but the only modification that would make this dress better is total dress replacement therapy."

Mom nodded in obvious agreement. Mom being on my side instead of Charlotte's was a rare occasion.

"No, really, I think if we could get the seamstress to let a little out here, and tighten it there . . ." Avalee pinched at a few areas on the dress like she was making mental notes.

"Everything genetics has cursed me with is only further sabotaged by this frock." When I took another look in the mirrors, this time I cringed. "Just help me out of this thing, okay? The sooner, the better. I'll figure out what to do about this disaster later."

Cynthia and Harper followed Charlotte while Avalee and my mom stayed with me.

"I'm sorry about this, darling. I should have asked to see what dress Charlotte had picked out for you." Mom fingered the pearls around her neck, rubbing them like they were a strand of worry stones.

"I don't think you could have changed her mind if you had." I lifted my arm as high as it could go so Avalee could get to the zipper.

"Probably not. Charlotte's always been competitive with you, Clara Belle, and sometimes she likes to take her shots whenever and however she can get them in. I'm sorry." Mom shot me a small smile, continuing to pull on her pearls.

I tried not to act startled by my mom's apology. I tried to pretend I was used to hearing them, but I wasn't. In fact, I couldn't remember the last time she'd apologized to me for anything, forgetting the name of the city I lived in every time she asked me how I was doing included.

So I cleared my throat and mirrored her smile. "It's okay. I think I'll survive. It's just utter and total public humiliation. Nothing I haven't achieved a few times in my lifetime."

Mom let go of her pearls and cleared her throat. "That reminds me, dear, now that we're alone, I was hoping to talk to you about Boone . . ."

My neck stiffened. Of course the topic of public humiliation would remind her of her firstborn daughter dating the boy who'd grown up in the double-wide that everyone knew about for a number of reasons.

"I was hoping we'd talked the subject to death by now, after last night and this morning at breakfast." I checked to see how Avalee was getting along with the zipper. Just thinking about talking about Boone with my mom was making me sweat. Sweat *more*.

"Yes, but with your father being the way he is, feeling the way he does . . . I was hoping we could discuss you two in a bit more civilized manner. Minus the testosterone."

Avalee grumbled beneath my armpit, tugging at the zipper but making no progress.

"I don't remember any of the conversations you and I have had about Boone being civilized, Mom."

"They weren't," she replied, her expression as unapologetic as her tone. "But you were a girl then and living under our roof and under our responsibility. You're a woman now and have proven yourself capable of making your own decisions." She waved at me, like me standing in front of her looking like a peach pumpkin was proving her point.

I felt at a loss, again, for how to reply. Was my mom talking to me like an adult? Was she talking *to* me instead of *at* me? Was she saying I was capable and accomplished and had proven myself?

"What do you want to know?" I found myself replying. Years ago, I would have marched off in a huff and slammed my bedroom door. I supposed, looking back, they hadn't been the only unreasonable ones.

"Why now?" she asked. "Why all of these years later are you two back together? Why after everything that happened . . . and with him just walking away from you like that . . ." She looked away, staring through the plate-glass windows lining the front of the shop. If eighteen years of experience hadn't proven otherwise, I would have almost believed she was close to shedding a few tears. "I don't want to see you get hurt again like that, Clara Belle. I don't think I can stand to watch you go through that kind of pain again."

Avalee stopped messing with my zipper long enough to exchange a look with me after glancing at my mom. I could tell she was just as thrown as I was.

Yeah, I remembered the pain—of course I remembered the tears and feeling like my heart was being shredded by a cheese grater in the months following Boone's and my fallout—but I never would have guessed my mom had been affected by any of it.

She hadn't given an indication otherwise. She hadn't offered a shoulder to let me cry my eyes out on or even a random hug when she'd found me spread out on the porch steps, staring at the end of that long driveway, just waiting for my life to end or for it to start again.

"That won't happen again. I know it," I said, shaking my head. "You don't have to worry, Mom."

"How can you be sure? He's done it once. He can do it again."

Avalee was back to pulling at the zipper, not so gently now.

"Not this time," I said.

"Why not this time?" Mom lifted an eyebrow and waited for me.

I couldn't exactly tell her I'd paid him to pose as my plus one so I wouldn't have to be publicly shamed for showing up to a Southern wedding in my mid-twenties without a husband or a date, but that was a secret I was happy to keep between Boone and me for the rest of our lives. I supposed I could tell her that he was a changed person and we'd matured and had moved beyond teenage intensity, but I knew she wouldn't be satisfied by any of those answers.

So I went with a different approach.

"He didn't just hurt me. I hurt him too, Mom. Just as badly."

She gave a little huff, like she doubted that very much. "You did nothing more hurtful than make a temporary omission. What he did . . . how he left you . . ." She threw up her hands and shook her head, unable to continue.

"That's behind us now. We've moved on as best as two people with history can. I'm not asking you to like him, I'm not asking you to like the idea of us—I'm just asking you to be civil. That's all. And it would be nice if you could sway Dad in that direction. Am I fool for thinking that's possible?"

Mom dropped onto one of the upholstered stools scattered around the dressing room and folded her hands in her lap. "You're probably a fool for hoping so, but I promise I will try. For you, Clara Belle. Only *you*, not for him. I don't hold a scrap of civility in my make-up for that boy and I never will . . . but for you, because you asked, I will *try*. No guarantees."

Avalee paused, looking up at me.

"I know," I mouthed at her. "That's progress, Mom. Serious progress. I'll take it."

She managed a smile but continued to squirm like she'd just found herself in a troublesome situation. Avalee gave another yank on the dress, so hard she wound up losing her balance and falling back a few steps.

"Easy there, killer," I said. "Are you okay?"

Avalee's face went a few shades lighter. "I'm okay." She held out her hand to reveal something that looked an awful lot like a part of a zipper. A *broken* part of a zipper. "But I don't think you are."

CHAPTER FIVE

"**I**f I die from suffocation tonight, please, Avalee, I'm trusting you to do this—please don't let them bury me in this thing. Please don't let this be what I spend my eternity wearing," I said as Avalee and I hung back from the other four in our group, who were already heading through the doors of The Half Shell restaurant on the pier.

After the long day we'd all spent together, even if it hadn't been for the dress restricting my movements, I would have chosen to hang back. Eight hours with my mom, Charlotte, and evil twin cousins was enough to grate on my every last right-versus-wrong perception of premeditated murder. That Charlotte was still breathing after the day she'd spent shoveling shit in my direction was a true miracle.

"You have my word," Avalee said, shaking her head for the billionth time that day . . . ever since she'd inadvertently ripped the pull of my zipper off when she'd been trying to lower it. "And can I just say, again, how sorry I am for what happened? If I'd known the zipper was a piece of crap, or that the shop didn't have a seamstress on call today, or that there'd be no other way of getting you out of the dress save for a busted zipper, I would have just left it alone." She kicked a small rock in our path, forgetting the open-toed sandals she had on. "I'm sorry. Again."

I grabbed her hand and gave it a squeeze. "If you were Charlotte, I'd know you had ulterior motives for busting my zipper, but you're Avalee, and I know Avalee Abbott doesn't have a mean, vengeful bone in her body, so don't worry. You're forgiven." I gave her hand another squeeze. "Again."

"You know, you don't have to stay in that thing until the seamstress gets to you tomorrow." Avalee stopped me before we headed through the restaurant doors. "You can always rip it off and drop it into the ocean." She lifted her chin toward the water. "I won't tell."

That option was beyond appealing, especially since I'd have to sleep in this neck-to-toe corset of a hot-mess, but I was making a point now, announcing my manifesto to the world, and more importantly, my sister. *Bring it, bitches. I'm not going down.* To the dress shop's merit, they had called one of their seamstresses to bring her in for an "emergency," but when I found out that meant she'd be pulled away from a day at the beach with her family, I said I could just wait until tomorrow when someone was scheduled to work. I didn't like garnering special conditions because of my family's name.

"Between you and me, I think the better way to piss Charlotte off is to smile and pretend like I've realized this dress and I were meant to be." I pulled on the high neckline to let in a little fresh air.

The one upside to being trapped in my bridesmaid

dress overnight was that I'd gotten to forgo the duo of waxing and body wraps my mom had booked for me. Instead, I'd spent the afternoon getting a hand-and-foot massage, followed by a relaxing facial. There's a silver lining to every situation, being confined within *Cosmo's* Top 100 Most Hideous Dresses Ever Devised included.

Avalee looked inside the restaurant, zeroing in on the back of our sister's head. She grinned. "You are oh so very right. You work that dress tonight. Own it. The woman doesn't let the dress wear her—she wears the fucking dress."

I held out my arms as far as they would go and looked down at myself. A giant round peach minus the fuzz. "Yeah, something like that . . . I'm just not ripping it off to spite Charlotte."

"Yeah, you're right. That thing . . ."—Avalee thrust her hands at my dress—"I don't care who you are or how many runways you've walked, there is no way that dress can be worn without overpowering the woman. Sorry, Clara Belle."

"No problem. I agree. Nice pep talk though." I went to open the door, needing to get yet another thing over with. Rip the bandage off had been the theme of my visit so far—and the theme of much of my life down here.

I wasn't sure how many people would be at tonight's shindig. I hadn't asked. I knew my parents had rented out The Half Shell and hired a band and spent more on food and alcohol for this one meal than most couples spent on their actual wedding, but the guest count I wasn't sure on. Judging by the number of Lexuses and Mercedes gleaming in the parking lot, I would guess at least a hundred.

One hundred people would get to bear witness to me

tromping around the place, eating crab claws and looking like a peach-colored sea cucumber. I could only imagine the clips that would be posted to YouTube and go viral come tomorrow.

One hundred people would also get to see that my sister could try all she wanted, but I wouldn't bow to her. They would see that I was made of stronger stuff than my family let on and there was more to the rich girl who'd once dated the poor boy than just her last name and trust fund.

After giving myself that pep talk, I pulled the door open.

"So," Avalee said, going in first when I held the door open for her, "did Boone survive the day with the guys? When I checked in with Sterling, it sounded like things might have been a little rough for him."

I followed her inside and let the door close. There. We were inside. Now all I had to do was mill about the room, waving and greeting a bunch of people while pretending I wasn't dressed like Bozo the Clown's mistress.

"I don't know. I haven't talked to him since this morning," I answered.

"Really? You didn't at least call to check in and see if he needed a rescue?" Avalee gave me a small shove. "That's cold, Clara Belle. You can't just throw a guy to Daddy and the rest of those guys, especially a guy named Boone Cavanaugh."

I shrugged, though it probably wasn't noticeable through the puffed sleeves of my dress. "Boone's always been a sink-or-swim type of guy. I'm sure he made it through just fine."

We caught sight of Sterling back by the bar with a

couple of other guys. He smiled and waved Avalee over. She lifted her finger to give herself a moment.

Then she turned and gave me a curious look. "Now. It's just you and me. Are you going to tell me what's going on between you two? Or am I supposed to keep believing you two just randomly reconnected and one thing led to another?" She crossed her arms and gave me a look that suggested she saw through it all.

"If there's anyone I could tell the whole story to, it would be you, but for now, I'd prefer to keep it under wraps." When she opened her mouth to protest, I added, "Plus, your *fiancé* looks like he's missed you and has that impatient come-hither look, and I don't want to feel rushed explaining Boone and me to you, okay?"

She exhaled and rolled her fingers across her arm. "I'd pressure you a few more rounds if I didn't already know that while you might have gotten Mama's good looks, you sure got more than your fair share of bull-headedness from our daddy."

Now it was me opening my mouth to object.

"And before you spend the rest of the night trying to convince me otherwise and demanding I take back what I just said, think about who else would do the exact same thing." Avalee's gaze didn't so casually move through the crowd until she spotted our dad with a glass of bourbon in one hand, his other shaking the hands of a bunch of guests.

"I'm stuffed inside a peach condom, Avalee." I did a not-so-graceful spin in the sausage casing of a dress to remind her. "Kicking me when I'm down is just not cool."

A laugh burst from her, but she covered her mouth to try to stop it. I pulled her hands away and laughed with her.

"It's okay. Laugh. This"—I did another spin, almost tipping over—"is funny if there ever was such a thing."

"I feel terrible for laughing," she said, though she continued to laugh with me.

"Well, it's a terrible thing," I teased before shoving her toward her fiancé. "Now go be a good future Southern wife and make him get you a drink."

She waved at me over her shoulder before rushing toward Sterling and throwing herself into his arms before he had them open.

This visit was becoming strange and unexpected in some wonderful ways. First my mom apologizing and now Avalee behaving like we were a couple of co-conspirators in cahoots to rise to world domination. Maybe my trip wouldn't be a total failure after all. Maybe there'd be something positive I could take from it.

With Avalee gone, I was on my own. I'd have to walk past the hostess desk and past the waiting benches and wade through the sea of people alone. I was used to going it alone in plenty of things in life, but not when I was dressed the way I was now.

I mean, what should I do first? Go over to my parents and mingle with them and their friends? Dart to the bar for a stiff drink and chug it before anyone could notice me? Head to the seafood buffet so I could be first in line for the crab claws that were longer than my arms? Or march right up to Charlotte and thank her for picking out, with such great care and concern, the dress I'd be spending the next fourteen to eighteen hours of my life trapped within?

The crab legs were calling my name, and since my mom had her back turned, maybe I could pile a plate up with them without being shamed into eating less. I was just marching toward the buffet line when I noticed one of the nearby restroom doors shove open, and out came a familiar face.

Boone took a few long strides before he noticed me. He froze in the middle of rolling up his sleeve and gave me a head-to-toe inspection.

I pointed at the zipper. "Zipper busted. Clara stuck."

Just when I couldn't tell if he was going to laugh or shudder, he raised his palm at me in a "stay there" kind of motion before disappearing back inside the bathroom.

He looked like he'd survived the day of golfing and country clubbing it with the boys, and if he was here now, he hadn't gotten himself arrested for breaking Ford's nose —as he nearly had back in high school—nor was he on the run for having murdered Ford as I knew he'd been fantasizing about for years. He was here, present, and accounted for . . . and hadn't wound up looking like he could play lead sidekick in *James and the Giant Peach*. Good for him. Sucked for me.

I wasn't waiting longer than a couple of minutes— and starting to get impatient when I saw people circling the crab legs like a bunch of vultures—when the men's bathroom door exploded open, and out came Boone . . . looking as I'd never seen Boone before.

"What in the hell happened to you?" I asked, shaking my head to see if my vision needed to clear.

"Let's see . . ." Boone kicked his foot up to show off a pair of knee-high lavender-and-mint-colored argyle socks that were pulled up to his knees, below which were tied a pair of matching golf shoes. "*Ford* happened to me. In case the pastel didn't give it away."

"Crap, Boone . . . they didn't make you wear this all

day, did they?"

Boone's jaw stiffened. "No one makes me do any-thing. Nobody." After adjusting his beret-looking golf hat, he pinched at the lavender bow tie. "I *chose* to wear this all day to prove to those elitist bastards that there's nothing they can do to make me feel inferior. As hard as they damn well might try."

I shook my head at his outfit, no longer feeling like the only one dressed like they may or may not have been under the impression that Halloween had come four months early. "What are those things?" I poked at the kha-ki-colored material. "Pantaloons? Britches?"

"If they have a name, I don't need to know it. I don't plan on stocking my wardrobe with every shade of them."

"I'm so sorry." I felt guilty I'd left Boone alone with my dad and the rest of the "elitist bastards." Here I thought I'd had it bad with the girls, and it turned out Boone had suffered for eighteen holes looking like a deranged metro-sexual had gotten his hands and glue gun on him.

Boone swatted away the tassel swinging from his be-ret when it bounced in his face. "But I'm not the only one standing here like the butt of every joke." He thrust his hands in my direction—my *dress's* direction. "What hap-pened to you?"

I was surprised he had to ask. "Charlotte happened."

Boone's eyes cut through the crowd of guests, land-ing on my sister. His eyes narrowed. "Well, aren't the little princess and prince just made for each other?"

"Perfectly made for each other."

"Why are you still wearing it if this was all Char-lotte's idea?" Boone leaned into the wall behind him and went to slip his hands into his front pockets. He wasn't wearing his typical worn-in jeans though, and the "panta-loons" were pocket-free. He muttered a curse.

"For two reasons." I gave the hem of his sweater vest a tug. "Because I want to prove to that elitist bitch that there's nothing she can do to make me feel inferior."

He lifted his chin and urged me on when I paused before giving him my second reason . . . which was more like my first.

I withheld a sigh and lifted my arm as high as it would go before I lowered my gaze to the zipper. "Avalee and I busted the zipper when we were trying to get it off of me, and the bridal store didn't have a seamstress on staff today—because why in the hell would they have one of those at the ready on a Saturday?—but there will be one available tomorrow to fix the zipper and free me from this thing."

Boone lifted a brow, gauging to see if I was done. "You don't need the zipper to get out of The Thing."

I shoved his arm when he used my designation for the dress, making it sound like the nemesis in some sci-fi flick. It was certainly my nemesis.

"Actually, I do, because in case you missed it, this thing is suctioned tighter to my body than the casing around a bratwurst." I give the fabric a pinch and pull to show him just how impossible it was to free it from my skin. I felt like someone had super-glued it to me . . . although the copious amounts of sweat I'd shed might have had something to do with that. "No amount of tugging, wiggling, sucking, or sliding will get The Thing off without that zipper functioning. Not even if I lathered my body with butter."

Boone smiled when I copied his ominous tone when

referring to the bridesmaid dress from hell. "Then why didn't you just cut, rip, or slash it off? That should show her what you think of the dress she picked out for her bridesmaids."

"Bridesmaid," I corrected, pointing at myself. "Just lucky me."

"You're the one she expected to wear This Thing? The *only* one?" The muscle running down Boone's jaw popped through his skin.

"Told you I was lucky."

Boone muttered another curse before grabbing my hand and tugging me toward the bathroom. "Come with me. I've got a pocket knife in my jeans. I'll get you out of This Thing, and when we're done slicing it into shreds, we'll go sprinkle the pieces into her lap."

"Hold up there, Eager Pocket Knife Man." I pulled against him just as we were breaking through the bathroom door. "Let's think this through. First, what am I going to wear when you free me from the confines of The Thing?"

Boone's face flattened with realization right before his mouth pulled into a crooked smile.

"And you can just delete that image from your depraved mind right now." I flicked his temple, not sure why knowing he was thinking of me in my underwear made me feel that strange stomach phenomenon. The one where it felt like it'd been invaded by a nest of hummingbirds extra high on nectar. I hadn't felt *that* feeling in a long time. So long I'd forgotten what it felt like. "Not to mention my sister will lose her shit if we sprinkle peach silk confetti into her lap and this is, after all, her special week."

Boone rolled his eyes but stayed quiet.

"And I'm not just wearing this because I couldn't

take it off by the conventional, non-pocket-knife-required, means. I'm wearing it because, like you, I'm sick of them making me feel like a puppet they can toy with whenever and however they choose." I was able to just barely shrug. "I'm tired of them sticking it to me—to us—just because they can and I've let them. This is my weird way of sticking it back."

Boone was silent for a moment, watching me like he was reading some sort of manual. He didn't stop staring until Charlotte's shrill, staccato laugh broke through the room. He cringed. "So we're sticking it to them together tonight? Have I got it?"

"You've got it." I pulled at the collar of the dress to let some air in. The restaurant was nice and cool, but it didn't seem to matter. The material didn't seem to breathe, and I was swathed in it from neck to ankle. "But quick question first, before we go make spectacles of ourselves in front of Charleston's finest . . ."

Boone pulled at his collar and bow tie and rubbed at the skin behind it. Even for formal dances, Boone hadn't worn a tie or buttoned his collar. He'd claimed back then that he didn't like anything around his neck and that collars were for dogs, so for him to be suffering through this, he must have been really trying to make a point.

"You came out of the bathroom in your regular clothes. You'd changed for dinner. Why did you change back into this when you'd already spent all day in it, sticking it to them, and are fortunate enough to not be trapped in it like I am in mine?" I tried not to grin when I noticed the argyle socks, but it was impossible. I doubted if Boone had let anything argyle come within a ten-foot radius of him up until today. "You had a choice tonight. Why choose this?"

He stalled for a moment, letting go of the door and letting it close behind us. He glanced at the main part of the restaurant, looking like he'd rather be there than standing in front of me with that question hanging between us.

"You didn't have a choice," he said at last, one of his shoulders lifting. "That's why I made my choice."

I felt my eyebrows come together. "So because I didn't have a choice when it came to This Thing, that made you choose to go change back into Your Thing?" They came together tighter. "That doesn't make sense."

Boone's eyes stayed focused over my shoulder. "We're a team in this, Clara. Like I told you last night, when it comes to you and your family, I'm always on your side. I'll always have your back, no matter what has or will go down between us."

I got it. It suddenly made sense . . . but this wasn't the Boone of present tense I'd gotten to know. This was the Boone of past tense I remembered. The one who seemed selfish to the rest of the world, but I knew was the least selfish one out there. The one who would give anything, and do anything, for the few people he loved.

That realization startled me more than the confines of the dress wanted to allow.

"You're doing this so I wouldn't be the only lightning rod for pointing and laughter, aren't you?" I asked, my voice having grown quiet.

"I just didn't want you to be the only spectacle and have all the fun tonight." He started to smile. "That's all."

For the first time since passing into the county, I felt so close to exhaling I could feel my lungs starting to contract. However, that was something else the dress wouldn't allow. Not without ripping the seams at least.

"Well? Should we get this over with?" I turned toward the main dining room.

"No." Boone shook his head as he came up beside me. "We should get this party started." Holding out his elbow, he waited for me to weave my arm around it before he led us into the restaurant.

"In case you were wondering, lavender's a good color on you." I nudged him as we walked. "It really brings out the feminine in your character."

He adjusted his bow tie so it was more crooked than straight. "Watch it there, peach cream puff, before I decide to call the debutante society and tell them you stole one of their gowns. From 1982."

"You weren't even alive in the eighties."

"I've seen Madonna videos. Close enough," he said as he climbed a couple of stairs before stepping foot in the lion's den. Also called the dining room.

I'd been right in my estimation of close to one hundred guests. Some of them were milling about the room with their cocktails in hand, some were staggered around tables and chowing down on the seafood buffet, and some were making their way to the dance floor where a jazz band was playing a Sinatra tune. They were all dressed in varying degrees of semi-formal wear that was fitting given the event.

Boone and I were the only ones not in some version of a suit and tie or cocktail dress.

That might have been the reason why everyone was staring at us like we'd gotten the wrong address. When we continued to move through the room, playing ignorant to the blatant points and stares, guests' gazes shifted in my dad's direction, waiting to see what Quincy Abbott would do about the party crashers.

My dad just stood there, continuing to carry on his conversation with the guy who'd been mayor when I'd been in high school and pretending like Boone and his daughter walking arm-in-arm through a roomful of his esteemed guests wasn't about to send him through the roof. I knew better. I could tell by the way he was clutching his glass of bourbon so tightly it looked like it was about to shatter.

"Looks like you and my dad made some progress in the growing-to-like-each-other department."

"Oh, tons." Boone twisted his index and middle finger together. "We're like this now."

"You and Ford too apparently." I nodded at the table where Ford was sitting with a crowd of his friends. Most of them were moving on from gaping at us to getting back to their drinks and bullshitting, but Ford was still staring at us, his mouth looking like he'd just bitten into a wedge of lemon.

"He was the one who informed me of the club policy regarding course attire, a fact he only brought up once we were there, and he's the same one who had some jackass in the pro shop lay out this getup for me in the dressing room."

I returned Ford's glare for a second before getting back to ignoring him. "You guys always were best friends."

Boone snorted, weaving us through clusters of guests toward the dance floor. "Always. But at least he footed the bill for this stuff. Someone would have had to pay me to take this stuff off of their hands, but I wasn't going to let them get rid of me so easily. I don't think they figured I'd call their bluff today. You should have seen their faces when I stepped out onto the green in this." Boone chuckled. "Priceless."

"And you golfed all eighteen holes too?" The few people who had been on the dance floor promptly left it when they noticed Boone and me heading there.

"Every last one."

"How did that go?"

Boone huffed. "How grown men can justify wasting five hours smacking a tiny speckled ball with a piece of over-priced metal while trying to get it into a tight little hole is a hint that they aren't getting laid enough. Or well enough when they do."

A burst of laughter shot from my mouth. The heads that were starting to turn away flew back.

"It's all making so much more sense now. I never understood the appeal with golf, but I get it now. It's a bunch of sexually frustrated men whacking out their aggression on some innocent ball before trying to get it in the hole. The universe makes sense again." I continued laughing, and Boone joined me. "So how did you do out there?"

"Terrible."

"I'm sorry for your terrible performance," I said as we came to a stop in front of the band.

"Why? I don't need golf as a substitute for other urges because unlike the guys who might have gotten an under-par score today"—Boone's head tipped in Ford's direction—"I'm getting my urges appropriately and sufficiently met."

"And thank you for that memo, but sharing time is over, Mr. Cavanaugh."

I put on a smile and tried not to think about what he meant by that. Was he banging half of the single female population? Maybe a handful of the not-so-single as well? Or was it someone else, someone serious, he was getting all of those "urges" so well met with? I should have let it rest, or saved it for a better time, but apparently I thought hovering on the dance floor of The Half Shell while Louis Armstrong blared a few feet away was the best time.

"So you're really not seeing anyone? Not even casually?" I asked, shouting above the music. When he gave me an odd look, I added, "Just so I know if I should keep my eyes open for some ticked-off kinda-girlfriend pulling out my hair in clumps if she sees us together."

"That implies I wouldn't have already told this kinda-girlfriend about our arrangement."

Boone's hand went to my wrist, and he moved us just far enough to the side of the band that I didn't feel like my eardrums were vibrating. It also made it easier to talk to each other instead of shout at each other.

"I wouldn't do that to someone I cared about," he continued. "I wouldn't go behind their back with someone else, whether it was a real or pretend relationship. I know what it feels like to be on the bad side of something like that, and I'd never do it to someone I cared about."

I stepped back from him, feeling too close given the accusation in his voice. "I never said you would."

"No, you just implied it."

I closed my eyes. "Boone—"

"Clara, there's no one. So you can quit with the interrogation already. I've already had enough of those to last me a few lifetimes."

"But you just said—"

"I know what I just said," he snapped.

When I noticed a group of Charlotte's old friends from high school pointing at me and laughing, I did a small spin followed by a stiff curtsy. They got back to their fruity drinks real quick after that.

"Then if you're not getting those urges met by some-*one,* that means they're getting met by some*ones.*" I paused long enough to let him either corroborate or argue my conclusion. He stayed quiet. "Am I right?"

He crossed his arms and looked away. He could try all he wanted, but looking tough in that outfit was a futile pursuit. "Maybe. Maybe not. But it's definitely none of your business."

"You're my plus one for my sister's wedding. I'd say it's my business to know just which cocktail waitress or hair stylist is going to give me the evil eyes because I'm 'with' her booty call."

"Cocktail waitresses and hair stylists?" Boone exhaled through his nose. "Is that what my league is? Are they the only types of women who would lower themselves enough to date the bottom-rung Boone Cavanaugh?" He shook his head and stepped away from me too. "You might pretend you're not one of them, Clara, but you're as Abbott as they get." He continued backing away, rubbing his hands in a washing sort of motion. "You can dance by yourself. I don't really feel like it anymore." Then he turned his back and powered away, the folds of his pantaloons brushing past guests as he wove though them.

My shoulders sagged as I sighed. I couldn't say or do much right when it came to Boone anymore. Not that he could say or do much right when it came to me either. After a whole day apart, we couldn't make it ten minutes without pissing each other off. What had we been thinking as kids pretending we could chase forever?

Stupid. That's what we'd been.

I left the dance floor and headed to where I'd wanted to go in the first place—the table with the crab legs. Before they were all gone. Weaving through the crowd this time was much more intimidating. Instead of sharing the stares with Boone, I bore them all. Instead of feeling my head held high, I felt it wanting to lower.

When I heard Ford calling my name, I pretended I couldn't hear him. I wasn't in the mood for him or my sister or anyone. I wanted to be alone for two minutes to forget about everything Charleston-related. I wanted to surgically remove that part of my life, albeit temporarily.

"Clara Belle, wait up there turbo jets." Ford had jogged up beside me by the time I made my way to the food table.

Most everyone who was planning on eating was already done at the buffet—a.k.a. the people who weren't my sister, Mom, and friends of a like-minded policy when it came to eating . . . or the avoidance of it—and thankfully there were still plenty of crab legs.

"What is it, Ford?" I said impatiently, snagging a plate from a tower of them. I grabbed another because why the hell not? I was having a rough week, a day from hell, and there was nothing like drowning my sorrows in crab meat dripping in garlic butter. Whoever said emotional eating wasn't an acceptable method of coping could just kiss my dimpled butt.

"Wow, ease up. I'm not your enemy." He held out his arms, clutching what looked like a mojito.

"No? You're just marrying the woman who is, right?"

"Charlotte's not your enemy, Clara Belle."

"Those who've spent the night gaping at the dress I'm presently stuck in might have a different opinion on that matter." I powered up to the ice baths of crab legs and piled them onto my first plate. When it was full, I thrust it into Ford's empty hand before filling my second plate.

"The dress is nice." Ford's voice was a key too high. "What's the problem?"

"No, this dress is Hitler reincarnated. It must be destroyed. And the problem, Ford, is that I don't like this town, and I don't like these people." I waved the tongs around the room as I scanned the table for the garlic butter. "And I don't like the weather. And I don't like coming back and feeling like I've been transported back in time two hundred years. And I don't like this restaurant . . ." Which clearly had neglected to supply butter with the crab legs, probably at my mom's request since she knew of my love affair with crab meat and butter. "And I don't like when I can't find the melted butter when I've got two plates of crab claws ready to be eaten."

Ford's face was blank. From the look of it, it had been that way for a while. Probably from the start of my spiel. *Nice, Clara. Way to act the part of the crazy person wearing the crazy dress. Way to really step into the role.*

While I worked on calming down my heartbeat, Ford pointed with his mojito at the table. "The butter's right there, Clara Belle. Crisis averted. The world's not going to end." Backing away with my crab legs still in hand, he nodded when I reached for the plate. "You need a drink. I'll be right back."

"I don't need a drink. I need my crab legs. That's it."

Ford continued toward the bar, ignoring me. "Coming right up."

Keeping a tight clutch on my plate of crab and bowl of butter, I headed for the outside dining area that just overlooked the water. I'd barely shoved through the door and felt the fresh air wash over my face, and I was already feeling better.

I sat in the first chair at the first table I walked by and was just breaking into my first crab leg when the door flew open and someone else stepped outside.

"A person generally isolates themselves like this because they want to be *a-lone*," I said, circling my finger around the empty outdoor area.

Ford let the door close behind him, and he moved toward me, clearly not grasping the whole concept of *a-lone*.

"Here, have this, and tell me if you're feeling less loner'ish after." Ford slid a fresh mojito in front of me before setting my second plate of crab legs next to my first. "Don't isolate. Intoxicate." Ford winked at me before pulling out the chair beside me and sitting.

"That sounds like a policy just screaming for twelve-step help." I scooted my chair over, not sure I wanted to be this close to Ford with no one else around. I wasn't even sure I wanted to be talking to him after what he'd said and done over the past twenty-four hours.

"What's going on with you, Clara Belle? Now that it's just you and me, you can sell me straight." Ford waved his finger between us like we were tight with a capital T. "What's the deal with Cavanaugh being back in your life? What's the deal with your business going national? What's the deal with you sitting out here when the party's inside?" Ford slid a flask from the inside of his coat jacket. "What's the deal with Cavanaugh?"

"You already said that," I said before pulling a piece of crab meat free and dipping it into the butter.

"I repeated it because you haven't answered it." He unscrewed the cap and brought the flask to his lips, peaking a brow at me before taking a drink.

"Why does everyone keep asking me the same questions? Why is everyone so concerned with my life these days?" I tossed the crab into my mouth, closed my eyes, and chewed. The night was instantly going better. Looking up.

"We've always been concerned about your life. All of us who really care about you."

I was pulling another chunk of meat free before I'd finished chewing my first. "No, you all have always been concerned about certain parts of my life. Not all of it as a whole. Nice try."

Ford rubbed the bridge of his nose and exhaled. "Why do you make things so difficult? Why do you act like you despise me?"

"It's not an act." I swirled the meat in the butter, cocking an eyebrow at him, then tossed the crab into my mouth.

Ford leaned forward, his eyes turning into a pair of smoldering embers. "What have I ever done to you, Clara Belle, besides look after you?"

I stopped chewing and had to resist the urge to pick up the largest crab leg I could and beat him over the head with it. Instead I grabbed the crab leg in question and broke it in half. "Gee whiz, I don't know, Ford. What ever could you have done to me . . .?" I tapped my chin before breaking another part of the leg in half. "Oh, that's right.

You were fucking my sister behind my back."

He threw his head back and groaned. "For the thousandth time, we were taking a break. How many times are you going to nail me to a cross for it? I'm marrying her, aren't I? Charlotte and I make a hell of a lot more sense than you and I ever did. At least she appreciates what she's got instead of pining after what she once had."

I felt as if my body temperature had just jumped ten degrees. I could almost feel my head sweltering. "I guess your and my definition of taking a break is different because, see, my definition includes not climbing into your little brother's bed less than seventy-two hours after said break went into effect." I shot out of my chair and waved what was left of the massacred crab leg at him. "And you're right, you and Charlotte do make sense. So much sense it's staggering. You two truly are made for each other."

Ford's face went blank before it morphed into something that looked like hurt. I didn't know why I was being so mean tonight. I was a better person than popping off nasty comment after nasty comment. Why was I getting caught up in it now?

While I stared at my plate of crab legs looking for an answer, Ford loosened his tie and sighed. "Listen, I'm sorry for the ways things went down. If I could, I'd go back and change how it happened because you're right, you didn't deserve that and it was a shitty thing for me to do . . ." His eyes narrowed on some distant spot in the water. "I guess I just got tired of playing second-string."

I wanted to deny what he'd just said, but I couldn't. It would have been as real a lie as ever there had been.

"He left you when you needed him most, and I spent

141

two years with a woman who was still hung up on the guy who'd bailed on her. I spent two years trying to prove to her I had her back and wouldn't bow out when things got tough. I spent two years flying across the country trying to prove that to her. I guess I was young and stupid and believed that with enough time, you'd come around." Ford pulled at his tie again, undoing his collar button as well. "I got tired of pretending I wasn't walking in Boone Cavanaugh's shadow. I got tired of waiting to see if you could ever love me the way you'd loved him. I know I went about everything all wrong—with your sister, when we'd only just taken a break—but I did love you, Clara Belle. Some part of me always will."

My eyes lifted from the crab to Ford. He was still focused on that distant spot in the night, taking another drink from his flask, but I caught a glimpse of the Ford I'd leaned on for support when Boone had left. The solid, unwavering Ford who would be at my side in a moment's notice and was on-call twenty-four hours a day if I needed him. He'd made his share of fuck-ups . . . but so had I. Maybe it was time to let go of the grudge and move on. Maybe it was time to accept not everyone in the world was out to hurt me, and that sometimes timing and poor decisions were more to blame than a person intentionally setting out to hurt me.

"I'm sorry." I shoved the plate of crab away and sat back into my chair. "I sound like a bitter, scorned woman, but that's not really how I feel, nor do I not want you and Charlotte to live happily never after. It's just that this damn place and these damn people bring out the worst in me. I'm happy for you two, and I wish you both the very best. Truly." I scooted my chair away from the table and stood. Enough fresh air for one night. The stuffy, air-conditioned kind inside the restaurant seemed like a better option than carrying on this awkward conversation with Ford. "Just ignore the bitter girl in the giant peach frock."

I backed away from the table in the direction of the door. Right after saying I was sorry, something started to lighten up inside me. Almost like I was being pumped up with oxygen and about to float away. *I'm sorry* . . . two words that were more therapeutic than I could have guessed. Maybe I should give them another go with some-one else I'd offended tonight, just to see what happened.

"You forgot your crab legs." Ford smiled as he swept his arm across the table. "And your drink."

"All yours," I replied as I pulled open the door. "Thanks again for the talk, Ford. It was . . . nice."

His smile stayed in place. "It *was* . . . nice. Let's do it again sometime soon, okay?"

When he lifted his brows, his smile shifting so it wasn't so straight, I shot him a wave and disappeared in-side. Too much was going on tonight for me to commit any time to deciphering Ford's looks and the meanings behind those looks.

I'd barely made it a few steps inside before Charlotte shot toward me out of thin air, looking as flustered as she ever got. "Have you seen Ford? I can't find him any-where." Even her voice gave away that she was stressed. Every other second, her head twisted from side to side, scanning the restaurant for him.

"Yeah, he's right outside." I threw my thumb over my shoulder.

Her eyes cut to the door. "Where did you just come from?"

I threw my thumb over my shoulder again. "Outside," I said slowly, because she seemed like she was having a tough time processing things. "That's why I know where he is."

Charlotte's eyes darted to mine. "You two were out there together?" she half-shrieked. "Alone? For how long? Why? What were you doing?"

At first I didn't understand why she seemed so frantic her head was about to spin, but it didn't take me long to understand why she was looking between Ford and me like we'd just been up to no good behind her back.

Charlotte might have been the one who'd cheated with him, but now she was committing her life to a man who was a known cheater. She'd probably spend their entire marriage wondering if that glint in his eyes was sparked by some other woman. She'd spend the rest of their relationship wondering if he'd do the same to her as he'd done to me.

For the first time in a long time, I pitied my sister. She might have been shallow and scornful and had only maybe one or two kind bones in her body, but she didn't deserve to live in that kind of doubt. I couldn't imagine what that would feel like.

"Charlotte, it's okay." I patted her arm a few times and tipped my head at Ford. "He's all yours. I promise."

She watched me for a minute, looking into my eyes like she was searching for the smallest fragment of a lie. When she seemed appeased, she let out a breath and moved around me. "Thanks for letting me know, Clara Belle." Her voice was stiff, and I knew from her inability to look at me that her words held more than one meaning. "And I'm sorry about the dress. You know . . . for the zipper breaking and everything."

She was still unable to look at me, and when she bit her lip, I knew there was also more to her apology for the dress than just for the zipper breaking.

Were Charlotte and I hinting around burying the hatchet? Was that even possible?

Before I could clarify it or consider it further, she rushed through the door toward her fiancé, who looked like he'd taken it upon himself to not let the drink he'd brought me go to waste.

As I moved through the restaurant, I didn't get nearly as many stares and points as before. People had either gotten used to The Thing or were too tipsy to notice or care. From the way couples were swaying and shouting on the dance floor, I guessed their nonchalance might have had more to do with the latter.

I didn't have to search the room too long for Boone. He was easy to find. Easy because he was the only person in the whole place who was sitting alone. Even the few tables around his had been vacated, like he was carrying the bubonic plague or something. Seeing him shunned all over again by the same people who'd done it to him years ago made something in my chest tighten. I knew for a fact, several instances aside, that he was the best person in the place.

From across the room, I noticed my mom and dad wave at me, motioning me over. I wasn't sure if they wanted to introduce me to some new acquaintances or some old ones, or just keep me away from Boone liked they'd tried to do for years, but I continued toward Boone. Nothing seemed more important at that moment than apologizing to him.

His back was to me, and he looked totally preoccupied with eating his dinner, but when I got within a few yards of him, his whole back stiffened. He had the same sixth sense with me as I had with him. He twisted in his seat slowly as I finished approaching him. He looked tired again, exhausted like when I'd first seen him last night in the bar.

The moment his eyes met mine, I spewed, "I'm sorry."

At the same instant, he opened his mouth and said, "I'm sorry."

A moment of surprise passed between us before we both smiled.

"I think I got mine out like a whole tenth of a second faster," I said.

"Yeah, but I think I hit just the right balance of sincere meets apologetic, so let's call it even." He scooted out the chair beside him and motioned at it. "If you're not scared to sit with the leper in the room, please."

"Since when have I been scared of sitting next to you?" I brushed his shoulder with my hand on my way to the chair. He was still tense.

"Since never," he said, resting his fork and knife on his plate. "And that's what I always loved about you, Clara, or what's made you so special to me. You didn't care what anyone thought because you wanted to sit by me, or wanted to be my friend, or wanted to be my girlfriend. You had my back when everyone else was taking stabs at it, and I'm sorry I forgot that when I went off on you tonight. I know you're not concerned with things like keeping to one's own kind or not seeing someone who's supposedly below or above you, so I'm sorry for accusing you of that earlier. Like I said this morning"—he thrust his thumb into his chest—"I'm a prick."

I took a drink from the water glass in front of me, which had remained untouched tonight. Along with the other nine glasses circling the table. "No, you're not a prick. At least not *all* the time. Just some of it."

He shot me a disparaging smile before shoving a plate toward me. "I got you some crab legs. You know, as a kind of peace offering if you made your way over." Then he scooted a not-so-small bowl beside the plate. "And I didn't forget the butter, because I still remember the way your mouth dropped when I forgot it the first time."

I studied the plate of crab and the bowl of butter in front of me. Something so simple, but it meant so much more given the context. Boone had been thinking about me, remembering what I liked and how I liked it. Fresh on the heels of an argument, he'd still thought to save me some food in the event I missed out.

I felt something tighten around my throat. Something that wasn't the dreaded collar of The Thing. Something that felt a lot like an emotion I hadn't felt in years, and one I wasn't eager to feel again for the man who'd left me without an explanation.

"What are you doing over here all by yourself? Is it by choice or by circumstance?" I asked as he slid a drink in front of me too.

This one wasn't a mojito like what Ford had brought me. I hated mojitos. Had Ford thought about it or asked me, he might have remembered, but Boone had remembered one of my favorite drinks from when I was a kid. It was my favorite even as an adult—Sprite with a splash of grenadine and two cherries.

"Both," he answered, waving toward my dad, who was trying very hard to ignore the two of us sitting together. "You know, there's that whole issue of your family hating me and me not feeling so fondly about them. Then there's that whole thing about them holding onto a grudge better than they do the past, and let's face it, when it comes to you and me, there's no shortage of topics to hold grudges on, especially from a father's perspective."

I was in the middle of taking a sip of my drink when I shook my head. "Please, Boone. I can't go back there. I can't keep kicking at it." I set the drink down, my eyes squeezing shut as I fought to keep the memories where they belonged—locked away. "I know it's asking a lot, and given what happened between us, I know I don't have a right to ask . . . but how would you feel about killing the past when it comes to you and me?" I forced myself to open my eyes and get on with the present, instead of fighting the past. When I did, I found Boone's face looked similar to the way I guessed mine did—tortured. "I'm not sure I can get through the next five days with my family clinging to it in every conversation like we know they will. If we could check our baggage at the door and pretend we've just met and from this moment on is the only history we have, it would make things a lot easier."

Boone searched my face for a moment, then he searched the room. Whatever he was looking for in these places, he seemed to find neither. "Are you asking or telling?"

"Asking."

He nodded to himself, and when his eyes drifted back my way, there was something new in them. Something I didn't recognize. This time when he searched my face, he

148

seemed to find whatever answers he was looking for.

"Then yes," he said with another firm nod. "Consider the past erased, history wiped clean. There's nothing between us except this moment on, Clara. How does that sound?"

Suddenly I found myself wanting to backtrack. I wondered if I'd made a mistake. Most of Boone's and my past was paved with the kinds of memories most people only dreamed existed, but there were plenty of the other kind too. Did I really want to let go of the good for the sake of easing up on a little, or even a lot, of the pain? Should the bad, instead of the good, dictate the past? Shouldn't it be the other way around?

Suddenly I wasn't so sure what I was saying. Or suggesting.

"I don't want you to think it's because I regret the past or regret you or us or anything like that . . ." I twisted in my seat to face him. The dress's seams stretched from the movement. Too many crab legs.

Boone gave me a sad smile. "I know. It's just too painful. Sometimes you have to know when to let go." His hand lifted to my cheek and formed around it carefully, like he wasn't sure how to touch me anymore, or if he even should. When his eyes locked onto mine, they mirrored his smile, then his hand fell away from my face. "Consider this our unified letting-go moment."

For one brief moment, I felt lighter, as if a burden had been lifted from my back. A moment later, I felt something heavier press down upon me. Something that felt more crippling than the weight of the past. Something that felt a lot like regret.

Boone tugged at his bow tie for the who-knows-how-many'th time that day and pretended to get back to his meal. All he did was shuffle piles of seafood from one spot to another; not a single bite made it to his mouth. "So this business of yours . . . there's quite a buzz in Charleston's upper echelon circle about it." Boone waved his fork at my father and his silver-haired, cigar-wielding counterparts. "What's the deal, Clara? I thought you were against all of that capitalist, bottom-line, going-public, high-profits-no-ethics style of making money. Are these expansion rumors true? Is world domination in the five-year plan for your business and, by the way, what *exactly* is your business?"

I pinched at the waist of The Thing in the hopes it would give a little. My stomach felt like it had been steam-rolled and vacuum-packed inside a sheet of rubber. "I'm sorry, Boone, but I can't do the future tonight either. To-morrow, yes, but tonight . . ."

I scanned the room. Everyone was trying hard, or try-ing not so hard, to not make it obvious they were talking about Boone and me, enlightening those who didn't know what had happened between us or speculating about what would happen between us now. I felt a hundred eyes on me, and none of them felt particularly kind or accepting.

"Tonight, I can barely make it through the here and now." I reached for my drink and sucked the rest of it down. I dug out the cherries when I was done and popped one into my mouth and held out the other for Boone.

He bit it right off the stem I was still holding. For some reason, I felt something contract around my navel when he did that. Something that wasn't due to The Thing.

"Oh-kay, so what do you want to talk about or do now?" he said, chewing on the cherry before swallowing it. "If you want to do or talk about anything."

I found myself eyeing the dance floor. It was empty again. A big shining floor for couples to dance, a live band playing sounds meant to move one's body, and enough food and drink to make the most ornery of people merry . . . and not a single soul was out there. Not even the bride-and groom-to-be, who were still outside from what I could see, flailing their arms and making faces that didn't lead one to believe they were playing charades.

"Let's do what we always used to," I said abruptly, shimmying out of my seat as fast as I could without ripping open a seam. I reached for his arm and gave it a tug.

"What was that?" he asked, not needing a lot of encouragement to go along with me.

I kept my hand wrapped around his wrist and pulled him toward the dance floor. From across the room, I felt my parents watching the two of us like they were watching history repeat itself. Like they were already scheming how to mitigate this scandal and keep the fallout a secret from the rest of the world. Who they'd have to bribe, threaten or owe a favor to in order to keep their daughter's reputation in pristine condition.

I picked up my pace, as difficult as that was with The Thing suctioned to my body. I didn't stop until we were in the center of the dance floor, where everyone in the restaurant would have a good view of us. The oldest Abbott daughter, stuffed inside a dress that had been in fashion three decades ago and was two sizes too small, standing with the infamous Boone Cavanaugh, who came from a family that was the proverbial gum on the bottom of these people's shoes, who was dressed like he'd spent the afternoon skipping through a field and shooting a commercial for some sit-com about escaped mental patients.

Boone cocked his brow a bit higher, waiting for my answer.

I shrugged. "Dance."

His smile started to form, the light in his eyes firing. He remembered. Not that a person could ever forget those times. The ones where two people just got up and danced or put on a show for a crowd to prove that they didn't give a flying fruit what anyone thought of them. Whether they were walking through a school cafeteria, or eating eggs and bacon at a downtown café, or mingling in a crowded room at my parents' New Year's Eve party . . . or being shunned by a roomful of family and friends-of-the-family years later. We gave them a show to prove they could stare all they wanted, but we weren't going to hide.

Boone fired a wink at me, bobbing his head to the beat of the song before throwing himself back onto the dance floor. His hands shoved off of it in quick succession, clapping every time he pressed off the floor. He still had the body of a teenager, and he could still move like one too.

Had I even been capable of performing the mad moves Boone was playing out for everyone, The Thing would have burst open at every seam if I tried now, so I kept my moves a bit more contained, though what I lacked in mobility I more than made up for in theatrics. As Boone popped out of his floor routine, moving onto a series of hip thrusts that would have disgraced a male stripper, I did something that was reminiscent of the sprinkler meets the mermaid, and every eye that hadn't been turned our way did.

Boone wrapped his arms around his head, popping his elbows forward in sync with his hips. A few whoops came from the circle of Charlotte's friends who'd been circling the bar most of the night.

"To us doing us," he said, his smile stretching as he watched me pinch my nose, shimmy my body lower, and do another mermaid.

Letting go of my nose, I smiled back. "To us."

CHAPTER SIX

Morning Two.

Two down, four more to go. That I was counting down the wake-ups until I could leave was an indication of just how unwelcome and uncomfortable I felt in the place I'd called home for nearly two decades.

When I went to stretch, I moaned when I found my arms restricted from their usual range of motion, along with the rest of my body.

"Yeah, me too," a sleepy-sounding voice answered from the floor.

"You also had the best sleep in your life?" I grimaced when I rolled onto my side toward where Boone had camped out on the floor again. My waist, along with my hips, felt either bruised or in danger of losing circulation. I wasn't sure how, but somehow The Thing seemed to have shrunk another size overnight.

"Positively the best," Boone said, moaning a bit louder than I had. "By the way, Clara, your floor? It's hard. I know there's carpet and everything and your parents probably made sure it was the expensive plush shit, and there's probably just as expensive and plush of a pad below it, but I've slept on hardwood floors and woken up with fewer knots in my back."

I tucked my lips between my teeth to keep from smiling. "You're saying this isn't the first time you've had to sleep on someone's floor? Big baby?"

"Not even close to my first time," he answered through a yawn. "Miss Pillow-Top Mattress."

I was just rolling over a bit farther to look at him when I caught myself. My eyes sealed shut before I glanced his way. "Hey, Boone?"

"Hey what?"

"Do you, you know . . ." I made a few motions with my hand that filled in the rest, starting and ending at the place south of his navel.

"No, we're good. It seems that along with my back, other parts of my body didn't like the sleeping arrangements." When my eyes stayed closed for another few moments, he exhaled. "That means you can open your eyes already. No morning wood to blind you with."

"Are you naked again?" I asked.

"Why? Would you like me to be?" His voice went down a few notes.

I grabbed the pillow behind me and launched it in his general direction. "Not unless you're planning on coating yourself in honey and rolling in a pile of feathers."

"I don't believe that's on my schedule. *This* morning."

I peeked one eye open. He still had the sheet tucked over him, but he had an undershirt on, so I took that to mean he was also wearing something that resembled boxers or briefs or whatever below that. I opened my other eye too, taking my chances. "What is on your schedule for to-day? I was supposed to be rehearsal-dinner dress shopping with my mom and sisters this morning, but since I'm still dealing with the repercussions of the dress I got forced into yesterday, I'm going to pass. Besides, I'll be camped outside of that bridal shop this morning, and God help me if a seamstress is not on staff today, I will declare myself one and pry This Thing off of me through whatever means are necessary."

Boone grinned at me, his eyes still looking sleepy. "You could always declare me a seamstress and I could do the honors."

"That sounds scary. I'm not sure I even want to imag-ine how you'd go about getting This Thing off of me."

Boone rolled up onto his elbow, his expression dark-ening just enough that the band around my stomach cinched tight again. It was like certain looks of his were hardwired to that invisible band, making it tighten and squeeze at just the right—or generally wrong—moment. Like when he was three feet in front of me, both of us still sprawled out in our respective beds, behind a locked door.

"It wouldn't be my first time freeing you from a dress, now would it?"

My throat flamed white hot. "So you're saying you've got this because of all your experience in the dress-freeing department?"

"Well, it wouldn't be from inexperience, that's for damn sure." His expression darkened another shade as he sat up, then that smoldering look was instantly replaced by one of pain. Reaching for his lower back, he grumbled as he rubbed it.

"You're way too young to be complaining of back

pain from sleeping on a floor," I said, feeling like I was about to break a sweat from keeping the unaffected look plastered on my face.

"No, not really. We're at that awkward, stuck-in-the-middle stage. The 'too old to be young, but too young to be old' thing." He continued to rub his back for another moment before throwing off the sheet and getting up.

"Old enough to know better, but too young to give a damn?" I called as he traipsed toward the bathroom. The way he was moving now, a person would never know he'd spent the last two nights sleeping on a hard floor.

"Something like that." He closed the door halfway.

Just when I was anticipating hearing the shower blasting to life, I heard the toilet seat lifting, followed by another typical morning ritual.

"Boundaries," I called, shaking my head. "They're a good thing."

"According to who?" he called, still letting it flow. "They seem like more an excuse for keeping people at arm's length, you know? Just another excuse for keeping your walls up when it comes to others getting to know the real you."

"An issue you clearly don't struggle with," I said right before I heard the toilet flushing and the toilet seat closing. At least he was a barbarian with manners.

"Hey, you get the good with the bad right from the start when it comes to me. I'm not going to wrap myself in gold paper and throw a silver bow on top and pretend my shit doesn't stink and the only flaw I'm in possession of is my affection for shelter animals." Boone snorted right before the shower fired on. "No wonder so many marriages wind up in divorce. A person thinks they're marrying one person only to find out they married someone else entirely. That's a bunch of crap. The woman who marries me is going to get the same me the day after the wedding as she had on the first date."

His undershirt and boxers flew out from behind the bathroom door and landed in a couple of heaps in the middle of the floor.

"Lucky lady," I muttered, rolling out of bed.

"So really though? What have you got going on today?" he hollered from the shower as I crossed the room to collect his dirty clothes. I tossed them in the laundry basket with my dirty clothes from yesterday. "Because I'm not looking forward to another eighteen holes of golf followed by a limo tour of the different distilleries around the city. Sunburned, dehydrated, and drunk—not the way I was hoping to spend my day. Plus spending it with a bunch of ass-clowns in the same condition."

I barked out a laugh. "Since I got a pass on the whole rehearsal-dress shopping outing thanks to my mom and Charlotte deeming my need to get helped out of The Thing an acceptable excuse, I highly doubt they'll let me bail on the afternoon of touring the local wineries." I stopped in front of my vanity to check my reflection, making sure I ignored what the mirror showed me from the neck down. My hair was messy, but after some brushing, it cleaned up enough to meet the passing bar.

I was about to sweep on some blush and a coat or two of mascara when the shower turned off, and I decided to sideline that idea. I didn't know why, but I didn't want Boone to see me putting on makeup. I didn't want him to think I was doing it for him. I didn't want him thinking, most importantly, about why I wanted to look my best around him.

"A winery tour? A distillery tour?" Boone's voice echoed in the bathroom. "Your family knows how to drink. I got to hand them that."

"You've spent a good chunk of time around them. It's a survivalist measure, the only reason we're all still alive and haven't been given life sentences for pre-meditated murder." I folded up Boone's blankets, sheet, and pillow and carried them into my closet so they wouldn't seem suspicious to any snoopy—a.k.a. my mom's—eyes.

Boone's chuckle carried out into the room. "God bless America and it's repeal on Prohibition."

"Please, my great-great-granddaddy was supposedly quite the puppet master in the bootleg industry in this part of the country. We present-day Abbotts would be well-stocked either way."

After making my bed, I slid into a comfy pair of sandals and scanned the room, looking for something else to do, or at least distract myself with. Boone had just charged out of the bathroom, steam billowing behind him, with nothing clothing him but a tiny towel cinched tight around his waist. His skin wet, his hair wet, his gaze landed on me, and that smile I'd been sure at one time had been created for me alone slid into place . . . I *needed* something to distract myself with.

"What have you got in mind for the day?" I turned away from him and headed over to my dresser to reorganize the porcelain figurines I'd been given every year on my birthday—a series of angels holding whatever age I'd turned that year. "Other than making fashion statements at the country club again and marinating yourself in a vat of premium scotch?"

From behind me, I heard what sounded an awful lot like a towel dropping to the floor. My instinct was to spin around to find out if I was right, so I made myself stay frozen, moving nothing but my hands as I moved the porcelain angels around.

"Well, I need to get back to my place sometime today to get a change of clothes. I turned my boxers inside out yesterday, but two days is really the limit for anyone's underwear, and I'd prefer not to go commando tomorrow too. Just because I like sleeping that way doesn't mean I like going about my day in the same condition."

I swapped the eighteen angel with the eight one, curling my nose. "That's disgusting."

"Oh, please, let's not act like I'm the only one recycling their underwear, because unless some sort of immaculate swapping miracle happened while we were both asleep, you're wearing the exact same panties you pulled on yesterday morning, Clara Abbott."

I felt my cheeks heat. He was right. In fact, I hadn't even been able to use the restroom thanks to the restrictive qualities of The Thing. I'd limited my fluid intake after learning I'd be trapped in it until sometime this morning, and the rest of my bodily fluid had been sweated out by the liter yesterday.

"Let's just mind our own business when it comes to our respective underwear habits," I said, swapping a few more angels around as I tried to pretend I wasn't so focused on what he was doing, I could pinpoint every part of his dressing ritual. The rustle of his old jeans as he pulled them on, one leg followed by the next, the sound of his zipper lifting, the flutter of his shirt as he tugged it over his head, followed by the stuffing sound of him tucking it in.

"How many times are you going to move that eighteen angel around?"

I nearly jumped when I heard Boone's voice right behind me. A glance over my shoulder revealed he was dressed and barely a foot away.

I hadn't realized I'd been moving her from one spot to the next for a while until Boone brought it up. I withheld a sigh and laid her on the desk close by. "Until she finds her place."

While I withheld mine, Boone didn't contain his sigh. "Come on. Let's get you out of The Thing. Since you're not thrilled with the idea of me ripping you out of it the old-fashioned way."

I heard the eyebrow wag in his voice, so keeping my eyes forward, I delivered an elbow jab into his stomach before heading toward the door. "I don't know what you're talking about, Mr. Cavanagh. Why, I just made your acquaintance last night, and I'd never let a man do that sort of thing to me on a first date." I opened the door and waited for him. We were a team, whatever else we were or whenever we'd "met." I knew that if I knew nothing else. "I'm not that kind of girl."

Boone covered his chest with his hand and gave me an appalled look as he crossed the room. "You say that like you're implying I'm that kind of guy."

"Not implying anything. Again, I only just met you. I don't know enough about you to make that sort of assumption." I waved him through the door before closing it behind us. Not that shutting it would do any good. My mom had never been one to adhere to the closed-door policy of privacy. "All I know is that you know how to tear it up on a dance floor and that you have troubling hygiene standards when it comes to your undergarments."

Boone's laugh rolled down the hall, seeming to spill down the stairs into the foyer. Like yesterday morning, the house was quiet, but today I knew the reason for the silence. Breakfast was being served outside, buffet-style, which was only about a million times more preferable than yesterday's crowded, stuffy counterpart. I might actually be able to take more than two and a half bites of my breakfast this morning.

"So is the future on the list of acceptable topics to be discussed today?" Boone asked as we headed down the stairs at an inchworm's pace.

In The Thing, stairs were next to impossible to maneuver with any speed. It probably would have been quicker and easier to roll me down.

"I got a good night's sleep. No one's yelled at me yet about my hair, my dress, or my weight, so sure, let's go crazy."

When I took the next step down, my toe caught on the step and threw me off balance a bit. Boone's hands were bracing me, keeping me upright, before I knew I was off-kilter. I thanked him with an embarrassed smile and slowed to a senior citizen inchworm's pace.

"You own a business. A successful one, from the sounds of it," Boone started, keeping his hands up—I guess in the event I decided to take another spill down the stairs.

"Yes, and yes, maybe," I answered.

He gave me a look that suggested he knew I was being modest.

"Okay, yes, it's been successful beyond what I imagined it would be," I admitted with an eye roll.

"Nice," he said, sounding like he actually meant it. If I'd admitted the same thing to the majority of my family, I'd be met with similar comments that would sound as if they meant the total opposite. "Warning you upfront here that I'm going to sound like an ignorant hick, but what exactly *is* your business?"

I smiled at the floor as we took the last step that put us in the foyer. "That doesn't sound ignorant at all. That sounds honest. Like the question most people would ask instead of pretending they know what the hell I'm talking about."

"So yeah, I'm an ignorant hick. Every one of my teachers' assessments of me from kindergarten through senior year study hall has been confirmed." He threw his hands up in the air like he was celebrating. "At last, I've finally lived up to someone's expectations."

I nudged my shoulder into his. "I've created a consulting business that works with large corporations to make them more energy efficient, ultimately saving them thousands, sometimes millions, of dollars a year, and doing my part to help the environment too. I see it as a win-win." I glanced at him and added, "And you're not an ignorant hick. God knows I've spent my fair share of time around them, but never has one minute of that time been with you."

He nodded as we moved through the kitchen toward the back door. "Your family is one of the oldest, wealthiest oil families in this country's history. Who would have seen their oldest child going into the business of saving the environment instead of advancing its demise?" He smiled at me, almost like he was proud I'd done one of the most outrageous, disgraceful things I could in my family's eyes by opening a business with the goal to lessen the country's dependency on oil, instead of doing everything I could to increase it. "And thanks for saying I'm not a hick, but that doesn't mean it isn't true. You can paint it white and braid its mane, but at the end of the day, you can't turn an ass into a unicorn, no matter how much glitter and flowers you sprinkle on it."

"You lost me around the glitter part there, but now you can understand why my visits home have been so infrequent. My dad couldn't talk to me without practically going cross-eyed after I told him about the company I'd started back in California."

"So pretty much the same look he gave you yesterday at breakfast when you told everyone you were expanding nationally?" Boone asked as we stepped through the screen door onto the back porch.

"Close, just a few notches less severe in the shock-and-awe department. Yesterday's look was three years ago's tamer version."

When we made it to the steps leading down into the yard, Boone and I stopped and surveyed the scene before us. Neither of us seemed in a hurry to throw ourselves to the sharks. We'd played the chum role long enough yesterday, and the whole apex of predators trailing us with bloodlust in their eyes had gotten old.

Boone sighed before looking at me in a way that suggested he was saying, *You first.*

I grabbed his hand and pulled him along, taking that first step down together.

"So you're hoping to rid the world of its need for oil?" Boone's voice was a bit louder than necessary, no doubt because he wanted every one of the oil-rich breakfasters to hear.

"I just want to save the polar bears. That's all." I waved at Avalee, who was camped out in a chair with a pair of dark glasses propped on her nose and an expression that indicated she was regretting certain aspects of last night.

She managed a wave back, but it was a short one before she grabbed her glass of ice water and lifted it to her temple. When I took a look at the rest of the half dozen tables dotted around my parents' backyard, it looked like a good portion of the breakfasters were in the same shape as Avalee. I was glad I'd stuck with Sprite and grenadine.

"Enough about mine, I want to know about your business," I said as we headed for the tables laid out with most of my favorite breakfast foods, starting with sticky buns and ending with a chocolate fountain. "I'm clearly the underachiever between the two of us when you consider I set out to save the polar bears while your goal was to save the children of the world."

Boone handed me a plate when we made it to the start of the buffet. From a couple of tables back, I spotted my parents from the corners of my eyes. They looked like they were in the middle of one of those spoken-under-their-breaths, frozen-expression type of arguments. Probably having something to do with Boone and me.

"Yeah, but unlike mine, your business is still *in* business and doing so well you're expanding. Mine barely managed to stay in business for two years, and during those years, there was never a month where it did well bottom-line wise." Boone waved me in front of him to go first.

"Why a kids' center?" I asked as I went straight for

the trays of pastries. I'd eaten more than my fair share of cage-free poached eggs with arugula for breakfast back in California. "I mean, I know you're a good guy and all and want to do your part to save the world without anyone knowing you give a damn about it"—I shot him a knowing look as I slid a sticky bun onto his plate, then one onto mine—"but I could have seen you opening at least fifty different kinds of businesses before I would have guessed a kids' center."

Boone paused in the middle of the buffet line, staring at the fruit salad with a look that redefined pensive. "When you grow up seeing what happens to kids like my sister, and what *could* have happened to me, all because we drew the short straw in life and wound up with a negligent mom and a TBD dad, you see things a bit differently. I guess I wanted a place where the Wren Cavanaughs of the world could find refuge. Even if it was only for a few hours at a time." He stopped staring at the fruit salad and turned to me, an entire ocean of emotion churning on his face. "You know?"

I moved closer to him and pressed a hand into his chest. I hadn't meant to touch him and I hadn't meant to touch him right where his heart resided, but I had. It had been an instinctive reaction.

"I know," I replied with a small smile, curling my fingers into his chest. I should have dropped my hand and walked away. I couldn't do either.

Boone was doing a better job of playing things off than I was, but I could tell he was rattled by the way he couldn't seem to look me in the eyes. "Just look at us. A couple of entrepreneurs. Who would believe it?" He scooped a heap of fruit salad onto his plate, which made it even more apparent just how ruffled he was. Boone had never been a fruit fan—something about it being too sweet for his tastes. "At least who would have believed it from me? I was unofficially voted least likely to succeed back in high school."

I laughed as we wound down the tables, eyeing the tray of petit fours at the end, when someone came up behind us.

"It wasn't unofficial. We actually held a vote." Ford's Kennedy smile was painted in place this morning. The rest of him from the neck down looked just as polished.

I counted to three in my head, reminding myself Ford and I had made some progress last night in the moving-on department. He was going to be my brother-in-law in a few days, and it would be nice to start out on the right foot. "Well, I guess you and your band of merry men were wrong about Boone, because look at him now." I waved the silver petit four tongs at Boone, peaking an eyebrow. "A business owner."

Ford meandered closer, clutching an empty plate. Clearly he hadn't jumped in line for the food. "His business went *out* of business. Therefore I'd say his 'unofficial' title is pretty damn poetic."

"Ford," I snapped, my grip tightening around the tongs like it was his neck.

"It's okay, Clara. He isn't dishing out anything I haven't been dished before," Boone said before turning toward Ford. "In fact, I kind of missed all that attention you gave me back in high school. I was starting to wonder if you'd moved past your fascination with me, but clearly"— he circled his finger at Ford's face, which was pinched together into folds of contempt—"you haven't."

Boone turned his back on Ford and let me pile a few petit fours on his plate. If fruit was too sweet for him, he would probably hate those, but he didn't say no. When Ford ambled up behind us again, with an expression that told me he was only getting started, I couldn't steer Boone away to one of the empty tables on the perimeter fast enough.

"People ever find it strange a single grown man was running a non-profit kids' center?" Ford said, matching our pace as Boone and I moved away from the food tables.

I held the back of Boone's arm, steering him toward an empty table. I felt it stiffen, and just when I thought he was going to break to a stop and take a swing in Ford's direction, he kept moving.

"What are you implying?" Boone said stiffly, dropping his plate on the table when we paused behind a couple of empty chairs.

Ford came around the other side of the table, just smart enough to realize that at this point in his goading-Boone-Cavanaugh agenda, he wanted something big and solid between him and Boone. "Nothing," he said with a lazy shrug. "Just that with the way your sister's let every cock in town take a dip and you prefer to spend your days playing with minors . . . something had to have gone down in that trailer of your mama's."

A gasp rushed out of me while beside me, Boone became a statue. One that could just as easily have been at peace on the inside as he could have been about to explode.

Going with the theme of this visit home so far—unthinking—I snatched an extra ripe strawberry from Boone's plate and hurled it across the table.

It landed square in the center of Ford's forehead. I'd been aiming for his mouth, but his forehead worked. Especially when the juice from it dripped down the sides of his nose, and when the strawberry fell, it managed to leave a few blobs of red behind on his sky-blue polo.

"What the hell was that for, Clara Belle?" Ford grabbed a white linen napkin from the table and rubbed at his crotch, where the strawberry had last touched before falling to the grass.

"Solid throw." Boone nudged me, his voice as even as his expression, despite what Ford had just said. "Nice aim."

"Why thank you," I replied, trying not to laugh as Ford's scrubbing efforts only smeared the strawberry juice, making even more of a stain.

"Just because you're running around with an animal doesn't mean you have to start behaving like one, Clara Belle." Ford wiped his forehead with the napkin, streaking strawberry juice across his eyebrows more than actually removing it.

"And if you don't have anything nice to say, then brace yourself for flying fruit." I crossed my arms. I felt the seam across my back pulling, so close to ripping open I could practically feel cool air trickling in.

Ford threw the napkin on the table and shook his head at me.

"You better stop shaking your head like that at her, or I will remove it from the rest of your body." Boone didn't blink as he stared down Ford.

"Oh, give it a rest, Cavanaugh." Ford snorted, but his head stopped shaking. "You got the girl in the end. Clearly." He made it a point to look between us a few times, not trying to disguise his disgust. "But it wasn't because you beat me. It was because I bowed out. I decided to stop wasting my time chasing one sister and moved on to a different one. One who's a little more discerning. One who didn't spread her legs for any piece of trash that came her way."

Before Boone could make it a step in Ford's direction, another strawberry splattered across Ford's face, exploding on his cheek and splashing juice all the way up his temple and down his neck. Boone froze in the middle of his journey around the table, giving me a chance to grab his hand and pull him back toward me.

"Goddammit, Clara Belle." Ford wiped at the strawberry carnage, blinking at me in disbelief.

"You still weren't saying anything nice. I thought you would have learned your lesson from the first one, but clearly not." When Boone tugged against me, I tightened my grip on his hand until it hurt. I wasn't going to let him take a swing at Ford in the name of "defending my honor." My honor was just fine, no matter what Ford wanted to spew this morning.

"Yeah, but you're out of strawberries now." Ford settled his hands on his hips.

"And I wouldn't underestimate the power of pineapple." I pinched a slice of it from Boone's plate and lifted it. "Especially when the spiny, prickly outside hasn't been removed."

Ford didn't look all that impressed by my pineapple threat, but it looked like he was just about to back away—and hopefully go in search of a change of clothes—when a familiar shriek sounded from a couple tables over. Charlotte had mastered the art of shrieking as a child, and she'd really perfected it in her teens.

As she charged toward Ford, appraising him like he was the center of a crime scene, she didn't miss what I was clutching. "Nice, Clara Belle. Way to really set the tone of the day. How immature can you be?"

"Only as immature as the things your fiancé was saying," I snapped back, dropping the pineapple slice when it became clear Ford was done.

Charlotte threw me a nasty look as she grabbed another cloth napkin, dipped it in one of the water glasses circling the table, and went to work rubbing his crotch. "God, Clara Belle, is there anything else you're planning to sabotage when it comes to my wedding?" She was rubbing so forcefully at Ford's crotch, his face started to crease with discomfort. "You know, just so I can mentally prepare myself."

"I'm not trying to sabotage anything," I said, realizing people were starting to notice what was going on at our table. My mom wasn't flying over here like sweet tea was in danger of being outlawed, so at least my parents hadn't noticed. Yet.

Charlotte huffed. "Since when?"

"What is that supposed to mean?" Now it felt more like Boone was the one holding me back, keeping me in place beside him.

Charlotte stopped scrubbing at Ford's crotch long enough to fire a look at me. "Just that you're one of the most selfish, self-absorbed people I've ever met. You figure out some way to throw a fit or make a scene or create a crisis if you aren't getting someone or everyone's full attention all of the time."

That was such a mouthful, it took me a few moments

to take in everything she'd just said. It took twice as long to figure out if she was being serious. When I determined, based upon the look on her face, that she was, I felt my blood heat.

"I think who you meant to say that to was yourself," I said, my voice shaking.

"No, I didn't."

My mouth fell open. "When it comes to selfish, you've got the market cornered." When she fired off another huff of disbelief, wetting the napkin again before going to work on Ford's face, I added, "Huff at me again. It won't change the fact that you were the sister fucking your sister's boyfriend for God knows how long behind her back." I hadn't meant for my voice to carry that way, but I couldn't control it. "So huff the hell at that!"

Boone glanced at me, but instead of gaping at me as Charlotte and Ford were, his look was more subtle. More one of him having my back. He gave me a quick wink.

Her rubbing was only making the stains on his shirt worse, so Charlotte threw the napkin on the table. Her shoulders slumped for a moment, like she was giving up, then her eyes dropped to the plate I was still clutching. "I'm done fighting with you for one day, Clara Belle. So why don't you just gobble up a few more sticky buns and see if you can get that dress another size too small. The seamstress will already have to let it out. Might as well take advantage and have her let it all the way out." Charlotte rounded her arms out around her pencil-thin frame, making it no secret of what she was getting at.

My appetite was gone. For food and for a fight.

Dropping my plate on the table beside Boone's, I watched her and Ford whisk away into the house. I wanted to call out to her. I wanted to apologize, if for nothing else, for ruining her morning. But the words wouldn't form.

I knew people were staring at me. I knew they were bobbing their heads, understanding just why I'd been labeled the black sheep of the family. After convincing myself for all of these years that my family was the enemy, I was starting to wonder if I was just as much their enemy. Was I selfish? Was I self-absorbed?

I'd just launched two pieces of fruit at my sister's fiancé because he'd been running his mouth—like Ford always had and always would. I'd just announced to whoever hadn't known that she'd been quote-end-quote "fucking" Ford while we'd still been together. All in all, I'd made a total disaster of what no doubt could have been a perfectly pleasant breakfast.

Why couldn't I just keep my mouth shut and accept that people were the way they were and no amount of shouting or fruit-hurling would change that? Why couldn't I stop fixating on other's mistakes instead of spending a little more time reflecting on my own?

And why in the hell, after being content to play oblivious to all of those deeply profound questions, was I getting around to asking them while I was smack in the middle of my own personal hell and bribing my ex-boyfriend to pose as my current one—an ex-boyfriend I had clearly not moved on from given the feelings I'd felt stirring the past couple of days?

The weight of my thoughts became too heavy for me to keep standing. Pulling my chair out, I collapsed into it. The sound of a sharp rip rang out right before a rush of cool air cascaded across my back.

"Clara . . ." Boone said quietly over my shoulder. The

sound of his button snaps ripping open followed.

"I know, Boone," I said as I felt his shirt fall into place around me. "I'm falling apart."

CHAPTER SEVEN

"**C**an you breathe now?" Boone asked as we stepped out of the bridal shop later that morning.

I smiled at my cotton sundress. My flowy, breathable sundress. I was free.

Then I tried to exhale.

"I *feel* better now at least," I said, pausing on the sidewalk and staring at the blue sky. "And I don't have to worry about my internal organs liquefying from being compressed so tightly. So there's that."

Boone shouldered up beside me and looked at the sky with me. "There's that."

The people passing us on the sidewalk kept looking up as they passed by, trying to figure out what had enraptured the two of us. Unless they were as moved by the hue of the sky or the wispy clouds as I was, they would wind up disappointed.

After Boone had whisked me away from the disaster known as breakfast, take two, he'd "borrowed" one of my dad's cars and driven me to the bridal shop. Our faces had been smashed against the glass door ten minutes before they opened, and Boone had rapped on it when they were thirty seconds late opening.

A half hour and a few hundred sighs later, the seam-stress had me free of The Thing. It probably would have taken a couple more hours if I hadn't accidently ripped the back open a good foot and a half. Once she'd unstitched me from the rest of it, she held the pieces of the dress like it was a dead animal and asked me what I wanted to do with it. I told her I'd let her know tomorrow, because to-day I didn't trust myself to answer with anything short of *torch it*.

"Should we head back to join the festivities now that we've freed you of The Thing's evil clutches?" Boone asked, stuffing his hands into his pockets while staring at the sky with me.

I stared up for one more moment before lowering my gaze. Everything around me was blurry with a blinding white haze. I tried blinking my vision clear. "Definitely not." I plucked at the skirt of my dress, wanting to twirl I felt so free. "I think Charlotte would appreciate a day free from me."

"I don't care what Charlotte would appreciate," Boone said.

"Well, I do," I replied, wandering down the sidewalk with no real destination in mind. "I'm not trying to make a mess of everything related to her wedding . . . but that doesn't change that I am, so I think I'll give us both a day off."

Boone wandered up beside me, matching my unhur-ried pace. "She was messing with Ford behind your back. She deserves whatever kind of wedding-week disasters you can toss her way. Intentional or not."

I waved at the drug-store owner sweeping the front stoop as we passed by. He waved back, greeting me by name.

"Charlotte didn't do what she did to hurt me. She didn't even do it to spite me."

Boone huffed his disagreement.

"Charlotte had been head over heels for Ford since long before he and I got together. I'd known it too." I studied the sidewalk as I continued, feeling like pieces long forgotten or repressed memories were coming back to me. "I didn't think much about it with her being so much younger than Ford—and that was such a big thing when we were kids—but I knew how much she liked him. I only had to listen to her go on and on about him every night from the time she was ten to the summer she turned fifteen and Ford and I . . . well, you know."

Boone nodded once, staring at the sidewalk. "I know."

"She'd liked him for years before I even considered liking him, and I didn't acknowledge that when Ford and I started dating. It was almost like I shrugged her feelings off as a girlhood crush. It was clearly more than that."

Boone rolled his head to the side, cracking his neck, but he stayed silent.

"Charlotte couldn't help who she loved any more than the rest of us. I guess I just chose not to see that until this morning when I watched her scrubbing at Ford's stained pants like a mad woman."

Boone's head turned in my direction. "Nothing like a woman waxing at a guy's crotch to define the concept of love."

I lifted my eyes. "That's not how I meant it. I just

meant . . . she *loves* him."

"Agreeing to disagree with you on that, Clara."

Boone and I slid to the side when a mom who had three more kids than she had hands for came stomping past us. It wasn't quite ten o'clock and she already looked ready for bed.

"Sometimes the people we're supposed to love are the hardest ones to. And sometimes the people we're not supposed to love are the easiest." I shrugged and continued through the crosswalk at the end of the block. "That's something I figured out years ago. I just didn't think Charlotte had figured that out too."

Boone came to a stop, reaching for my arm. His face was a mask of confusion. "Was that just you paying your sister a sort of compliment?" His voice matched his expression. "Did you suggest that Charlotte might not be the root of all evil?"

I answered him with a shrug.

"And now I've seen and heard everything." He smirked at me before continuing down the sidewalk.

"It's amazing how perspective can change when you try looking at a situation from the other person's shoes. In Charlotte's case, her size-seven daffodil-suede Milano pumps."

"Is there a reconciliation on the near horizon?" Boone threw his arm out in front of me when I went to step into the next crosswalk, just to make sure the car that had stopped to wait for us was really stopped and waiting.

"I launched a couple of juicy berries at her fiancé's face at breakfast in front of a bunch of close friends and family. Right before ripping open the back of the bridesmaid dress I'd been suctioned inside of for close to twenty-four hours." I winced as I replayed the more stand-out scenes from the morning. "I think *distant* horizon is more likely."

Boone waved at the car once we'd made it through the crosswalk. "Well, good for you. I might never be convinced that Charlotte isn't the seed of Satan, but I'm not surprised you see things differently."

"Why's that?"

"Because you've always had a way of seeing the best in people. That's just what makes you so great, Clara Abbott."

A laugh spilled out of my mouth. "Oh yeah. I'm totally awesome."

I hadn't realized we'd reached the edge of the commercial part of the street and were about to head into a residential area until Boone stopped and looked around. I thought we were both realizing where we were for the first time since we'd started walking.

"Do you want to just keep going until we hit Georgia, or did you have something else in mind?" he asked, sounding like he was up for either.

"I want to see the kids' center you started," I said, checking his face to gauge his reaction. I wasn't sure how he'd feel about discussing, let alone seeing, his hard work gone away. "If that's okay with you."

His brows pinched together as he studied me. "Why would you want to see that?"

"Because I think I need a reminder that there are still good people doing good things."

"You mean you need a reminder of what happens when people of questionably good origin attempt to do something good and all of it winds up going belly up?"

I backed up down the sidewalk we'd just ventured down, heading toward the bridal shop where my dad's old Chrysler was parked. I didn't know where Boone had opened up his place, but I guessed it wasn't within walking distance. The area we were in was so upper-class uppity, they would have staged a revolt had anyone suggested someone had applied to open a kids' center in the area.

"Come on, I want to see what you've been up to since graduating high school."

"Since *narrowly* graduating high school." He sighed as I continued down the sidewalk. After another moment, he followed me.

"Is that a yes?"

"I like how you ask that like there's a hint of me still having a choice." He gave me a look before ringing an arm around the back of my neck and pulling me along. "You were always good at that."

I flashed my hands up at my sides. "It's the Abbott in me."

I smiled at him as we continued down the sidewalk. It might not have hit him the way it was hitting me, but Boone and I had walked these streets what felt like hundreds of times just the way we were now: side by side, his arm hanging around some part of me, both of us so in our own world that the one we were actually inhabiting faded away. Without knowing I'd been missing it for all of these years, my heart seemed to sigh with contentment.

As we got closer to the Chrysler, Boone pulled the keys out of his back pocket and swung them around on his index finger. "I gotta say, I was kind of expecting a repeat of the last time I 'borrowed' your dad's car during winter formal."

"Are you talking about me getting grounded for the rest of my natural life? Or my dad calling the cops and them finding us at Peach Point, steaming up the windows?"

Boone's eyes changed when he stared at the car, his smile going higher. "I'm talking about the sheriff rapping on the back window when my head was buried under eighteen layers of taffeta."

I felt my face go flat as heat shot up my neck. I'd remembered that night . . . without remembering the night detail-by-detail. Now that I was remembering it that way, I felt like I was reliving it by the way certain parts of my body were contracting.

"Memories," I said, my voice high. And why couldn't I make eye contact with him like he could with me?

"Sorry. I didn't mean to . . . you know, bring up the past again," he said as he unlocked the door for me. His fingers brushed the metal of the door handle and lingered there.

"It's okay. It's not like that memory is one of the many we can file in the Forget and Move On box."

When Boone tipped his head at me, almost smirking over the fact I wouldn't label the first time he'd given me head as something I wanted to forget, I couldn't contain the flustered expression I'd been holding back. Reaching for the handle he was still holding, I threw the door open and leapt inside the car.

Only to be reminded why one shouldn't throw their bare skin onto a leather seat that had been baking in the sun for the past hour without doing a few taps to get used to it first.

"Hot?" Boone winced as I rolled onto my side.

"Scalding." I rolled onto my other side, keeping the rolling motion going.

"Air conditioning coming up." After slamming my door, Boone jogged around the front of the car, threw himself inside, and had the engine on and the air running before I could complete another roll back and forth.

"How far is your center?" I could have sighed with relief when the cool air rushed across my face.

"How far is what *used* to be my center? Not far. Or kinda far." Boone threw his arm over the back of the seat, angling his head back too, before backing out of the parking spot. "Depends on your definition of far."

"Is that your subtle way of saying it's a matter of perspective?" I quirked an eyebrow in his direction as he gassed down the street.

"That's my not-so-subtle way of saying everything's a matter of perspective."

Boone waved at the classic Mercedes that had just passed us after the driver waved out the window first. As we passed, the driver gave us a strange look. Probably because he was used to seeing my dad behind the wheel, not some young guy with hair tucked back into a ponytail.

"When you went to lift a car from my dad this morning, why this one?" I asked a few minutes later, after we'd made it from the wealthy part of town into one that was distinctively middle-class. I liked this part of Charleston better. More public parks, way more kids, and more dogs being walked on leashes. Not the kind that could be stuffed in a ridiculous-looking baby stroller.

Boone's fists slid up and down the steering wheel, like he was thinking. "I've driven this one before, so I felt reasonably certain I wouldn't destroy it like your father believes I've destroyed the other things in his life."

I smashed my lips together and nodded. "That makes sense." I smiled as we passed a city park stuffed as full with children bouncing around the toys as there were trees. "I was just thinking it might have been for another reason . . ."

At the same time, Boone's and my gazes shifted to the backseat for a moment.

He nodded once. "And because of the memories. The good ones." He'd left his arm draped over my seat back, and when his hand draped over the cusp of my shoulder, I flinched.

"Sorry." His hand moved back to the seat.

"No, that's not why I jumped," I said quickly. "It felt good." Clearly I was saying things *too* quickly now, as was confirmed by Boone's expression changing into something I couldn't quite translate. But no matter what, it didn't mean anything good when he was looking like that, inside this car, talking about *those* memories. "I mean, I was surprised it felt good."

Boone's brows knitted tighter together.

I groaned silently and slumped into the seat. "Never mind. I can't put together an intelligent thought to save my soul today."

After another minute of shifting around in my seat, the growing silence shifting from uncomfortable to unbearable, I noticed the corners of Boone's mouth twitching before a smile moved into place.

"Good to know my touch still feels so good it makes you jump."

When his eyes slid in my direction, right before he winked, my mouth dropped open. "Good is a generous way of putting it."

His eyes rolled, calling my bluff. "You might be paying me ten grand to pose as your date for the week, but that was for free." Another wink matched with a roguish smile. "You're welcome."

I wanted to swat his chest, but I knew better than to touch him. Not with the way I was feeling—like everything he did pulled me closer instead of repelling me as it should have. "A little more driving, a little less gloating please."

"Just so you know, my hand's here for your feel-good pleasure." Boone kept a straight face and lifted his hand that was still just behind my shoulder.

I ground my teeth together. "The only way that hand could give me any more feel-good pleasure is for it to never touch me again." When Boone glanced over to check my expression, I hoped he found one as convincing as I'd intended.

After one final glance at me, Boone chuckled. "God, Clara, it's no wonder your parents figured the two of us out. You aren't just a bad liar, not even an exceptionally bad one." Boone shook his head. "You are certifiably incapable of lying."

His laugh continued to fill the cab, and though I knew he was only teasing, I felt my feathers ruffle. "I seem to remember getting a few lies by you when we were kids."

I wanted the words back. I wanted them stuffed deep back inside me, never to be uttered again. From the look of Boone, he wouldn't have minded that either.

All lightness left his expression, his laughter coming to a halt. "Withholding the truth is different than telling a lie, Clara."

"Not much," I whispered, staring out my window and trying to see what was happening right then instead of what had transpired in the past.

After that, we were quiet. Too much past had been brought up. The present couldn't hold any more without bringing everything to a screeching halt.

Only a few minutes after that, Boone pulled into an empty gravel parking lot and parked beneath a patch of shade thrown by one of the big trees lining the property.

"We're here," he announced, staring and clutching at the steering wheel like he wasn't ready for whatever was coming next.

In front of us was nothing but what looked to be a mass of undeveloped land, but behind us, just past the parking lot, I saw a large building surrounded by what looked to be several overgrown sports fields. My gaze ran the length of the steeple. "Is that an old church?"

"Yeah, it had been vacant for close to a decade though, and with all of the empty land around it and its proximity to the neighborhood, its past use was easy to overlook." Boone's fists continued to slide up and down the steering wheel, his gaze unwavering.

I took a look around. Though its location was just on the edge of the city, there were still plenty of houses well within view, and plenty more well within walking distance. This was a part of town I'd rarely visited—only when I'd been with Boone.

"Can I see it?" I asked softly.

Boone's knuckles were so white, the bones looked about to break through his skin. "Of course." He cleared his throat. "That's why we came here, right?"

"If it's too hard, I understand."

Boone looked at me from the corners of his eyes. "I've been through harder."

I swallowed and nodded. I knew he had.

After a few more seconds, he let out an exhale that sounded as if he'd been holding his breath the entire drive here, then he threw open his door. He didn't say anything else, but he waited for me at the bumper of the Chrysler. I found him leaning into the trunk, his arms crossed loosely and his expression almost peaceful as he inspected the property in front of us. Whatever tension he'd felt inside the car was erased now that he'd given himself permission to look at the center.

"The Charleston Center for Kids," I read the sign out front, which looked as though it had been freshly painted not long ago.

"Yeah, the legal people told me I should go with the word children instead because it was more 'dignified' sounding, but I told them I didn't want kids to come here thinking they had to be dignified. The whole point was for them to be able to act like kids for however long they were here . . . not behave like *children*."

I smiled as I read the sign again. Boone had put more thought into the name of this place than I guessed he'd spent during an entire year's worth of high school geometry.

"It's amazing, Boone." My gaze swept up and down the fields—for soccer, football, and baseball—and ended on the converted church. It also had what looked like a fresh coat of paint, and the windows gleamed from having been recently cleaned. "When you said you'd owned a kids' center, I envisioned something a quarter this scale."

Boone nudged me before starting toward the building.

"You wouldn't be the first person in my life to underesti-mate me."

I followed him, liking the way the gravel crunched beneath my sandals. It sounded like a musical instrument, something living and something that was happy to be alive. I hadn't stepped foot outside of the parking lot, and already I was in love with the place.

Boone paused at the edge of the parking lot to pluck a few weeds popping through the gravel. "It's amazing how something so small can take over an entire area in no time at all if you don't take care of it." He plucked a couple other weeds before continuing toward the building.

The wooden steps didn't even creak as we climbed to the entrance of the center where, by the looks of it, at least a hundred kids had dipped their hands in paint before pressing them onto the walls. Little hands, big hands, a couple hands missing a finger, in every hue and shade that ran the length of the rainbow. It was an inviting place, somewhere I imagined a kid would grin as they entered, unlike the handful of centers and shelters I'd visited in other parts of Charleston. Where somber and melancholy had seemed to be the themes at those centers, warmth and joy had clearly been the themes here.

When I read the yellow notice stapled to the large front door—essentially announcing the center was closed and now owned by the bank—my smile dimmed. One of the few businesses in this part of town, in this entire city, that had made and could have continued to make a signifi-cant impact in the lives of so many had been forced to close its doors because it could no longer afford to pay the monthly expenses.

Where were the wealthy families who wrote checks at

fundraisers and auctions like dropping a hundred grand for a non-profit that donated wool sweaters to homeless dogs in India was no bigger thing than walking into a gas station and buying a Coke? Where were the wealthy people who reached the end of the year and realized they needed to give such-and-such dollar amount away to charity for tax benefits? Where were they?

I didn't need to ask Boone how much it had cost him to run this place to know it hadn't taken much. Or not much in the scale of the kind of wealth I knew flowed through this city. I wanted to rip that notice off the door and burn it . . . though I knew doing so wouldn't make a difference. The center was closed. Boone had lost it.

"This is really amazing." My voice came out as a whisper because I was too choked up to say anything louder.

"Yeah, you said that back in the parking lot." Boone riffled for something in his back pocket, giving me a peculiar look like he was worried I had a fever. "All you've seen is the parking lot and the outside of the building."

"And it's all been amazing," I replied as he stuck a key into the lock. "Didn't they make you turn over all of your keys?"

Boone wiggled the key a couple of times before turning it and shoving open the door. He smiled. "Sure, they did. And I gave them all to them." He slid the key out and held it in the air. "Except for this one."

"Such a rebel." I passed through the door and waited for him to close it once we were inside. "Who would have guessed you would have owned and run a place like this?"

"No one." Once he'd closed the door, he left it unlocked. "Not even I would have up until a few years ago."

"Let me guess—it came to you in a dream?"

He shook his head as he flicked a light switch up and down a few times. The lights stayed off. There was enough light coming through the various windows spread around the old building for us to see clearly, but I didn't have to check his face to know he was disappointed that where lights had once burned brightly, they now didn't burn at all.

"It actually came to me in the form of my sister stumbling into my place late one night, boozed up, bruised, and bloodied."

"Oh my God. What happened to her?" I knew that his younger sister, Wren, had been drinking alcohol for as long as she'd been drinking apple juice, but the bruised and bloodied thing hadn't been such a regular occurrence back then.

Boone had to work his jaw loose before he could reply. "Her boyfriend. That's what happened to her."

I touched his arm. "He beat her?"

Boone looked around the hallway, inspecting everything that wasn't anywhere close to my direction. "He beat her. He'd been beating her. Just like most of our mom's boyfriends had beaten Mom" He shook his head. "It was like I was watching my kid sister become my mom. Making the same mistakes. One bad decision at a time, paving her way into a living hell with her own hands."

I wanted to squeeze his hand or give him a hug or give him something to indicate his pain was evident and I was acknowledging it. My feet seemed glued to the floor though. "And seeing your sister like that made you think of creating this place?"

He turned his back to me and shook his head. "No,

not so much what had happened to her that night, but what had happened to her *before* to drive her to a place where dancing for dollars and dating guys who dealt with problems with their fists was all she expected out of life."

My back stiffened when he looked at me over his shoulder. I knew what he was getting at. "You mean what happened to her when you were kids?" I had to pause before I could say anything else. "Her . . . *abuse*?"

Boone didn't answer, and when he finally did, it was with a single nod.

"You thought that if Wren had had a place like this, as a sort of refuge, she could have been saved from what happened to her?" The ceilings were high out here in the hall, making my voice echo around us, but the words I was saying I wanted to keep quiet.

"No, I didn't think something like this could have prevented what happened to her, or stop what happens to thousands of other kids. It just got me thinking how her life could have been different if she'd had something in her life that lifted her up instead of constantly tearing her down. If going somewhere and being around people and activities that made her feel good about herself could have . . . you know, changed how she ended up." Boone angled around, more facing me than turned away. "I couldn't save Wren or the other Wrens out there from what happened to them, but I guess I was hoping to even the scales. I wasn't ignorant enough to believe I could erase the past with fresh cinnamon rolls and soccer games. I was just trying to make a difference in their here and now, and maybe give them a leg up when it came to their futures."

I couldn't keep looking at him saying what he was saying without welling up, so I looked away. I still welled up, but at least he couldn't tell. "You wanted to be a force for good."

Boone exhaled. "I think it had more to do with not wanting to be a force for evil. There's enough of those already."

I continued to stare down the wall, dabbing at the corners of my eyes like I was trying to pluck out an eyelash that had fallen into my eye. "So are you going to show me around? Or are we going to keep discussing forces of good and evil in the entryway?"

A chuckle vibrated deep in Boone's chest. "Come on. Let's get this over with before the police show up and charge me with breaking and entering in addition to vehicular theft."

"I'd get charged as an accomplice."

"Yeah, right. Your dad would tell the sheriff I kidnapped you, so I guess you could just add a third charge to my arrest." When Boone passed me, he grabbed my hand and led me down the hallway.

Instead of allowing him to let me go when we got to wherever we were going, I knit my fingers through his and held on tightly.

"This is the dining room and kitchen," Boone announced as we stepped into a large room at the end of the hall. From the way the inside had been framed and redesigned, once a person was inside, they never would have known they were in a church.

"The most important room in any place, right?" I smiled at the dozen or so tables staggered around the room. They were all round, some lower to the ground than others, and in one of the corners was a pretend kitchen complete with an army of dolls and stuffed animals still propped into chairs and high chairs at their own table.

Boone caught me staring at it. "Yeah, I just couldn't find a way to tear it all down and tape it into boxes. I'm an idiot for leaving it all behind for the bank to own now too, but I think I'm deluding myself into believing someone else will step in, buy it, and keep things exactly the way they were, Tinkerbell and Winnie the Pooh dining side-by-side included." Boone motioned at the table full of eclectic guests.

"So what would you do in this room?" I asked, milling around and peeking into the kitchen area. It was a large, well-equipped commercial-grade kitchen from the looks of it. "I mean, other than the obvious."

Boone smiled at me. "If by obvious you mean we used to see how many marshmallows a kid could stuff in their mouth and still say chubby bunny, and wind up with more fruit smashed into the floor than in the jars when we'd teach them how to make jam, and we'd hold award ceremonies for who was the most brave when it came to trying new foods resembling a healthy, leafy kind of nature." Boone rubbed at a handprint on the stainless-steel countertop with the cuff of his sleeve. "A few of the more *un*obvious things we used to do in here included prepping, preparing, serving, and eating meals."

I rolled my eyes at his smile. As difficult as it had been for him in the parking lot, now that we were inside and he was moving around the center, it was like I was with a whole different person. "How many meals did you serve on a typical day?"

He didn't have to narrow his eyes in concentration or crease his forehead to calculate. "Seven days a week, we served breakfast and dinner, and on the weekends, we also served lunch, so in total we were doing close to fifteen hundred meals a week. More in the summer when the kids were home from school."

My eyebrows lifted—I hadn't guessed half that many. "We're talking hot dogs, pizza boats, French fries, and canned vegetables, right? Think school lunch a rung or two better?"

Boone's gaze searched the kitchen, seeing something that was invisible to my eyes. "My goal wasn't to give them what they expected. What everyone else thought they deserved. Food-bank quality meats and soggy peas from a can was not the environment I wanted to create here."

"So you went with frozen peas instead?" I tried to calculate how many pounds of frozen peas a person would go through weekly trying to keep up with fifteen hundred meals.

"Fresh. Whenever we could get them. Homemade. Whenever we could. Fruit that was more than just a brown banana or a bruised apple." Boone moved out of the kitchen into the dining room, his smile still in place. "You should have seen the kids' faces when we served kiwi for the first time. Half of them tried eating it like an apple, fuzzy brown skin and all, and the other half wouldn't dare take a bite until they'd watched someone else do it first." Boone's laugh echoed through the large empty room. "I wanted them to know that there was more to life than everyone else's hand-me-downs and second bests. I wanted them to realize that they were worthy of the good stuff in life, even if that lesson was subtly passed to them in the form of a glass of milk that had been poured from a carton instead of powder mixed into water."

I followed him into the dining room, wanting to say

so much. Wanting to gush and praise and condone and compliment him until I was blue in the face. I wanted him to know that even though I knew in his eyes he failed because he'd lost the center, he'd succeeded.

"How many people did you have working at any one time?" I asked, instead of going with the gushing thing.

"There were usually three people working the kitchen at any time and a few more helping with the activities we had going on throughout the day, so usually five to eight people depending on the time and day."

Boone slid a chair back under a table as he headed out of the dining room. The tour was moving on, and based upon what I'd already seen, I couldn't wait to see the rest.

"Is that including you?" I asked as I came up beside him.

"That's including me."

"What sort of schedule did you have?" I asked as he opened the first door we came to in the hall. This room didn't have as many windows as the kitchen had, so it was a bit darker. I was hesitant to enter, but when he went in, I followed.

"If the center was open, I was working. That was my schedule." From the way his voice wasn't echoing as much as it had in the kitchen, I guessed this room was half the size of the dining room.

"What were the center's hours?"

Boone's footsteps moved around the room, then fresh light cut into it. And then more as he lifted the shutters covering the windows. "Monday through Friday, we were open six in the morning to nine at night. On the weekends, we opened an hour later and stayed open an hour later."

"You were open fifteen hours a day?" I moved about

the room more comfortably, letting my eyes adjust to the light. "Seven days a week?"

"Yes and yes."

"So your work weeks were a breezy one-hundred-and-some-change hours?"

Boone settled against one of the window wells and looked around the room. Now that my eyes had adjusted, I saw it was a kind of library. Rows of bookcases had been shoved against walls, all of them brimming over with books, and in the center of the room, a bunch of beanbags and colorful floor rugs had been laid out.

"That sounds about right," Boone answered.

"When did you sleep?" I paused when I came up beside a tie-dyed beanbag that still had *Anne of Green Gables* propped open on it.

"Whenever I wasn't working," he said, lifting his shoulders. "Sometimes by the time I'd finish with the cleaning and the bookwork and the ordering, I'd be too bushed to make it back to my place, so I'd just come in here, snuggle up, and lights out." Boone eyed one of the larger beanbags that had clearly seen its share of use.

I shook my head, baffled. The Boone I'd loved could have done no wrong in my eyes, but the Boone of today . . . he was something else. Someone who had made so much of his life. Someone who had beaten the odds and chosen to put good into the world when it was so much easier to go with the other option.

"You're a saint," I said, turning around slowly.

"No one gets to be a saint without first being a sinner." Boone shoved off of the window well, heading for the door. "Funny thing, isn't it?"

I crouched beside the beanbag with the book. I was

tempted to pick up the book and put it away, but at the last moment, I stopped. I stood, turned around, and left the room just the way it was—ready for the young person who'd left the book there to come back and finish reading it.

"In this room, we mostly did arts and crafts." Boone carried on down the hall, opening doors as he passed them. "And this one, which was a coat closet when this place was a functioning church, was my office." He glanced at me when I peeked my head inside the cramped space. "I couldn't stretch my arms behind me without banging my hands into the wall."

"I'm surprised you could turn around at all in here." I crinkled my nose when I estimated that while the space was on the longish side, it couldn't have been any wider than three, maybe four feet.

Boone laughed, grabbing my shoulders and steering me away from the coat closet of an office. "But what I'm really excited to show you is what's just outside."

"The sports fields?" I asked as I let him lead me through a different room that looked to have a bunch of educational materials before he threw open a door that led outside. "Those are great, Boone. They look really well-kept, and I love the bleachers you have lining the base-ball field."

"The fields are great," he said, guiding me down a few stairs before steering me in the opposite direction of the fields. "But this is what you're going to think is *really* great."

He didn't have to guide me much farther before I caught sight of what he must have been talking about. From the parking lot, it hadn't been visible, but from what

I could make out here, it looked to be a large area fenced in by honey-stained fence posts.

"A fenced-in yard?" I said, moving closer. "This is what you think I'm going to think is really great? I'm more of a fenceless yard type of person. Open spaces and no boundaries type of thing."

Boone pinched my shoulders, still guiding me along. "The fences are to keep out the deer and other animals. I wouldn't choose to have them either if it wasn't necessary."

"Keep the deer out of what?"

When we stopped outside the fence, Boone reached over the top and opened the gate. He invited me to go in first. I gave him a suspicious look before taking a hesitant step inside.

My second step wasn't as hesitant. "A garden," I whispered, twisting around to try to take it all in. I couldn't though. Something of this magnitude couldn't be taken in all at once. "You put in a garden."

Boone answered by stuffing his hands into his pockets and shrugging.

The space was easily as large as the inside of the building. If I had to guess, probably twenty-by-forty feet large. Raised beds lined the perimeter, and tomato cages and trellises wound through the center rows. A rudimentary walkway of river rocks had been woven through the garden, and there was such an abundance of fresh fruit and herbs and vegetables, I understood how Boone had been able to feed so many kids so much fresh food.

"How has it stayed alive with the bank owning the property?" I crouched beside a healthy tomato plant bursting with hefty scarlet globes.

"Someone on the next property over may or may not be coming in and hand-watering it daily." Boone moved around the garden, plucking a couple of weeds and dead leaves away.

The tomato was so ripe, I barely had to touch it for it to break free of the vine into my hand. "You live next door?"

"As next door as places are out here."

Boone's mom had lived, and I guessed she still lived, a few miles in the other direction. I assumed he wanted to be close to her without being too close. I'd been more of the mindset that I wanted to be far away from my family, as far as the country would allow.

"How long have you lived in your place?" I asked.

Boone continued pruning with his back to me. I was temporarily distracted from the plants by watching him. Before the past two minutes, I hadn't known Boone knew what it took to tend to a garden. To keep so many different types of living things alive and thriving. I couldn't figure out if that was my impression because he'd never outright admitted to not knowing the root of a plant from its flower, or if it was because I couldn't recall a single living thing growing outside or inside his mom's trailer, a stray piece of crab grass included.

"I bought it from my uncle when I was eighteen, but I didn't move in until a couple years after that." Boone shuffled down the row of herbs, tearing off little bits of each and collecting them inside his shirt pocket.

"Why didn't you move in right after you bought it?" I remembered Boone's uncle who'd lived out here—crotchety was the way most people who knew him described him—but I'd never known Boone had bought his house from him.

"I wasn't ready," Boone answered, continuing down the garden, getting farther away with every shuffle.

I stood and wiped the tomato with my dress. "Can I see it?"

He was quiet. I was almost convinced he hadn't heard my question until I noticed him nod.

"I've got to get some fresh clothes sometime this week, right? Before your family realizes I really do own nothing more than the shirt I've got on my back." His tone was light, but I knew there was a heaviness in his meaning.

I was just about to bite into the tomato and eat it like an apple when something flashed at the other end of the garden. The sun was catching something just right. My eyes watered from its brightness, but it didn't stop me from moving closer. Every step I drew closer, the light became less severe, and it was bearable when I was a handful of steps back.

It was a sign made out of different kinds of metal and welded together by someone clearly skilled with a blow-torch. I'd only known one person in my life who could wield a blowtorch like most kids did a pencil.

"What is this?" I hollered at Boone, who was still fussing with the herbs.

When his head tipped in my direction, his back went rigid. "It's a sign."

I crossed my arms and continued to study it. "Thank you for that world-shattering revelation, but my question had more to do with what it says."

"What do you mean?" Boone lifted himself up but stayed where he was.

"'Clara's Garden,'" I read. "That's what the sign

says."

"It does."

I couldn't stop staring at the sign, puzzled over why it was there and what it meant. "Is that Clara as in me . . . or a different one?"

I saw Boone slowly making his way in my direction, but there was no urgency in his steps. "I've only known one Clara in my life so far."

"So that means . . .?"

"Yes, I named the garden in your honor." His boot-steps padded closer, cushioned by the thick layer of chest-nut soil.

My eyebrows pulled together. "Why?"

Boone came to a stop. "Because you always wanted a garden of your own, and I wasn't sure if you'd ever have one. So I guess this was my way of making sure you did." He tugged his shirt free from his pants and wiped the soil from his hands. The soil was so rich with nutrients and water, more of it streaked his hands than brushed clean of them.

"Really?" I asked, brushing the sign with the tips of my fingers. It was hot from baking in the sun, but none of the metal edges were sharp.

"Really. Plus, you were responsible for making me feel that I was worth more than what the rest of the world was going to give me. My goal was to give these kids here at this center the same thing you did for me, so in a lot of ways, I couldn't have given the garden a more fitting name."

"You didn't need me in order to do great things with your life, Boone. This center proves that." I looked at him and lifted the tomato.

"No, but I did need someone else to believe in me first, before I could believe in myself. That person was you. You gave me the time of day when no one else from your circle would. You showed me that I was worthy of someone's love and trust. How you saw me . . ." Boone shook his head. "It was like you were seeing me for the man I could be, instead of the floundering boy I was. That was what this center was about, that was what you did for me, and that was the reason I named the garden after you. No other reason." Boone's gaze fell on the sign, and almost immediately, the skin between his brows creased. He looked away.

"Whatever your reasons," I said, smiling at the sign before turning and inspecting "my" garden, "thank you. I did always want to have a garden, and you were right—I still hadn't gotten one."

Boone stretched out his arms. "Well, you've got one now." His arms fell back at his sides. "If only in sentiment, since Clara's Garden now belongs to The First Bank of South Carolina."

"Sentiment works just fine for me." I felt shy when I turned to face him. I wasn't sure why; shy was one of the only emotions I'd never felt around Boone. "Thank you."

He plucked a tomato of his own from a vine before lifting it to his mouth and taking a bite. "You're welcome." He did another slow spin, inspecting the garden, before tipping his head toward the gate. "You've seen it all now, and fresh clothes aren't going to pack themselves. Ready to move on?"

"No." I shook my head. "But I don't think I'll ever be ready, so we better go before my feet take root with the rest of the plants in here."

"I guarantee you you won't have to worry about the same thing happening at my place," Boone said as he moved toward the gate.

"What does that mean?"

"It means the house might have a roof that doesn't leak and a functioning air conditioner, but my place isn't exactly what most people would consider welcoming. Or inviting."

"What would they call it?" I asked as he held open the gate for me.

"Marginally hospitable."

"I'm sure it's just fine." I finally took a bite of my own tomato. It was so juicy and sweet, it made the ones I'd bought at the farmer's markets in California seem like they were red circles of air and seeds.

"As the owner and sole occupant, I'm not even sure it's fine, but thank you for being nice."

When we came out of the garden, Boone turned toward the back of the center's property and started powering in that direction. I wasn't in heels, but even in my flat sandals, I couldn't match his pace. It felt like he was marching off to war and couldn't wait to get there so he could get it over with. I huffed and puffed, trying to keep up.

We hadn't been walking/tromping for more than a minute when a structure came into view. It wasn't as bad as Boone had led on, not even by half. Like the center, it looked freshly painted and the windows gleamed. It didn't have much of a yard, but the landscape made up for it. From the looks of it, there were just as many old oaks draped in Spanish moss surrounding the perimeter of Boone's place as there were on the entire fifty acres of my family's estate.

Boone glanced back, and he broke to a stop when he saw me so far behind. Apparently he'd been too distracted to realize he'd left me in his dust.

"Sorry," he said as I got closer. "I guess I'm in a hurry."

"A hurry for what?" I asked, trying not to sound like my heart was beating through my chest.

Boone's gaze shifted from me to his place. A sigh followed. "To get this over with." Offering nothing else, Boone continued toward his house, his pace slower.

The old truck he used to drive in high school was parked off to the side, looking exactly as I remembered it, save for the addition of another rust spot or two above the wheel wells. There was a detached garage behind the house, just as well tended, and in addition to the glider on the house's front porch, I spotted two rocking chairs on the other end.

Boone caught me looking at them as we climbed the front steps. "For when I have company," he explained, like owning two rocking chairs was a crime. "Every decade or two."

I fell a step behind him thanks to my lungs being about to give out from the sprint through the field. "At least the kind of company that doesn't come tiptoeing through your back door in the middle of the night, clutching their panties in one hand and their stilettos in their other, right?"

Boone's back seemed to stiffen, but I couldn't tell if that was because he was wrestling a set of keys from his pocket or because of what I'd just said. It had been more in jest than anything, but jokes aside, there had been no shortage of girls who'd wanted in Boone's pants when we were teenagers. I could only imagine how much longer that list had become since he'd become a man.

"You can just wait out here for me and stay cool. I'll be quick, and the furniture out here is the most comfortable stuff I have anyway." Boone turned the lock over with the key, but he didn't open the door. It seemed like he wasn't sure how to open it with me standing right beside him. "You should wait here. I won't be long."

"It's a furnace out here, Boone. I think I'll wait inside." I wiped at my forehead to prove my point. It was a rare day when it was anything cooler than a furnace during the summer in Charleston, but I could tell he didn't want me to go inside. That made me want to go in that much more. It wasn't like I was going to snoop through his dresser drawers or anything. I just wanted to see the place he'd spent the last five years of his life in.

"I turned the air conditioning off when I left a couple of nights ago, so it's going to be stifling inside. At least out here you've got air movement, *and* I'll bring you a cold glass of lemonade. Unless your preference has changed and you'd rather have sweet tea now." Boone rubbed the back of his head with his hand, his other hand still stalling with the key in the lock.

"I lived eighteen years in the South and never once did I take to drinking sweet tea. If that didn't have the ability to change my tastes, seven years in the anti-sugar state certainly won't either." I leaned into the side of the house and gave him a pointed look, but he wouldn't look at me. "I'd love a lemonade, thank you, but I'd love to have it inside. I'll take my chances with the stifling."

Boone exhaled.

"Come on. Do you think I'm really going to care if you've got a bunch of dirty laundry piled around the place? Or if every dish you own is piled up in the sink?" I shook my head and waved at the door. "I just want to see inside for a minute. No snooping around, I promise. I won't round up the dirty underwear and start a load of wash either. Or run a sink of soapy water for the dishes."

"You? Willingly clean up a mess—someone else's or your own?" Boone pushed on the door, opening it a crack as he smiled at me. "Yeah, that's something I'm not worried about."

My mouth dropped open right before I gave him a shove. "Is that your way of hinting that I'm messy? Because in case you were wondering, it hasn't been the Cleaning Fairy visiting and picking your clothes off of my bedroom floor."

Boone's eyes rolled. "Just that you're not a clean freak. Nothing more, nothing less." The door was halfway open, but we were both still on the porch.

"We all have our downfalls," I said. I might have been a tad on the messy side as a kid, but that had changed, which he might have realized if he'd stopped to think about who'd picked up his discarded clothes and shoes every morning.

"Yeah, and we all don't grow up with a houseful of maids trained to clean up our every mess, further enabling us." Boone fired a wink at me before lunging through the door before I could take a swing at him.

I was too busy chasing him, pretending to be outraged, to realize I was inside his house until I was halfway through the living room. Boone had already disappeared down the hall and rounded into what I guessed was his bedroom when I slowed to a stop to look around. Boone's house. I was standing in the middle of it.

That was something I never thought I'd be doing, not after everything that had happened between us.

In keeping with the outside, the inside was clean and tidy and decorated with a clear focus on function rather than aesthetics. A sofa, a couple of chairs, and a few side tables and lamps made up the living room. From what I could see of the kitchen, a basic wooden table surrounded by four chairs was all there was to it. There were a few pictures staggered around the walls and tables, mainly ones of him and his sister from when they'd been kids, and one that looked to have been an old senior photo of his mom.

"If you want to make a truce, I'll brave coming out into the open to grab you the lemonade I promised," Boone shouted from inside the room he'd disappeared in-to.

I lifted my eyes to the ceiling. "Truce."

He stuck out his head, studying me to gauge if I could be trusted not to fire my half-eaten tomato at his face. Tempting . . . but nonetheless, I lifted the tomato before backing up and slowly setting it on one of his end tables.

From the look on his face, it was like I was holding a loaded weapon and could open fire on him at any second.

"Truce," I repeated, cocking an eyebrow.

Boone grinned, then stepped the rest of the way out of the room. "Darn." He pulled something out from behind his back. "I was really hoping you were going to go the other way with that." He tossed the tomato into his other hand. "Because my tomato's bigger."

"You men and size. Even when it comes to your produce."

Boone tossed me his tomato when he walked by. I caught it, but barely. "You say this like you're surprised."

"Not really," I replied, setting his tomato beside mine while he headed into the kitchen. "Just restating the obvious."

He laughed as he opened the fridge. "Make yourself at home . . . or at least make yourself comfortable."

"Need any help?" I started for the kitchen. Like the rest of the house so far, the walls were painted white.

"I think I can manage a couple glasses of lemonade. You know, growing up without an army of maids and all."

I narrowed my eyes at him, but he was still half buried in the fridge, riffling through it. "Watch it."

Another laugh followed me as I wandered down the hall. The first door I came to was the bathroom. Small, practical, and again, the walls were white. It was just as tidy as the rest of the place, not so much as a water spot dotting the mirror or a dirty washcloth stuffed into the corner.

I kept going. The next room I came to was his bedroom. I didn't wander in or give it more than a cursory look—for a lot of reasons; the main one being I didn't want him to feel like I was sneaking around what was generally considered the most private room in a person's house.

There was only one more room left, and it was directly across from Boone's bedroom. The door wasn't open, but it wasn't quite closed either. So I let myself in.

I studied the walls, trying to figure out why they were painted a soothing shade of seafoam when it had not a single piece of furniture to give any indication of its purpose.

There was a nice picture window on the opposite wall, and a set of white sheer curtains had been hung, though they seemed just dusty enough to hint at Boone not frequenting this room.

On the wall to my right was a closet. Moving toward it, I slid the door open, expecting to find it empty.

It was not.

My hand went to my mouth as I stared, feeling all of the dammed-up emotions I'd held back for years pushing against my walls, threatening to break through. I couldn't stop staring at what was inside the closet, not even long enough to blink. My heart felt as if it had stopped beating, and I was fairly certain the burning I felt in my eyes was from my efforts at fending off tears.

I wasn't sure how many times he'd called my name before Boone rounded into the room. He was in the middle of calling my name again when he broke to a stop, the last syllable of my name cut short.

This time when he said my name, there was no question mark in his tone.

"What is that, Boone?" I asked, though why I did, I wasn't sure. I knew what it was.

He paused for only a moment. "A crib."

My eyes stung harder. "Why is it in here? Why is it in this empty room?" My voice sounded like it was mere words away from breaking. Like it was teetering on the edge of a dagger.

He didn't pause this time. "I bought it for the center when we first opened. Just in case we had any little ones show up and needed a spot for them. I wasn't sure, and I thought it would be good to have on hand." He backed up, stepping into the hall before leaning into the doorjamb.

"We never used it, so when I had to close up, I packed it up and stuffed it inside the closet. I totally forgot it was in here. Out of sight, out of mind, I guess."

I couldn't stop staring at the disassembled pieces of the crib. Boone couldn't seem to give them one fleeting glance. "You left everything else. Why not this too?"

I heard the ice cubes clink in the glass Boone was holding out for me from outside the door. "I don't know. I guess I thought it would make a nice baby shower gift for someone one day or something. It's not like it was ever used." Boone's tone took on a sharp edge, one that sliced right through me.

How one little thing could be responsible for undoing years of repression. How one inanimate object could make me feel like it had just been hardwired to my heart and then pressed the destruct button. How I'd gone so long without thinking about what had happened, how it had, what had happened as a result . . .

"I'm sorry, Boone," I said, swiping at the tear that finally gave up hanging on and decided to let go.

"Sorry for what?" he said, shoving off the doorframe. "It's not a crime to stick your head inside a room and look through a closet. No harm, no foul. Just forget about it."

The sharpness in his voice that he was trying to veil with a dismissive tone kept cutting through me. "Boone —"

"Just forget about it, Clara," he snapped. "I mean it."

I shook my head, not sure I ever could, but if he needed me to pretend for his sake, I could do that. I owed him that after how I'd hurt him, despite how he'd hurt me back. His mistake wasn't mine to atone for; mine was.

That was why I managed to look away from the object in the closet and close my eyes. "Okay, I'll try."

"Could you close the closet door please?" he asked, but from the sound of his voice, he was already halfway down the hallway.

I didn't reply, nor did I do as he'd requested. Instead, I kept the doors open, the crib in view for when and if he ever chose to stick his head in this room again. I wasn't sure why, but the crib affected Boone as much as it did me, and I didn't doubt those reasons stemmed from what had happened in our past.

A person couldn't just stuff something in a closet and close the door and pretend it was forgotten. It wasn't that simple.

As I left the room, I left the door half open, the way I'd found it, and made my way down the hall, recomposing myself as best as I could in the span of a dozen footsteps.

When I found Boone, he was in the kitchen, leaning into the edge of the counter and chugging a glass of lemonade like he wasn't really tasting it. The other glass was resting on the table, already beading with condensation on the sides.

"You've got a nice place," I said, moving for the lemonade and trying to pretend that whatever had happened in that room was behind us. "Thanks for letting me see it."

He nodded as he tipped the glass higher, drinking up the last drop of lemonade. He practically slammed the glass on the counter when he was done, before powering through the kitchen. "I just have to grab my bag and then we can get out of here. You ready?'

The sharp notes had been leeched from his voice, but

he still sounded removed, distant even. His eyes wouldn't come close to me.

"I'm ready," I said softly. I lifted the glass of lemonade and took a drink though, like Boone, I didn't really taste it either.

He disappeared into his bedroom again and was out in less than five seconds, the strap of a duffel bag hanging off his shoulder. He marched down the hall faster this time, heading for the door like he couldn't get out of these four walls fast enough.

I took another long drink of my lemonade, rushed to the sink, and dumped out the rest before following him. I knew I wasn't rushing because he was eager to leave the house—it was me.

I found him waiting at the door, holding it open with an expectant look. I moved by him quickly, almost afraid to say anything. It wasn't until Boone had shut the door, locked it, and turned around to take a deep breath that his body started to relax. His expression followed last.

He was in the middle of taking in his second deep breath, and looked like he wanted to say something to me, when a phone rang.

I didn't have my purse, so I knew it wasn't mine, and I hadn't heard or seen Boone on his phone yet these past few days. I was almost surprised when I saw him pull one out of his back pocket and check it. He sighed before answering.

"I was just about to call you and wish you a Happy Wednesday as well, Han—" He must have been cut off, because Boone stopped talking with his mouth still open. His expression didn't really change. Whatever the caller on the other end was saying, none of it must have come as a surprise. "Yeah, okay." Another sigh. "I'll be right there."

Boone didn't say anything else before slipping the phone back into his pocket.

"Is everything okay?" I asked.

"I don't know about okay, but everything's normal." Boone rubbed the bridge of his nose a few times before setting his jaw and jogging down the front steps. "Having to pick up my mom from her favorite dive bar has pretty much been a weekly occurrence since I turned twelve and my feet could reach the pedals and I could see over the steering wheel." Boone dug my dad's Chrysler keys out of his pocket and tossed them at me. "I've got to go get her before Hank calls the cops and, in addition to picking her up, I have to post her bail. Do you think you can make it back to your dad's car okay?" Boone was flying around the house, throwing his duffel into the bed of the truck before I'd made it all the way down the steps.

"I'll go with you," I said, no room for negotiation in my voice.

"You've gone on these excursions before. Once you've seen one, you've pretty much seen them all." He threw open the driver's side door and leapt inside the cab. "The only difference is that she's added another seven years of liver spots to her skin."

I broke into a run when I heard him fire up the engine. Before I'd come to a complete stop, I'd thrown open the door and tossed myself inside the cab.

He gave me a look that would have shriveled a lesser woman into nothing. "Get out."

"No." I buckled the seatbelt around me and sat up straight.

"Now, Clara."

"Stop bossing me around, you big jerk." I crossed my arms.

"Stop forcing me to boss you around. Listen, for once." Boone reached across my lap, trying to shove open my door.

At the last second, I jabbed my elbow into the lock and lowered it. "Drive."

Boone's mouth snapped open, but nothing spewed out. I had enough experience with the two of us going at each other in the past that I could imagine what words were on the tip of his tongue, but they didn't come. Somewhere along his seven-years' journey, he'd picked up a little self-control.

Something I was still struggling to grasp.

"Why can't you ever listen to me? *Ever*?" he said at last, peeling out of the driveway.

"Because if I listened to you back then, we never would have gotten anywhere. Because if anyone listened to what you asked them to do, no one would ever get close to you." I uncrossed my arms and relaxed, despite Boone barreling down the dirt road at close to fifty miles per hour. He'd always been a crazy driver. I'd gotten used to it. *"That's* why."

"You're the very reminder of why I don't let people get close to me, so be careful how you're lecturing me, got it?" Boone glanced at me. "Now is not the moment to be preaching to me about opening myself up to people because I've been burned, by you, and I'm not going to let anyone do that to me again."

"Me included?"

"You *especially*."

I stared out the window at the trees blurring by, and I stayed quiet when the last thing I wanted to do was stay still and silent. Maybe Boone wasn't the only one who'd picked up some self-restraint. The longer I stared out the window, concentrating on calming down, the more I found it actually worked.

Boone hadn't said where we were going, but I didn't need two guesses to figure it out. Dolly Cavanaugh had been frequenting the same bar since the night Boone and Wren's daddy left them when Boone was four and Wren was still a baby. I couldn't begin to count the number of times I'd camped out inside Boone's quiet cab while parked outside The Bar—yeah, the owner really was that creative—waiting for him to escort or carry his mother out. How they exited depended on the night and how many painful memories Dolly hadn't been able to keep repressed.

I mostly remembered Boone carrying her over one shoulder, his head held high but his eyes cast downward. He didn't want anyone to see his shame, but to anyone who looked closely enough, it was unmistakable in those blue eyes of his.

"Why are you being so quiet over there?" Boone asked a minute later, his voice back to normal.

I continued to stare out the window. "I don't have anything to say."

"You might not have anything to say, but God knows you've got something to argue." There was enough doubt creeping into Boone's voice that I could tell he was as surprised as I was that I'd chosen the more peaceful resolution to our spat.

"I don't." I lifted my shoulders. "You're right."

His head twisted in my direction. "I'm right about what?"

"You did open up to me, and I did hurt you. You have no reason to want to do that with me or anyone else again." The trees were becoming less of a blur, which meant we were slowing down. Which meant we were getting closer. I didn't want to be battling Boone right before we threw Dolly into the mix. Back when we were kids, I knew I could rely on him to intervene if she decided to take a swing at me or wrap her hands around my throat and drain the life from me like I knew she'd been fantasizing about ever since an Abbott started dating her son.

This time, after everything . . . I couldn't be quite so sure Boone would be in the same kind of rush to intervene.

"Are you being serious right now? Or ironic?" he asked, the truck making a sharp turn into the bar's rudimentary parking lot. "Maybe a punchline on the horizon, or am I just failing to pick up on your sarcasm?"

"Yes, no, no, and no," I replied. "I get where you're coming from, and I respect it." I made myself look away from the window and focus on him.

After he parked the truck out front of the bar, he stared inside, but didn't seem in a hurry to go in.

"But you did the same to me, Boone. I trusted you. I opened up to you. When there was no one else in the world I felt like I could talk to, there was you. And then everything fell apart, and you wrecked me too." I kept looking at him, waiting for him to turn his attention my way. "So please stop pretending you were the only casualty in the game of you and me. Because I bled just like you did. I died a little that day too."

Boone's fingers clenched the steering wheel, twisting

up and down on it. "I guess we weren't as alone as we thought."

I followed his gaze toward the bar. I'd be stalling too if I had to go into that packed place and drag my mom out kicking and screaming. "I guess not."

Giving a nod, Boone sucked in a deep breath then threw the door open. "Wait here. I'll be right back."

I'd heard that phrase so many times from him, it had become branded into my memory. "I'll go with you. To help."

Boone gave me a look as he crawled out. "Thanks for the offer, but your presence while trying to haul my mom out of her favorite bar isn't going to help."

"How do you know? I haven't seen Dolly in years, and from the sounds of it, she's probably five drinks past facial recognition."

Boone cracked his neck, holding his arms against the top of the truck and bracing himself. "My mom wasn't exactly fond of you when we were together."

"Not exactly fond of me?" I twisted in my seat and peaked an eyebrow. "Boone, she would have flipped the switch on the electric chair if I was strapped into it. With a smile on her face."

His eyes reached me. "Yeah, well, along with that smile, now she'd dance a jig and throw an after party for the entire state. You should stay here." He shoved away from the truck and lifted an outstretched palm in my direction. "She doesn't know you're back. She doesn't know we're together. 'Together,'" he clarified, making air quotes. "With her so drunk Hank's threatening to call the cops, I don't want to add you into the mix when I go in there. That's like masterminding some perfect storm."

I reached for the door handle. "You used to be able to tell me what to do and I'd listen. Not so much anymore."

His hands settled onto his hips as he angled away from me. "I don't want you to see this, Clara. I don't want you to have to see this ever again. It's humiliating. For my mom. For me. Please," he said, still facing the bar more than he was facing me, "please stay."

My hand stayed on the handle, wanting to push it open. "Are you asking or telling?"

He looked at me over his shoulder. "Asking. Always asking."

My hand fell from the handle to wave him on. "Go get her. I'll stay here. Wishing I'd packed my full body armor, which I would have, had I known I'd be coming face-to-face with Dolly tonight."

Boone's chuckle was barely detectable, but I didn't miss it. "Don't worry. I've got your back. Anyone takes a swing at you, my mom included, they'll have to get through me first."

I lifted my fist and circled it a few times. "Who says I haven't been taking kickboxing, jiu jitsu, and tae kwon do classes the past seven years?"

"Please, with those skinny little arms?" Boone shook his head. "No way."

"Little arms?" I lifted my arm and inspected it. "You might be the only person in Charleston who would call these arms little. My mom will have you chained to a stake and burned for heresy if you repeat that in her presence."

Boone rolled his eyes. "Just because your mom says your arms aren't little doesn't mean they're not. And just because your family tries to make you feel little doesn't mean you are. People will always want to tell us what we are and who we are, but no one can tell you who you are. That's your job."

I watched him for a moment. I stared at him for a few more moments. "When did you go and get so smart, Boone Cavanaugh?"

He held out his arms, backing away. "When I stopped being a dumbass."

Giving a wave, he lunged up to the bar's entrance and paused just outside the door, looking like he was working up his courage, before shoving inside.

He'd left the truck running, and after a minute, I thought about turning it off. That was when he came out, Dolly hanging over his shoulder and looking so limp I guessed she was passed out. That solved the problem of facial recognition and explaining why I was here with Boone.

As Boone moved through the door, a chorus of cheers and shouts followed him. Clapping exploded through the bar. They were applauding. The patrons of the bar were glad she was gone. Or they were goading him. Or they were being their typical brand of prick and sticking it to someone else instead of focusing on their own pathetic little lives.

Boone left the bar the same way I remembered him leaving it when we'd been teenagers: head high, eyes cast down. My eyes burned as I watched the man before me shift into the boy I'd once loved. He'd changed some, I'd changed some, but some things never would.

Dragging Dolly out of a bar late on a weeknight never would change. The way doing so made him feel probably never would either. The way I felt watching him do it apparently never would as well. It was a strange mix, a potent blend of sympathy and intense pride as I watched him carry his mom, time and time again, out of the place she'd chosen to work out her issues. Some chose therapy, others elected for repression—Dolly Cavanaugh turned to a cheap bottle of whiskey.

When he was halfway to the truck, I shoved open the door and held it open while he came around the front bumper. Before, I'd just sat sandwiched between Boone and Dolly on the bench, sometimes with her drooling into my hair and sometimes with her trying to rip out my hair. This time though, I didn't want to be pressed so tightly against Boone. Not with the swirl of confusion I felt around him when it came to certain feelings trying to resurrect themselves.

I was just stepping aside, about to climb into the bed of the truck, when the very passed out Dolly came to life. No kidding, it was like she'd just been struck by lightning and zapped to life Frankenstein-style. Her head jerked up, her eyes latched onto me, and if I'd seen hate before, it was redefined right in that moment.

"What in the hell is that uppity hussy bitch doing standing in front of me, Boone?" Dolly shouted, her words more slurred than said. "I might be buzzed, but I'm not so buzzed to be imagining things."

"You were buzzed ten shots ago, Ma," Boone said, keeping his tone even and calm. I remembered that too, his steadfastness in the face of a storm. The louder she got, the calmer he became. "Right now you're drunk enough I'm worried if we don't get some fluid down you other than the eighty-proof kind, you're going to get alcohol poisoning."

Without him asking or even glancing my way, I snagged one of the plastic bottles of water from the case he had stuffed in the bed. When I twisted the bottle open and held it out for Dolly, she took it.

And she threw it in my face. "You better not try to give me anything again with that judgmental look on your face. I didn't tolerate it when you were a bratty teenager, and I sure ain't going to tolerate it now with you being a bitch of a woman."

I wiped my face, sweeping the water away.

"Shit, Ma, you're just begging for the cops to come haul you away tonight aren't you?" Boone backed up from me a few strides before lowering her from his shoulder. "I told you the last time I bailed you out that was the very last time. You go in again, and you're going to be sitting in that cell for a while."

Dolly patted Boone's cheek, staggering enough he had to reach out to keep her from falling. "You've been saying that for years, sweetheart. You're too good of a boy to leave your mama to rot. I raised you right. Unlike the other folks in this town I'm not going to name."

"Can I do anything to help?" I asked Boone, Dolly's back to me as she continued to sway in place.

"You can turn around, put one foot in front of the other, and don't stop until you fall off into the face of the ocean," Dolly snapped at me, looking ready to spit in my face. "That's what you can do to help this family out."

I took another step back. "Hi, Dolly. How's it going? Nice to see you too."

I waved at her before stepping up onto the back wheel of the truck and climbing into the bed. I didn't want to be so close to Boone, but I didn't want to be anywhere close to Dolly. With the way she was wound up, she might turn her murderous dreams into reality.

"You can just fuck off now, Clara Belle Abbott, and fuck off tomorrow, and fuck yourself off into eternity. That's how it's going."

"Ma, enough," Boone said, checking to make sure I was in the bed before clamping his hands on Dolly's shoulders and guiding her toward the cab. Apparently he was of a like mind when it came to keeping us as far apart as possible.

"Don't expect me to pretend to be civil, Boone. Don't ask me to play nice with the girl who took a sledgehammer to your heart." Dolly stumbled forward, guided by Boone's steady grip. "You're a good boy, the best kind out there, and you didn't deserve to be treated like trash. Not with everything you did for her."

I should have bit my tongue. I should have tried to bite it harder. "And treating him like trash doesn't include having him haul your ass out of the same dive bar every week while the crowd jeers at you both like you're a couple of clowns?"

Boone's face pulled into a wince, but he was anticipating Dolly hurling herself my direction. His hold tightened on her shoulders right as she threw herself toward the bed, looking ready to leap inside headfirst if that was the fastest way to get to me.

"Goddammit, enough!" Boone shouted, pulling her back and twisting her body around until she was facing the cab again. "Get in now, or I'm leaving and the cops can deal with you."

Dolly looked at her son, her eyes unable to focus on him thanks to the alcohol, and she patted his cheek gently. Almost affectionately, though Dolly was about as affectionate as a rabid wolverine. Over her shoulder, she said to me, "You better not compare what you did to my son to what I've done to him. We all have our faults, but at the end of the day, I love my son."

My fingers curled into my palms. Dolly Cavanaugh had always had a way of getting under my skin. Not just because she was the mother of my once-upon-a-time boyfriend, but because she used love as an excuse for everything she did.

"I loved him too!" I shouted as Boone lifted her into the cab. "But at least I didn't keep making the same mistake over and over, excusing it with love. The same mistake every other happy hour."

From the looks of it, Dolly put up a bit of a fight to get out of the truck to come at me, but her strength was waning. She'd likely gotten a punch of adrenaline after seeing me, and now that that had tapered off, she was probably only a few seconds away from passing out into a whiskey coma.

Boone shot me a look as he held his mom, keeping her where she was. His look was more pleading than stern, one that said he already had to deal with one person he could barely handle and he really didn't need another one. I sealed my lips for him, then I turned around and threw my back against the back window of the truck. It was a little easier to ignore Dolly when I wasn't looking at her and she was more snoring than spewing.

Dolly Cavanaugh had been a five-foot-two tornado with fiery red hair for most of her life. From the sounds of it, she'd come into life making a ruckus, and I knew from experience she was likely to leave the world the same way. A person couldn't miss her walking around town. She might have been petite, but she had a way of holding herself that made her seem half a foot taller. Plus she was top heavy and all legs, and she knew how to dress to further showcase her genetic advantages. She'd never been shy with her affections for men, just as they'd never been shy in return.

That was probably why there'd been a long-standing rumor circling the community that Boone and Wren came from different dads. To look at them, a person could easily be convinced, but the rumors had never gotten to Boone. Wren was his sister, and no one could try to tell him otherwise.

When Boone came around to the driver's side after buckling his mom in and getting her door shut behind her, he paused. "Are you okay?"

"I'm okay." I nestled a bit lower into the bed to get comfortable. The drive from here to Dolly's place wasn't far, but riding in the back of an old truck while bouncing down washboard roads that hadn't been repaved in over a decade wasn't the definition of comfortable.

"You don't look okay."

"Gee, thanks. I guess I probably don't." I glanced at him from the corners of my eyes. He'd moved close to the bed, draping his long arms into it as he watched me. "But when I woke up this morning, I wasn't anticipating getting called an uppity bitch before half a bottle of water was launched into my face." I could still feel the water on my hairline and the neckline of my dress, but I wasn't really upset over that. "I guess I'm just a little surprised. For your mom to have gone from hating me to loathing me with every fiber of her being, you must have told her what happened between us . . . even though you promised you wouldn't tell anyone." I had to shift my position in the bed. There was nothing comfortable about this.

"I promised I wouldn't tell anyone, Clara, and I didn't." Boone's voice was so low it was almost a whisper. "But instead of telling her how things really went down, I told her you left me—that it was you who ultimately walked away."

My forehead folded into creases. "Why would you tell anyone that?"

"Do you really think anyone would believe that I was the one who'd walked away from you?" He let that hang between us in the muggy Charleston night. "Do you really think anyone in this town would have bought that Boone Cavanaugh broke up with Clara Belle Abbott?" He shook his head. "No one would have believed that, and those who did would have figured out real fast there must have been one hell of reason for me to do so. I didn't want any-one to do too much digging to get to that hell of a reason . . . so I told everyone what they'd all been anticipating since the day we walked through the county fair the sum-mer we were sixteen, holding hands—you got your slum-ming out of your system and were moving on to bigger and better things."

My head shot in his direction. "I *never* once treated you like you were trash, Boone, so don't try to staple your insecurities to me. Where you came from and who you came from didn't matter to me. All I cared about was where you were going and who you'd become."

Boone hung his head between his arms, kicking at one of the tires absently. "Yeah, well, no matter what you thought of me, I was well aware what the rest of this town thought, and the easiest way to explain what happened be-tween us was to tell everyone what they'd been waiting to hear. It was simpler that way. Less explaining involved."

I curled my knees to my chest and wrapped my arms around them. "So you never told anyone? About what really happened?"

Boone didn't reply right away. Just when I thought he was going to climb into the truck and pretend the question had never been posed, his head lifted, his eyes landing on me. "I made you a promise, Clara. I never told anyone, and I never will."

I rolled my head to the side to look at him. Where had we gone wrong? Where had all of that love gone? I knew about the mistakes we'd made, sure, but how had we let them tear us apart? Why had we let them break us? Fast forward seven years to us living separate lives on opposite sides of the country, and I still felt like every part of me was being pulled in his direction, not so much by choice but by something that ran deeper, something between instinct and destiny.

"Thank you. For not telling," I said. "I'm sure that must have been hard, not being able to talk with anyone about what happened."

"I figured enough people already knew." Boone's hands curled around the edge of the truck bed. "And the only person I would have wanted to talk to was you . . . and you were gone."

From inside the cab, I heard Dolly's familiar alcohol-induced snoring. "I guess that explains why your mom's affection for me has only increased. Although the way she used to talk, I thought she would have thrown a celebration when she found out I finally took her advice and left her son 'the hell alone.'"

Boone's gaze shifted inside the cab, where his mom's

head was slowly falling from sight. She'd be curled up on the bench before he climbed in. "You would have thought so, right? I guess people can't decide what they want in the end."

"I guess not," I agreed, though I didn't really. At that moment, I felt as if I knew exactly what I wanted.

"Why don't you climb into the cab? From the smell of her breath, Ma won't be waking up until about noon tomorrow." Boone held out a hand to help me out, but I stayed in place.

"Thanks, but I'm not going to take my chances." I scooted my hands under my backside to form a kind of seat and settled in. "Something tells me that if Dolly Cavanaugh thought she could break through dimensions to get to me, she would. I don't want to be in a vehicle flying forty down some back road when she snaps awake and decides to shove me out the passenger-side door."

Boone shook his head, smiling. "I won't argue with you there. My mother does hold a rare kind of hate for you in her heart." He stared inside the cab where his mom's head had disappeared from view. "You want to trade places with her? It's not like she's going to notice she's in the back of a truck."

I shook my head. "She's your mom. Leave her where she is."

"And yet here I am, still playing parent to her." He glanced at the bar and let out a quiet sigh. "I'm just so sick and tired of this same old shit."

"Then why keep doing it?"

"Because I love her. I don't just stop loving someone because they make a mistake, or the same mistake every other night. When you love someone, do it right and love them forever. Don't leave them wondering the whole time when it's going to run out or expire."

I tilted my head back to stare at the sky. It was a clear night. The kind that made it seem like a person could see all the way to the far end of the galaxy. Whatever else was out there, I knew there was no other place I'd rather be than right here—camped out in the back of Boone's truck after having just come to Dolly's rescue.

"Your mom's lucky," I said.

Boone gave a huff. "Lucky is not a word I'd ever use to describe my mom."

"She's lucky to have you is what I meant."

Boone gave another huff, this one sharper. "I'm even more sure lucky is not a word I'd use to describe someone who has me in their life."

My eyes landed on the North Star. How many people had clung to that beacon as their compass? How many times had it steered a person in the right direction, keeping them from the wrong path? I stared at it for a moment before my eyes went back to Boone. He'd always been more of my North Star than anything else. "I would. I'd say a person is lucky to have you in their life."

I couldn't tell if he'd heard me, because he slid into the cab before I'd finished my sentence, but from the stiffness of his shoulders, something told me he had. Boone had never taken compliments well. I supposed he'd never had a chance to get used to them.

After he fired up the engine, he opened the back slider window and craned his head through it. "Just holler at me if it feels like I'm going too fast or your spine feels ready to snap from the potholes."

I lifted an eyebrow at him. "I might have been a California resident for the past seven years, but that doesn't mean I've gotten soft."

Boone adjusted Dolly on the bench seat, managing to wrangle a seatbelt around her lap. She didn't move or startle awake once; she just continued to snore.

"Glad to hear it," he said after clicking the belt into place.

When Boone pulled onto the road, I swore he looked both ways half a dozen times before pulling out. There hadn't been a single car in sight, but I wouldn't give him a hard time for his vigilance, overkill or not. Once on the road, the truck kept what I guessed was a steady twenty to twenty-five miles per hour instead of the posted forty-five. For as wash-boarded as I remembered this road being, the ride was as smooth as I'd ever had in the back of Boone's old truck.

Every once in a while, I'd catch Boone glancing at me, seeming to exhale when he confirmed I was still there. It was a strange thing—where did he think I was going to go when I was stuck in a truck bed going down a middle of nowhere road late at night?—but it seemed more of a habitual tic than a situational one.

Almost like he'd been looking for me for years.

It took longer than the ten minutes I remembered it taking to get from Dolly's favorite bar to her trailer in one of the parks on the edge of town, but when we finally pulled into the Diamond Trailer Park, I saw that nothing had changed here either. The same rusted and broken swing set Boone and Wren had played on as kids was still in the community's ten-by-ten foot "park," looking so rusted it might just crumble into pieces and blow away with the next breeze. The same neon letters that had been burnt out the last time I'd visited here—the summer before I'd left for college—were still burnt out. The same shells of cars from decades past were decaying beside the same trailers, becoming more one with the landscape than an invention of human industry.

When I glanced at Boone, I found his expression flat and his back stiff. He hated it here. Not because it was a trailer park and he was ashamed of the stigma that came with that being one's home address, but because of the things that had happened here. The lives that had been twisted and shattered, the moments that had been bled of hope and happiness.

Boone turned off his headlights when he was halfway through the park, creeping down the narrow road until we reached the gray trailer covered in more moss than paint. He came to a slow, rolling stop and turned off the engine.

"I'll be right back," he whispered through the open window as he unbuckled Dolly's seatbelt.

"I'll help." I stood slowly to get my balance before heading toward the tailgate to crawl out. The drive hadn't been particularly bumpy, just long.

"I don't need help," Boone replied in a louder whisper once he'd stepped out of the truck. "But thanks."

"You're welcome," I said, swinging my leg over the tailgate and stepping onto the bumper before leaping to the ground.

He paused with Dolly tucked in his arms when he heard my footsteps shuffle up behind him. "I said I don't need any help. I'll be right out."

I raised my shoulders and followed him up the creaky wooden steps to the trailer's front door. "I heard you."

"Then why are you following me?"

"Because I don't believe you," I said simply, bouncing up the steps until I was standing beside him, careful to stay just out of claws' reach in case Dolly caught my scent and went all wild animal on me again.

"Don't believe what exactly?" Boone stayed square in front of the door, trying to rifle through the purse wrapped across Dolly's chest.

"That you don't need help." Abandoning my claws'-distance policy, I stepped up and pulled Boone's hand out of her purse before slipping my own in.

Holding his drunken mother on the steps outside her trailer that looked months away from being condemned couldn't have been easy. Fishing around for a set of keys in her purse while maintaining his hold on her was impossible.

When I pulled out the keys, I held them up. "See how helpful I can be when I put my mind to it?" I smiled in an attempt to ease the heaviness from his face, but it did nothing. "What's the matter?" I tried a few keys in the doorknob before getting the right one.

He didn't answer right away. "I didn't want you to see us like this again."

I'd opened the door and was about to step inside, but the smell that rushed at me from inside kept me in place, trying to get used to it before getting assaulted by it at maximum strength. "What do you mean?"

"All this time that's gone by . . . you've really done something great with your life. You've made something of yourself." Boone gave a small shrug, his gaze sweeping around the trailer before landing on him holding his mom. "But look at us. The same seven years have passed us by too, but nothing's changed. Same old shit, different day.

Having you here, seeing this"—he motioned down at Dolly with his eyes—"it's humiliating."

My eyes closed as he uttered the last word. Boone had been through a lot and survived a lot. He'd had so much thrown at him from those who deemed themselves better than him and others who just plain thought judgment was their calling in life. Most people would have assumed he was no stranger to shame and humiliation, but the truth couldn't have been further from that.

Boone had never let others box him into feeling any certain way. He'd never let circumstance or situation dictate his sense of self-worth. He'd never admitted to feeling humiliated, not once . . . until right this moment.

I hated that I was the reason he had to experience it.

"You *have* made something of yourself. How can you not see that?" I kept my voice quiet as a force of habit. I wasn't sure if the old woman who used to keep her window facing Dolly's trailer open so she could eavesdrop on every word, curse, and shattered bottle still lived next door, but I wasn't giving her any snooping pleasure if she still did.

"I tried," he replied. "And I failed."

I stepped closer and lifted my finger. "And you'll get back up and try again because that's the kind of person you are. So why don't you stop acting like you're this defeatist nothing and get on with it already? I'm tired, and I'd like to crawl into bed soon, so if you'll be so kind, can we get her settled so we can be on our way?" I waved my arms inside the trailer, waiting.

He stayed frozen on the porch for another few seconds, then he stepped inside. He had to lower his head so as not to bang it on the top of the doorframe, but he'd had to do that since he was sixteen.

"What makes you so convinced I'm going to get up and try again?" he asked as I followed him.

I tried to breathe through my mouth and not through my nose. The scent was so pungent, I could actually feel it swirling in my stomach. "Spending close to ten years watching you get up every time you got knocked down." I stopped behind him as he lowered Dolly onto the same brown couch I remembered.

"I never learned when to stay down and admit defeat, did I?" Boone chuckled as he snagged the afghan hanging over the old rocking chair missing one of its arms. He draped it across his mom's body and tucked it around her.

It was hotter than Hades in here, but I knew Boone tucking that blanket around his mom had more to do with his deep-seated need to look after her and protect her in whatever ways he could. He might not have been able to save her from the slime of mankind she was drawn toward or keep her from the bottle, but he could tuck an old blanket around her as she slept.

My throat tightened as I watched him. He didn't deserve this. He deserved so much better. Life had spent the last twenty-five years cheating Boone Cavanaugh, and I was sick and tired of watching it play out.

"Why haven't you left, Boone?" I whispered as he carefully slipped off her boots. "Why didn't you ever escape this place like I did?"

Boone stepped back from the couch, staring at his mom with a conflicted expression. "Because if I left, she'd have no one." His forehead creased deeper. "And everyone should have at least one someone who gives a shit about them."

I shouldered up beside him, staring at his mom with him for so long, I didn't even notice the smell around us. It didn't take long to get used to. Not with the years of experience I had.

I didn't like Dolly Cavanaugh. I'd go so far as to say there were moments in life when I'd flat-out hated her, tonight bordering on that designation. From where I stood, she'd only done one thing right in life and that was managing to bring the kind of person Boone was into this world. That was all I could give her credit for though, because she'd done little else for him. Other than take him for granted and do everything in her power to keep him from becoming the good person he was today.

"And who's the someone who gives a shit about you, Boone?" I asked, though it was a question I'd meant to keep to myself.

He sighed but cut it short. Turning around, he headed for the door like he suddenly couldn't get out of this place soon enough. "Hell if I know."

He waited for me at the door and sealed it closed behind us. He stayed close to me as we moved down the stairs and didn't start the truck until I was in my seat and buckled up. We didn't say anything else the entire drive back to my parents' place.

I was as content with the silence as he was.

The house was dark and quiet when we pulled up, which made both of our shoulders relax. I'd missed plenty of calls and texts from Charlotte wanting to know what I was doing and where I was when I was supposed to be spending the day with "the girls," and I knew I didn't have the patience to explain anything to her in phrases that weren't peppered with words I'd wake up tomorrow regretting.

Instead of parking beside the handful of guests' cars around the side of the house, Boone pulled up the driveway to the front door, keeping the engine running as he lifted his chin at the front door. "I'm going to run back and get your dad's car. I don't want it to get lifted or graffitied overnight."

I shook my head. "It's late. You've had a long day. We can get it in the morning. My dad's got five other cars he can drive if he needs to go anywhere."

"But he's only got one '72 Chrysler."

"Tomorrow."

Boone shook his head, keeping his hands on the steering wheel. "It's the right thing to do. I borrowed it today. I should return it today as well."

I twisted in my seat to face him. "And since when have you and my dad been under some kind of 'doing the right thing' policy when it comes to each other?"

"Since I decided to grow up and start acting like a man instead of a boy."

When I laughed, it seemed to echo in the cab. "How very evolved of you."

As I opened my door and slid out, Boone cleared his throat. "I shouldn't be long, but don't worry about waiting up for me." He cleared his throat again. "You know, if you were thinking about doing that . . . which I'm sure you probably weren't . . . and yeah, shutting up now." Rubbing the back of his head, he clamped his mouth closed in a dramatic fashion.

Right after I closed the door and was about to head up the porch steps, I stopped. I couldn't take another step. Not until I did something. Turning around, I stuck my head through the open passenger window. "Hey, Boone?"

He was already watching me. "Yeah?"

"I'm someone who gives a shit about you." I bit my lip, dropping my gaze. "You know, just in case you needed a verbal confirmation."

CHAPTER EIGHT

If another phallic-shaped sucker or candy or Jell-O shooter got thrown my way, I was going to self-detonate. And I was taking out the rest of the sucker-licking bitches with me.

Avalee stumbled in my direction, throwing herself onto the pink leather couch beside me. She was the first person who'd been brave enough to take a seat next to the girl who'd been called so many variations of party pooper and prude, I wondered if these girls really *had* spent as much time in college hitting the books as they had banging the quarterback.

"Can you at least pretend you're having a good time?" Avalee giggled, curling up to me by throwing an arm and leg around me. She was a fun drunk. A touchy-feely one, but a fun one nonetheless.

I circled my finger around my face, trying not to wince when the next song blared through the club. Apparently the DJ was under the impression the Top 40 list was the be-all end-all of music. "This is me pretending. See? Pretending to have fun face." I circled my face again and cocked an eyebrow at my grinning-like-a-fool little sister.

"Come on, this is a bachelorette party. If you can't lighten up at one of these, you're truly doomed to a sad and miserable existence." Avalee waved at the party table, which had so many penis-shaped balloons attached to it, it was a miracle the table wasn't floating. Situated front and center was the—who would have guessed?—giant penis cake.

Our mom wasn't here tonight, and thank god because she would have keeled over from a heart attack if she set sight on a tenth of the gifts Charlotte had opened tonight—or a hundredth of the provocative photos that had been snapped of her demonstrating her oral skills pertaining to a certain piece of male anatomy.

"Sad and miserable existence"—I held out my arms —"take me, I am yours."

Avalee giggled again, tickling my sides.

"Would you stop pawing all over me? You've got a fiancé for that." I shoved her hands away even though I was fighting a laugh. My sides had always been ticklish, and I'd be damned if I gave any indication I'd enjoyed any part of this hellish night.

"You want to help me cut the cake?" she asked, trying to sit up. She collapsed right back beside me on the couch.

It was a good thing the maid of honor—aka Avalee—had had the foresight to rent one of those chauffeured party buses—which I'd refused to ride in because *gross*—because the only person who wasn't ten sheets to the wind was me. After the comments I'd had fired my way all night, I wasn't feeling exactly eager to make sure these girls made it home in one piece.

"Do I want to hack into a penis-shaped red velvet cake with beige frosting, complete with pieces of black licorice rope as an especially graphic accent to a certain round area on said cake . . .?" I tapped my chin. "Let me think. Why yes, yes, I do."

Avalee gave a little squeal, clapping as she attempted to sit up again. I had to help her or it would have been a long night.

"See? You're not doomed to a totally sad and miserable existence. There's still a streak of reckless abandon buried inside there somewhere."

I grabbed Avalee's elbow to steer her toward the cake table. She was directionally-impaired at the present moment. "I just don't trust you wouldn't cut your fingers off if I didn't help."

She blew out a huff of protest, waving at me like I was crazy.

"Why don't you wrangle up the wannabe pole dancers before they hurt themselves and tell them penis cake's being served? That ought to bring them running." I pointed the cake knife at Charlotte and the other girls, who were obviously trying to set bachelorette party records for debauchery and general hedonism. From my estimates, they were well on their way to making history.

Avalee answered with a couple of thumbs-up before heading in more of a zig-zag type direction for them, slipping past the sheer pink curtains lining our personal party cabana. I didn't see the point of paying the extra few grand to rent out a "private" space when the curtains were so sheer anyone in the club could have seen who was inside and what was going on. Maybe that was the point though. To be seen, but to keep up the pretense that a person didn't want to be seen.

Either way, it was a waste of money, especially since I'd been the only one who'd spent any real time camped out inside the cabana.

As I glanced at the cake, I grimaced. It was the most repulsive thing I'd ever seen. Who had Charlotte found in town who was willing to disgrace themselves to this level of low? I couldn't imagine my family's go-to caterer, who made an art of food, agreeing to something like this, but who knew? The Abbott dollar had a solid exchange rate in this part of the country.

"Here they are!" Avalee announced proudly, swaying her hips to the off-beat as she dragged a few of the girls past the curtains.

Now they had glow-in-the-dark penis necklaces. Was there no end to the number of items one could purchase in the shape of a Johnson?

"Yay," I said flatly, waving a pretend pom-pom. "Who wants penis cake?"

Every hand flew into the air, followed by shouts requesting which part of the anatomy they wanted their piece sliced from. Since I was the only one sober enough to be holding a knife, they were getting what I gave them—the shaft.

Go figure a group of women who behaved like dessert was to them what garlic was to Dracula, were acting famished for a slice of good old-fashioned cock cake. Just couldn't wait to get it in their mouths, I guess.

"Have you heard from Boone yet?" Charlotte said as she stumbled up to the table. Her eyes were glazed over and her lipstick was smeared. I didn't want to know why.

"No," I said, chopping into the ridiculously long shaft

of the cake. "Why?"

She winked at one of the girls beside her. If it was meant to be subtle, she missed the mark. "Just wondering."

"Since your fiancé pretty much forced-slash-kidnapped him into going to his bachelor party, I at least hope he's enjoying a nice big slice of clitoris." I took another hack at the shaft before freeing a piece so large, it could have fed an entire agency of runway models for a month. I dropped it onto a plate and held it out for Charlotte. "Enjoy the shaft."

"I don't know about the cake, but I'm sure he's about to enjoy something . . . though enjoy might not be the right word for it." Another wink was exchanged, this one less subtle than the first.

I rolled my eyes, then covered my mouth and gave them a show. "Oh no. Not a stripper. Please say the guys didn't hire a stripper for their bachelor party." My eyes went wide. "But Boone's innocent eyes! Why, he's never seen a naked woman before. I can't stand for it. I won't allow it. I must go save him."

Charlotte and her friends were all tipping their heads at me, half of them looking like they believed my act.

Flattening my face, my eyes went back to normal, along with my voice. "Yeah, not worried. Or jealous if that's the emotion you were trying to conjure out of me." I hacked off another chunk of cake, the same size as the piece I'd just flung at Charlotte. Maybe if I fed them enough cake, we could all look like a bunch of sausages in our gowns on the wedding day. "I don't care who shakes their fake boobies in his face or how much glitter is left on his crotch from her thong. I think our relationship can survive the lap dance waters."

Charlotte stabbed her fork into her chunk of cake, twirling it around until she'd successfully pierced her slice of shaft. "Well, *you* might not mind whose fake titties are in his face tonight, but *he* might mind."

The girls around Charlotte giggled, which sounded more like a chorus of cackles with the way it mixed with the next Top 40 song blasting through the club.

"Especially when it's his sister's fake titties doing the shaking."

I froze, the knife mid-slice. The club was hot from all of the bodies, but an icy chill ran through my veins. "His sister?"

Other than mine, Avalee's face was the only one locked in shock. The rest of the girls had expressions more resembling the smug one plastered on Charlotte's face. They'd known. All of them. That was the whole reason Ford hadn't taken Boone's first fifty nos tonight. The only reason he'd wanted Boone to tag along so badly was because . . .

My stomach turned in on itself.

"Wren," I said, not realizing I'd lifted the knife until Avalee came up and nudged me. I didn't lower it. "She's the stripper?"

"And if she's prompt"—Charlotte checked the screen of her phone—"the glue on her pasties is probably drying as we speak."

A dollop of frosting plopped onto the floor from the knife. I found myself wishing it was Charlotte's blood instead.

"Why?" I asked, my voice quivering.

Charlotte shrugged, still laughing. "Why *not*?" She checked her phone again, probably waiting for the photo evidence Ford would no doubt send her. "Can you imagine the look on Boone's face?" She shook her head, scrolling through something on her phone. "Actually, you won't have to, because I'll have the photos soon."

Charlotte and the other girls kept laughing, shaking their heads at me like I was missing out on the humor of a great joke. I wanted to go all chop suey on every last one of them, so instead, I took my violence out on the cake.

After hacking off another serious piece of cake, I had to balance it on two plates to make it fit. Throwing the knife aside, I picked up the plates about to collapse from the weight of the cake and shoved them into Charlotte's hands. I might have shoved the cake a bit harder than necessary, but getting frosting all over the top of her dress had been part of my plan.

"God, Clara Belle." Charlotte gaped at the plates of cake in her hands and frosting splattered across her dress. "Do us a favor and start doubling up on your meds."

"What can I say, Charlotte?" I grabbed my purse from beneath the table and flashed my arms at the chunk of cake she was still gaping at. "You've got balls. A serious set of big, hairy, ugly ones."

I didn't hang around to derive any satisfaction from the rage that no doubt crossed her face, because I knew I didn't have a second to spare. From the sounds of it, I'd probably be too late anyway, but I had to try. I had to at least try to save him from what was coming.

I flew out of the club, freeing my phone from my purse and dialing Boone's number the moment I broke through the outside doors. It went straight to voice mail. I tried again. Same thing.

After shrieking with frustration, I exchanged my

phone for my keys buried in my purse and hustled into the parking lot. The party bus was parked front and center, just waiting to pick up the party where it had left off inside, but when I'd witnessed that thing rolling up my parents' driveway, I'd uttered something to the effect of *Hell no* and told the girls I'd catch up with them at the club.

Unless someone did a comprehensive sanitation of the inside of that bus after every party, I wasn't stepping inside without a biohazard suit, and something told me The Party Bus wasn't exactly known for its cleanliness.

My dad had let me take his old Chrysler to the club— because he hadn't known. I would have asked, but he was out twilight golfing and my mom was nowhere to be found. Besides, I wasn't planning on drinking tonight and having my own mode of transportation meant I could escape whenever I wanted.

Whatever level of reprimand I'd receive, it would be well worth it.

Once I was inside the Chrysler, I fired up the engine and peeled out of the parking lot. I hit ignore when Avalee's call came in on my phone, and I tried Boone again before firing off a quick text. His phone was off or disconnected. Either way, getting ahold of him was clearly out when it came to warning Boone.

That might have been why I felt okay breaking a few speed laws as I gunned down the highway toward Ford's family's lake cabin. The guys were supposedly going to be spending the night drinking and having a bonfire and night fishing and basically acting like Neanderthals. Of course I'd expected a stripper would be involved somehow, but I'd never arrived at the possibility that she would be one of the party guests' sisters.

My fingers curled around the steering wheel so hard I felt as if I could rip it straight off. From childhood into adolescence, Ford had always derived a great deal of pleasure from tormenting Boone, but despite what I'd seen over the past few days, I would have assumed his venom would have wilted in adulthood. It had never made sense for Ford to pay Boone so much attention anyway, with the way Ford seemed oblivious to those he deemed "beneath him," but Boone, for whatever reason, had been the exception.

And here we were, years later and so-called adults, and I was refereeing the same kind of shit I had as a kid. If Boone didn't strangle Ford for this stunt, I was planning on it. Actually, I was looking forward to it.

By going twenty over, I got to Ford's cabin in just under twenty minutes. A record, and not to mention a miracle I'd made it without getting pulled over and ticketed.

The cabin sat on the edge of Clear Lake was more an estate than what a person envisioned when they thought of a lake cabin. Three stories, two thousand square feet per floor, and complete with a tennis court out back, this was not how one "roughed it" at the lake for a weekend.

A few cars were staggered in the driveway, all of them in the six-figure category save for one: a beat-up Honda I'd walked by countless times when visiting the Cavanaughs' place.

I hadn't known Wren had grown up to be a stripper until recently, but I guess it wasn't a great surprise. Boone's little sister had been tough and bullheaded like him, but she hadn't had the hope and optimism Boone had always carried to some degree. She'd been a troubled child who grew into an unruly youth. With what Boone suggested had happened to her at the hands of Dolly's boyfriends, her behavior made more sense now.

I'd been too young and perhaps too close to the situation to see it then, but the blinders of youth and love were off.

I skidded to a stop right behind the bumper of Ford's Jaguar. The urge to ram into it became so overwhelming, I forced myself to take a few deep breaths before I turned off the Chrysler and slid out of the car. If I'd had a baseball bat, that would be one thing, but I couldn't damage my dad's prized possession in the name of revenge on his future son-in-law. Tempting though it was.

The night was cooler out here, less sticky with heat, and the lake was flat and still. The night was quiet and calm. That all ended the moment I tore toward the front door, running as fast as my short, embarrassingly out-of-shape legs would take me.

As I rounded the front of the house, gunning for the front door, and prepared to drag Boone out of there if I had to, I heard shouts coming from the back of the cabin, where I'd just been. I paused, waiting to hear the voices again. When I did, my heart sank. One of the voices was Boone's. The other was a woman's.

I was too late. Too late to save Boone from being the butt of another cheap joke dealt from Ford's hands. Too late to save him from the humiliation of discovering his sister was the entertainment for the night. Too late to save him from being treated like a second-class citizen all over again by a bunch of guys who were a long fall from being first-rate themselves.

Spinning around, I sprinted back in the direction I'd just come, the shouts becoming louder. The Cavanaughs

weren't known for their propensity for peaceful resolutions
—they were better known for their tempers doing the talking. Or in this case, the hollering.

I found Boone and Wren around back. Boone had his
sister tucked beneath one of his arms with a blanket draped
around her, guiding her toward her old Honda. I slowed to
a walk and approached them from the side, ignoring the
feeling that my heart was about to malfunction. Neither of
them noticed me.

"You said you were going to stop," Boone's voice
bellowed into the still night as he continued steering Wren
to her car. The blanket was so tightly drawn around her
body, she looked like a nun in a habit. "You promised me
no more of this shit when you had to call me after the last
one got out of control."

Wren struggled against Boone, but she was as short as
I was and had always been rail-thin. She might as well
have been trying to move the Hoover Dam with a team of
mules. "I didn't call you, Boone. You showed up all on
your own at that one, dragging me out in the exact same
way."

"And it was a damn good thing I did show up, because what would have happened if I hadn't?"

They'd made it to Wren's car. Boone managed to
throw open the driver's side door and still maintain his
hold on her.

"I would have made the other two hundred dollars I
was planning on making that night, and there would have
been a jack-off line out the bathroom after I left." Wren
shoved at Boone's side, squirming against him. "God,
Boone. When are you going to stop acting like I'm a kid?"

"When you stop behaving like one," he growled.

"This is my job. This is how I make my living. This is me being an adult and leaving the kid part behind. Why can't you see that?" When Wren shoved him again, she caught him just enough off guard he staggered a bit. "Thanks to your Save the Little Sister routine again, you cost me another thousand bucks tonight. That's one thousand singles I had plans for."

"Plans for shooting up your arm?"

Wren managed to free an arm from the blanket and didn't waste a moment slapping Boone's cheek. The slap echoed across the lake, making me wince.

If anything registered on Boone's expression right then, it wasn't pain.

"You're a son of a bitch." Wren's voice quivered, more from what I guessed was anger than sadness. "And in case you didn't catch the first five thousand hints, here's me saying it out loud—leave me the hell alone."

Boone's jaw set, but he stayed silent. I wanted to move in, but my feet were stuck to the ground.

"You couldn't save me then, and it's too late to save me from whatever it is you think I need saving from now. A person has to want to be saved for it to work, big brother, and does it look like I'm screaming for help?"

Boone's arms had fallen away from Wren when he stepped back from her slap. Lifting her arms, she threw off the blanket and did a small spin in front of her brother. If it made me wince to see Wren in her outfit—if that was what one could call it—I couldn't imagine how Boone felt. How he'd felt when all of those guys inside had seen his little sister the same way.

"Wren—"

"Don't, Boone. Just don't." Wren kicked off her clear

platform heels and chucked them inside the Honda. Without them on, she barely came up to his shoulders. "I'm sick of the hero act. You've been playing it your whole life, and it's never been that successful of a role for you." Wren shook her head at him. "You can't even save yourself."

My feet were finally able to move. The sound of my footsteps crunching through the gravel made both of their heads turn, though Boone's moved as if a weight had been strung to it.

"Oh, goodie. Clara's here." Wren's eyes narrowed at me as I approached. There was very little of the girl I remembered in the woman before me now. Apparently she felt the opposite from the way she was glaring at me. "You can run along and save her now. She was always your main priority anyway."

I tried to ignore that the woman in the high-leg purple sequined thong and matching pasties was the same girl I'd seen camped out in front of the television in Dolly's trailer, a coloring book and box of crayons colored down to nubs in front of her. It was next to impossible though.

"God knows she needs all the saving she can get." Wren shook her head at me next before disappearing into the car and slamming the door.

"Wren, stop." Boone lurched forward and rapped on her window.

She answered by waving her middle finger at him, sputtered the Honda to life, and as she gunned it out of the driveway, it didn't seem as though she were trying to avoid hitting me with her 80s Accord. It looked more as though she were trying to make me a hood ornament.

I dove to the side, but it wasn't necessary. At the last

moment, she steered the car to the side. She might have wanted to scare the shit out of me, but she didn't actually want to maul me. It wasn't one of the more comforting realizations I'd come to, but at least I wasn't roadkill.

"Shit, are you okay?" Boone yelled as he lunged toward me.

When I said I'd dove to the side, I meant it. I'd actually dove. "Yeah, I'm good. Other than a little road burn and being reminded of my lack of grace, I'm just fine."

Boone reached for me, and I took his hand and let him pull me up. He didn't seem to blink as he watched Wren speed away, the blanket flapping in the wind, its corner caught inside the driver's door.

"Are you okay?" I asked, dropping my hand on his arm gently.

My touch made him flinch, but his shoulders relaxed the moment after. "It's been so long since I've been okay, I don't think I remember how it feels."

The cheek Wren had slapped was red and sparkling with specks of what I presumed was body glitter. I wiped his cheek lightly to dust off a few flecks of glitter. His skin was warm, more so where Wren had hit him. "Sorry, that was probably the dumbest question I could ask you after what just happened."

"No," he said, still watching her car. "If you didn't care, you wouldn't ask. It's nice to know someone cares."

Wren's taillights disappeared from sight, far down the road.

"I care," I said.

The night didn't seem so quiet anymore. The crickets were chirping so loudly their calls seemed to vibrate in my ears. The frogs croaking and the waves lapping at the shoreline joined in the deafening symphony. From inside the cabin, I could make out the sounds of laughter. After a few moments, it went quiet again right before another round exploded into the night. I could only imagine the things they were saying, the image they were reliving, the pictures they were comparing.

If Boone noticed the rounds of laughter coming from the cabin, he didn't show it.

"I'm sorry, Boone." I angled myself in front of him, to try to get his attention.

"What are you sorry for?" he asked, blinking. "That my sister's a stripper or that I had to be reminded just now that she was a stripper?"

"I'm sorry for what happened."

I couldn't tell if the reason he wouldn't look at me was because he was afraid to look away from where Wren had disappeared or afraid to look at me. "And I'm sorry for a lot of things too, but a lot of good that does." Turning to the side, he walked down the driveway.

"Boone, wait," I called, realizing I was repeating the last thing he'd said to Wren.

"I need to be alone right now, Clara." When he reached the end of the driveway, he turned left instead of following Wren's car back to the highway. He was taking the long way around.

"I didn't know they had that planned. I just found out." I panted as I chased him. He was only walking, but I had to jog to catch up with him. His legs were twice my size and seemed to move ten times faster. "I tried calling to warn you. I tried getting here before—"

"It's not your fault. Wren is who she is, and Ford is who he is. I should have seen it coming."

Even at my present jog, it became clear there was no way I could keep up with him and keep up a conversation. "Will you please stop?" I was more hyperventilating than panting now. "Will you please just talk to me?"

His shoulders rose a few inches before falling. "There's nothing to talk about. I'll see you back at your parents' later. I need to think."

Walking away when things got sketchy—a favorite pastime of Boone's. This time, I wouldn't make it so easy for him to walk away. "If that's the direction you're planning on taking to get back to my parents' place, I hope you've got a lot to think about. A whole week's worth."

Boone continued powering down the dirt road, getting so far out in front of me I was losing him to the dark. "I've always got that much to think about. Good night, Clara." Picking up his pace, he disappeared in another few steps.

I came to a stop, stomped my foot against the road, and roared.

He wanted to be alone, he wanted to think . . . code words for him wanting to fester and brood.

Spinning around, I made use of whatever my legs had left to give me and jogged back to Ford's cabin. Laughter was still ringing inside the cabin, and as much satisfaction as I would have derived from charging in there and stringing them all up to the rafters by their nut-sacks, I forced myself into the Chrysler and went after Boone. He might have said he didn't need anyone, and he might have thought he meant it, but I knew better.

It seemed like the people who cried the least for help were the ones who generally needed it most. Boone hadn't asked for help a single time in his life for all I knew.

I peeled out of the driveway, making sure to leave a

few unsightly tread marks on the light concrete, before I made a left and barreled down the road after Boone. I'd gone close to a mile by the time the headlights cast their light on him.

He didn't look back. He didn't slow down. He just kept moving forward.

I rolled the Chrysler up beside him and cranked down the window. "Now try jetting away from me," I said, revving the engine a few times.

Boone kept his head forward, though I noticed his eyes drift off the road toward the numerous trampled trails animals had made through the trees.

"Don't think I won't follow you in there too." I gave the engine one more rev. "Come on. Talk to me. Say something. I know you'd prefer to pretend like nothing happened and you didn't just have to drag your sister out of the bachelor party she was scheduled to strip at and that Ford McBride isn't still an immature, petty asshole whose goal in life seems to be to make yours as unbearable as possible, but I know you feel something." I hung my arm out of the window, glancing at him. His face was flat, his eyes matching. "I know you feel lots of somethings. Name one. Any one. Just give me something, for crap's sake."

"Frustrated," he growled. His jaw returned to its former position—clenched so tight, it made the sinews running down his neck look as if they were going to pop through the skin.

"Frustrated, okay, yeah, sure, I can understand that." I nodded and gave the car a little more gas. He was really trekking. "I'd feel the same way if something like that happened to me."

"I'm not frustrated with them. I'm frustrated with

you." He glanced at me from the corners of his eyes.

"With *me*? Why are you frustrated with me? I'm not the one who hired your little sister as the main attraction at Ford McBride's bachelor party." I edged the Chrysler closer to him. He wanted space? I wasn't going to give it to him.

"I'm frustrated because I told you I wanted to be alone, and here you are, stalking me down some dark back road in your daddy's car. I'm frustrated because you're pretending to care when all you care about is me showing up and standing by your side at the right time for your family to see you're not some poor, single, just-got-dumped woman. But mostly I'm frustrated because I'm not so sure you picked me to pay ten grand based on your limited options that night, and it had more to do with you wanting to piss off your family and everyone else all over again. I'm frustrated because I feel like a damn puppet in your master scheme of waving your middle finger in your family's face."

I hadn't realized I'd come to a stop until Boone had to shout his last words back at me. I had to shake my head to clear it enough to make sure that when I reapplied pressure to the gas pedal, it didn't ram all the way to the floorboard. Still, the car jumped forward faster than I'd intended. Boone shot to the side of the road, throwing me a look like I'd been trying to hit him.

"If I wanted to run you over, I would have done it years ago," I snapped, making sure the car was in park before I threw open the door and burst out. "I can't believe you'd say that to me. Any of that!" I flailed my arms at him as I stomped toward him.

Boone took a few steps back, not as though he was

afraid of me, but more like he wanted to keep his distance.

"Me choosing you back then had nothing to do with wanting to piss off or please my family. It had nothing to do with them at all. And me choosing you this time definitely didn't have anything to do with that either."

Boone made a face. "Forgive me if I'm not convinced. I'm a little jaded from the two years we spent dating and how you spent that whole time making sure you were holding my hand when Daddy walked into the room, or we were making out when your mommy got home from her rotary club brunch. You weren't content unless we were wrapped around each other whenever anyone from your inner circle was close by. I was too young and dumb to see it then, but I see it now. Find someone else to be your puppet. I've done my time."

It was a good thing he'd put so much distance between us, because he'd just earned himself a slap on that other cheek of his. "How dare you, Boone Cavanaugh. How dare you say I was using you when I went through hell that entire time we were together."

"Yeah, yeah, I'm sure it was so hard for you having everyone whisper behind your back about how you just needed to get it out of your system before settling down with some guy like Ford McBride. I'm sure it must have been torture for you to face your parents' disapproval when it came to your choice in boyfriend, and yet still get that fancy convertible when you turned sixteen and spend two weeks every winter in Vail and four weeks in the Hamptons every summer. I'm sure that was so hard for you, Clara. All I had to deal with for dating outside of my league was having the sheriff pull me over anytime we passed each other on the road, or getting cut from the damn football team every single year because the other guys didn't want me on it and their daddies had plenty of sway in the community. Then when we did finally break up, I couldn't find a girl to date me in this county or the next one over. The ones who were supposedly in my league didn't want me because they took me being with you as intentionally shunning them, and the girls in your supposed league looked at me as used goods."

When he finished, I stood in front of him, arms crossed and insides fuming, but I stayed quiet. There was so much I wanted to say, so much I wanted to spew right back at him, I needed to figure out what I wanted to argue with first.

"Are you done?" I said, raising my brow.

"You asked me to talk." He held out his arms. "I'm talking."

"I asked you to talk about what you were feeling." I lifted my brow higher. "Not what you've imagined up in that depraved head of yours"

"So what do you want to hear? What do you want me to tell you? I remember that game. I'm sure I can settle back into that role easily enough." He stepped closer, coming within arm's reach.

I cinched my arms tighter around myself to keep from slapping him, because my God, if he ever deserved it, now was the time. I shook my head furiously. "If you told me what you thought I wanted to hear, that's on you. Not me. All I ever wanted was to know you, the real you. I knew enough about people plucking at my strings and wanting me to act this way and say that and do this. I never wanted you to feel that way with me."

"No, you just wanted me to say and do and act how

you wanted me to, and say it was who I really was and what I really wanted."

I marched closer, my eyes narrowing. "You go ahead and keep on believing whatever it is you think you know. That won't change how I really felt about you and why I wanted to be close to you. Asshole," I tacked on when he gave a huff of dissent. "And just for your information, when I reached for your hand, it was because I damn well wanted to hold it. And when I lifted up onto my tiptoes to kiss you, it was because I damn well wanted to kiss you. And since I'm on a roll when it comes to setting you straight of all your preconceived—totally erroneous, by the way—notions, when I made you that offer a few nights ago, it had nothing to do with wanting to piss off my family. If that had been my goal, I would have made sure we had a couple of rings settled on our left hands before marching through those front doors."

Boone made another face, one that implied he didn't believe a word I'd just said. "Then why don't you clear up why you did make me that offer? I'm still a little sketchy on that."

Of all the things I'd just fired at him, I hadn't expected that would be the part he'd cling to. The one he'd ask for clarification on. It seemed like the most harmless of the list, but I knew better, and from the look on his face, so did he.

"I told you already," I said, angling myself so I wasn't square in front of him. "You were the only one in that sorry excuse for a bar I could get through my parents' front door without them calling the cops." When Boone cocked a brow, I added, "Or at least the only one who wouldn't have warranted an immediate call to the psychiatrist in charge of committing new patients that night." His other brow lifted. I sighed and rubbed my temples. "My options were limited. At least I knew you and guessed I could trust you not to stab me in the middle of the night before running off with my parents' crystal and silverware."

He was staring at me. I could feel it, but I wouldn't let myself meet his stare.

"That's a pretty speech, Clara, but dress it up all you want. It won't change the fact it's a lie."

"Are you implying that I'm lying?"

"Not implying, more stating a fact, and yeah, I am."

"Well, you've accused me of just about everything else tonight, so why not?" I backed up toward the Chrysler. If this was how he wanted to treat me when all I'd done was try to help him tonight, then fine, he could have his alone time.

"You could have picked anyone to ask to be your date to your sister's wedding, forget the ten grand. Why did you pick me?" His voice was closer but softer.

The sudden change in tone took me by surprise. "I'd flown into the airport a whole forty minutes before walking into that bar for a drink. I had a whole fifteen minutes to spare before my family was expecting me to arrive. Not only was I limited on applicants for the plus-one job, I was also a little short on time."

Boone's boots moved closer, crunching the dirt and gravel. "You said you and your boyfriend back home broke up a few days earlier. That gave you a few days to put together a back-up plan. Why wait until you were minutes away from your parents' front door? Why would you care about having a plus one so badly anyway? The girl I remember didn't care what people thought about her."

I reached for my temples again, but no amount of massaging would make the pulsing dim. It was as if everything I'd kept hidden inside me was trying to break free—their preferred path being through the spots I was rubbing furiously.

"Clara?" Boone's voice was closer, even softer.

"You know why," I whispered, sealing my eyes closed. "Stop pretending like you don't. Stop with the questions. You *know*."

I heard his breaths behind me, slow and steady. "I know what?"

I went to clamp my mouth closed, but it was too late. "Why we're here now. Together."

I didn't hear his breathing for a while after that. "I need you to give me your explanation for that, because I have my own ideas, but I'd like to hear yours first."

It was late. I was tired. And life was short.

Those were the reasons why I wound up giving him my answer, despite knowing it should have remained a secret I took with me to the hereafter. "It doesn't seem to matter how far away I go or how many years go by. I'm starting to accept that there will always be some part of me that is going to hold on to some part of you." I just barely glanced over my shoulder to make sure he was still there. He was. "And you're here right now, saying these hurtful things, trying to push me away, because some part of you has held on to some part of me too."

Boone remained frozen behind me, his breathing silent. The night seemed to circle in tighter around us, relentless. The longer he stayed quiet, the more tempting my desire to leap inside the Chrysler, speed to the airport, return to California a few days early, and never come back to this godforsaken part of the country again became.

Boone had been my source of strength for much of my life. He'd been just as much my weakness. I wasn't sure what he was more of now, but I also wasn't sure how much longer I could wait with my words hanging between us before I ran away and, this time, stayed away. For good.

A half a lifetime had passed, and Boone was still silent. I guessed he would stay that way, no matter how long I hovered on this dirt road.

My lungs had felt like withered balloons for years now, but I couldn't feel them anymore. The part of me that was responsible for keeping the rest of me alive had disappeared. I'd been losing parts of me for a while. Scattered pieces of Clara Abbott were strewn all over this county. I only had one piece left, and I was leaving it on the side of this dusty Charleston road.

I managed to take a step and then another, the second harder than the first. By the time I was taking my third and closing in on the car, my legs felt as if the moon had been tied to one and the sun to the other. Moving seemed impossible, but somehow, I did it.

My arm was reaching out for the door handle, and just when my fingers were about to curl around the kiss of cool metal, something intercepted their path.

Warm fingers tied through mine, his firm palm pressing into mine. Boone's footsteps crunched closer. Nothing but the sound of the car's engine, the sounds of the night, and his slow and even breathing filled the air. But he had my hand. He'd reached for me. He hadn't let me walk away. Instead of his grip loosening, it grew stronger.

"You were right." His voice echoed into the night, his body so close to mine I felt the warmth of his words on the crest of my shoulder.

I tipped my head back. He was closer than I'd guessed. "Right about what?"

His other hand lifted to my face, his thumb tilting my chin up until I was looking at him. The veil that had been shading his eyes since I'd seen him in the bar was gone. The boy I fell in love with was in those eyes, in the man standing before me now.

His thumb swept up the line of my jaw, his forehead drawn together, before all at once, he seemed to relax. "About everything."

My heartbeat thrummed in my ears, slow and steady and strong.

"I'm going to kiss you." He spun me around slowly, his hand on my hand and the other one lowering into the bend of my neck, anchoring himself to me. "And I see you've got two options for how you can react to that."

My eyebrows came together, my chest rising and falling heavily between us. "I do?"

Boone nodded, his eyes glimmering. He slid closer until our chests were just barely touching. I felt the car brushing against my back. "You can slap me across the face like I know you were desperate to do a few minutes ago, get in that car, and drive away. You can leave me in the rearview and the dust, and this is where I'll stay if that's what you want."

I was about to ask what my other option was, because as much as I might have known leaving was what I should have done, it was the very last thing I wanted to do.

Boone pressed closer, cocking a brow and not letting

my eyes leave his. "Or . . ."

But he'd said enough. The instinct that resided deep within me broke to the surface, and before I knew it had escaped, I was lifting onto my toes, my fingers curling around the material of his shirt and pulling him to me at the exact moment I was pushing myself closer.

My lips pressed into his, lingering there for only a moment before I lowered back onto the balls of my feet. It had been an innocent kiss, unexpected and fleeting, but it had sent a torrent of emotions cascading through me. One simple kiss. That was the only simple aspect of it.

"Or you can kiss me back," Boone finished his sentence, looking not quite as surprised as I guessed I did, but surprised enough for me to assume he'd been bracing for a slap just as much as he had for a kiss.

So many things fired to life inside me, places I thought had gone dormant, hidden caverns I'd forgotten about. I felt as if I was coming to life, shedding the shell I'd been traipsing around in the past seven years.

I pressed my body into the car, not trusting myself to listen to reason and behave if I remained so close to Boone. Instead of heeding the fresh distance I'd put between us, Boone moved closer.

His lips were parted, his breath coming in quick pulls, but no other part of him told the tale of a man being rattled. He was as solid as he'd always been. "I do believe I said *I* was going to kiss *you*."

His smile was more crooked than straight. Our bodies locked like I remembered, two pieces made to fit together. My jagged pieces accepted his. His rough edges smoothed out mine.

"It didn't seem like *you* were in a hurry to kiss *me*." I

returned his smile.

"It's been seven years since our last kiss. I stall for two seconds, and its one too long?" His fingers curled into my neck lightly.

"Like you said, I've been patient for a long time." I slid one hand up his chest and let it curve around his shoulder. "I'm done with patient."

His smile stretched, then his head lowered toward mine. His smile dissolved, replaced by a look I loved even more—the intent one he got whenever he was about to kiss me. The one that made me feel like I was and always would be his beginning, middle, and end.

"Then let's be done with it together," he whispered right before his lips brushed across mine.

It wasn't really a kiss, but it was something just as good. His lips brushed mine again, this time from the opposite direction, and made my heart scramble as it seemed to have forgotten its purpose. When he repeated the same thing, the sensation of it—just as satisfying as it was insufficient—made a gasp slip past my lips as my body suddenly trembled.

Either the shudder or the gasp pulled something from Boone. His lips stopped teasing mine with slow, gentle brushes, and his mouth pushed into mine with as much intention and strength as his body pressed into mine. Pinning me to the car, Boone's hands tightened around me while mine did all they could to hang on to him.

I felt the cool metal of the top button of his jeans through the light material of my dress. I felt his narrow hips holding my fuller ones in place, anchoring me. I felt his urgency in every touch, every kiss, every breath . . . yet I also felt his careful hold on his restraint. He wanted more. From the way I'd started to feel him slide himself against me before easing back, he wanted it all, but where we'd shown next to no restraint as kids, we seemed to have picked up some as adults.

I wasn't sure how much longer I could take all of this kissing and innocent touching before my body combusted, but it felt closer to the short end of the spectrum than the long. Leaping, I managed to wind my legs around him without skipping a beat of returning his kisses. Boone's hands lowered around my backside, a deep grumble crawling up his chest when I pitched my hips against his.

"The backseat." I turned my head to reach for the door handle.

Boone's mouth moved from mine to the base of my neck, sucking at it in ways that made it seem as if that part of my body was directly hardwired to what resided between my legs.

Boone shook his head, still playing with my neck. "No."

"The front seat?" I panted as his mouth moved lower, just skimming along the neckline of my dress.

"No," he said with another shake.

A groan of frustration was almost immediately followed by a gasp of pleasure when his mouth found a very sensitive area on my body. His tongue circled it, drawing wet patterns through the thin material of my bra.

"I'm not going to fuck you in your daddy's car like I might have been content to do when I was a kid."

My inner thighs contracted. His legs spread them back apart.

"Why not? Backseat, front seat, hood, bent over the bumper . . . all sound like good options to me."

When he pressed himself between my legs, hard and ready, my head fell back against the roof of the car. I swore if he would had just moved against me a few times right there, fully clothed, I would have come.

"Because I'm not a boy anymore, Clara." Boone sucked my nipple, toying at it with his tongue.

My legs tightened around him, my lap pressing hard against his. He gave a sharp grunt, nipping at me before releasing me.

"Fine, I get it."

When his mouth moved to my other breast, giving it the same attention he'd just given the other, I forgot what I was saying, or what I'd been about to say. I was reminded when his hips flexed against mine, giving me the friction I wanted in the exact place I wanted it.

"Then fuck me like a man. Whatever the hell that means." My arms wound around his head and my fingers wove into his hair, smoothing through it or pulling it based on whatever his mouth and hips were up to. "Take me out into the woods, throw me up against a tree, and show me what this screwing like a man thing is all about because right now . . ." He'd just gotten to the nipping part again. My back sprang into an arch, inadvertently creating more friction in the space between my legs. I could feel it—my orgasm was starting to spiral. "I don't care how you do it, just so long as you do."

Boone nodded once as his head lifted above mine. His eyes were wild, his expression the same. His lips were dark and wet, his breathing rushed and shallow. "I don't want to hurry. I don't want to rush. I don't want to feel like we're moments away from getting caught or like we're doing something wrong. I want to take my time. I'm sick of feeling like I'm two minutes from sharing my last ones with you."

I bobbed my head in agreement, knowing I would have agreed to him tying me up to a tree and painting me in honey before doing whatever other freaky things the freaks of the world performed, just so long as sometime tonight, I got to feel him inside me. "Sounds good. Perfect. Why are we still standing here when the woods are over there?"

Boone's face shifted into a smirk as he stared at me spread out on the hood of my dad's car. "You've always been the most beautiful thing I've ever seen, Clara." The backs of his fingers ran down the length of my cheek. "That still hasn't changed."

I was just sitting up as he was winding his arms around my back when a pair of headlights appeared down the road. They started out small and became large so quickly, whoever was behind the wheel of that thing had to have been cruising. We barely had time to adjust our bodies and clothes before the car slowed to a crawl and swung around us. It was a gun-metal Jaguar. A couple of heads popped out of the open windows.

"Hee-haw!" Ford's drunken voice echoed around us. "I see I wasn't the only one worked up into a hot and bothered mess after seeing your sister's fine titties flashed in my face."

Boone's body went rigid in my hold, his expression shadowing in a familiar way. "You're lucky to still have the use of your jaw after what you pulled, Ford. Keep jabbering, and I won't show the same level of restraint I showed back there."

When Ford's gaze drifted to me, all flushed and

clothes twisted around me, his expression turned sour. He looked away like he was disgusted. I looked away from him because I felt the same.

"Hey, Boone!" one of the guys stuffed into the backseat hollered out the window. "This whole time I've been curious about your sister being a natural redhead." He stuck his head out and waggled his brows. "Let's just say my curiosity has been sufficiently squashed."

Boone lowered me to the ground quickly and rounded the back of the Chrysler. I didn't need a glass ball to know where this would go, and I also didn't need one to know that no matter who might have started it or how many were pitted against him, Boone would take the fall for whatever went down tonight.

Rushing around the car faster than him, I said, "It's a Friday night, guys. Why don't you all just go jerk yourselves off like you usually do, before making a bowl of popcorn and watching your old football games for the millionth time as you relive the glory days?"

The loud mouth still hanging out the back window shook his head at me. "Nah, I'd rather go find myself that fire-crotch and play hide-the-hot-dog." A round of chuckles rang inside the car. "God, there sure wouldn't be a shortage of hiding spots with the tits and ass on that thing."

Boone charged ahead, not saying a word, but that was how he did it. Why waste words when talking wasn't what he had in mind?

I threw out my hand, splaying it against his chest. It shouldn't have stopped him, but somehow it did, albeit temporarily I knew.

Since the guys in the car didn't seem to be in a hurry

to leave and Boone wasn't going to tolerate much more of those assholes talking about his sister, that left the responsibility of forging a peaceful resolution to this stand-off in my not-so-capable hands.

The only option I could think of wasn't exactly peaceful, but I was hopeful it would get Ford to screech off and leave us alone. Leaning over, I removed one of my shoes and moved toward the back of Ford's car. All eyes shifted to me, most of them staring like they had no idea what was coming next. To me, it seemed pretty straightforward.

When a girl approaches a guy's car, his most prized possession, with the expression I had and armed with a heeled shoe—whether a five-inch pump or the chunky one incher I was aiming—what did they think was going to happen?

Pulling my arm back, I crouched into position right behind the Jaguar's right taillight, and I swung my arm down hard. It took me a few hard stabs with the heel to get the taillight to break, but it worked.

Ford dropped a series of curses while the other guys in the car watched me like they were both appalled and enraptured. I was making my way over to the other taillight when the Jaguar's wheels spun out right before the car sped away.

Ford stuck his head back out the window and hollered, "Crazy bitch!"

I didn't take my eyes off of the car until its one intact and one broken taillight disappeared. From the look and sound of Ford, he was in no condition to be driving. I should have done the honorable thing and called Charlotte to let her know her fiancé was about to drive himself—and the rest of his soon-to-be extinct kind—into a tree, but I didn't.

I believed in natural selection, and it clearly hadn't caught up to the Ford McBrides of the world yet. Tonight might have been the night.

"Glad he finally figured that out," I said as I slid my shoe back onto my foot.

"Figured out what? That he's a dead man walking?" Boone moved up beside me in the middle of the dirt road, staring at the spot where their car had disappeared.

"That I'm a crazy bitch," I shrugged.

Boone's shoulder brushed mine. "Did you just do that because you hate Ford or because you like me? Because I'm pretty sure what you just did could be charged as a crime."

So much adrenaline was surging through my system from what had just happened and what had just been about to happen before Ford and his gang of future dodo birds showed up, I felt drunk with it. "I might hate Ford McBride, but I just went 'crazy bitch' on his taillights because I like you."

Boone smiled at the ground, kicking it with the toe of his boot. "That's the sweetest thing you've ever said to me."

"I'm not sure I just like you, Boone . . ." The adrenaline was giving me courage, making me heady with power.

Boone's shoulder tensed right before he moved toward the car, leaving me straddling the middle of the road all alone. "We should get going," he said, his voice flat. "We don't belong here."

CHAPTER NINE

I was in my bedroom, sitting on the edge of my bed, wringing my hands in my lap, and waiting for Boone. The sensation of déjà vu was so violent and intense, it almost knocked me over.

A lifetime had passed since that day seven years ago, and even though I wasn't the same girl I'd been then, she was still a part of me. I'd waited for hours that afternoon, not giving up hope until I woke up the next morning not having remembered falling asleep. Boone hadn't come that day. He'd left me waiting.

Part of me felt like I'd been waiting for seven years, but for what, I wasn't sure. An answer, maybe? An explanation in the least? Some reason that would justify why he left me after what he'd found out.

That was what I felt like I was waiting for now, on the edge of my bed again. Answers. Yet another part of me wasn't waiting for answers that might explain the past, but answers for right now. What had happened between us only a short hour ago. What had been *about* to happen between us. What might happen between us going forward.

Answers. That was what I needed.

That was what I hoped Boone would be willing to give me.

The shower shut off, and I heard him step out of it and pad across the bathroom. Unlike the past few days when he'd left the bathroom door cracked open, tonight it was closed. I didn't have to test the handle to guess it was locked as well.

Another closed and locked door hanging between Boone and me. Another one to add to the pile. I was a fool for believing we might have a chance for something different. Our pasts might not have predestined our futures, but they certainly made it predictable.

He took his time in the bathroom; I couldn't be sure exactly what he was doing, though I guessed it had plenty to do with avoiding me. We hadn't exchanged a word since sliding into my dad's car, driving back here, and trudging up to my bedroom. We might have had plenty of things we wanted to say to one another, but I wasn't sure where to start, and I guessed he felt like he'd already said too much through his actions.

When the door did finally open, I heard the click of the lock clicking free first. He'd locked me out, as I'd suspected. Why? Had I gotten too close? Had he let himself get too close?

It was all such a clusterfuck of confusion, I felt like I was staring at a never-ending field of wheat and expected to find the single stalk made of gold.

Boone emerged from the bathroom, the usual billow of steam missing from the portrait.

"Enjoy your cold shower?"

He padded across the room, hair wet, wearing his

usual pajamas—a pair of boxers. "It was better than the alternative."

My feet stopped bouncing. "What alternative was that?" My tone was on the chilly side, not needing an actual verbal confirmation of the conclusion I'd arrived at.

Boone didn't answer me. When he looked at me, his eyes told the story.

"So what? Out there on some back dirt road, you were all ready to fuck me 'like a man,'" I lowered my voice in an attempt to sound like him, "and an hour later, back in my bedroom, you're all for cold showers and silent treatment?"

Boone threw a few blankets and pillows on the floor, making his bed. "What do you want from me, Clara?"

"Well what I wanted earlier sure isn't the case any more." I grabbed a pillow from my bed and threw it into the pile he was making on the floor.

"Good, because that's never happening between you and me again. I mean it."

"Really? Because it sure didn't seem like you were so conflicted when you had me pinned against my dad's Chrysler."

He kicked and punched the blankets and pillows around, making a bigger mess than when he'd first heaped them into a pile. "I don't want to talk about it."

"And why would you? Since your preferred method of 'working things out' includes you turning your back and walking away." I motioned at him to prove my point, not that he saw it.

He was crouched on the ground, his back to me. "It's a better method than letting myself say the things I want to sometimes."

My feet were back to bouncing. I was so wound up, it was a miracle I was able to stay seated. "That sounds like a convenient excuse."

"Call it whatever you want, but it's the truth." He managed to keep his back to me as he moved around the room, turning off one light after the next. He was shutting down and closing up in every way possible.

When he reached for the lamp on my nightstand, my hand snapped out and caught his wrist. "It might have been easier on you, leaving me without an explanation, but I swear to you it was the opposite on me."

My back stiffened, the rest of my body following, when the memories came spilling back. How could I still feel the things I did for the man beside me after everything? How could my skin touching his make me feel like I'd come home?

I wanted to cry. So I glared at him instead.

"You have no idea what I wanted to say to you. What I *still* want to say to you sometimes." His jaw set as he stared at the spot on the wall just past my shoulder. "Believe me when I say it was better for us both that I went the way I did, instead of the way I wanted to."

"And is that why you're acting like this now? Closing up and refusing to talk?" I shoved his hand away from the lamp and away from me. The moment I did, I wanted it back. "Is this your way of punishing me for what happened back then or for what happened tonight?"

"I'm not trying to punish you."

"Then what in the hell are you doing?" I couldn't stay sitting on the edge of the bed anymore. I leapt up and moved to the end of it, pacing up and down by the footboard. "I was starting to think that we were patching things up between us, that we might be able to become friends again, then tonight happened and it became pretty clear that we both might have been interested in exploring the more-than-friends thing. Whatever it was, impulse or recklessness or nothing more romantic than wanting to get laid, I know you felt what I did. I know you felt it before we even put our hands on each other."

Boone stayed crouched beside my bed, his jaw set and his chest tense. "You've sure got yourself convinced you know everything I'm thinking, don't you?"

"You felt that connection. The one we had and the one that's still there. I know you did." I was probably talking too loudly. I was probably going to wake up anyone who had been asleep. I would probably regret saying all of this in the morning. That didn't stop me.

"Yeah?" His forehead formed into three deep creases. "What makes you so sure?"

I stopped pacing. I stared at him still drilling holes into the wall across from him. "Because of the way you looked at me right before you kissed me, and because of the way you're refusing to look at me right now."

"It doesn't matter what I felt or what you *think* I felt tonight," he said, the muscle running down the side of his neck quivering. "I won't do that to myself again."

"You won't let yourself do what again? Fall in love with someone who loved you back?" A sharp huff rushed from my mouth. "Because yeah, that must have been real rough on you."

Boone's head shook stiffly as his hand clenched into a fist around my comforter. "I won't let you rip me open, gut me, then leave me to pick up the pieces and try to figure out where they went in the first place."

My pacing came to an abrupt stop again. "*I* left *you* ripped open and gutted?" I scanned the floor. Where was a shoe when I needed to throw one? "Please say you're fucking with me. Please don't tell me you're serious about me doing that to you."

Finally, he turned to face me. His face held such a foreign expression, he didn't look like Boone anymore. "Do I look serious?"

That question didn't require an answer. The longer I stared into his face, the more I felt my anger crumble. The anger that drained from me was replaced with confusion. I'd had so much confusion in my life, I found myself wishing back the anger. At least it came with an explanation as to the place from which it had been derived.

I knew, or at least I thought I knew, where some of his anger came from, but years later, it still didn't add up to why Boone had left me when he knew how we'd felt about each other. I was only seeing one part of the picture, or else I'd underestimated his affections for me.

"I know I should have told you sooner. I know I shouldn't have kept that kind of secret from you, but I was eighteen years old and terrified. I didn't understand what was happening, let alone how to explain it to you." I started for my dresser, where those numbered angels rested. In comparison to the rest, the number eighteen angel had always seemed to have such a sad face. I guessed now that that probably had more to do with my experience than the sculptor's. "I was scared, but I should have you told you before you found out from someone else."

I ran my thumb across the angel's face and felt a ball clog up my throat. I could relive a lot of memories and remember the past in all its shapes and forms, but this was the period I kept locked down as a general policy. These memories had the ability to turn a person's blood to poison and encase their organs in cement.

"You're sorry for what exactly?" Boone's voice had a sharpness to it, one I hadn't been expecting. "That you got pregnant, or that you weren't sure who the baby's father was?"

My thumb froze as it was stroking the angel's face. "What?"

"I think you heard me."

My fingers curled around the angel. There was so much tension in them, I felt as if I could break her into pieces. "I heard you, but my *what* was more of an *excuse me?* and not one of a *repeat what you just said* variety."

"Come on, Clara. You were a kid back then. If nothing else, age gives you something of an excuse for lying, but you're old enough to know better now." The mattress springs groaned as I guessed he shoved off it to stand, but I wasn't going to look at him. Not with what he was accusing me of. "Plus, we're not together anymore, so you don't have to worry about me breaking up with you if you tell me you were fucking Ford at the same time you were giving it to me."

One of the wings snapped off of the angel from my grip tightening around her. She couldn't hold herself together when that much pressure was applied. Everything had their breaking point, and this angel had just found hers. I'd found mine years ago.

"What?" Anger made my voice tremble as I lifted the angel from her spot in the back row. Her broken wing stayed behind.

"You. Heard. Me."

I told myself to take a breath. I *ordered* myself to take a breath. I should have known better. I hadn't managed to take a single breath since arriving. When the breathing exercise failed, I spun around, angel in hand, and hurled it across the room. Right at him.

"Fuck, Clara!" Boone hollered, ducking just in time. The angel whizzed over his head and smashed into the wall behind him. "What the hell?"

He stayed crouched, making sure I wasn't armed with another, before inspecting the carnage behind him. Contrary to what I'd expected, she hadn't shattered into a million pieces and powder. She was scattered across the floor in a good dozen different pieces.

She'd wound up being stronger than I expected. Those porcelain angels had always seemed so fragile, but it was only the way they appeared, not what they were really made of.

"That's what you get for accusing me of sleeping with Ford when we were together." My voice shook, filling the room and seeming to echo off the walls. "How dare you. How fucking dare you." I paced again, so much adrenaline mixed with anger pouring into me that I felt as though it would erupt right out of my skull.

"He told me. The bastard came to me, looked me in the eye, and told me, Clara. He told me how long, how much he cared about you . . . he even fucking apologized." Boone's voice was quieter, more controlled, but his expression was not. Behind that even voice, the same storm was brewing inside him as was in me. "He told me, so you can stop lying. It's ancient history as far as I'm concerned."

"Is that why you're bringing it up then?" I spat, glaring at him before pacing to the opposite corner of the room. Too much emotion. Too little air to breathe. Too much temptation to pick up another one of those angels and fling it at him.

"I'm only bringing it up because I'd like to hear you admit it. I'd like you to look me in the face and tell me yourself about you and Ford." Boone slowly stood, rising to his full height. He seemed impossibly imposing with the way he was facing me, with the way he was staring at me. "You know, this whole time, everyone's felt so bad for you because your boyfriend was banging someone else behind your back—and sure, their case might be a bit more juicy given the other woman was little sis—but all I have to say is that what goes around, comes around."

I crossed my arms and backed into the corner. That was about as far as I could get from him. "You really have no goddamned idea what you're talking about, do you?"

"I think I've got a pretty good idea."

"You might think you know, but the story I know is just a teeny bit different." I glanced at the door. My longing to walk through it and never have to see him or this room or this place again became as irresistible as a siren's call. The past was gone. I didn't want to relive it. I didn't want to talk about it. I didn't really even want to set the record straight. I just wanted to go.

"How different?" Boone's voice was a note quieter.

"Are you asking for the sake of continuing our argument, or are you asking because you actually want to know?" My voice had gone quieter as well. Barely three minutes into a fight, and we were both already worn out. As kids, we could have gone on for hours. Either we'd learned our lessons as adults or just didn't possess the same amount of energy.

"I'm asking because I'm willing to hear your side of the story." Boone opened his stance some, keeping his arms crossed.

"How generous of you. Too bad you didn't think to stop and ask me the same question years ago." I shook my head, blinded by the light that was finally being shed on why Boone had left me.

"I was a little busy seeing red after finding out the girl I fucking loved was screwing some asshole behind my back. I was a little busy trying not to commit murder when I found out you were pregnant and the guy I hated most in the whole entire world could just as easily have been its father as I could."

"And while you were busy doing that, I was busy being alone and scared and . . ." When my vision got hazy, I shook my head. I'd cried enough tears over that time in my life. I'd reached my official limit 1.5 million ago. No more. "And did I mention, I was scared and alone?" My voice broke, so I stopped. I had so much more to say, but I didn't want to say it if my voice was going to break into a bunch of pieces.

"What did you think was going to happen?" Boone cracked his neck.

"Not what actually did happen," I whispered.

Five seconds of silence passed between us. I knew because I counted them. It felt like the only way to keep the tears at bay.

"I've forgiven you, Clara. I forgave you a long time ago. That's not why I'm bringing this up now." Boone shuffled forward a small step. "I'm bringing it up because it explains part of the reason why I can't do this again." He waved between the two of us. "Why I can't do *us* again. Forgive is one thing. Forget is another. I'm not the forgetting kind."

My eyes closed. I wondered just how much of the world had been built and crumbled by miscommunications. How much of our history had been built upon a foundation of assumptions and lies and crossed wires. I was getting a good idea of just how much of my history had been marred by it.

"Well, thank you for the forgiveness, but you should have saved it for someone else because in terms of what you're under the impression I needed it for, you're sadly mistaken." I pinched the bridge of my nose, feeling tension so thick throughout my body, it felt like molasses. I wanted to set the record straight. I wanted to tell him my side of the story, but it felt like it would take so much energy to do so, and right then, I was down to my last ounce.

"I didn't sleep with Ford."

There. I'd said it. My side of the story. Now he knew. What he'd choose to do with it and if he'd choose to believe it, I didn't know. But at least he knew, for whatever it was worth.

"I think I'm going to need a little more clarification than that." Boone's arms relaxed to his sides, but his shoulders stayed tight.

"I. Didn't. Sleep. With. Ford." I blinked. "How much more clarification is needed?"

He held up his hand, counting off on his fingers. "You didn't sleep with him before we were together? After we got together? You didn't sleep with him the month you got pregnant? You didn't sleep with him after you got pregnant? Or you didn't sleep with him as in that's a boldfaced lie but your way of telling me what you think I want to hear?"

The door. Why wasn't I throwing myself through it right now?

"How about this? Since you're having a tough time understanding simple sentences right now." I made myself look him in the eye, and I lifted an eyebrow. "I didn't sleep with Ford before, during, or after you and I were together, Boone Cavanaugh. So why don't you put that in your Book of Facts and see how it cross-checks with the story you've been told."

Boone's brows pulled together. "What do you mean, you and Ford never slept together?"

"Exactly what it sounds like. I've never fucked Ford. He's never fucked me." I made myself hold his stare for one more moment, despite the cold sweat I could feel about to break out from the effort. "Any more questions?"

From the way he looked, it seemed as if someone had just told Boone that everything he'd known about life was untrue. That the members of his family were really strangers and that his life had all been a lie. The expression that molded his face made it seem like he was lost in the middle of the Sahara with no compass or map to guide him.

"But you two dated for a couple of years after we broke up . . ."

I couldn't tell if he was talking to himself or to me.

"And people can date without fucking. You know, in case you weren't aware of this."

"But—"

"But what? Just because I was screwing you at sixteen automatically meant I was going to screw any future guy I dated? What kind of a girl did you think I was?" I shook my head and took that first step toward the door. From Boone's expression, he was still reeling, still trying to catch up to a train barreling down an open set of tracks while he had bricks tied to his feet. "Oh yeah, that's right. You thought I was the kind of girl who'd screw some other guy behind the back of the guy I loved. I guess it's not that big of a stretch to leap to the conclusion I'd fuck just about anyone else who came along, right?"

Boone lifted his hands. "Clara—"

"Please don't try to Clara me in that tone. Please just don't." I bit the inside of my cheek and took another step toward the door. "Not after accusing me of what you did. Not after what happened between us earlier. Not after everything we've been through. Please just don't ever say my name again, okay?"

He scrubbed his face with both hands, either not knowing what to say or searching for the right words. "Are you saying the baby was mine?"

My eyes shut. The baby. That was a topic just as, if not more, painful than the one of Boone leaving me. "If it wasn't yours, then it was immaculate conception. How's that for an honest answer?"

His hands fell from his face, his gaze lowered to the ground. "It was mine," he whispered.

"It was yours," I whispered back.

He spun away from me, clamping his hands behind his neck. "Goddammit."

A tear fell from the corner of my eye. I'd cried another one. When I closed my eyes, a few more wound their way down my cheeks. I hadn't cried over this in years. I'd cried so many tears over this during those first few years I could have raised the Gulf another foot. I wasn't sure what I was angrier over: that I was crying or that it was because he'd brought it all up again. A person couldn't just bury something, then choose to excavate it any old time they chose to. Buried things should stay that way.

Keeping his back to me again, he paced the room as he shook his head, and I hit my limit.

"I'm kind of relieved, you know? In a weird way." I barely gave my angels a second look as I passed the dresser. "All this time I thought you left because I was pregnant. I thought the baby and the responsibility and too much too fast drove you away."

Boone stopped pacing, but his arms stayed curled around his head.

"When really, all along, it had to do with some giant miscommunication. You taking the word of, as you put it, the guy you hated most in the whole entire world, no questions asked, without running his story past me. You believed him. You had so little faith in me that you were willing to accept that I could look you in the face and tell you I loved you in the morning, then slip into his bed that night." I paused on my journey to the door. Even now, looking at him and having so many of the missing pieces filled in, I still couldn't hate him. I wanted to, but I couldn't. My heart wouldn't let me. "It's a relief knowing what really happened and why you really left."

Boone's head tipped back some. "How is that a relief?"

I waited a moment before answering. "Because now I can let go of the what ifs and the occasional moments I miss you. You didn't run away because you were a typical eighteen-year-old boy, scared shitless of becoming a dad.

You ran away because you took the word of an asshole and never had the consideration or the respect or the foresight to ask your girlfriend about it. I didn't lose a scared boy that day, because you know what?" I swiped at my lower lashes before the next tear fell. "You can't lose something you never had in the first place."

When I reached the door, I only hesitated for a moment before opening the door and escaping. Tonight, I was the one walking away.

And I learned being the one who left was just as hard as being the one left behind.

CHAPTER TEN

'd moved on from being unable to exhale to completely suffocating. The thick night air felt as though it were pressing down on me, ready to grind me into the ground. That future didn't seem all that bleak in comparison to the possibilities.

When I'd finally come back after my night walk that wouldn't end, it was morning and my room was empty. I might have been the one who left, but he was the one who was gone.

There hadn't been a sign he'd ever been there either. No curled up socks abandoned in a corner, no blankets and pillows left on the floor, no second toothbrush balanced on the ledge of the sink. Boone had left my life as seemingly suddenly as he'd come back into it.

I should have been relieved. I should have been thrilled I wouldn't have to deliver some awkward good-bye at the end of this whole plus-one charade after what the two of us had learned last night. He'd left me because of a lie, while I'd spent the past seven years believing he'd left me because he couldn't handle being a teen dad.

Knowing the truth should have made things easier, but instead it made them harder. We hadn't come between ourselves—someone else had come between us. We'd *let* someone else come between us. Who knew what would have happened if Ford had never told Boone what he had. Our breakup could have been inevitable, it could have been worse, but either way, it was tragic.

I'd dated Ford after Boone. For a couple of years even. How could he look me in the eyes when he'd done what he had? How had he been able to just forget the past, the lies he'd told, and try to make a future with me when he knew the scars Boone had left me with?

I hadn't been able to look at Ford once all day. In fact, I knew better than to put myself in the same general area as him—unless I was looking to get myself arrested for aggravated assault.

That was why I was camped out on the back porch stoop, where the hired help passed through, instead of mingling with the rest of Charleston's finest at the Abbotts' version of a rehearsal dinner.

The Abbott version didn't include renting out a room at the local buffet or barbecuing some ribs down at the public park or being served pot roast in the basement of a church, like the handful of other rehearsal dinners I'd attended. No, the Abbott interpretation of the rehearsal dinner included fine champagne ordered by the case, a surf and turf dinner where only the best cuts of beef and largest lobster tails would be offered, and about one server to every two guests.

Not to be forgotten, the Abbott family rehearsal dinner had a theme, and it wasn't a half-assed one either. Tonight's theme was the Roaring Twenties, but instead of feeling like actual history books had been consulted for inspiration, I felt more like I'd stepped into one of the more opulent scenes from the latest Gatsby movie.

Everything was excessive or over-the-top or some mix of the two. Everything was golden or sparkling in some jewel-toned color. A band played '20s music, and most of the guests were wearing some style of fashion that harkened back to that time period. A few of the guests had even rolled up in old cars from the '20s. It was a ridiculous show of money and abundance. Everyone loved it.

Except me.

That was why I'd holed up on the dark stoop—to avoid the party, the party-goers, and most importantly, the party-throwers. I hadn't told my family about Boone leaving, not that they wouldn't have thrown the celebration if I had, but because I didn't want to give them the satisfaction. I didn't want them to know I'd made the same mistake twice with the same man they'd warned me against twice.

I didn't want them to know I'd lost him all over again. I'd done a decent job of dodging them all day, and my plan was to keep up the trend tonight. Actually, keeping up the ruse until I was lifting off and flying in the opposite direction of this place would have been nice. I knew better than to hope for that though. I'd learned the hard way what happened to a person when they put their faith in hope.

I was busy picking at my version of a '20s dress—a simple cotton sundress that Charlotte had informed me was not anything close to resembling the era before thrusting a different gown, heavy with beads and contempt, at me . . . which was why I was wearing the cotton dress.

I noticed the shadow moving in my direction, but I assumed it was one of the catering company's staff needing to step into the kitchen for a fresh tray of caviar and crackers. That was when I noticed the orange glow of a cigar. For some reason, that pulsing orange glow was one of the few good memories I had of home and my family.

"What are you doing camped out back here, Clara Belle? Everyone's looking for you." My dad's voice filled the night around me.

"Hiding," I answered, because if I'd ever been able to admit the truth to anyone in my family, it had been my dad. More because he could see through a lie before it had been aired than because of his aptitude in understanding and compassion.

"Hiding from what?" When he moved closer, enough of the light streaming outside from the kitchen cast onto him. In true Abbott style, he was dressed to impress with his pinstriped, double-breasted suit and cap shoes.

"Hiding from everyone," I said, twisting the toe of my shoe into the ground. "And everything."

"Hiding only delays the inevitable. It sure doesn't make it go away. Better to just confront whatever it is you're hiding from and get it over with."

"Does that wisdom apply to me wanting to stab a cocktail fork into the groom-to-be's right eye, then his left, before burying it in his throat?" I hadn't really intended to verbalize my dark fantasies, but I was tired of the whole lip-service thing.

Instead of shaking his head like I was being emotional and immature, or grunting in tired disapproval, my dad moved closer and took a seat beside me on the second-to-bottom step. I scooted over to give him space, and I pretended I wasn't surprised my dad was sitting beside me—willingly—on the back steps of the staff entrance.

"Where's Boone?" he asked, shifting around on the step like he couldn't get comfortable.

I shouldn't tell him the truth. I should keep up with the lie. I was tired of both.

"Gone. I think we're over. Again."

Dad was quiet for a moment, silently working on his cigar. "When something doesn't work out the first time, there's not much hope it's going to work out a second time." He stared out in the night in front of us like he could see things I couldn't. "You're still you, and he's still him. People don't change, Clara Belle. Not because they don't want to, but because they can't. Boone is who he is, and you are who you are. I would have warned you not to make the same mistake twice if I'd known you were even considering letting Boone Cavanaugh into your life again. Or if I thought you might actually listen to me . . ."

I ignored his last comment, knowing he was right. I did have a bad disposition when it came to listening to anything my parents tried telling me. "Yeah, but I think the whole reason we didn't work out the first time was because of a lie. The same lie that's coming between us now."

Dad shifted on the stair. "What lie?"

I was about to shake my head and wave in a forget-it kind of way before encouraging him to go enjoy the party, but I felt the truth rise up in my throat. It was done being bottled up. "Ford told Boone we were sleeping together and implied in not so many words that the baby could have been either of theirs."

Dad's face pulled up into a wince, probably because

we didn't talk about the baby. I was as guilty of keeping that topic under lock and key as they were. I hadn't said anything about it since that summer I'd left, and it was clear from the look on his face that he thought he'd never hear about it again.

"I'm sure Ford had the best intentions when he told Boone that." His voice was too controlled, too even. "Ford's always cared about you, Clara Belle, and while what he did might have been the wrong way to go about it, you can't fault him for trying to do what was in your best interest."

I felt anger boil in my veins. I shouldn't have expected my dad to side with me, but I sure hadn't been prepared for him defending Ford. "He told Boone that I was sleeping with him." I twisted on the stair, facing him. Dad didn't move; he just kept staring out into the night like a movie reel was flashing before his eyes. "How can you say that Ford telling my boyfriend something like that when I'd just found out I was pregnant was in my best interests?"

Dad took another long pull on his cigar before blowing out a series of smoke rings. "You and Boone Cavanaugh were never going to wind up together. You both knew that, right along with the rest of us. Ford just happened to be the one to step in and bite the bullet."

"He had no right to."

"Right or not, he did it. And I'm not sorry to admit I was relieved. You deserved better than that boy, sweetheart." Dad's voice went quieter, edging into the soft realm. "You deserve better than any boy God's seen fit to make, but I knew Boone would only become a bigger black hole in your life if he stayed."

I crossed my arms over my knees and dropped my head onto them. Seven years later, and I was still about in tears talking to my dad about Boone Cavanaugh. I prayed I wouldn't find myself in the same situation in another seven years. "He was never a black hole. He was pretty much the one bright spot in my universe. You guys never got it, but that's the way it was."

Dad snorted. "What do you call him getting you pregnant when you were both a couple of kids then?" He shook his head as he popped off another snort. "If that's not a black hole, I don't know what is. What were you two going to do if you had stayed together? Have that baby, let this whole city see you as a single teen mom pretending to play house with a boy whose five-year plan was staying out of prison? I wanted more for you, baby. I wanted the world." He threw his arms out in front of us like the world was right there, just waiting for me to grab it. "Not some run-down shack in that trailer park he grew up in."

"Don't you see, Daddy? I had the world. *He* was my world. He was everything I wanted, and Ford took that away from me." I didn't realize I'd started to cry until I felt my dad's arm wrap around my shoulders. It didn't feel forced or unnatural; it felt like a concerned father trying to comfort his daughter.

He patted my back a few times before his arm returned to his side. "Don't play the victim. Ford didn't take anything from you. You just didn't have a hard enough grip around it. Because somewhere inside you, you knew what we all did. Boone wasn't your future." His words weren't gentle, but his voice was.

"I loved him."

"I know baby." He sighed. "I know."

Swiping the tears away, I felt anger shoot back into my blood. I was on an emotional roller coaster and couldn't find my way off. My dad was going to wish by the end of this conversation that he'd never sat beside me. "I loved him so much, and he just left. He took Ford's word and walked away. Didn't answer my calls, wouldn't answer the door no matter how hard I pounded on it. He just seemed to forget all about me."

My dad shifted beside me right before he worked the top button of his shirt undone. "That, baby, might not have been all Ford's doing." He stopped to put out his cigar. "I wasn't planning on telling you this, your mama doesn't even know, but I think you should know something about Boone you don't."

My heart stalled. "What?"

"He came back."

"Wait." I shook my head, feeling like I'd just been dropped in the middle of the desert and wasn't sure which direction I was facing. "When did he come back?"

"A few days after the big scuttleloo."

What he called a "scuttleloo" I called the worst day of my life—the day Boone and I had broken up.

Dad continued, "I suppose he needed a few days to cool his jets or whatever, but he came back to the house late one night, looking for you. I was out on the porch and caught him before he climbed that tree to sneak into your room."

"Did you talk to him?" My voice was barely audible.

He gave a burly-sounding grunt. "I wanted to run him off with my shotgun, but it was locked in the safe. Your mama made sure of that after all that went down between you and Boone, guessing I'd shoot him on sight when and if he showed back up."

"Daddy . . ."

"What?" He looked at me with an innocent expression. "That's what any boy deserves who doesn't take the proper precautions and responsibility to prevent an unwanted pregnancy."

"It wasn't unwanted." I looked him straight in the eye, unyielding. "Unexpected, but please don't ever call it unwanted again."

He returned the unyielding stare, the master I'd probably picked mine up from. "You were eighteen."

"It was my baby."

He blinked and looked away. "So Boone wanted to see you. Right then and there, at half past midnight. I told him no and to get lost. He said he wasn't leaving until he saw you. I told him you were asleep and I'd be damned if he ever saw you again. He said he'd wait outside until you woke up and that he'd be damned if he let me keep him from seeing you." He waved his hand in an et cetera motion.

"So it was about a typical conversation between you and Boone."

"Up to about this point. That was the day after . . . you'd lost the baby. You remember?"

The air shifted then, becoming less sticky and more chilly. Instead of encasing my skin, it felt more like it was attacking it. "I'll never forget," I whispered.

"You were catatonic and hadn't left your room all day. I was worried, beyond worried." Dad kicked at the same patch of earth I'd been working to death with the toe of my shoe. "You were dealing with so much, and I thought bringing Boone back into your life would set you off into a tailspin. You were fragile."

My shoulders lifted then fell. "I'd lost a lot in a matter of four days."

"I didn't know what or who would be the one to pull the pin from you, baby, but I knew if I wasn't careful, it would happen. Boone seemed like the most likely suspect, so I did what I had to do to keep him away."

I swallowed and hugged my body. It was barely nine at night in the dead of summer in the south, so why did I feel like I'd been locked inside of a walk-in freezer? "What did you have to do?"

"Offered him a stack of cash. A thick stack." He pinched his fingers together to show just how thick.

"You paid him off to stay away." I should have known. I should have at least guessed.

"I would have done so much more." He clasped his hands together and let his shoulders drop. "I *did* do so much more."

"What does that mean?"

He was quiet for so long, I was almost convinced he wasn't going to answer me. I knew from experience that trying to pry something from my dad was about as successful an endeavor as trying to pry a cub from a mama grizzly bear's paws.

"I told him you lost the baby." His eyes narrowed as he studied the night in front of us. "I told him it was gone. You should have seen him, Clara Belle. The life drained right out of his face. I'd never seen a person fall apart like that, right in front of me." Dad stared at that space like eighteen-year-old Boone was in front of him all over again. "That lasted for about a minute, then he made a run for the door. He's always been one strong son of a bitch, even for a kid, and I couldn't hold him back. So I told him what I had to in order to get him to go away."

My heart was beating so loudly, it drowned out the music from the band on the front lawn. "What did you tell him? What did you tell him, Daddy?"

He shook his head, glaring at that space in front of him like he was cursing it. "I told him that you'd had an
—"

"Abortion." An imposing shadow stepped out of the same space my dad had been staring at. "That you'd walked into some clinic and had our baby aborted."

Dad shot to a stand, holding out his hand as he stepped in front of me. "Now, Boone, you're walking in on the tail end of this conversation. I'd suggest you take a step back, cool that hot head of yours, and listen to what Clara has to say."

My father's posture indicated he was trying to protect me from Boone. From what, I didn't know, but didn't he see? I hadn't needed protection from Boone—I'd needed protection from my family. From my father, and whatever lies he'd woven that were just as responsible as Ford's for tearing Boone and me apart. From telling Boone I'd . . .

What had he just said? Abortion? My mind was lagging behind, not quite capable of keeping up with the moment.

When Boone looked at me, betrayal drowning in his eyes, I finally got it—why he'd left me like he had. So sudden. So final.

"I'm done listening to what she has to say," he said, backing away from me like I was a viper about to strike.

He hadn't just bought one lie back then—he'd bought two. He'd listened to Ford and my father, not even thinking to confirm what they'd said with me. I suddenly felt like that viper, ready to spew venom in Boone's direction.

Thrusting off the porch, I stood as tall as I could. "You've never been ready to hear me out, Boone. You've been too busy listening to everyone else."

And then I walked away. Again. For the second night in a row. I was hurt and confused and felt betrayed by so many people for so many reasons.

I didn't really know where I was going until I wound up in my bedroom and slid the window open. I'd worked out so many problems and tears on this roof, it should have collapsed from the weight years ago.

After crawling out and finding a good spot, I told myself I wasn't going to cry. Not over this. Not again. Not after finding out three men who'd held important roles in my life had all betrayed me. For whatever reasons—selfish or unselfish—they'd hurt me and cut me out of the equation, leaving me to be the victim of their outcome instead of the creator of my own.

I ordered myself not to cry again. I cursed and belittled myself, threatening that if I dared cry another tear over the past, I'd hurl myself over the roof and give myself a broken leg or something. I was already crying when I made my threats though, and they only made me cry more.

I'd come to a place in my life where I'd been certain I'd left all of this behind. I'd left Charleston and Boone and the baby behind. But if that was the case, why did I feel like I'd just been gutted at the same time my heart was attempting to exit my body via my throat? Why did I feel like everything I'd known had been a lie and everyone in it had been a liar?

I was trying so hard not to cry, because each tear that

rolled down my cheek seemed to make it more real. Each one gave more credit to what had happened instead of allowing me to rebury it in the unmarked grave I'd been content to ignore for seven years.

I should have listened to the warning siren in my head and never come back here. I should have listened to it after I had come back and it kept going off, warning me to leave before things got worse. Because things had impossibly gotten worse.

We're talking bottom floor of the Worse Building.

From the corner of my eye, I noticed a big shadow crawl through the window toward me, but I was going to ignore him. Maybe if that was the policy I'd applied to Boone Cavanaugh all those years ago, like my parents had ordered me to, I wouldn't be here now—on top of my childhood home and crying my eyes apart.

He didn't say anything. He didn't even look over. He just sat beside me, leaving a couple feet of space between us, and stared into the darkness that he seemed immune to. Whereas the dark had always seemed to envelop me and take me under, Boone had always been able to wade through it.

After a minute, I couldn't take the silence anymore. He'd come looking for me and crawled out here for a reason. He should have had the balls to announce that reason without drawing out the waiting game.

"What are you doing here? I'm just your slut ex who got an abortion." I'd been going for venomous hate, but my voice fell more in the overwhelmingly sad realm.

"You're right. I never did stop to hear you out." Boone looked at me. "Or listen. I would have done anything for you back then, but when it really mattered, when we probably both really needed to talk and listen to each other, I failed." I wasn't looking at him—not really—but even from the corner of my eye I could see his jaw go rigid. "I'm ready to listen now."

I curled my knees up to my chest and wrapped my arms around them. Sitting like this, on the roof next to Boone, transported me back in time, to a place I both wanted to never leave and never visit again. "But maybe I'm past being willing to explain."

"Maybe." He nodded. "And that's on me. So if that's the case, I'll understand."

"You seemed less 'understanding' down there."

Boone shifted so he was almost facing me. He might have been ready to face this, but I wasn't sure I was.

"Well, like your dad said, sometimes I just need to give myself a moment to cool my hot head." One of his shoulders lifted. "Plus, he might have threatened to turn me into a shotgun target if I didn't get up here and hear your side of the story."

"I bet he was disappointed when you listened."

Half a smile moved into place. "I've never seen a man so disappointed."

He was wearing on me. Wearing me down or wearing me ragged, he was getting to me. It could have been the partial smile, or it could have been him, again, being the only one to ever come find me when I left, or it could have been that I'd never been good at saying no to Boone Cavanaugh. Whatever it was, it seemed that after years of silence and misguided beliefs, I was ready. Ready to talk, explain, and finally bury this all for good.

"Tell me this first," I started slowly. "If what you believed was true, about what I'd done, why did you take me up on my offer?"

"The money." His answer was immediate, but his voice gave him away.

"Oh yeah? The fat check you still haven't cashed? That was your reason?" My brows lifted in his direction. "Well, paint me skeptical."

"Seven years have gone by. That's ancient history for all I care." His tone was still off, barely, but it was enough to give away that he wasn't telling the truth. At least not the *whole* truth.

"And that's why you're acting like it all happened yesterday?" I waved at him, his posture tense and his eyes darting over everything but me. "Well, slap a double coat of skeptical on me."

That was when his eyes finally moved in my direction. They didn't dart away. "You know why."

"I know what?" I pressed, not about to make this easy on him. Why start now after years of trekking down the hard road?

"The same reason we touched on last night."

My heart stopped climbing up my throat and dropped back into my chest where it belonged. It was beating harder than I was used to though, and faster. "We touched on a lot." I sounded almost out of breath. "What reason are you *specifically* referring to?"

Boone glanced at me, waiting for me to say it so he didn't have to. I kept my lips sealed.

"The one having to do with that damn connection of ours," he half-shouted, throwing his arms into the air. "The one I wish to hell I could wash away, but it's immune to everything I try to destroy it with. The connection I thought could be killed with the things that happened back then, but here it is, still pressing down on me and making me crazy." He rolled his head like he was trying to diffuse his feelings. "I want to scream at you as damn badly as I want to lay you down on this roof and kiss you until I'm goddamn done." He took a deep breath, his body finally relaxing. When he glanced at me again, his expression had softened. "Which might take a while."

When he flashed a sad smile, I swallowed and smiled back. It felt as sad as his looked. We were both sitting in front of each other's what-could-have-been and realizing that what could have been could have been amazing had things not gotten fucked up along the way.

"I didn't have an abortion." The word took my breath away. "I had a miscarriage."

Boone's eyes closed as his forehead creased. "Your dad," he said with a nod, "he told me."

I found myself twisting around so I was almost facing him. His expression . . . he looked like he was experiencing the kind of pain few people ever experienced.

"I didn't know until tonight what he'd told you," I explained. "I mean, I knew he told you I'd lost the baby, but not that you'd showed up at our house looking for me, and not that he'd told you I'd lost it voluntarily."

The muscle running up his jaw went rigid. "That man is a son of a—"

"I know."

"Why would he do something like that? Why would he lie about—" Boone closed his mouth like nothing good could come from what he wanted to say next.

"I'd just miscarried the day before," I said softly. I'd come up here sure that I was the one who'd been cheated, and a few minutes later I found myself realizing I hadn't been alone. "I'd lost my boyfriend, the father, a few days before that. My dad was under the impression I might have been in a bit of a fragile state."

"I get that. I do." He kicked at one of the shingles. "But why not tell me the truth? If anything, that would have made the situation better instead of worse."

I didn't have an answer. At least not one I wanted to give any dignity to by verbalizing it, because I might not have agreed with what my dad did, but I knew why, in his mind, he'd done it.

"Never mind," he said, realization dawning on his face. "I know why."

"You do?" I hoped he didn't. I hoped he'd arrived at another conclusion than the actual one.

"He wanted me gone, and that was his chance." Boone's arms went around his head, his fingers lacing at the base of his neck. "Same thing Ford did to me, but your dad's tactic actually worked."

My eyes closed. Of course he'd figured it out. My family had never made it much of a secret that they'd do anything to weed Boone out of my life. Stooping to lying about an abortion included. "He might have wanted you gone, but I didn't."

A moment of silence passed between us. The kind that reminded me of standing at a headstone and saying a silent farewell. I wasn't ready to say another farewell, silent or otherwise. Not now that we'd finally sorted through the shit that had ripped us apart in the first place. Not now that we'd figured out we'd been lied to, manipulated, and deceived. I wasn't ready to say good-bye.

"Why aren't you pissed?" I asked, my voice louder than the small distance between us warranted. "Why aren't you doing your usual beating your chest and grunting thing now?"

"Because I understand." Instead of angry, his voice was calm.

"You understand why my dad lied to you about me having an abortion? You understand why Ford lied to you about us fucking behind your back?" If he wasn't going to get angry, I was. What had happened was deserving of unrestrained anger.

"Ford's a piece of shit I'm going to punch in the face when I see him next," he cursed. "But your dad . . . I understand what he was doing."

"Which was what exactly?"

Boone looked at me. There it was—that good-bye in his eyes. "Protecting his daughter."

My head shook so violently my hair whipped into my eyes. "Protecting me from what? Heartache? Pain? Depression? Feeling like all that love I'd had for you had been for nothing?" I was glaring at him, but another tear slipped out. I swiped it away so fast it didn't count. "He protected me from nothing."

"He protected you from me."

I huffed, frustrated at what he was saying and why he wasn't letting himself get pissed like I was. I was frustrated at everything tonight, the stars and moon included.

"Come on, Clara. Look at me. Look at you." Boone waved between us like he was comparing an apple to a rotten banana. "You wouldn't have gotten where you have if your dad hadn't stepped in and taken a butcher knife to the bond tying us together."

"How the hell do you know that?" My tone was biting, arsenic in audible form.

"How can you keep denying it?" He paused long enough to give me a chance to respond. When I didn't, he continued. "Look at what I've done with my life. Other than age seven years and move into my own place, not a hell of a lot. I'm still sputtering through town in that same relic of a truck. I'm still as single as I have been since the day we broke up and as I will be until the day I die. I'm still getting calls to come rescue my mom, and I'm still an utter failure at saving my sister. Shit, even my business, the one good thing I tried to do with my life since you and me, failed. That's what I am, Clara, a failure. It might have taken me a while to see it and you might be blind to it, but your dad has always seen it. He wanted better for his daughter than some failure. I would have wanted the exact same for mine had ours been born a daughter." When his eyes sealed shut again, he forced them back open. "I can't fault him for what he did."

"Well, I can." I sounded like a child. One who hadn't gotten her way and, instead of moving on, was going to pout about it for the next lifetime and a half.

"Why?"

I actually grunted in frustration at his iron-clad calm resolve. This wasn't the way I was used to these kinds of talks/arguments going between Boone and me. "Because you might choose to see yourself as a failure, but that's not what I see when I look at you. That's never been what I've seen. Even a few days ago, even still being under the impression you'd left me because I'd gotten pregnant, I didn't see a failure when I looked at you that night in the bar."

He laughed. "I am what I am. Not what you think I am."

That, perhaps more than anything else that had been said or discovered tonight, was what pissed me off the most. The person I'd looked up to for years was incapable of seeing just how great he really was.

My hands curled around my legs. "That's right, Boone. You are what you are. Not what you *think* you are."

Instead of laughing, this time he sighed his disagreement. "You know, all that time, I was so worried about protecting you from your family and the rest of this town, I didn't see where the real danger really was. It was right beside you."

"You weren't a danger."

Boone shifted so he was at the edge of the roof. When he looked down, it was almost like he was contemplating what it would feel like to drop from this high up. I found myself creeping closer, ready to grab him in case he did something crazy.

"Tell that to the guy who just found out he walked out on the girl he loved when she was pregnant because he believed the lies of two people who he knew better than to trust," he said.

"It's strange, isn't it?" My anger was dissipating now that I'd run out of adrenaline. I was back to feeling sad and betrayed. I would have rather been angry. "Realizing we've both been living with the wrong idea of what really happened back then."

"Strange isn't the word I'd use to explain it."

"What word would you use?"

He glared in front of him. At nothing. Or at everything. With Boone, the enemy was as obvious as it was invisible. "Devastating," he said at last, like the word had drained the last of his energy.

"I'm sorry I didn't tell you sooner. I should have." I scooted closer, until I could have reached out and touched him if I wanted to. "The moment after I found out. I should have told you before my parents found out and before Ford found out and he told you."

"Why didn't you?" His voice was muffled and his expression tired, as if someone had plunged a hose into him and siphoned the life right out of him. Down to the last drop. "Why did you wait to tell me?"

I glared out at the same darkness, knowing my eighteen-year-old reasons for not telling him weren't the same reasons the twenty-five-year-old version of me would have used. "I'd only found out a week earlier, Boone. I think I was paralyzed those first few days, then I just felt so many things, I couldn't tell what I felt most. I couldn't explain what had happened to myself yet, so I wasn't sure how to go about explaining it to you."

"How far along were you?"

"Ten weeks," I answered. That hung in the air for a moment.

"And I just left you."

"You came back. You might not have made it through the front door and I might have only just found out about it, but coming back counts for something."

He shook his head. "I should have stayed away. I should have listened to your dad and your friends and this whole town when they told me I'd bring nothing but destruction into your life."

In the background, the music got louder. Laughter and celebration was echoing from one end of the estate to the other. The Abbott family was having the time of their lives while mine felt like it was ending. Again. Some stories just kept repeating themselves.

"You brought more of the good stuff to my life than anyone else ever has," I said, looking at him so he could see how serious I was. When he wouldn't turn his head, I knew I had two options: I could leave and try to put all of this into a sealed folder marked The Past, or I could stay and ask all my questions until I didn't have any more. I went with the latter option before realizing I'd made my decision. "Why did you come back?"

Boone rolled his head to one side, then the other. "I decided I didn't care about the Ford thing. Or which of us was the father." He wasn't looking at me, but when my eyebrows lifted as high as they'd go, he added, "Okay, so I might have cared, but I wasn't going to let that stop me from being with you and being a father to that baby."

"And what was your plan? To marry me and move me into a two-bedroom house in the country?" I asked, scooting just a bit closer.

"Actually, yeah, it pretty much was."

My face ironed out. "Oh, Boone, I'm sorry. I didn't mean it like that . . ." I hadn't meant to tease him, but he'd clearly taken it like I had. "But were you really?"

"I still have the microscopic-sized-diamond ring to prove it."

Good-bye, beating heart. It was nice knowing you. Hopefully the vultures enjoy the taste of bitterness. "I guess you didn't make it to the house part then."

"Actually . . ."

"Oh, God, Boone. Tell me you didn't . . ."

"It's okay. It all worked out." He shrugged like none of this was any big deal. Like him buying an engagement ring and a house to marry his teenage girlfriend who may have been knocked up with his childhood nemesis's baby was what anyone else would have done. "It was actually my uncle's place, but he'd been trying to sell it for years, and it was such a project. No one wanted to put the time and effort into it. He worked out a rent-to-own thing with me and handed over the keys."

That was when Clara Belle Abbott started to cry. Again. Round 2. It didn't quite hit the body-rocking-sob territory, but it came close. Finally, I had Boone's attention.

"This is all so damn unfair," I cried, wiping at my face with the back of my arm, but it was no use. The tears were on full-bore. "I think I might want to go back to the way I believed things were before. I think I'd rather have my opinion of you being an asshole back, rather than this new one of you being prepared to spend your life with the person you thought cheated on you, raising a child that may or may not have been yours."

He nodded, looking like he was wrestling with the choice to wrap his arms around me or keep his distance. God, I knew that feeling too well. I'd been steeped in it this whole week.

"I think it might be easier for me too," he said, going with the wrapping-his-arm-around-me option. "If I still thought you were that other person."

"I'm sorry about the house, Boone." I was still crying, so I didn't know how he was able to understand what I was saying, but he did.

"It turned out okay. Really." He nudged me gently, rubbing circles on my back. "It's the one you were in a few days ago. It took me five years to turn it into something decent, but it worked out. The ring though?" I felt his shoulders rise. "Maybe I should have tried to return it or pawn it or hell, throw it into the river, but I couldn't."

"Why?" I sniffed.

"I guess I wanted to hold on to some part of you. You were right about that the other night, about me holding on to a piece of you. I've tried letting it go. God, I've tried, but I just can't."

"I've tried too. Same result." The tears were slowing, though they hadn't stopped. "So where does that leave us?"

Beside me, Boone took a deep breath. I never heard him let it out. "In the exact same fucking spot."

My body froze, but that beating thing inside me froze faster. "Which is?"

That was when Boone let out the breath he'd been holding. "Nowhere. It leaves us nowhere." He pressed a quick kiss to my temple before standing and moving for my open bedroom window.

"So that's it?" I popped up in place too, feeling like I was playing a game of tug-of-war I could never win. "You're leaving and all of this is just going to haunt us for the rest of our lives?"

Boone paused with his hand on the window frame. "Where should it leave us?"

"I don't know. Maybe with a second chance?"

He paused long enough for me to believe he was really considering that. But when he looked at me, I knew his answer. I might have believed in second chances, but Boone didn't. I should have known. He'd stopped believing in fairy tales before most kids even learned what they were.

"You live in California. You have a successful, growing business," he said. "I live here. I'm unemployed. I get calls from the bartender to pick up my mom, from the sheriff to come pick up my mom, or from bill collectors wondering why my water bill's late. Taking our past out of the equation, our current lives don't leave much hope for us either."

I stood staring at him, wanting to hold on and knowing I had to let go. "When did you start caring about shit like that?"

"When I realized shit like that matters." He swung his leg through the open window and crouched to lower the rest of him inside.

I lunged forward a few steps, but part of me knew that no matter what I said or how I tried to hold him down, Boone was already gone. "What matters is how we feel about each other. What matters is what we could be together."

He was already on the other side of the window—in a different world—when he tried to look at me. He tried again. But he couldn't. Just when I thought my heart had been ripped apart, frozen whole, transformed into vulture carrion, and wrapped tightly in barbed wire, I realized that couldn't have been true, because how could it break the way it was now if it hadn't been whole before?

Boone tried to smile, but he couldn't do that either. "What matters is that I didn't deserve Clara Abbott back then, and I sure as hell don't deserve her now."

CHAPTER ELEVEN

I was suffocating.

The humidity was nearing the eighty-percent margin, and the temperature was nearing ninety. I was encased in The Thing, staggered around the back lawn with my family as the wedding photographer prepared to take the family photos. But I didn't want to have my photo taken with my family for the family photo. After everything I'd learned last night, I didn't feel they deserved the title of my family anymore . . . or maybe I didn't belong with their family anymore. One of those things.

My dad had told a terrible lie to the person I cared about most when I was seventeen, a lie that drove him away. How could I ever look my father in the eye without being reminded of that?

Charlotte had stolen my boyfriend right out from beneath me, betraying me in ways arch nemeses would have hesitated over first.

My mom, who had no direct fault tied to her pertaining to Boone's and my breakup, had been quite the opposite of supportive the entire time we had been together.

Avalee was the only Abbott worth a darn, me included, but next spring, she'd be the one leaving the Abbotts.

My family was more a formality at this point.

The wedding was still a couple of hours away, and once Miss Charlotte Abbott officially became Mrs. Charlotte Abbott McBride, the four hundred wedding guests would flock from the big white church in town back to my parents' house to dance and eat and celebrate an evening that my parents had shelled out a cool million to bring into being.

It was excessive and obscene and appalling. Caviar wouldn't be on the menu at my wedding should that day ever come, nor would fifty-year-old scotch for the men and elegant charm bracelets for the women be party favors.

I didn't want the fifteen-person symphony playing Mozart and Beethoven, and I didn't want the towering ice sculptures that would be decorated around the west lawn by the time the reception started, and I certainly didn't want the Grammy-award-winning singer my parents had booked as a surprise for the newlyweds to serenade them in their first dance.

I didn't want excess. I didn't want show. I didn't want the veneer of perfection when all one had to do was scratch at the surface once or twice to see that nothing about the Abbotts was as it seemed.

My parents were being ushered into position with Charlotte and Ford, my mom's hand draped around Charlotte's elbow while the photographer positioned my dad's hand around Ford's shoulder. It went there naturally. It stayed there just as naturally.

Ford was the type of person my father approved of.

The kind who was deserving of Quincy Abbott's respect and one of his daughters. Ford McBride, the man who'd lied to Boone that he'd been in bed with me too, implying what he had to drive Boone away . . . the same person who'd cheated on me with my sister . . . this was the type of person who deserved my father's respect?

No wonder Boone had never gotten a lick of it from him. He didn't measure up in the immoral and devoid of decency categories.

Boone. Just thinking his name made my heart wring hard enough I had to shuffle back a few steps and lean into the giant oak behind me. He'd left last night after our roof-top talk, leaving the check I'd made out to him on my nightstand.

He was gone. Again. At least this time I had an explanation for why, but it didn't change the way my heart felt like it was twisting over itself, attempting to wring itself dry.

I found myself staring at my dad's hand cupped around Ford's shoulder, the two of them smiling for the camera like they were best friends and life was just all so grand. I couldn't take it. I'd managed to keep up appearances up to now, but I wasn't sure how much longer I could. Charlotte's wedding day might not have been the ideal time for me to drop the façade, but I just couldn't do it anymore. Not after everything I'd learned last night.

"The Abbott family?" the photographer called to the small group staggered around the yard, waiting their turn to smile and suck it in with the bride and groom. "I need the sisters now too."

I hung close to the tree, wishing a few more layers of Spanish moss would magically appear because that might have been thick enough to keep me hidden from them.

"The other sister? Where's she?" The photographer had the kind of voice that made a person believe he spent half of his life waiting and the other half of his life being bored. With the way he'd been hollering orders and commands all afternoon, hearing him continue to call for the "other" sister was making me want to wrap a few layers of duct tape around his mouth.

"Clara Belle?" First my mom, then my dad, called out.

"Clara Belle?" Next Avalee called, and finally Charlotte joined in, although hers was edged with annoyance.

"I'm here," I said under my breath, making myself shove off the tree and start in their direction. "I'm right here."

"What took you so long?" Charlotte asked as I approached, fanning herself with her bouquet, although I didn't know why. I'd never once seen Charlotte's hairline damp with sweat, or her face flushed from the heat, not even as kids after we'd sprinted circles down the driveway in the middle of the day in August. The perks of being someone who had ice running through her veins.

"Just trying to figure out if I was still a member of this family," I answered as I headed toward where Avalee was lining up beside my mom.

"Of course you're a part of this family, dear," my mom replied with a nervous chuckle. I wasn't sure if she knew what had happened last night, but she could sense the tension. "You'll always be a part of this family."

"I meant that more in the way that I'm trying to figure out if I still *want* to be a member of this family," I said matter-of-factly, to no one in particular but to all collectively. It might have been me, it might have been them, but I knew one thing—I didn't fit. I really never had, and after this past week, I knew I never would.

I felt both of my parents' eyes on me as I lined up behind Avalee, relaxing my stomach muscles instead of contracting them like I knew everyone else in line was. The seamstress had supposedly let out The Thing, but where she had I couldn't tell because I still felt like my body had been vacuum-packed inside a layer of satin.

"Oh no, that won't work." After messing with a few dials on his camera, the photographer came rushing over to us.

Guiding my mom out of line, he stuffed her behind Avalee and started to pull me to the other end of the line. I dug in my heels when he tried to stuff me between Ford and my dad. That was like being tossed into the snake pit and the lions' den at the same time.

"I'm not standing there," I said, shaking off the photographer's hold on my arm. "You want the 'other' sister to smile for the family portrait, you put me somewhere else."

Ford let out a sigh while my father shifted. My father knew why I was fighting this, and he knew I had every right to. He stayed quiet, which was a first for my dad when it came to getting one of his family members to "fall into line."

"Oh no, that won't work." The photographer shook his head.

"Yeah, you already mentioned that. Why not?" The humidity was clinging to me, coating my skin in what felt like twelve layers of sweat.

"Well first, because we need to have an even number

on either side of the bride and groom." The photographer waved his finger down the line, like that should have been obvious.

"Here, I'll stand down there and Clara can be here." Avalee stepped out of line and started to slide between Ford and our dad.

The photographer grabbed her hand and pulled her out. "Eh, no. That will not work."

"Why not?" Avalee and I asked at the same time.

Next he pointed at my dress, his nose curling just enough to give away what he thought of my bridesmaid gown. "I can't put that shade of . . . whatever you want to call it next to the shade of pink the mother of the bride is in. All anyone would see when they looked at the family portrait would be the clashing colors."

"Sounds like an accurate depiction of the family," I added, not as under my breath as I'd intended.

"Clara Belle, why can't you ever, for just once, do something without putting up a fight?" Charlotte stepped out of line and angled herself toward me.

The photographer opened his mouth as he tapped at his watch, but Charlotte lifted her bouquet into his face to shut him up.

"My whole life, all I've ever done was what this family wanted me to do, and be who this family wanted me to be, and smile when told to"—I threw my arm in the direction of the photographer—"never once putting up a fight except when it really mattered."

"Oh yeah, that's right, you had to fight for your one true love, Boone Cavanaugh." Charlotte threw her hand on her hip. "A hell of a lot of good that did you because you lost him then and you've clearly lost him now. Maybe you

THE FABLE OF US

should pick your fights a bit more carefully in the future."

I heard Avalee hiss Charlotte's name, but everyone else within hearing range looked too shell-shocked to say anything. There it was, the great war of the Abbotts about to take place on the east lawn while family portraits were being snapped two hours before the first sister got married off. No one could say I didn't have style when it came to my timing.

"I am picking my fights carefully." I eyed the empty space between my father and Ford, the place meant for me. I'd been trapped between those two, a victim of their lies and falsehoods, for enough of my life. No more. "I'm not standing there. You want me to be a part of the family photo, choose somewhere else."

"You could just *not* be in the family photo at all." Charlotte's gaze cut to Ford, whose gaze was clearly focused on me. That would explain why I felt the urge to simultaneously shiver and throw up.

"You won't hear an argument from me. I won't even shed a tear to pretend like I am heartbroken." When I went to settle my own hand on my hip, I only made it to my upper thigh. The Thing was more like The Strait Jacket.

Charlotte's face started to go red. "Get into line, Clara Belle!"

I tried crossing my arms. Same result. Couldn't move. "No."

"Now." Charlotte stabbed her finger at the empty space between Ford and our dad.

"Order me, threaten me, beat me, try to force me"—I shook my head hard—"I will not stand there."

"Get into line, Clara Belle or so help me God—"

"God's long past helping you, Charlotte, so no need

for the idle threats."

Her face went another shade of red, the serpentine vein running down the center of her forehead beginning to pop through her skin. "Get into line, damn it!"

As she lost her cool, I got cooler. "No."

Half of a shriek, half of a grunt of frustration came from the bride. "Stop being so stubborn and thinking of what you want for once in your life! There is more to this family, to the world, than the needs, wants, and tragedies of Clara Belle Abbott, for God's sake."

Her words hit me like a slap. So much so, I almost reached for my cheek to rub it. At the same time I tried to convince myself her accusations had no merit, I knew to a degree they did. But that wasn't what I wanted to focus on. That wasn't what I wanted to tackle as the photographer continued to stare at the spot between Ford and my dad, flashing me expectant looks in between stabbing his finger at his watch's face.

I went for the quickest way I knew to throw Charlotte off balance, if only for a few moments. "You want me to stop behaving like the moon orbits around planet Clara? Fine. Why don't you stop sleeping around with your sister's boyfriends?"

Charlotte's mouth fell open and a sharp gasp came from it, followed by a collective gasp circling the rest of the family. They all knew the first low blow would come at some point, but it almost always came from Charlotte.

I'd taken them all by surprise. Though it wasn't exactly in the way I'd intended.

Charlotte took a step closer. Then another. Looking at me with such contempt in her eyes, I could have shriveled up into a pile of sand if I hadn't built up a sort of immunity to her brand of hatred.

"Stop getting knocked up by the town trash." She enunciated each word painfully slowly, looking me up and down like I was the town trash in question. "Please, did you really think Ford was actually going to marry you after that? You were nothing but used goods, a rung on his climb to the Abbott sister who hadn't defiled herself with the likes of Boone Cavanaugh."

Another gasp circled my family. My mom covered her mouth and shook her head, backing away a step. Surely this wasn't the way she'd envisioned the wedding day of her first daughter to get married going.

I was the only one who hadn't gasped or responded with some level of shock. Mainly because I knew what Charlotte was capable of. After finding her and Ford together like I had, words were nothing. She could throw them all at me, woven tightly together in as cutting a way as she could, and I doubted I'd flinch.

"What's it like being the most spiteful person on the planet?" I asked, lifting an eyebrow and waiting a moment for her answer. It didn't come. "You got the guy, but you and I both know who he'd rather have standing next to him in that pretentious white dress." I let that settle in, making sure her gaze was good and locked on mine before adding, "And it's not you."

I stepped back when she lunged forward, but she didn't slap, punch, or claw me like I'd been expecting. Instead, the red slowly drained from her face, the fire in her eyes dimming to a smolder. She took one more step closer.

"Look where you're standing, Clara Belle." Charlotte waved at our family and Ford behind her before flashing her arms at me, where I stood separate from them all. "Alone. You're standing alone. You've always been standing alone." Charlotte stepped back, aligning herself between Ford and our mom. "You *will* always be standing like that. Alone. So stop taking it out on us. It's not our fault you're alone and have driven away everyone who has or might have cared about you. Being alone's an outcome, Clara Belle, not a choice like you'd like us all to believe."

I stood in place, taking in just how separate and apart I was from the people standing across from me. We were bound together by things like blood and experience, but that didn't seem like the kind of bond that could hold if no other ties were formed. Why I felt tears wanting to form, I didn't know, but realizing that I'd driven my family away as much as they'd driven me away might have had something to do with it.

I felt everyone watching me, waiting for me to say something or respond in some way. By either melting down and rushing away or by firing back something equally as nasty, continuing to play this potentially never-ending game of insult volley. Both were appealing options. Both were ones I found myself struggling to set aside as I accepted what I wanted most was to give each of my family members a hug before saying good-bye.

I'd say it, leave this place, leave Charleston, and never come back. It was the only way we could all live in peace. Not just myself, but them as well. I was as guilty of messing up their lives as they were of messing up mine. No one had to come right out and say it for me to realize that. It was written in my dad's brow line. It was etched into the corners of my mom's eyes. It was stamped all over every square inch of Charlotte's face. It was hidden beneath the warmth Avalee was trying to look at me with now.

I was just as much to blame for my actions as they were for theirs.

I felt stuck, unable to turn and walk away, and just as incapable of moving forward to say good-bye. That was when five fingers knitted through mine before a warm palm pressed against mine. His body settled closely beside mine, his arm running the length of mine.

"She's not alone."

The surprise of him being there, coupled with the surprise of his touch, should have rattled me, but it didn't. Instead it seemed to ground me. When I looked over, I found him locking eyes with each member of my family, ending on Ford. Charlotte had a thing or five hundred to learn from Boone when it came to contempt.

"I think you're in the wrong place, Boone." My dad's voice didn't resonate as it normally did.

"I'm exactly where I'm supposed to be." Boone pointed at the ground, his palm pressing harder against mine.

"Well, lobster and free booze are on the menu tonight, so I figured you'd make your appearance somewhere along the way. You never could pass up a free lunch, could you, Cavanaugh?" Ford had stepped out of the family line-up a few steps.

I wasn't sure if Ford knew Boone and I had figured out he'd lied to us, but my guess was that if he didn't shut his mouth and step back, Boone was going to inform him with his knuckles.

But Boone's gaze didn't flicker Ford's way. His expression didn't change. It was as if he hadn't heard a single word coming from the man not ten feet in front of us. Like Ford was invisible and Boone was deaf, there was no recognition. Not even a flicker firing in Boone's eyes.

"I know you're hot on ruining lives and all, Cavanaugh, but I'm going to have to insist you don't ruin my wedding day. Leave, or I'll have the sheriff I just so happen to have on speed dial make you leave."

Ford stepped closer still, his voice elevating, but Boone didn't acknowledge him in word or action. All that did was drive Ford further up the pissed-off pole. He looked close to marching up and forcing Boone off the premises, one shove at a time, when my dad cleared his throat.

"You need to leave, Boone. This isn't the time or place to be making a statement." Dad pointed his chin in the direction of the driveway. "Now go on and get."

Boone's hand flexed around mine, so strong it made me wince, but he loosened his grip a moment later. "Because you are the father of the woman I love, I will let that one go, but if you order me to leave her again, I won't be so willing to overlook it." Boone stepped forward, taking me with him. "I might have been a stupid-as-shit boy back then and listened to you when you told me to leave, but I'm not making that mistake again."

"And we're supposed to believe you're any less stupid-as-shit now than you were then?" Ford nudged my dad, trying to garner a chuckling companion, but my father's face stayed cemented in hard lines.

"You think you know about love, but the truth is, all you've learned is how to run away from it when life gets tough," Dad said. "I won't ask to be forgiven for wanting more for my daughter than some man who's going to cut and run every time life puts the pinch on him. You don't deserve her, Boone, so don't try strutting in here and hoping to convince me otherwise."

"You're right. I don't deserve her." I shook my head, about to object, but Boone kept going. "And I know there's nothing I have done or could do or could do in my next ten lifetimes to deserve the woman standing beside me, but fuck deserving and fuck the past. I love her."

Dad didn't blink. "You mistake love for infatuation."

"No, you're mistaking the two. I'm all clear on the subject." Boone stepped in front of me, turning his back on my family and Ford. His hand stayed in mine, and he stared at me like there wasn't anyone around for miles. He stared at me like there weren't a good twenty sets of eyes staring at us without blinking. "I love you. So much. And I'm sorry I've been too scared or proud or stupid to say it, but it's the truth. I've loved you since the first day I saw you. I always will."

"If this is the part where you add something about being born to love her, you can save it, son. Clara Belle's all grown up and not some impressionable girl anymore."

Boone didn't glance back at my dad, but he shook his head, still staring at me. "Not born to. Just made to."

A sharp huff came from my dad.

Boone continued to stare at me, waiting. "You haven't said a word."

I felt my collapsed lungs struggle to fill. They couldn't. "That's because it's been difficult to get a word in."

"You don't have to say anything, Clara Belle," my dad piped up, his forehead drawn into so many lines it looked like an old washboard.

For once, I saw feelings on his face. Concern. Worry. Nervousness. He was afraid I was going to fall for Boone all over again, get hurt, and be wrecked just the same way I had been before.

My dad . . . *cared* about me. In more ways than just how I influenced the Abbott family image?

A lot was coming at me, and none of it was slowing down, but instead gaining speed.

"I've got my thumb on Sheriff Cooley's number. Give the nod, and he'll be here as fast as his cruiser can send him." Ford lifted his phone, quirking a brow at me.

"You're *still* not saying anything." Boone guided us a few steps away from everyone, pressing the pads of his fingers deeper into my cheek. Reaching around his back, he fumbled with his shirt before pulling something out and holding it in front of me.

My eyes cut from him to what was in his hand. It didn't seem possible. I'd seen it shatter. Hell, I'd been responsible for it shattering. I was sure I'd never see it whole again. I was sure I'd never see it again at all, yet there it was, pieced back together, within my grasp.

"What once was broken can be fixed." Boone lifted the angel with the number eighteen at her feet. I could still see every crack from the break, but she was fixed. "It'll always bear the scars, but at least it's whole again."

When he held it out for me to take, I did. Carefully. Looking at it, a person's instinct was to believe it was extra fragile due to the breaks. It seemed more delicate, not as strong or able to withstand as much as it had before being fractured.

"People say we're weak where we've been broken, but I say we're stronger." Boone traced the long jagged line running right down the center of her. "We're stronger because we know our weak spots and can protect them more carefully the next time."

I nodded as I turned the angel over in my hands. *Miraculous* was all I could think as I inspected every fissure and crack. They had all been repaired. They would always be visible, but the angel had survived the crash. It wasn't perfect anymore, the innocence of it had been lost, but that was life's policy. The good came with the bad, the highs brought on the lows, the idyllic days were balanced by the ones that made us want to give up and crawl into a hole.

Life wasn't about learning how to deflect the bad, but learning how to hunker down and weather it until it passed. I supposed . . . no, I *knew*, it was the same way with love.

"Just so I don't hold my breath for too long"— Boone's voice was quiet, almost unsure—"are you going to say anything? Eventually?"

"Maybe she doesn't have anything to say to you besides good-bye and get lost." Ford's voice rang out behind us.

Neither of us bothered to acknowledge him.

"Thank you," I said, smiling at the angel, feeling like the muggy Charleston air was dispersing and thinking about finally letting me breathe. "Thank you," I repeated, louder since I wasn't sure he'd heard me the first time.

"You're welcome." His shoulders relaxed as he ran his finger down a few of the cracks. "I figured since it was kind of my fault it broke, it was my job to fix it."

"It wasn't just your fault. I'm just as much to blame as you are." I lowered the angel to my side and turned my attention to him. My hand found its way around the back of his neck. As I moved closer, so did he. Our bodies were connected, so close together they were one. "You were right, you know."

"I was right about what?" His hands slid over the peaks of my hips, tying together at the small of my back.

I smiled at him. "Everything."

Something gleamed in his eyes. "Everything?"

"Every." I raised an eyebrow. "Thing."

"Even the part about you feeling the same way about me? Even the part about me telling you—"

"I love you." I didn't hesitate. I didn't look away. I didn't blink or blush or squirm. I looked him right in the eye, stood my ground, and was confident I'd never been more certain of anything in my life.

"Clara Belle . . ." My dad's voice rolled across the lawn, but before he could say anything else, I shook my head.

"I love you, Dad," I said, looking over Boone's shoulder at him, refusing to release my hold on Boone. "But no."

"Clara, sweetheart, don't—"

It was my mom's worried eyes I locked onto next. Somewhere in the course of unearthing what had really gone wrong between Boone and me, I'd uncovered where my family and I'd seemed to go wrong. Both cases were chock full of good intentions gone horribly awry, bound together by an unending yarn of miscommunications. I found myself forgiving them as easily as I had Boone.

"Mom, I love you," I said in the most soft, firm voice I was capable of, "but no."

I couldn't miss Charlotte bouncing in place, rattling like a volcano on the cusp of exploding. "But no, Mom.

But no, Dad. But no. But no. But no?" She thrust her bouquet my direction. "What does that even mean, Clara Belle?"

Boone turned us a quarter turn, almost like he was trying to deflect Charlotte's spite, but it was unnecessary. Along with my parents, I think I was finally understanding who Charlotte was, not just who she appeared to be. She wasn't borderline vicious because she was just plain mean, but because she was plain scared. Scared of playing the middle child role her entire life, never measuring up to the firstborn and never being as infectious as the third. Scared of being alone and abandoned and discovering all she'd worked for had been for nothing. While I'd never quite fit in in this family, Charlotte had been the one desperately trying to.

I cleared my throat. This was her wedding day. *Her* day. Whatever Boone and I had to figure out, she didn't deserve to be caught up in the middle of it today.

"It means I love you all, but please stop interfering in my life and just let me live it the way I want, with who I want to live it with," I said.

For a long moment following that statement, my family stared at me. At me in The Thing. At me with Boone's arms twined around me. Every moment that passed, another grain of acceptance sifted into their expressions.

It was my dad who cleared his throat and backed toward the driveway first, just as the line of limos arrived to take everyone to the church. "Clara Belle's right. We all interfered enough the first time around. Let's do our best not to this time." As my dad backed away and looked at me, a rare smile formed. "So if you two make it or not this time, you'll have no one but yourselves to thank or blame for it."

I returned his smile. He held out his elbow for my mom, and Charlotte and Avalee followed them, Charlotte's train billowing behind her as the photographer checked his watch, cursed, and rushed after them. So much for the family photo; I guessed showing up for the actual wedding was more of a priority. Ford's family and the rest of the wedding party dashed after everyone else. It was a beautiful sight, everyone in their formal wear running across the expansive green lawn toward a line of sparkling white limos. It would have made a perfect picture if the photographer had stayed around long enough to see it.

One figure lingered on the lawn, watching Boone and me with the same grimace I'd grown used to as kids. Ford lumbered forward a few steps, clucking his tongue. "Bad choice, Clara Bella. Such a bad one." Ford motioned at me in Boone's hold like I was a chick caught in the talons of a raptor.

"Ford—"

"I tried to help you. I went out of my way to help you." Ford thrust his arms in my direction. "And look at all the good it did. You're right back where you started. In the arms of a nobody who knocked you up and waved good-bye. When it happens again, don't come crying to me. My sympathy's run its course with you."

Boone's arms tightened around me, his jaw going rigid. I was just about to snap something back when Boone let me go and angled toward Ford.

"You know, you bringing that up reminds me that I owe you something," he said, stopping a couple feet back from Ford.

Ford fired off a disgruntled huff, crossing his arms.

"What the hell could you possibly owe me?"

At the same time Boone's mouth opened, his arm wound back. "This," he snapped a moment before his fist connected with Ford's face.

CHAPTER TWELVE

I was alone again. Sprawled out in a chair at a wide empty table, watching from the sidelines as a bunch of people had a grand time.

Avalee was tearing it up with her fiancé on the gleaming teak dance floor; Charlotte and Ford were in the middle of the floor, swaying together in slow circles to a fast-paced song; and my mom was playing the indelible, tireless hostess.

But me? I was alone.

For the first time in a while, it was out of choice.

After dancing and talking and singing and having what constituted one hell of a time, my feet were throbbing, my skin was sticky with sweat, and my body was spent. I needed a moment alone if for no other reason than to wipe my armpits with a couple of napkins and massage a few knots out of my feet.

Leaning back in my chair, I realized this was the first minute I'd had to myself to relax and attempt to take in everything that had happened throughout the day. Besides my sister marrying my ex-boyfriend, who my present one had given an impressive black eye to an hour before the ceremony, I'd managed to come to some sort of understanding with my family. The Abbotts, not exactly your typical American family on the surface, but beneath all of that, we struggled through the same rivalries, good intentions going off course, resentment, and misunderstanding, and finally—or at least where I'd wound up—understanding and acceptance.

I'd dreaded this week for a dozen different reasons. I'd come up with just as many excuses not to come. This week hadn't just been a pivotal one in Charlotte's life, but in mine as well. To miss it would have meant spending the next however-many-years of my life perpetually avoiding my family and my memories of Boone.

To have lived this week made all the difference.

My "plus one" had disappeared after not letting me leave the dance floor for fifteen songs, and yes, I had been counting. When a woman was stuffed into a sausage-casing type dress (alterations and everything, the dress was still tight) and shoes that could only be described as the root of evil, one started counting songs after the first three.

Boone. He was in my life again. Maybe he'd never really left it, but he wouldn't continue to be a ghost haunting it. Instead, I'd have the real living, breathing, grinning-like-there-was-always-some-secret Boone Cavanaugh. How would it work? I didn't know. How long would it work? I didn't know. How often would we see each other, and would that be enough, and where would this journey take us? I came up empty in the answer department there as well.

All I knew was that those were just details. Bullet points in the grand scheme. We'd let enough details muddy the waters between us; I wouldn't make that mistake again. As Boone had said, the places we'd been broken before reminded us of what we needed to be careful to protect.

I would protect our weak spots. I would protect the strong ones too.

I was just slipping out of my other shoe to massage my other foot, which had grown its own heartbeat and was throbbing in pain, when I noticed someone whisk up to the center of the long bridal party table and crouch down to rustle through her clutch. Charlotte's train had been gathered so she could dance, and her veil had been removed from the delicate tiara combed into her hair. Her skin was flushed from the heat and what I guessed was happiness, and her eyes gave away just how excited she was, despite her face holding an expression of mild amusement carefully in place.

When she slid a compact out of her clutch, she opened it and took in her reflection, immediately going to work combing a few strands of loose hair back into place and dabbing at the hollows under her eyes. A few cheek pinches followed, along with some more hair fretting.

"You look really beautiful, Charlotte." I felt my eyebrows come together—I hadn't known I was going to say anything, yet there I was, reassuring her and telling her she was beautiful.

Her back had been angled my way—I didn't think she'd even noticed I was there—but it stiffened for one moment before it relaxed. "Really?" She tipped her face from side to side, getting a good view of all angles, sounding as doubtful as she looked.

"Just as beautiful as you looked this morning, and just

as beautiful as you have your whole life." I turned in my seat to face her, wondering if I'd be less surprised if a leprechaun fell out of the sky into my lap than by the fact that I was attempting to make some kind of peace with Charlotte.

"Okay . . ." she said slowly, clicking her compact closed before sliding it back into her clutch. "Thanks, Clara Belle. I mean, thanks, *Clara*." Charlotte sat on the edge of her chair and angled herself somewhat my direction. There were still four empty chairs between us, but it felt like the closest Charlotte and I had been since when she was seven and sick. Mom had been out of town, so I'd stepped in as the mother hen, pressing cool washcloths to her forehead and reading her stories. "Is that what you prefer? Clara?"

I felt my smile move into place. "That's what I prefer. Though after years of saying that, Boone and now you are the only ones who've seemed to listen."

"I remembered you correcting us when you still lived at home. But you stopped bringing it up after you left." Charlotte crossed her ankles and leaned forward. "Why?"

"Because no one would listen."

Charlotte seemed to mull that over. "No one ever listened to me either."

"What a terrible childhood you must have endured." I peered at her, watching her fight her smile. Charlotte had always fought her smiles like they were an enemy. It was nice to finally watch her lose a battle to one.

"Probably about as terrible as yours," she replied, having to look away when I laughed. Smiling was one thing, but laughing was uncivilized in Charlotte's book.

"But just look at us now." I waved my finger between

her and me. "Listening to each other."

"Who would have thought it?"

"Not me."

Charlotte shook her head. "Me neither."

Shifting on her seat, she started to stand. She looked as though she was reeling from our truce, and I knew I was, but she didn't seem in a hurry to get back to her wedding reception.

"Charlotte?" I called before she could move. "I don't think I've gotten a chance to tell you yet . . . but congratulations." I paused, having to take my time to get this out. Not because the words were feigned, but because I actually meant them. "I'm happy for you, and I hope you and Ford have a wonderful life together."

Her face went flat, followed by her eyebrows knitting together how I guessed mine just had. Perplexed seem to be the tone of things tonight. "Thank you?"

That made me laugh. "You're welcome?"

Charlotte came close, but she didn't quite laugh. Waving at me, she'd just turned to head back to the dance floor when she paused. Her hand went to the back of her chair, and she looked over her shoulder. "I'm sorry about the dress, Clara Be—" She cleared her throat "Clara. I'm sorry. That was a cheap shot."

I smoothed my hands down it, having gotten used to it twenty hours of continuous wear ago. "I'm sorry Boone hit your husband in the eye right before you said your vows. He should have waited until after at least."

Charlotte's and my gazes drifted to Ford. His eye wasn't swollen shut, but the injury wasn't exactly subtle. He'd deserved it, but the timing could have been a bit better. At least they'd gotten the majority of their portraits together taken beforehand.

Charlotte stayed where she was, hovering behind her chair. "I'm also sorry for what I did." She chewed at the corner of her mouth. "What Ford and I did to you—"

I cut her off with a hard shake of my head. I was done revisiting the past. Unless it had to do with fond memories or funny ones, I wasn't lingering there any longer. "You've loved Ford McBride from the time you were seven years old and our families vacationed together that summer in Nantucket. I knew you loved him. I knew you still loved him when Ford asked me out. I guess I just wasn't thinking about that when I said yes, you know?"

Charlotte stopped gnawing at her lip. She nodded. "I knew you two were together when Ford and I started spending more time together. I knew you were technically still a couple when we . . ." She swallowed, still watching him out on the dance floor. "But I guess I just wasn't thinking about that when he leaned in, you know?"

I smiled as she walked away, heading for her new husband flagging her out onto the floor. "I know," I said to no one but myself, because at the core of it all, I needed to be told that the most.

She rushed as quickly as she could to Ford, both of them smiling at each other like there was no one else around. I might not have liked Ford, I might not have wished him on my worst enemy after finding out what he'd done, but it didn't matter what I thought about him. My sister loved him.

I'd been the victim of people scrutinizing me for who I wanted to give my love to. I wouldn't do the same to my sister, no matter what asshole she chose to love.

That was when I finally caught sight of Boone. He

hadn't disappeared to escape the stifling air that traveled with my family and their friends. Instead, he was camped out beside my dad, talking to him in a way I'd never before seen them converse. It was a peaceful, bordering on respectful sort of conversation. I wasn't sure how long they'd been talking, but when Boone shook hands with Dad before walking away, his shoulders relaxed with what I guessed was relief.

He didn't scan the crowd for me. He didn't search the tables. He just headed in my direction like he knew exactly where I was without needing sight to guide him. Our connection had always run deep. Beyond attraction. Beyond friendship. It landed somewhere in the realm of the soul's bearing.

He was still in the same jeans and shirt he'd showed up in, but he didn't seem to care that he was in casual wear while everyone else had donned their most formal. Kind of like I'd gotten over the fact I was parading around in the most unflattering dress for my body type. We'd had plenty of experience dealing with other people's disapproval and didn't seem too concerned about changing that trend now.

"So? Did you win him over?" I called out as he lunged up toward the head of the table.

It was only then that his eyes drifted my way. They were lighter than normal today. As light as I'd ever seen them. "I think it's safe to say we can be in the same room together without attempting to kill one another now."

I smashed my lips together and nodded in approval. "Progress."

"Serious progress." Boone crashed into the chair beside me, reaching for my seat and pulling me closer. He wound his arms around me and pulled me into his lap.

He'd never been stingy with his affection in the past, and that was one thing I was happy had travelled with him to the present.

Somewhere in the midst of him settling me deeper into his lap, arching my back far enough so our mouths were aligned, I heard it. The sound I'd been dreading but knowing somewhere along the way, it was bound to echo in my ears.

That sound was the tearing of the seams stitching together The Thing. Again. The seamstress had done what she could, but it still didn't fit right. I doubted any amount of letting out or rebuilding would make it fit.

"Ah, shit." Boone winced, returning me to a more upright position. "I think I just killed The Thing."

I felt cool air rushing against the side of my body where the tear must have been. From the feel of it, the rip spanned from my hip to my armpit. "And this is something to be sad about because?"

Boone ran his fingers down my freshly exposed skin. His extra-light eyes went darker. "Because I was looking forward to tearing it off of you later. Alone. You. Me. Minus the five hundred people who keep mistaking me for the hired help."

I felt my heart pick up speed. "There's still plenty of dress left for the tearing."

He grinned at me as his fingers slid through the tear to cup my back. "Was that you and Charlotte I saw making what looked an awful lot like a truce?"

"I think so, yeah." My heart jacked up again when he leaned his face closer to mine.

"You making amends with Charlotte. Me shaking hands with your dad." He paused just long enough to drop a lingering kiss onto the side of my neck. The sensation of it lingered a while in other areas. "I think that's our cue to leave."

"I thought our cue to leave was you talking about tearing dresses off of me."

"I'd say we've had more than enough cues. Let's get out of here." In one smooth motion, Boone had me on my feet and had popped to a stand beside me. Weaving his hand through mine, he started to lead me away from the table and through the reception festivities.

We were both grinning as we rushed through clusters of people, feeling like a couple of kids skipping classes on a Tuesday afternoon. I felt light, a floating kind of light that would have no doubt sent me into the sky if Boone hadn't kept his hold on my hand.

We'd just made it to the edge of the party and were almost free when I heard our names being shouted from behind us.

"Keep going," I instructed, letting my feet take me as fast as I could.

Boone listened, keeping our pace, but when I heard my dad shout after us again, I found my pace slowing.

"Clara, sweetheart, hold up a minute!"

Boone slowed to match my pace right before we both came to a stop. He looked at me staring at my family waving us back, and he sighed. "It's like they know. Every single time. I swear they've got built-in radar when it comes to you and me trying to sneak away."

"I'm surprised you're only just figuring this out." I winked at him and gave his hand a tug back toward the reception.

As we drew closer, I saw why I'd been called back.

THE FABLE OF US

The photographer had managed to round up all of the Abbotts, along with Ford, to get the family photo he'd been trying to get earlier. This one though would be more fitting than the picture-perfect, all-white smiles and perfect posture one would have been.

This one would be an accurate depiction of the Abbotts. Me in my ripped dress, which was ugly as sin but my sister had forced me to wear as a bridesmaid. Ford with his glaring black eye, earned from being a regular dick and all-around asshole. My dad with his bow tie a little cock-eyed, half-drunk tumbler of scotch in hand. Even my mom . . . she'd kicked off her heels and was padding around the grass in her sheer pantyhose.

"Come on, honey. We've got to get a family photo to remember the day." My dad motioned me over as everyone else clustered up in a way that was not wedding-photographer approved based on the way the photographer was gaping at the scene forming in front of him.

I started their way, Boone following me until he stopped beside the photographer. He couldn't stifle his smile as he inspected the group before him.

The photographer was just getting into position to snap the photo, when my dad lifted held up his hand. "What are you doing over there, Boone?" He waved him over. "You better squeeze your way into this circus too."

My head twisted toward my dad.

Boone's brows touched his hairline. "I thought it was a family photo."

My dad circled his finger around all of us and shrugged. "It is." He gave Boone another wave. "Now get the hell over here."

Boone didn't pause to think that over. Jogging to my

337

side, he squeezed in between my dad and me, cinching his arms around me. His mouth lowered to my ear as the photographer fired off a series of sighs before returning to his camera.

"Thanks for asking me to be your plus one."

I looked back at him. He was looking at me. "Thanks for being my date."

The photographer snapped the photo.

CHAPTER THIRTEEN

Frozen in time. Moments could be seen through the shutter of a camera, but eventually we all had to move on from the past. Willingly or forced.

For the first time in years, I was marching forward of my own doing, content to leave the past exactly where it belonged. It was a revelation. One that set me free at the same time it grounded me.

Another two hours had gone by, my family refusing to let Boone and me sneak away like we'd attempted earlier. Well, they let me sneak away for a few minutes, but it was only to change out of The Ruined Thing into something more comfortable. After a few more rounds of photos, a few more spins on the dance floor, and the three Abbott sisters taking the stage to serenade the guests as they slowly made their way back to their cars, we finally got our moment.

He didn't say a word. He just took my hand and led me across the lawn toward where his truck was parked out in the field. The night was more morning than evening by that point, almost silent but for the sounds of the night coming to an end and the sounds of morning not quite ready to come alive. It was the time when a person could almost be made to believe in magic. The time of the night when a person could almost be swayed into believing in foolish notions and fairy-tale endings.

"Are you sure you don't want to stay?" Boone asked as we came around the side of his truck.

I brushed his stomach as he swung the door open for me, and I stepped inside the truck. "Let's see. I like all of my family right now. They all like me. I'm not going to press my luck."

"Sounds like a solid policy," he said before closing the door.

As he loped around the front of the truck, I settled my number eighteen angel into my lap, nestling her between my legs so she wouldn't bounce to the floor and break again when we hit a pothole.

After launching himself inside the truck, he fired it up, put his hands on the steering wheel, studied the empty space in front of us and the quiet road behind us, then glanced my way. "Well? Where are we heading?"

"I don't know. How long of a journey did you have in mind?"

"As long of a journey as you plan on taking, that's how long." Boone punched the truck into reverse, sending a spray of dust and gravel around us before he fired his old truck down the road. Down the road that led west. The direction I had in mind.

"Have you ever thought of visiting California?" I peered at him as I hung my arm out the window. Even the muggy air seemed to have taken a temporary break.

"I've been thinking of visiting California for the past

seven years." He gave the truck a bit more gas, until the rearview mirror was rattling from the speed we were cruising down the gravel back road. "I think it's about time I got there."

"Funny you say that, because I've been wondering when you would visit California for these same past seven years. I think it is about time you got there too."

Boone smiled at me, keeping his eyes on the road. "I don't know how long I'll be able to stay—I have some things to take care of back here too—but I should be able to sneak away for a while."

"That's good to hear." I snapped open my clutch and pulled out something I'd stuffed in there earlier that morning. I dangled the set of keys, tinkling them just outside his ear. "Because you've got some big responsibilities to see to when you get back. Rest and relax with me in California —my bed's the perfect place for that—because you're going to be busy when you get back."

The corners of Boone's eyes creased when he glanced at the keys. His eyes returned to the road for a moment, and when they drifted back to the set of keys I was holding out, recognition dawned on his face. "Those keys . . ." He swallowed, eyeing them. "Are those what I think they are?"

"Well if you think they're the keys to a brand new F-350 Super Duty, then no, sadly they are not." I jingled them again. "But if your next guess leads you to wondering if they're the keys to the Kids' Center, then ding! Ding! Ding! . . . you are correct."

At first, he didn't say anything. His chest just rose and fell in heavy pulls. "Clara—"

But I cut him off. "I believe in you. I always have."

Lowering the keys to the steering wheel, I looped them around his thumb. "It's time you did too."

He was quiet again, his grip tightening around the steering wheel enough to make his knuckles go white. After a minute, he opened his hand and let the keys fall into his palm. He wrapped his fingers around them. "How did you manage it? The bank? The short timeframe? How did you do it?"

I shrugged. "I'm an Abbott. I had to cash in on my name at least once in my life."

Boone shook his head. "No, you're Clara. The girl I grew up loving, and the woman I'll die loving." His hand, the same one still holding the keys, found mine, and he managed to knit his fingers through mine and still maintain his hold on them. "You're the best person in the whole world. *That's* who you are."

I tipped my head back against the headrest, letting my hair whip around my face from the wind rushing into the truck, and I wondered how long it would take us to get to California. What I realized then was I didn't care. Where we were heading didn't really matter—what counted was that we were on our way.

This time, when I went to suck in a breath, my lungs responded. They filled with air to capacity, strong and solid. I exhaled.

I could breathe again.

The Charleston city limits sign was still miles down the road.

I took another breath and stared across the seat at Boone. The boy I'd grown up loving, and the man I'd die loving. "I was just thinking the same exact thing about you."

The fable of us had been rewritten. With a spin that had exposed the truth. Instead of the happily never after we'd been dealt or with the happily ever after that was a lie, we were retelling the ending. Boone and Clara— happily *even* after. It was a great story. The greatest one I'd ever heard.

THE END

Thank you for reading THE FABLE OF US by NEW YORK TIMES and USATODAY bestselling author, Nicole Williams.

Her next novel, COLLARED, will be released in Spring 2016! Check her social media sites for updates on the release date.

Nicole loves to hear from her readers.
You can connect with her on:

Facebook: Nicole Williams (Official Author Page)
Twitter: nwilliamsbooks
Blog: nicoleawilliams.blogspot.com

Other Works by Nicole:

CRASH, CLASH, and CRUSH (HarperCollins)

UP IN FLAMES (Simon & Schuster UK)

LOST & FOUND, NEAR & FAR, HEART & SOUL

FINDERS KEEPERS, LOSERS WEEPERS

THREE BROTHERS

HARD KNOX, DAMAGED GOODS

CROSSING STARS

GREAT EXPLOITATIONS

THE EDEN TRILOGY

THE PATRICK CHRONICLES